... Book Award 2014 – Winner

'Br

Books by Chris Bradford

The Soul series (in reading order)

THE SOUL HUNTERS

THE SOUL PROPHECY

The Young Samurai series (in reading order)

THE WAY OF THE WARRIOR

THE WAY OF THE SWORD

THE WAY OF THE DRAGON

THE RING OF EARTH

THE RING OF WATER

THE RING OF FIRE

THE RING OF WIND

THE RING OF SKY

THE RETURN OF THE WARRIOR

Available as ebook

THE WAY OF FIRE

The Bodyguard series (in reading order)

HOSTAGE

RANSOM

AMBUSH

TARGET

ASSASSIN

FUGITIVE

THE SOUL PROPHECY

CHRIS **BRADFORD**

PUFFIN

PUFFIN BOOKS

UK | USA | Canada | Ireland | Australia
India | New Zealand | South Africa

Puffin Books is part of the Penguin Random House group of companies
whose addresses can be found at global.penguinrandomhouse.com.

www.penguin.co.uk
www.puffin.co.uk
www.ladybird.co.uk

First published 2022

001

Cover art by Paul Young
Cover images © Shutterstock

Set in 10.5/15.5 pt Sabon LT Std
Typeset by Jouve (UK), Milton Keynes
Printed and bound in Great Britain by Clays Ltd, Elcograf S.p.A.

The authorized representative in the EEA is Penguin Random House Ireland,
Morrison Chambers, 32 Nassau Street, Dublin D02 YH68

A CIP catalogue record for this book is available from the British Library

ISBN: 978–0–241–32672–5

All correspondence to:
Puffin Books
Penguin Random House Children's
One Embassy Gardens, 8 Viaduct Gardens, London SW11 7BW

To the Roses,
because you deserve more than an acknowledgement :-)

The Darkness that once was will be once again,
For it's the Light that casts a shadow and the Shadow that casts out the Light . . .

The Soul Prophecy

Prologue

Los Angeles, present day

Siren wailing, lights flashing, the ambulance threads its way between the traffic as the Californian sun sets over Huntington Park. The vehicle pulls up sharply to the kerbside, its doors fly open and two paramedics leap out.

A body is sprawled on the sidewalk.

The paramedics push through the knot of onlookers surrounding it and approach a well-built man in a crisp suit and dark glasses who has his hands pressed firmly against the casualty's chest. Blood seeps between his fingers.

'Alex has been shot!' barks the man, a desperate yet determined expression on his rugged face.

One of the paramedics, a young woman with copper-red hair tied into an efficient ponytail and a name badge identifying her as BAILEY, kneels down and sets to work assessing the injury. Releasing his hold on Alex's chest, the suited man moves aside to allow the medic to do her job. 'Single entry and exit wound . . . nine-millimetre calibre round, at my guess . . . significant blood loss . . . Let's get some pressure bandages and vented seals on fast.'

The other paramedic, an older man with a trimmed beard and shaved head and the name badge CARTER, tears open a packet of sterile dressings and starts tending to the wounds.

'Alex, can you hear me?' asks Bailey, but she gets no response. She checks for vital signs, while her partner inserts an IV drip and runs in vital fluids. 'The casualty's no longer breathing,' she says, and immediately begins CPR.

Carter pulls out a portable defibrillator from his med-bag and attaches a pair of electrode pads to the victim's chest. As soon as the unit powers up, the ECG monitor bleeps a rapid and erratic rhythm.

'The heart's gone into cardiac arrest,' says Carter. Then as a light flashes red he warns, 'Stand clear!'

Bailey takes her hands away as the defibrillator delivers an electric shock. Alex's body jolts slightly, but the graph on the ECG monitor continues to spike out of control . . . before flatlining entirely. The heart monitor sounds its ominous drone and the paramedic hurriedly resumes CPR –

Alex watches this life-or-death struggle from above with an almost indifferent attitude – as if it's happening to someone else. In fact, it's the man in the tailored blue suit and sunglasses who seems the most concerned. He's talking rapidly into his mobile phone, an intense and troubled expression on his rugged face. What's his name? Clive, is it? . . . No, not Clive . . . Clint!

But, unlike Clint, Alex no longer feels any pain, worries or cares. After all the struggles and stresses of life, this sense of detached calm is blissful . . . welcome, even. The connection between body and soul is now little more than a fine silver thread in the growing darkness.

As Alex observes the two paramedics working frantically to resuscitate their casualty, a bright, warm light appears at the end of a long tunnel. Drawn towards the light, Alex leaves the body lying sprawled on the sidewalk and glides away down the tunnel, the silver thread connecting body to soul becoming thinner and thinner . . .

'Adrenaline shot!' orders Bailey, and her partner dives into his med-bag looking for the syringe. 'Hurry . . . or we're going to lose this patient for good!'

In the distance the wail of police sirens closes in from all directions while Bailey continues to pump away with a combination of chest compressions and rescue breaths. Locating a suitable vein, Carter pulls the cap off the syringe and injects the stimulant to kickstart the heart . . .

The fraught scene on the sidewalk fades, the colours and sounds muting, until the two paramedics and their patient are little more than a silent black-and-white movie flickering in the distance. Alex drifts further and further along the tunnel, the celestial white light growing brighter and more vibrant with each passing moment.

But, as the end of the tunnel approaches, a long, spindly shadow blocks the light.

Alex hesitates, not recognizing the soul that has suddenly appeared. Hello? Do I know you?

No, *comes the sharp reply.* But your death is my beginning.

Moving with frightening speed, the shadow rushes forward, devouring all light and suffocating Alex's soul with its cloying darkness . . .

'Still no response,' announces Carter after administering a second adrenaline shot.

Exhausted and out of options, Bailey is forced to abandon CPR and declare the patient dead at the scene. The suited man swears and throws his phone to the ground in a fit of rage and grief.

Then – just as Carter is disconnecting the defibrillator – a faint bleep sounds on the monitor.

'Hang on, we've got a heartbeat . . .'

1

St Petersburg, Russia, 1904

'AND NOW, LADIES AND GENTLEMEN!' the ringmaster bellows. 'The act you have all been waiting for . . . the Famous, the Fantastic, the Fantabulous, the Phenomenal . . . Yelena, the Flying Firebird!'

To thunderous applause, I run out into the circus ring. My spikes of flame-red hair and glittering costume draw everyone's eye. Dmitry, clad in a silver leotard, is at my side as we cartwheel, flip and somersault in unison to land in the centre of the ring. The crowd cheer and wolf-whistle before the ringmaster quells them into a hushed silence.

'Prepare to be astounded by feats of physical daring,' he says breathlessly. 'Within this ring, you see a dastardly array of deadly obstacles. The Wall of Knives! The Pit of Glass! And the infamous Flaming Hoops of Hell! Our Firebird must survive them all!'

Dmitry takes up a lit torch and ignites a series of hoops mounted on iron stands, the fifth and final ring so small that my body barely fits through it. The searing heat from the hoops is enough to force the front row to lean back, but the rest of the audience are on the edge of their seats as I prepare to run the lethal gauntlet.

I survey the first hurdle ahead of me – a wall made entirely of knives, their points protruding from the top like a row of shark's teeth. Taking a deep breath, I start sprinting towards the bladed barrier then vault high into the air. I tuck in my legs and perform a neat somersault over the glinting points, landing safely on the other side.

The audience barely have time to applaud as I run towards the next obstacle – a trench filled with broken glass, above which are suspended three parallel bars. Bouncing off a wooden springboard, I propel myself up, catch hold of the first bar and do a full spin, before launching myself on to the second bar. Here I perform a straddle cut then swing for the third bar and, using my momentum, lift into a perfect handstand. Now the crowd do have time to clap. I steady myself over the sea of glass that I know lies below me, waiting to pierce my snow-white skin if I should fall. After a few seconds I drop out of the handstand and execute a double flip to touch down just beyond the pit.

At last, I'm faced with my final challenge, the Flaming Hoops of Hell – a circus feat no other acrobat in the world dares perform. The heat is so intense it almost scorches my skin as, in a deft series of jumps and rolls, I dive through each of the hoops in turn. The smallest requires every ounce of skill to pass through without getting burned to a cinder. Then before I've even caught my breath, Dmitry throws one last ring of fire high into the air and with an elegant leap I somersault through it to land, arms spread like an eagle, beside him.

The crowd are on their feet, whooping and clapping. As I soak up the applause, my eye catches a dour-faced woman in the front row. She alone sits dead still, staring at me, her hands resolutely in her lap, the only person it seems who isn't impressed by my daredevil performance. But it isn't her lack of appreciation that troubles me.

It's her eyes.

Pitch-black and horrifyingly empty.

'Hey, are you OK?' whispers Dmitry, noticing my look of alarm.

'I . . . think I see a Soul Hunter,' I reply under my breath.

'Where?' Dmitry is suddenly alert, his body tense like a tiger.

I look back into the audience but the woman is clapping now, her eyes a pale green. I blink hard. Had it just been the blaze from the hoops causing blind spots in my vision? 'No . . . I was mistaken,' I say uncertainly.

'Yelena, don't worry,' assures Dmitry softly, resting his hand gently on my arm. 'We've kept on the move and in disguise these past six months. Left Tanas and his Hunters far behind –'

'LADIES AND GENTLEMEN!' booms the ringmaster above the fading applause. 'Prepare to be even more amazed, astounded and astonished as our flame-haired Flying Firebird now attempts the death-defying Trapeze of Terror!' With that, he points towards the two swing bars suspended high above everyone's head.

As the audience look up, Dmitry draws me close and whispers into my ear, 'But to be sure, once this show is over, we'll lie low for a while. We can always join another circus.' Then with a reassuring wink of his sparkling blue eyes he heads over to one of the rope ladders and nimbly climbs to the uppermost reaches of the circus tent.

'Do note, ladies and gentlemen,' the ringmaster announces ominously, 'that there is NO safety net! The slightest mistake by Yelena will mean her certain DEATH!'

He glances at me, no doubt wondering why I'm still standing in the ring. I break into a wide smile for the crowd, which masks my lingering unease at spotting a possible Soul Hunter, and run to the other ladder. I climb up to a small, raised platform, where, once high and safe from the reach of others, I shake off my fears and prepare for our routine.

Dmitry is hanging upside down by his legs from the catch bar, swinging easily. 'Gotov!' *he shouts, indicating he's ready for a catch.*

I take hold of the swing bar and leap from my board. The rush as I fly through the air, free and untouchable, is exhilarating, and I quickly forget all my troubles. I forget about Tanas and his hunger for my soul. I let go of the constant fear of being discovered by his Hunters. I release my panic at seeing that woman with the pitch-black eyes . . .

As I reach the top of my arc for a second time, I let go of the bar and execute a double-twisting, triple somersault before Dmitry catches me by the arms. We swing away, then back towards my bar, where I perform a two-and-a-half pirouette return. Below, the crowd burst into rapturous applause. Landing neatly on my platform, I glance down and wave in acknowledgement – then freeze. Even from this heady height, I can spot several new members of the audience sitting statue-still, their stone-cold black eyes staring up at me.

However, before I can register my horror, the audience start laughing.

'What's this?' cries the ringmaster.

A wild orange-haired clown has tumbled into the ring. He waddles up to the Wall of Knives and with a large, white-gloved hand tests the tip of a blade. Howling in mock pain, the clown shakes his injured hand, spraying fake blood over the people in the front row. More laughter erupts from the crowd.

As Dmitry swings towards me, I hear him shout, 'What's Gretto doing, barging in on our act?' but I've no idea.

Then Gretto looks up at me. His face is painted bone-white, his false nose as red and bulbous as a boil, and his lips are stretched into a grotesque smile. But it's his eyes – coal-black eyes – that send a jolt of terror through me.

'That's not Gretto,' I cry. 'It's Tanas!'

The demonic leader of the Incarnates continues to play his role as circus clown. Choosing several knives from the wall, he begins to juggle them as he heads towards my rope ladder. The audience laugh, then clap, then laugh again with every knife he fumbles and every finger he pretends to lose.

But Dmitry and I both know that it's no act. The clown's intentions are clear. With the remaining knife clamped between his teeth, Tanas ascends my rope ladder like an insidious spider.

'To me!' shouts Dmitry, swinging hard in my direction.

For several seconds I can only stand and stare in pure panic at the black-eyed clown scurrying up towards me.

How has he found us? We've risked our lives crossing Siberia to escape his clutches. We've seen no sign of Watchers or Hunters for months. We've changed our names, our appearance, our location almost every week . . .

'YELENA!' shouts Dmitry in desperation.

His voice breaks the spell. I turn and launch myself from the platform. But the first swing is never enough to set up for a catch. The bar is already returning just as Tanas mounts the board. He makes a grab for my legs, but I kick him away and swing back out across the void. For a moment Tanas teeters on the edge of the platform, arms windmilling as he tries to regain his balance. The crowd laugh delightedly, believing these antics to be all part of the act.

'Gotov!' *cries Dmitry, his hands held out, ready for the catch.*

But I can't. Tanas's grab at me has put our swings out of sync and, unable to release my grip on the bar for fear of falling, I return once more towards the platform. Tanas is waiting, his balance regained. There's a ghastly grin on his red-painted lips and the knife is now clutched in his gloved right hand.

'Come to Gretto!' he says, his tone as twisted as his smile.

However, as I pass within his reach, Tanas doesn't try to grab me again. This time, he slashes with the knife. I twist my body away, lifting one hand off the bar. The blade misses me by a hair's breadth – only to slice into one of the ropes attached to the bar!

As I flail in mid-air, the audience gasp in sudden horror. Using all my strength, I get both hands back on to the bar and swing towards Dmitry. He's ready for me, arms out, fingers splayed for the catch.

'Trust me!' he shouts. 'Your life with mine, as always.'

But as I leap for his outstretched arms, the frayed rope snaps and the fly bar drops. I scream in terror. I see Dmitry immediately release his knee grip on the catch bar to hang solely by his ankles. He reaches out. His hands go to clasp mine –

Our fingers brush against one another –

But I slip from his grasp and plummet to the ground.

2

'I'm falling . . . falling . . . endlessly . . . no ground beneath me . . . just a terrifying black void . . .'

A click of fingers and my eyes flicker open. My pulse is racing, my breathing fast and shallow.

'Calm yourself, Genna,' soothes a gentle voice. 'You're perfectly safe.'

I glance around nervously. I'm lying on a leather couch in a pastel-green room with sunlight filtering through a set of bamboo blinds. There's a tall flowering pink orchid in one corner and on the far wall a framed picture of a snow-capped mountain with the words: *You never know how strong you are until being strong is the only choice you have.*

'That was most enlightening, Genna. Tell me, how are you feeling now?' asks a man with slate-grey hair. Reclining in an armchair opposite my couch, he peers at me over his wire-framed glasses. A notebook rests in his lap, his slender fingers clasping a silver fountain pen.

'Erm . . . a little disorientated,' I reply, sitting up. He makes a note of this. My mind is clearing now and I recall that I'm in my post-trauma therapy session with Dr Larsson at his counselling clinic in west London.

'That's understandable,' he says kindly. 'For those receptive to hypnotherapy, it can be quite a profound experience, as well as a very effective treatment, of course. Can you see now how those past lives – or *Glimmers* as you call them – are the products of your subconscious?'

I frown deeply, shaken by my first experience of hypnosis. 'I *imagined* all that?'

My therapist nods.

'But I've never been a circus acrobat, let alone visited Russia!' I argue.

'Your subconscious works in metaphors,' Dr Larsson explains. 'Don't you remember, before I put you in a trance, we talked about your gymnastics training? It's quite reasonable to assume, considering your success in inter-school competitions, that in your mind you identified yourself as an acrobat. Have you ever been to a circus before?'

'Yes, but years ago, when I was a little kid,' I say.

'There you go,' he replies with a self-approving smile. 'You've also told me you read lots of historical novels. Is there one in your collection about Russia?'

I visualize the bookcase in my bedroom. 'Tolstoy's *Anna Karenina*. It's set in . . . St Petersburg . . .' I trail off. I'm just proving his point.

Dr Larsson leans forward in his chair. 'Genna, these past lives you believe you've had are conjured up by your mind to help you cope with a stressful and traumatic experience. That's nothing to be ashamed of. Anyone who's been through what you've been through is bound to develop coping mechanisms. And, may I say, you've coped wonderfully.'

My throat tightens and hot tears prick my eyes as I recall the attack by Damien and his gang in the London park, how he tried to kidnap me for his so-called master, Tanas, and how that evil and twisted priest almost murdered me in a horrific sacrificial ceremony. Even now, six months later, I can still taste the bitter wax potion that Tanas poured into my mouth; feel the deeply unsettling separation of body and soul as he performed the ritual; and recollect my sheer terror as he attempted to cut out my heart with an ancient jade knife. A shudder runs through me at the nightmarish memories.

Dr Larsson hands me a tissue and I dab away the tears. 'Are you all right to continue?' he asks.

I nod. 'It's just hard when I think back to that moment in the crypt.'

His tawny eyes soften with sympathy. 'And it will be, for some time,' he says. 'But you've come a long way, Genna. You're far tougher and more resilient than the frightened and confused girl I first met. The circus vision you just experienced proves that.'

'How?' I ask.

Dr Larsson settles back in his chair. 'Well, this is how I see it,' he begins. 'The vividness of your dream is a result of the intense emotions associated with your trauma. As I've already indicated, the setting is influenced by what you've read, by your childhood experiences of the circus and your talent for gymnastics. From our previous sessions and today's, it's evident that being a gymnast is when you consider yourself to be strongest and most capable. So your role as an acrobat in the vision shows a positive mental shift from seeing yourself as a victim to a survivor and, given time, on to being a thriver.'

I sit up a little straighter on the couch with a sense of empowerment that I've not felt in a long while.

Dr Larsson glances down at his notes. 'The boy, Damien, no longer seems to feature in your thoughts, unless he's represented by the dour-faced woman you described seeing in the front row. But, even if that's the case, he's merely an observer and no longer an active participant. Most significantly, though, you've started turning your greatest fear, Tanas, into something comical – a clown.'

'He was still terrifying,' I point out.

'Yes,' concedes my therapist. 'However, the audience were laughing *at* him and you were actively fighting back. That's another positive sign of progress. Finally, the boy you say rescued you –'

'Phoenix,' I interrupt, and a smile immediately blossoms on my lips. In my mind I picture his long waves of chestnut-brown hair, his high, defined cheekbones and his worldly-wise, knowing grin. Above all, I remember his unusual dazzling eyes, as blue as sapphires against his olive-tan skin. Phoenix Rivers, the Latino boy from Arizona who declared himself to be my Soul Protector. The boy who almost laid down his life to save mine.

Dr Larsson returns my wistful smile. 'Yes, Phoenix. Well, he appears to be represented by the trapeze artist, Dmitry. He was there to catch you, but he didn't –'

'Phoenix *did* save me, though,' I say, somewhat fiercely. Even now I feel protective of him, despite it supposedly being his role to protect me. 'In this life and in my other Glimmers – I mean visions, or whatever they are.'

'That may be the case. But in this particular circus vision he *didn't*,' reminds my therapist. 'And I interpret that as a good sign. Perhaps this is your mind finally letting go of the past.'

I lean back on the couch, allowing its soft leather to cradle me, and stare up at the ceiling as I absorb my counsellor's assessment. Over the past months, I've resisted much of what he's said, preferring instead to believe in my own perceived truth and the experiences I shared with Phoenix. But, with the benefits of time and therapy, I'm beginning to gain perspective on what happened and how it may have affected me and even altered my grip on reality. As the pain and trauma dissipate, so too does my attachment to the idea of past lives. *Maybe it is all in my mind*, I think.

'But it seems so *real*,' I say.

'Doesn't a dream seem real when you're sleeping?' suggests Dr Larsson. 'And I assure you, these visions you've experienced are no more real than a dream.'

'Maybe ... But dreams fade,' I say, 'whereas these Glimmers remain in my mind like memories.'

Dr Larsson taps his pen thoughtfully on his notebook. 'Aside from the one just now, have you had any other visions in the past six months?'

'None,' I admit, unable to keep the disappointment out of my voice. Despite their unnerving intensity and their often fraught and frantic nature, the Glimmers also give me great comfort, like I'm reuniting with a missing part of me. 'The last one I had was when I said goodbye to Phoenix at the airport.'

'Which implies two things,' says Dr Larsson. 'One: that such visions are triggered by a state of heightened emotion or extreme stress. And two: that this boy Phoenix – who first convinced you these visions were past lives – is the one influencing and implanting them, in a similar manner to how I induced the Russian circus through hypnosis.'

I bite my tongue to stop myself immediately leaping to Phoenix's defence. The doctor's argument is persuasive. I can't deny that Phoenix's sapphire-blue eyes do have a mesmerizing quality. Indeed, some of the most intense and early Glimmers occurred when we were eye-to-eye. Nor can I ignore the fact that I haven't had a Glimmer since he returned to the United States. I find myself wondering whether Phoenix hypnotized me and feel almost conned at the thought.

'I guess you're right,' I concede with a sigh, and a weight seems to lift from me. 'What you're saying about my subconscious processing the trauma makes sense – at least a lot more than believing I've lived a load of previous lives!'

Dr Larsson closes his notebook and sets it aside. 'Well, Genna, I think you're making excellent progress. In fact, I'll be recommending to your parents that we reduce your sessions to once a month going forward.'

Feeling I've made a breakthrough, I swing my legs off the couch. 'Thank you, doctor, for all your help.'

He points the tip of his silver pen at me. 'No, it's *you* who helped yourself.'

With a lighter step than when I entered his office, I head for the door. However, as I reach the threshold, I stop and turn back to him, seeking a final confirmation. 'So . . . I really just imagined all my past lives?'

Dr Larsson takes off his glasses and studies me hard. 'In my professional opinion, yes, you did,' he says. 'But that's no bad thing, Genna. It enabled you to survive.'

3

'We're *so* proud of you,' my mum enthuses as my dad pulls away from the clinic in our silver Volvo. Turning in her seat, Mum reaches over to gently touch my knee. 'For a while I didn't think we'd get our Genna back,' she admits, tears welling in her soft blue eyes. Then, like a ray of sunlight on snow, a tender smile warms her face.

I clasp her outstretched hand and give it a squeeze, reassuring her that, yes, her daughter is back. But I can't quite manage to say it out loud. While I may have recovered from the worst of the trauma, I'm not the same as I was and I never will be. Like a scar, the wounds to my psyche have healed but will never completely disappear. And, even though I've come to accept that the Glimmers were created by my subconscious, I can never forget them either.

Now, however, the idea that I am a reincarnating soul from the dawn of humankind – a First Ascendant tasked with carrying the Light of Humanity, as Phoenix claimed – does strike me as somewhat far-fetched. So does the thought that there is a worldwide network of Incarnates – Soul Hunters and Watchers – who are searching for me in order that their leader, Tanas, can tear out my soul and extinguish this so-called Light. I smile at the absurdity of it all. Thinking back to the explanation Phoenix gave me in that air-raid shelter, I really should have trusted my own instincts rather than what a stranger told me.

Dad glances in the rear-view mirror and catches my eye. 'We're so glad you stuck with the programme, Gen,' he says. 'I know it's not been easy for you. It's not been easy for us either, for that matter. But together, as a family, we've pulled through.'

'Thank you, Dad,' I reply, thinking of all the sacrifices they've made: the multiple trips across London for my counselling sessions; the many sleepless nights they endured comforting me from my dark nightmares; the hours of desperate research to find a way to heal my trauma; their helplessness as they watched me fall apart time and time again, both of them at a loss what to do. 'I'm just sorry –'

'No, there's no sorry,' my dad interrupts. 'Life is meant to test us. But remember this, Genna: when you walk over a mountain, your legs get stronger. And you've walked away from this ordeal stronger and more resilient than ever. So, whatever challenges you face in the future, you'll be more prepared, more capable of tackling them.' He beams a proud smile at me in the mirror. 'In my eyes – although you'll always be my little girl – you're growing into a truly fine young woman.'

I feel a glow in my heart at his words. Seeing both my parents happy and genuinely smiling for once is a great relief. For so long they've been strained and stressed, unable to hide their fear that the trauma I suffered may have run too deep to be treated and that I might regress and plunge back at any moment into depression. But the months of therapy have paid off, and the whole family seem to have healed with me. Perhaps we're even closer now than we were before.

Mum looks at me, a twinkle playing in her eyes. 'So, to celebrate your recovery, we have a surprise for you,' she announces.

'What?' I lean forward eagerly in my seat.

She performs a dramatic drum roll on the dashboard, before announcing, 'Weeeeeee're . . . off to Barbados!'

For a moment I just stare at her as the news sinks in, then I yelp: '*Barbados!*'

Dad nods. 'Yes, a two-week holiday, and we'll see all my family while we're out there,' he says, his grin now as broad as mine. 'Your great-grandpapa can't wait to see you. Nor can your cousins.'

'I'll see Papaya again!' I cry, delighted. The last time we visited Barbados I was a toddler and couldn't pronounce 'Great-grandpapa', so I ended up calling him Papaya instead and the name stuck. Dad has often talked about returning to his roots, but we never seem to have had the money. I frown at him. 'But I thought we couldn't afford fancy holidays . . . especially after the expense of my therapy sessions.' A twinge of guilt twists my stomach. I'd caught a glimpse of the private doctor's bill when my dad was paying and the final figure was by no means small.

Mum waves away my concern. 'Life's too short to be worrying all the time about how much it costs to live it,' she replies. 'What's happened has reminded us of that. So we've dipped into our rainy-day savings –' she glances through the windscreen at the grey drizzle falling outside – 'and it sure looks like a rainy day to me!'

'When do we go, then?' I ask eagerly.

'The weekend after next,' replies Dad. 'I've already reserved the plane tickets and will confirm our booking as soon as we're home.'

'It's going to be the break we *all* deserve,' says Mum, affectionately patting my dad's thigh and planting a kiss on his cheek. 'Darling, I'll need a new swimsuit . . .'

'Of course. I'll need new swim shorts too!' He laughs, slowing down to a stop at a set of traffic lights.

As my parents chat away excitedly, I lean back in my seat and gaze out of the window at the rain and passing traffic. My reflection gazes back at me, my thoughtful expression framed by ringlets of light brown hair. I still look like the young, smooth-skinned teenager I am, but I know my hazel eyes have noticeably aged. They appear older, wiser and more world-weary. I peer closer, searching . . . but there's no blue-white sparkle to them like I glimpsed in the roadside cafe mirror when I was on the run with Phoenix. My amber-brown complexion, an even mix between my mother's and father's skin tones, masks the weariness I feel deep inside. After a long therapy session I'm always a little drained, and today's was more demanding than usual. But the thought of heading to Barbados on holiday lifts my spirits. Warm sunshine, golden sands and crystal-clear seas are just the therapy I need right now. A smile breaks across my face at the thought of being among my extended family again, and my hand instinctively reaches for the amulet round my neck.

Tugging on the slim gold chain, I pull out the Guardian Stone that Phoenix gave me. This protective amulet saved my life during Tanas's ritual, or at least that's what I thought it had done at the time. But its power – if it had any to begin with – is now spent, a crack fracturing its circular blue marbled gemstone. It's my one and only keepsake of Phoenix and I have kept it close ever since he was deported back to the United States. Whatever the truth of my strange ordeal, whether I imagined past lives or not, I didn't imagine the connection between me and Phoenix. That *was* real . . . wasn't it?

But if it was, then why hasn't he contacted me? I know he doesn't trust technology or have a mobile phone, but that's no excuse not to even write a letter. Phoenix said he was returning home to Flagstaff, Arizona, or else going to hang out on a beach in LA. Neither place is exactly in the middle of nowhere. Surely, if I did mean something to him, he would have sent a message to at least say he'd arrived safely.

A heavy, heartbroken sigh escapes my lips as a painful realization hits me. If my past lives were all just a fantasy, then maybe our connection was too. Early on, my counsellor diagnosed that my intense attachment to Phoenix was a result of Stockholm syndrome, and that my positive feelings towards him were another means of surviving and coping with my situation. Perhaps he's right about that as well . . .

I yank the chain from round my neck. For a moment I consider tossing the amulet out of the window, but, not wanting to alarm my parents with any erratic behaviour, I stuff it into my back pocket instead.

It's time for me to move on.

Thinking of our imminent holiday to Barbados, I force a smile back on to my face and imagine being reunited with Papaya and the long hugs and chats we'll share –

A loud toot from the car horn snaps me out of my reverie. 'Get out of the way!' mutters my dad irritably.

There's a man in a hooded raincoat standing in the middle of the pedestrian crossing, solitary and still. Dad hits the horn again, but the man refuses to move, despite the rain spitting down on him. Cursing with annoyance, my dad spins the steering wheel and drives round the stubborn pedestrian.

As we pass him, my smile drops. His cloaked appearance and dark demeanour remind me of Damien and his gang. From within the shadowy cowl of his raincoat, the man's gaze seems to follow me. Rain drips down his beaked nose and glistens on his unshaven chin. As my dad drives off, I turn round to look out of the back window. The man is still standing there in the middle of the road, his hidden eyes never leaving me.

Just like a Watcher.

Goosebumps creep across my skin as a deathly cold shiver runs through me. I try to shake off the unnerving feeling.

It's just my imagination . . . isn't it?

4

'Barbados! You lucky thing!' says Mei upon hearing my news. 'Any room in your luggage for your best friend?'

I close my school locker and smile. 'Of course! Not sure you'd pass through security though.'

'What are you saying, exactly?' exclaims Mei in mock offence. 'It's not as if I'd take you over the excess baggage limit, is it?'

I look Mei up and down. She's as a slender as a vine, with long, black, arrow-straight hair and piercing tiger-brown eyes. 'No, you're more like a dangerous weapon,' I say.

'You're right there,' she says, springing into a kung fu stance. 'My brother's been teaching me some wicked Wing Chun moves. Did you know that Wing Chun was created by a woman? According to legend, an abbess of the Shaolin Temple called Ng Mui taught it to her student Yim Wing-Chun as a way to defend herself against unwanted advances.'

'No,' I reply, 'I didn't know that . . .' Mei's words, however, do stir a vague memory of a temple in the mountains and of monks in saffron orange robes – but I push it aside. *Just another figment of my overactive imagination.* I give my friend a searching look. 'Since when did you become so interested in history, anyway?'

Although Mei's parents are famous archaeologists, she doesn't share their passion for antiquities. For me, on the other hand, it's a subject that holds great fascination; in fact, Dr Larsson considers my deep interest in history to be a possible explanation for the detailed and varied nature of my Glimmers.

'Oh, I'm not really that interested in it,' Mei admits. 'But after what happened –' she hesitates, then continues awkwardly – 'to you, well, my parents insisted I join the kung fu club Lee goes to. Our sifu is keen on us learning the history and philosophy of Wing Chun, as well as its techniques. But, to be honest, I just want to know how to fend off boys.'

As she chops and punches at the air, I glance around the locker area. A stream of students flows past. Aside from a few odd looks at Mei, no one's really paying us the slightest bit of attention. 'Yeah,' I say. 'I can see we're having trouble fighting them all off.'

Mei shrugs. 'Not our fault if none of them have taste, is it?' She picks up her school bag and slings it over her shoulder. 'Shall we head to lunch?'

I nod and follow her along the corridor. As we turn the corner, we bump into a group of girls coming the other way. Anna's freckled face is among them. Having not really seen or spoken to her since my return, I've got the sense she's been avoiding me. I offer her a tentative smile, but she just ignores me.

'Watch out, everyone – it's the Teenage Terrorist!' taunts a short-haired girl with a stud in her nose. She dramatically holds everyone back.

'You're so pathetic, Lozza,' retorts Mei. 'Why can't you give it a break? Or is your brain stuck in reverse?'

Lozza makes a face. 'Ewwww, defending the Clapham Killer, are you? Careful she doesn't run you over!'

The other girls laugh, including Anna, and my cheeks flush hot. I know I shouldn't get upset, but Lozza's name-calling is a sharp reminder of everything I'm trying to forget. Unbidden, the memories flood back . . . *Damien's attempted abduction of me . . . Damien shooting an innocent bystander . . . his reckless pursuit of Phoenix and me through Clapham market in the white van . . . the driver knocking into people in her attempt to run us down . . .*

Suddenly I'm short of breath. My heart is pounding hard and fast. My hands begin to tremble as the girls' mocking laughter rings in my ears. I haven't had a panic attack for weeks, but I recognize the signs. With the emotional floodgates in my mind opening up, the fear and anxiety I'd experienced at being on the run comes rushing back – the police assuming the van was part of a terrorist attack and linking me to the incident; the newspapers, initially sympathetic to my plight, turning against me when it emerged I was fleeing with Phoenix of my own free will, and concocting headlines like 'Teenage Terrorists' and 'Clapham Killers', which they plastered all over their front pages along with my photo and those of the other suspects.

'Genna didn't kill *anyone*,' says Mei fiercely as I battle to calm my chaotic thoughts.

'Yeah, but her boyfriend did,' Anna points out. You can tell she looks up to Lozza like a needy puppy seeking approval. 'That's why he was deported.'

'Phoenix had no choice. He was saving my life!' I burst out, unable to hold my tongue any longer.

'So, he *was* your boyfriend, then,' Lozza replies with a smug grin, then in a sing-song voice teases me with, 'Genna and Phoenix sitting in a tree, *K - I - L - L - I - N - G!*'

I clam up, my lower lip quivering. I don't want to give that bully the satisfaction of knowing that her taunts are riling me. But it's difficult. While the therapy may be helping me deal with the trauma, six months on from those events Lozza and her cronies still won't stop goading me. Their constant needling is opening up the very wounds Dr Larsson is trying to heal.

'Lozza, aren't you depriving a village somewhere of an idiot?' snaps Mei as she sees me struggling to hold myself together. 'Ignore her, Gen – she ain't worth it.' And, taking my arm, she quickly leads me away. Jeers of 'Teenage Terrorist' and callous laughter echo after me down the corridor.

Once out of view, I can no longer keep it in and the tears spill down my cheeks.

'Genna, don't let them get to you,' says Mei, putting an arm round my heaving shoulders. 'They've no idea what you went through.'

'B-but Anna does!' I sob, surrendering to her embrace. 'I just don't understand why she's acting like that . . . She used to be my friend . . .' I close my eyes and force myself to breathe deep and slow, counting to ten as Dr Larsson taught me to do whenever I feel overwhelmed.

Mei's grip on me tightens. 'In a situation like this, Genna, you never lose friends. You simply learn who the real ones are.'

Gradually the panic attack begins to subside, and I glance up at her. 'You're more than a friend to me, Mei. You're like the sister I never had.' On saying these words, I feel a profound love and deep sense of gratitude towards her, one that seems to fill an inexplicable hole in my heart. Just the idea of Mei being my sister gives me strength. 'Thanks for sticking by me. I know I haven't been myself these past months, but I –'

My breath suddenly catches in my throat . . . Through the prism of my tears, I've glimpsed a tall boy standing at the furthest end of the corridor. His hands are clasped in front, his head bowed, his face concealed by a dark grey hoodie.

'But you what?' asks Mei, then she sees my shocked expression.

'*D-Damien!*' I manage to stutter.

'What are you talking about?' she says, her back to the frightful figure. 'That creep's locked up in a young offender institution.'

'But I swear that's *him*.' Furiously wiping tears from my eyes, I look again. Mei follows my gaze. The boy is still standing there, dark, dangerous and intimidating. I feel the panic rise in me again.

'Oi!' shouts a teacher. 'Put that phone away and take that hoodie off! You're in school!'

The boy glances up from his mobile. Begrudgingly, he pockets his phone and flips back his hood to reveal a tangle of ginger-blond hair. As he's briskly ushered out on to the sports field, I let out an unsteady, relieved sigh. No, it definitely wasn't Damien. My tormentor's hair is as black as a raven and his complexion is far paler than that boy's sandy skin.

'See?' says Mei. 'It's just a sixth former.'

I nod, swallowing back the lump in my throat. 'Sorry. For a moment I was thought it was him.'

Mei shakes her head in pity. 'That stupid Lozza really upset you, didn't she? Try not to let her drag you down like that,' she advises kindly. 'Remember, you're safe now. It's all in the past.'

5

With the hooded image of Damien still haunting me, I head into the lunch hall with Mei. We each grab some pizza, a bowl of salad and a juice before joining our friend Prisha at a table in the far corner. A waft of garlic and cardamom rises from her lunchbox.

'Smells good,' I say, peering at the steaming dish in front of her. 'What's on the menu today?'

'Chole,' Prisha replies, scooping up a spoonful of homemade chickpea curry.

Having tasted her mother's cooking, I can't help but compare Prisha's mouth-watering lunch to my limp piece of pizza, its appeal fading fast.

But Mei isn't put off hers; she tucks hungrily into it. 'Have you heard? Genna's going to Barbados,' she mumbles through a mouthful of pepperoni.

Prisha glances at me in surprise, then grins. 'No, when?'

'Next weekend, for two weeks,' I reply, taking a sip of my juice. 'My parents have permission to take me out of school.'

The smile on Prisha's face falters. 'Oh . . . does that mean you'll miss my birthday sleepover on the Friday?'

For a second my mind goes blank. I totally forgot about it in the excitement of a Caribbean beach holiday. 'No, course not . . . That's still fine,' I reply optimistically. 'We don't fly out until Saturday evening.'

'Ah, good!' says Prisha, happily resuming her meal. Then she notices my reddened, puffy eyes. 'You all right, Gen?'

Mei answers for me. 'We just bumped into Lozza. She was her usual delightful self.'

Prisha snorts her distaste of the girl and offers me a sympathetic look. 'Oh, Gen, why won't she leave you alone? That girl's a nightmare! No wonder you're upset.'

'Not only that,' says Mei, lowering her voice and catching Prisha's eye over her pizza slice, 'Genna thought she spotted Damien in school.'

Prisha abruptly puts down her spoon. '*Damien?* I thought he was locked up.'

'He is,' I say. 'It was just my imagination. I was having a panic attack and not thinking straight. Yesterday I even thought I saw a Watcher!' I add, letting out a self-conscious laugh.

Mei and Prisha exchange worried glances.

'But I know that's impossible,' I say hurriedly. 'Even if the whole past life and First Ascendant story *was* true, Phoenix said that when Tanas dies so does his hold over his followers. Any Soul Hunters or Watchers become inactive – at least until Tanas reincarnates again, and that won't happen in this lifetime . . .' I trail off under my friends' troubled gaze.

Reaching across the table, Prisha takes my hand, her gentle touch warm and reassuring. 'Gen, I think this holiday is exactly what you need,' she says kindly. 'A break from it all. A fresh start. A line in the sand. When you come back, you'll be as good as new.'

'I hope so,' I reply with an uncertain smile. 'Dr Larsson says I'm recovering well, that I've progressed from victim to survivor. But I could do without these flashbacks of Damien and my kidnapping. In my last session, Dr Larsson managed to prove that my Glimmers are products of my subconscious.'

Prisha's brow furrows either side of her bindi. 'He did? How?'

'He induced a new one through hypnosis,' I explain.

'What was this Glimmer about?' she asks, leaning forward with keen interest. Prisha has always taken my story of past lives more seriously than anyone else. So I recount my vision of the Russian circus, my act as a daredevil acrobat and trapeze artist, and how I fell to my death escaping Tanas.

'That's fascinating,' says Prisha, breathless. 'You describe everything in such detail. No wonder you believe the Glimmers are real.'

I shake my head. 'Not any more. I've accepted Dr Larsson's explanation. Reincarnation isn't real.'

Prisha stiffens slightly. 'Hindus believe in reincarnation,' she counters, her tone a touch offended. 'As do Buddhists and Sikhs.'

'But that's about belief, not proof,' says Mei, finishing off her pizza and setting aside her plate.

'No, it's been proven,' Prisha replies earnestly. 'There was a girl from Delhi in the nineteen thirties who claimed to have had a past life. A commission set up by Mahatma Gandhi himself concluded her story was true. They –'

'Prisha, you're *not* helping,' interrupts Mei, shooting her a warning glance.

Stabbing at my salad with a fork, I push a tomato round the plate with no real desire to eat it. I'd read about that particular girl online when I was searching for answers to explain my strange visions with Phoenix. Shanti Devi was her name. The case was highly convincing and, when I read about it, it gave me great comfort. But now Shanti's story only makes me question things all over again.

'Sorry,' mumbles Prisha with a contrite look, 'but you can't dismiss the possibility of reincarnation just like that.'

'Nor can you trust one story from, like, a hundred years ago,' replies Mei pointedly.

'You're both right,' I say, picking listlessly at my salad. 'But now I don't know what to think.'

'Look, there may be a way we can settle this, once and for all,' says Mei with determination.

'How?' I ask.

'With a bit of detective work,' she replies, pulling out her laptop and booting it up. As we gather round her screen, Mei opens up her browser and types in a web address. 'So, this supposed past life in the Russian circus,' she says, turning to me. 'When was it?'

'In the early nineteen hundreds.' I frown thoughtfully as I try to recall the exact date.

'That's good enough,' says Mei, entering the period 1910–20 into the search box. 'And you said the circus was in St Petersburg. What was the name of your act again?'

With a slightly embarrassed grin, I reply, 'Yelena, the Flying Firebird.'

Mei raises an amused eyebrow. 'Catchy! That shouldn't be too hard to check out.'

'So what exactly are you looking for?' Prisha asks as Mei types in the location and key words.

'Well, if Genna's Glimmers are real – which I very much doubt – then her death as a famous acrobat should have been reported in the newspapers at the time,' explains Mei, hitting the enter button and beginning the search. 'My parents often use this archive website when hunting for clues to lost treasures. Every available paper from around the world has been scanned in, going back as far as the eighteenth century. If it made it to the newspapers, then we'll find it on this site.'

Within a few seconds a list of relevant hits fills the screen. My pulse races a little faster as we scan the search results. Most are references to performances of the ballet *The Firebird* by the Russian composer Igor Stravinsky. There are also a number of articles about a magical burning bird from Slavic folklore. My heart even skips a beat when I see the name Phoenix in a link, before realizing it's just another reference to the mythical firebird. But there don't appear to be any hits for a Russian circus performer called Yelena.

Leaning back in her chair, Mei laces her fingers behind her head and declares in a satisfied voice, 'There. Point proven. Genna's Glimmer isn't real.'

Despite an underlying pang of disappointment, I can't help but feel an immense sense of relief. Dr Larsson's assessment really is beyond doubt now.

But Prisha folds her arms and shakes her head. 'This doesn't prove it didn't happen,' she argues. 'Just that it wasn't reported.'

Mei scrolls again through the long list of links. 'This search is pretty comprehensive, though. And I'd have thought that such a dramatic death would've been mentioned in the obituary section of a newspaper somewhere at least –'

'Hang on,' I interrupt, my heart thudding as my eye catches a subheading. 'Go back a page – stop! What's that?' I point to a reference within the summary of another link, titled 'Famous Flamebird Fails to Fly'.

Mei clicks on the link and a scanned article from an edition of *The Daily Telegraph* dated 23 October 1904 is highlighted on the screen:

Famous Flamebird Fails to Fly

In a tragic accident last month, renowned Russian acrobat Yuliana Petrovski, known to all as Yuliana the Flamebird, died during a circus performance in Yamburg, Russia. During her famous and death-defying trapeze act, witnesses say the line snapped and she missed her partner's catch. Her funeral took place in St Petersburg five days later.

A chill runs down my spine. I exchange a shocked glance with Prisha, whose eyes are as equally wide as mine.

'Well . . . it's not one hundred per cent conclusive,' argues Mei, shifting awkwardly in her seat. 'The name's wrong, to start with.'

Prisha gives Mei a look. 'You have to admit they're quite similar, though.'

'OK, but there still are too many differences,' Mei insists. 'I mean, even the location is different.'

'Granted,' admits Prisha. 'But the fact still stands: a famous acrobat died in Russia falling from a trapeze in the early nineteen hundreds. Just like in Genna's Glimmer. That's quite compelling evidence of a past life.'

'Or it could just be pure coincidence,' Mei shoots back. 'I know how much you'd like this to be true, Prisha, but remember that it was Genna's counsellor who induced this Glimmer.'

Prisha shrugs. 'So? He could have stirred up a past-life memory.'

'Or, *more likely*, it's a figment of Genna's imagination,' declares Mei emphatically. 'We both know Genna's a history buff, so she could've read about this story in one of her books, or heard it on the radio, or even seen it in a movie!'

'Perhaps,' says Prisha, relenting under Mei's resolute glare. 'Or perhaps accepting the Glimmers for what they really are is healthier than trying to deny or suppress them.'

'You're not Genna's therapist, Prisha!' snaps Mei, causing the lunch hall to fall suddenly quiet at her outburst.

'No, I'm her friend,' Prisha replies, her voice trembling slightly and her cheeks reddening. 'And, like you, I'm trying to help her.'

As my two friends lapse into a tense silence, I continue to stare at the newspaper headline, transfixed by the surreal possibility I may be reading my own obituary from a past life.

6

'Happy Birthday, Prisha!' I say, feeding her a small piece of birthday cake before stepping away to allow Mei to do the same. Their quarrel earlier in the week has been forgotten and, likewise, I've dismissed the idea that I was once some Russian acrobat in a previous life. For my own sanity, I have to believe that the news story was merely a strange coincidence.

Prisha, in a vibrant lilac sari and with her long black hair combed into a high sheen, grins between mouthfuls as the other guests partake in this cake-feeding tradition. Prisha's mother and grandmother have already performed a number of other Hindu rituals: anointing her with a sprinkling of dry rice and a dab of orange-red paste on her forehead; circling a small flaming diya lamp on a silver tray round her head in an Aarti ceremony of light; and bestowing upon her an abundance of prayers.

Once the last guest has honoured the birthday girl with cake, Prisha's father, a wiry man with a bushy moustache and a thick head of hair, stands up and clears his throat.

'Dearest family and friends,' begins Mr Sharma, surveying the room and smiling broadly, 'it gives me great pleasure to celebrate the birthday of our eldest daughter,

Prisha, and I thank each and every one of you for coming today. I'm sure you'll all agree with me that she looks most wondrous and is a credit to our family . . .'

As everyone claps, he fishes into his jacket pocket and pulls out a ream of paper, whereupon Prisha's mother, clearly alarmed that her husband is about to launch into one of his legendary long lectures, politely announces that dinner is served. After a delicious feast of colourful curries, bowls of steaming pilau rice, and plates piled high with samosas and onion bhajis, everyone retires to the living room, where Prisha's uncle produces a sitar and performs in honour of his niece.

I take the opportunity during a lull in the festivities to move my overnight bag up to Prisha's room ready for the sleepover. But, as I'm heading back downstairs to rejoin the party, my attention is caught by a strong scent of sandalwood tinged with the lightest fragrance of rose. The distinct aroma is familiar, yet I can't place where or when I remember it from. Curious, I follow the trail of scent down the hallway to Mr Sharma's private study. The door is partly open and, enticed by the smell, I can't stop myself from peeking inside. Now the aroma grows stronger and, along with the scents of sandalwood and rose, my nostrils fill with a rich earthy odour and the tang of sweat.

As if drawn by an invisible thread, I'm compelled to step into the room. I notice that the window overlooking the garden is closed and there doesn't appear to be any incense burning. *So where is the smell coming from?* I wonder.

I glance around, spotting Mr Sharma's planned birthday speech on his desk. Then, looking behind me, I discover to my astonishment an array of ancient weapons on the wall. There's a curving double-edged dagger decorated in gold; a pair of lethal knives, their sharp triangular blades protruding from H-shaped hand grips; a large heavy wooden club almost the length of a man's arm; a round polished shield, paired with a long silver sabre; and – the strangest-looking of the lot – a carved wooden stick resembling an elephant's trunk with a hilt and handle. *I get now why Mr Sharma's study is usually locked and out of bounds!*

Gazing at the impressive weapon collection, I'm reminded of the time I first encountered the Guatemalan jade knife at the museum exhibition organized by Mei's parents. That time I imagined that I smelt singed hair and heard screams, distant thunder and pounding drums. Phoenix convinced me that that was my Wakening, my first true Glimmer. But here, aside from the lingering smell of rose and sandalwood, I hear nothing alarming. Just laughter, sitar music and chatter coming from the party down the hall.

I feel a sudden urge to hold one of the weapons.

Phoenix had me believe that certain objects could be Touchstones to a past life, that skills from a previous incarnation could even be transferred into the present through Glimmers. From a battered medical box during my time as a nurse in the Second World War, I apparently gained in-depth knowledge of first aid, enough to patch up Phoenix's gunshot wounds. From an incarnation as a Cheyenne, I seemingly learned to ride a horse bareback. And from my training as a samurai warrior, I somehow acquired remarkable fighting abilities; those combat skills enabled me to escape my captors.

But now, after all my therapy, I question those abilities and wonder if it was just in my imagination. I haven't ridden a horse since, or attempted any first aid, and the fight with Damien and his gang in the crypt is a hazy memory at the best of times. I have to remind myself that Tanas drugged me with his wax potion, so I must have hallucinated everything.

My eyes sweep again over the display and rest upon the carved wooden stick. Feeling the need to disprove Phoenix's claims beyond any doubt, I reach out to grab its hilt –

'*Genna!*' barks a harsh voice.

Jumping out of my skin, I spin round to discover Prisha's father standing in the doorway, his dark mud-brown eyes narrowed, his moustache bristling. 'What are you doing in my study?' he demands. 'It's private. You don't have any right to be in here.'

'M-Mr Sharma, I-I'm sorry,' I stammer. 'I . . . was just admiring your *otta*.' I indicate the S-shaped wooden stick.

He continues to stare at me.

'Y-you have an impressive collection,' I go on, speaking rapidly in my embarrassment and to fill the awkward silence. I point at the curved gold dagger crowning the display. 'That's a beautiful *bichuwa* . . . and that pair of *katar* are exceptional . . . along with the *gada* club, and the *val* and *paricha* shield . . . You must have a passion for . . .'

As I babble away, I notice his stern expression melting into a beaming smile. 'You certainly know your Kalarippayattu weapons,' he says, his tone at once turning warm and friendly. 'Genna, if I'd known you harboured such an interest in the mother of all martial arts, I'd have introduced you to my collection moons ago.'

I blink, surprising even myself at my knowledge of the weaponry.

Joining me beside the display, Mr Sharma lifts the wooden stick from its cradle and offers it to me. 'This is my own personal *otta* from my training days as a youth. Here, you may hold it if you so wish.'

Hesitantly I take the *otta* from him, bracing myself for the unsettling shift into a Glimmer . . . but nothing happens. I remain present in the room, clasping the long curved stick, feeling a complete fool.

Touchstones were clearly just another delusion.

Mr Sharma studies me intently. 'Have you ever trained in Kalari?' he asks.

'No,' I reply, weighing the weapon in my hand. It feels light yet strong, almost like a natural extension of my own arm.

'I ask because you're holding the *otta* in a perfect reverse grip,' he observes.

'Am I? I've never –' I flip the club over into a normal forward grip without thinking – 'held one of these before in my life . . .' My voice trails away.

'Really?' His moustache twitches and he raises an incredulous eyebrow. 'Well, in that case you must have an innate talent,' he declares. 'The *otta* is considered to be the master weapon of Kalarippayattu. It's a great pity we're not in Kerala, otherwise I'd recommend you to my old guru to train. She'd be delighted to have such a naturally gifted student in her school.'

I return the weapon to him, unnerved. 'Thank you, Mr Sharma, but I'm not a born fighter.'

He looks deep into my eyes. 'Then you do not see what I see, Genna.'

I shift awkwardly under his unwavering gaze. Rarely have I spent so much time alone with Prisha's father. He usually keeps himself to himself, working in his study.

'I know we haven't talked about what happened to you,' he continues, placing the *otta* back in its place on the wall. 'It's none of my business. But from what little I do know, it seems you've demonstrated great *vignesva* as we'd say in Kalari training – real strength.'

I smile hesitantly. 'I don't always feel that strong,' I admit.

'*Tsk!* Don't do yourself such a disservice,' he chides, turning back to me. 'Strength doesn't always come from the things you can do; it comes from overcoming the things you thought you couldn't.' He gives me another searching look. 'Prisha tells me that you believe you may have had past lives. Is this true?'

I shake my head vehemently. 'No, no, I don't think that any more. That was just silly stuff.'

Mr Sharma furrows his brow in mild disapproval. 'I wouldn't be so quick to discard such beliefs,' he replies softly. 'For, as it is written in the Bhagavad Gita: "Just as a person discards worn-out clothes and puts on new clothes, the soul discards worn-out bodies and wears new ones." In my humble opinion, you've certainly got the heart and spirit of a Kalari warrior. So, who knows? Perhaps you were one in a past life.'

And, with a knowing smile, he presses his palms together in front of his heart and inclines his head. Intuitively I return his gesture of respect, then hurriedly leave the room, feeling more bewildered than ever.

7

'I hope he didn't upset you,' says Prisha as we lay out our beds for the night in her room. 'My dad can be quite intense.'

'No, not at all,' I lie. 'It's more the fact that I recognized each weapon and knew their names in Hindi that's odd.'

Mei rolls out her blanket. 'You've been to Prisha's house countless times. Surely Mr Sharma's talked about his weapon collection at some point?'

'Not that I remember,' I reply, setting up my pillow and sleeping bag on the floor beside hers. 'But, even if he has, that still doesn't explain how I knew the correct way to hold the *otta*.'

'Come on, there can't be that many ways to hold a stick!' retorts Mei with a laugh.

'According to my father,' Prisha says earnestly, 'it takes twelve years to master the *otta*.'

Mei rolls her eyes. 'Guess there's more to it than I thought.'

'And what about the smells?' I go on. 'Where did they come from?'

With an exasperated sigh, Mei turns to Prisha on her bed. 'You burn incense all the time, don't you, Prish?'

Prisha nods. 'Yeah, I've got some here, in fact,' she says, pulling a long thin box off a bookshelf, the container clearly labelled SANDALWOOD.

'See? There you go,' Mei says triumphantly. 'You probably smelt that when you dropped off your bag.'

'Maybe,' I concede, 'but the scent reminded me of somewhere specific. If only I could remember where . . .'

'Well, if objects and places can potentially trigger these Glimmers, then perhaps smells and tastes can too?' suggests Prisha. 'We could try again with my incense.'

As Prisha lights a stick of sandalwood along with a couple of small diya lamps on her bookshelf, Mei shoots her a sceptical look. 'Is that really wise?'

'You were the one who googled her death as an acrobat!' Prisha points out.

'Yes, but I was simply trying to disprove the concept of Glimmers,' argues Mei. 'You're attempting to make one happen. There's a big difference.'

Prisha offers a strained smile. 'OK, I guess you're right,' she admits, and climbs into her bed.

Under the soft flickering glow of the lamps, we chat quietly about her party, her mother's exquisite cooking, her uncle's skill at the sitar, and the many fabulous gifts she's received, including tickets to see the Rushes and a once-in-a-lifetime pilgrimage trip to Varanasi, the sacred 'City of Light' in northern India.

'So, d'you wanna come?' Prisha asks me.

'*What? To India?*' I gasp.

'No, dummy!' she says, laughing. 'To see the Rushes.'

My jaw drops open, even more amazed. 'Err . . . they're, like, only my favourite band! Of course!'

'How about you, Mei?' asks Prisha.

Mei puts on a pained expression. 'Er, thanks, but I'd rather shove glass in my ears.'

'They're not *that* bad!' I protest.

'I suppose they're all right . . . to look at, I mean,' Mei teases with a glance at the poster on Prisha's wall. 'But can any of them actually sing?'

'Yes! Brandon has an awesome voice,' I reply defensively, and the two of us fall into our usual argument over music. As our debate heats up, Prisha tactfully interjects, 'So, you must be excited about going to Barbados tomorrow, Gen?'

I nod and grin, my heart immediately warming at the thought of seeing Papaya again. 'I think my parents are even more excited than me. They've been packing all week.'

'I sure envy you dodging school,' says Mei, stifling a yawn. 'Do spare a thought for us poor souls toiling away, while you're sunbathing on the beach.'

I stare at her with a totally blank expression. 'Er, sorry, who are you again?' At that, Prisha and Mei both laugh.

We continue to chat into the night. After a while Mei drops out of the conversation and we glance over to see her flat out on her blanket, snoring lightly.

'Guess it's time for sleep,' whispers Prisha, yawning and rolling over. 'Night, Genna.'

'Night,' I reply.

I lie on my back, but sleep evades me as troubled thoughts whirl round my head. I've put on a brave face for my friends, but the encounter with Prisha's father and the

Kalari weapons has unsettled me to my core. It was only a week or so ago that I finally accepted my Glimmers were created by my subconscious. In the time since then, I've imagined I've seen a Watcher, spotted Damien, read what appears to be my own obituary as a circus acrobat, and now I seem to possess innate knowledge of a martial art I'd never heard of before this evening. On their own these events don't mean much, but together they're much harder to explain away. *Surely they can't all be figments of my imagination?*

But why now? I've had six months with no Glimmers. Maybe I'm simply decompressing. Dr Larsson did warn me that I may relapse or experience flashbacks as my mind accepts the truth and I adjust back to normal life. Perhaps Prisha is right. I need this holiday – a break from everything, time to find myself and come back anew.

Pushing my concerns aside, I focus on my imminent trip to Barbados and the thrill of seeing the Rushes in concert when I return. As I fantasize about going backstage and meeting the band, a waft of sandalwood incense drifts over me. I roll on to my side and gaze at the trembling flames of the diya lamps on the bookshelf. Some fresh flowers are arranged round a small golden statue of the elephant-headed deity Ganesh. For some reason, the shelf reminds me of a *puttara*. The word pops unbidden into my head.

For a moment I lose track of my backstage daydream and see a flash of a thatched wooden building with an earthen red floor . . . then my eyelids begin to droop. The diya lamps flicker, their flames guttering out. In the semi-darkness, I watch the glowing red tip of the incense and the faint wreaths of smoke as they curl lazily into the air . . .

The dawn sun peeks through the slatted windows of the kalari and on to the hard-packed earth of its sunken floor. Trails of sandalwood incense smoke swirl as I bow before the puttara *and place my offerings of rose petals on the altar. Having paid my respects to the kalari's guardian deities, I begin my daily training with a series of stretches, twists, low stances and high kicks.*

Soon my lithe body glistens with sweat as well as the sesame oil that I rubbed on to warm my muscles and which gives my skin the sheen of deep burnished bronze. I wear only a white cloth langoti *round my waist; still, the heat of the day is already building and making me sweat even more. All the while my guru sits in the corner, her chin resting upon the hilt of her* otta *as she observes my progress.*

'Aarush, swing your arms to give yourself more momentum,' she instructs as I try to increase the height of my kicks. Her face is lined like the bark of a walnut tree, and she is just as hard. Although she may be old, she's practised Kalarippayattu since she was seven years old. There is not one man in the whole valley who would dare take her on in a fight.

Once I'm limbered up, I turn to a small leather ball that's suspended from the ceiling by a rope, the other end of which is clasped in my guru's hand. The ball hangs just above the height of my head; the target set for the first of my high kicks.

Easy, *I think to myself with a grin.* I don't even have to jump for it.

A high flick of my foot sends the ball swinging. But, as soon as the target settles, my guru lifts it a couple of inches.

This time I need to spring off the ground to make contact. With each successful attempt, she raises the ball higher. I cope for the next three kicks until she puts the target well beyond my usual training height.

'Are you expecting me to fight an elephant?' I ask, incredulous. The leather ball is now halfway to the beamed ceiling.

'This isn't about the size of your opponent,' she replies, waving the trunk-like otta *at me. 'It's about the range and reach of your attack. The higher you can jump, the stronger you are.' She points the stick's rounded tip at the target. 'Now kick that ball!'*

With a deferential bow, I set myself up for the impossible. Taking a run at it, I leap into the air and kick out with my foot. I miss the ball completely and land heavily on my back, where I lie, winded.

'You won't move it with breath alone,' she chides, a small smile curling the corner of her mouth.

Dusting myself off, I prepare to make another attempt. This time as I leap into the air, I swing my arms harder. My toes almost brush the bottom of the ball. I look to my guru, hoping that it's close enough. But she shakes her silver-haired head.

'It's no good tickling the nose of a warrior,' she says. 'He'll just laugh in your face before bashing it in!'

Knowing that my real training won't begin until I manage to connect with the ball, I keep trying to hit the target. The sweat pours from me, the rich earth of the floor sticking to my back with every fall. Then, in my dogged determination, I overextend a kick and land in an awkward, painful heap. Exhausted by my efforts, I turn to my guru to plead for a break, but her dark-brown eyes, always ringed with a starlit gleam, are closed and she breathes in the slow, steady rhythm of deep sleep.

It seems my lesson is over for the day. Limping quietly up to her, I reach out to take the rope from her grasp. But before I even lay a hand upon her, I feel the sharp thrust of her otta *in my chest.*

'Ow!' I cry, falling on to my backside on the packed earth. The attack was so swift and sudden that I barely saw it. But I certainly felt it; my whole chest is crushed with pain.

Stirring, my guru opens her soulful eyes. 'One who is an expert of otta *cannot be touched, even in sleep,' she says sagely.*

I rub the middle of my chest where the rounded tip of her stick struck me. The pain won't fade. In fact, like an unchecked fire, it's only growing worse. 'What – did you – do – to me?' I gasp.

She rises to her feet with an ease that belies her age. 'I hit you in a marma point,' she explains. 'The hridaya *to be exact. It's a potentially lethal blow.'*

'What?' I'm beginning to struggle for breath.

'Marma are vital energy points in the human body,' she continues, lecturing me like she's delivering a normal lesson. 'While these points are used in Ayurvedic medicine to heal, the word "marma" literally means "a point that can kill".'

'Well, I think – I'm dying!' I cry in agony.

'Oh, Aarush, do stop your whining.' My guru sighs. With the palm of her hand, she massages my chest, then

using her thumb presses down hard on another marma point. The pain and pressure instantly ease.

I stare at her in amazement. No wonder every man fears her. 'Please, will you teach me the marma points?'

'Maybe, when you prove your worth,' she says. 'But there are two rules I live by as a Kalari guru. The first is never to tell anyone everything you know.'

'What's the second?' I ask, breathless.

My guru responds with an arch, silent grin, then turns and walks out of the room.

8

'It must have been a dream,' says Mei as we make our way back home from Prisha's the following morning. The sun is out and the streets are bustling with Saturday shoppers, but I can't shake last night's vision of the kalari from my mind. The sunken hall's distinctive smell still lingers in my nostrils and even my muscles seem to ache from the training.

'How can you be so certain?' I say, wearily shifting my overnight bag to my other shoulder.

'Because you were a boy!' replies Mei, laughing as if the answer is obvious.

Crossing the road, we head down a quieter side street and into the leafy residential area of Clapham where I live. 'Why should that make any difference?' I ask.

'In every Glimmer so far you've been a girl or a woman,' Mei explains in a patient tone. 'Isn't it a bit odd to suddenly be a boy?'

A silver-grey cat jumps up on to a nearby garden wall and demands my attention. I stop to give it a stroke. 'But surely if I've had lots of past lives, there's no reason why I couldn't have been a boy at some point,' I argue as the cat purrs loudly and rubs against my hand. 'Doesn't my incarnation as Aarush make it *more* likely that it was a Glimmer?'

Mei shakes her head in dismay at my renewed fixation on Glimmers. 'For what it's worth, I believe Dr Larsson is right about these being figments of your rather vivid imagination. Just as he induced your circus vision, so Prisha's party inspired your dream. The sandalwood incense, the Indian food, the clothing and music, Mr Sharma's weapon collection . . . Your brain absorbed all these things during the course of the evening. Then at night your mind was processing that information, storing it as memories. That's what dreaming is, as I understand: the events of –'

As Mei is talking, the cat suddenly stiffens and hisses. Unsettled by its reaction, I glance over my shoulder, following the cat's line of sight. But the tree-lined street is quiet. There are no other cats or dogs around, no people either, so I'm at a loss as to what has spooked it. Then I notice the tips of a pair of white trainers sticking out from behind one of the nearby trees. The cat hisses again and I too feel unnerved, the hairs on the back of my neck rising.

I turn to Mei, but at that moment her mobile rings. 'Hi, Dad,' she says, answering the call. 'What's up?' Her face drops. '*Are you serious?* When?'

I watch as her expression grows ever more shocked. I snatch a look back down the street but can no longer see the white trainers. Either the person has gone or I was mistaken – perhaps there was no one there in the first place. The cat, however, remains alert and watchful at my side.

'OK, I'll come straight home,' says Mei. She pockets her phone.

'What's happened?' I ask.

Mei gazes at me in angry disbelief. 'Our house was broken into last night!'

'*What?*' I gasp. 'Anyone hurt? Anything taken?'

Mei shakes her head. 'My parents have only just got back home from an overnight conference. My brother's still at his mate's house, thank goodness. Dad's office is in a right mess, he says. It seems like whoever did it was searching for something in particular. Or otherwise plain stupid, because even though they broke into his wall safe they ignored the collection of Spanish gold doubloons he kept in there. Those coins are worth a fortune!'

I raise an eyebrow in surprise. 'Perhaps the burglar was disturbed,' I suggest. 'Still . . . I guess your dad must be pretty upset.'

Mei nods slowly. 'It gives me the creeps to think some stranger may have been in my bedroom,' she murmurs, a shudder running through her.

'It's a good thing we were over at Prisha's last night,' I say quickly, giving the cat a departing stroke before taking Mei's arm and leading her down the road. 'I'll ask my mum if she can give you a lift back.' But, as we turn the corner to my street, I spot two police cars . . . and an ambulance – *and they're parked outside my house!* Mei and I exchange frightened looks.

'What the hell's going on?' she says.

I don't bother replying. We dash along the road up to a small cluster of onlookers who have gathered outside on the pavement. My heart racing, I push through them, and Mei and I duck under the police tape that is cordoning off my house. Before anyone can stop us, we sprint up the driveway and burst through the open front door.

'Mum! Dad!' I shout. But there's no reply.

Halfway down the hall I stop dead; my bag slumps to the floor with a thud. Ahead of me, through the half-open kitchen door, I see a pair of legs. My mother's legs. The rest of her is hidden behind the door – and lying beside her I can see my father, his hand outstretched, as if trying to protect her. Then I notice the kitchen floor. I swear the tiles weren't so dark red –

'*Oh my God* –' gasps Mei. I feel her hand tightening round mine as my whole world caves in on me. The hall floor buckles under my feet, my stomach lurches and my vision warps . . . *A brief but vivid flash of two bodies (my parents yet somehow not my parents, since the people I suddenly see are both olive-skinned) sprawled across a Grecian-blue mosaic floor, their ivory-white togas stained red with blood* . . . The next moment the nightmare vision has vanished.

A police officer appears from the living room. 'No, girls! Not in there,' she says, swiftly ushering me and Mei into the adjacent dining room. She guides me over to a chair and sits me down before I fall. My legs are weak, my head heavy, my heart hollow. Mei is close beside me, trembling, her hand still clasping mine as if afraid to let go and lose me to my despair.

The police officer kneels down in front of me. Her honey-brown eyes are gentle and kind. 'I'm guessing you're Genna,' she says softly.

Grief and shock coursing through me, I nod.

She turns to Mei. 'And you are?'

'Mei – Genna's best friend,' she replies in a far-off voice.

'Well, it's good she has a friend with her,' says the police officer, and she smiles mournfully. Then her gaze returns to me and she swallows hard. 'This won't be easy to hear, Genna, but there's no easy way to tell you. It appears someone broke into your house last night. There was a struggle and, I'm so sorry to tell you, your parents were both killed.'

I sit numb and silent, the hard wooden dining chair digging into my back. Mei squeezes my hand even more and puts an arm round my shoulders.

'W-was it a-another burglary?' Mei asks, her voice hitching.

The police officer gives Mei a puzzled look. 'What do you mean, *another*?'

As Mei tells her about the break-in at her house, I stare vacantly at the family photo of me, my mum and my dad on Brighton beach. It's a gloriously sunny day, the sea is glistening and we're all smiling, ice creams in our hands. The photo was only taken a month ago – I remember just moments later a seagull swooped down and stole Dad's ice cream. How we'd all laughed, for the first time in a long while . . .

Then the photo blurs.

Tears are rolling freely down my cheeks and dripping on to my jeans, but I'm too choked with sorrow to make a sound. I hear a car pull up on the driveway, then the clunk of car doors opening and closing followed by the crunch of footsteps.

'Anyone found the daughter yet?' demands a sharp female voice from the porch entrance.

'Yes, good news, ma'am,' responds a gruff male voice in the hallway. 'According to the family calendar, she was staying at a friend's house last night: a Prisha Sharma. I've just come off the phone to Mr Sharma. He says Genna left there half an hour ago.'

'OK. Inform me as soon as you make contact, officer.'

'Yes, ma'am,' the police officer replies. 'We've also determined that the weapon used in the attack was some sort of knife. Judging by the victims' wounds, its blade appears to be quite unusual . . .'

As the policeman proceeds to deliver his report, the officer with us quickly gets to her feet. 'Mei, will you look after Genna for me? I need to inform the detective inspector that you're here.'

'Sure,' says Mei, her arm still round me.

The policewoman goes out into the hallway, leaving the dining-room door ajar. Through the gap, I can spy the detective inspector in the hall mirror. Her charcoal-black hair is pulled into a tight bun, her tailored navy-blue suit is as crisp and as sharp as ever. There's a small scar marking her forehead, the only visible sign of the car crash she was in when Phoenix liberated me from her custody. As DI Katherine Shaw listens attentively to the police officer's report, she takes off her tinted glasses to clean the lenses, and in the process reveals what I was dreading. Her keen grey eyes have pooled once more into oily black holes.

9

The shock of seeing DI Shaw cuts through my grief like a knife and I leap to my feet. I suddenly know, beyond all doubt, that my therapist was wrong. 'The Hunters are back!' I gasp. 'But how can they be? Tanas is *dead*!'

Joining me as I hide behind the dining-room door, Mei lays a gentle hand on my shoulder. 'Shh, calm down, Genna. What are you talking about? What Hunters?'

'Can't you see her eyes?' I whisper, peeking nervously into the hallway. DI Shaw is still being updated by the first officer, while the policewoman stands behind them, impatiently waiting for him to finish.

Mei glances at the detective inspector's reflection in the mirror. 'What about her eyes?' she whispers back.

'Can't you see? They're completely black!' A familiar panic is rising in my chest. 'She's a Soul Hunter!'

Mei frowns at me. 'Genna, her eyes look normal to me,' she replies in a slow, deliberate tone.

'Yes, of course they do,' I mutter, more to myself than to Mei. 'The change must only be visible to those with Soul Sight.'

This realization has suddenly hit me and it explains a great deal: how the Hunters can move through society undetected; how they can infiltrate the police and other key organizations; and how they can recognize and communicate with other Incarnates. I guess the same is true for the star-like blue gleam of Phoenix's eyes and mine – invisible to everyone but people like us: Soul Protectors and First Ascendants and, worst of all, to Soul Hunters like DI Shaw.

'I think I should get our police officer back,' suggests Mei, reaching for the door handle.

'No!' I cry, grabbing hold of her arm to pull her away. 'You *have* to trust me. I'm in grave danger. My very soul is at risk!'

'Genna, I understand you're deeply upset,' she says as she extricates herself from my grip. 'Your parents have just been killed in this attempted burglary –'

'No, it wasn't a burglary,' I correct her. 'My parents were *murdered* because the Soul Hunters were looking for *me*. And DI Shaw is one of them.'

'OK, you're seriously worrying me now,' says Mei firmly. 'You're having a panic attack. You need to breathe deep and slow.'

'No, I'm completely lucid,' I reply. 'Phoenix was speaking the truth. He always was. The Glimmers are *real*! Soul Hunters are *real*!'

Eyeing me with concern, Mei backs away towards the door. 'I'll only be a second. Wait here.'

'Mei, STOP!' I beg. '*Please* trust me on this. I need your help if I'm going to survive.'

'I *am* trying to help you,' Mei replies patiently.

'Then create a distraction while I escape.'

‘*Escape?*’ she exclaims, disbelief marking her face. ‘Why would you want to run from the police? They can protect you.’

‘Believe me, Mei, they can’t,’ I reply, peering over her shoulder into the hall mirror. The officer is stepping aside now to allow the policewoman to talk to DI Shaw. ‘There’s only one person who can protect me. Now, listen. I need to grab a few things and go. Just delay them. Please. That’s all I’m asking.’

Mei hesitates, her hand on the door handle. ‘Why should I?’

I look at her imploringly. ‘Because you’re my best friend. Because you’re the only person, aside from Phoenix, I can trust. And because you owe me for that time I covered for you when you were in trouble with the police for shoplifting.’

Reluctantly Mei releases the door handle. ‘Fine,’ she mutters through clenched teeth. ‘But don’t make me regret this.’

‘I promise you, I won’t.’

So, leaving a bewildered and troubled Mei in the dining room, I crouch low and slip out of the door. Thankfully, our L-shaped hallway means I can’t be seen from the front entrance as I scurry up the stairs to my bedroom. My suitcase and backpack are spread out on my bed, half-packed for our – for our family holiday that will now never be. The sharp pang of loss hits me again . . . Blinking back fresh bitter tears, I stuff a pair of spare jeans, a few tops, a jacket and some extra underwear into the backpack, the trauma of everything I’ve lost today spurring me on. Lastly,

I pack my old fluffy bunny Coco for comfort and Phoenix's amulet too for good luck. Then I dash into my parents' room. Their bags are ready and waiting by the door, and all our travel documents are set out neatly on top of the chest of drawers. Both Mum's purse and Dad's wallet lie untouched – more proof if ever I needed it that this was no burglary. I grab my passport, the plane tickets, a currency envelope stuffed with US dollars and my mum's credit card.

Below me I can hear voices.

'Where is she?' DI Shaw is demanding.

'In the downstairs toilet, I think,' replies Mei. 'She said she was feeling sick.'

'Genna, are you OK in there?' asks the female police officer, rapping on the toilet door.

I make one more sweep of my parents' room, shoulder my backpack, then head out on to the landing. From the top of the stairs, I can spy DI Shaw, the police officer and Mei standing downstairs.

'Let me have a go,' I hear Mei say, leaning close against the toilet door. 'Genna . . . it's me. I know you're upset, but you do really need to come out. I'm worried about you. I understand how much of a shock all this is, especially after everything that's happened this year, but I'm here for you, and the police can help you, so . . .'

Playing for time, my best friend even tries the door handle and pretends it's locked. *Dear Mei, you really are my best friend. Thank you!* The extra seconds she's given me to escape may prove vital. Since I can't leave the house via the stairs, I retreat to my bedroom. My sash window overlooks the back garden, which is clear, save for the cherry tree and the shed. But the drop down to the ground is a good five metres. The tree isn't close enough to climb down ... *but could I jump to it?*

Now a fist is pounding on the downstairs toilet door. I glance over at my bookcase and my gold trophy for gymnastics. My agility may be impressive in a gymnasium, but to reach the tree and land safely I really need to be an acrobat – or trapeze artist ...

'Genna!' barks DI Shaw's voice from the hallway. 'Come out *now*, or we'll have to force this door.'

Once more I must put total faith in my Soul Protector, Phoenix. If he's right about skills transferring from past lives, then my Glimmer in the Russian circus means Yelena's abilities have passed to me. But if on the other hand he's wrong – well, I could easily break my neck.

'This is your last warning, Genna,' declares DI Shaw.

A few seconds later, I hear a splintering of wood and the policewoman exclaim, 'Oh! She isn't in here, ma'am!'

I'm out of options.

I lift up the sash window. It squeals loudly. Now the thud of feet is thundering up the stairs ... Clambering on to the windowsill, I leap for the tree. I fly through the air, arms outstretched, and imagine myself as a trapeze artist ... reaching for Dmitry's grip. With an assured grace, I grab hold of a branch, swing from the bough and somersault to land neatly on the lawn, arms spread wide as if performing for an audience. I can almost hear the echo of applause –

I laugh to myself. I really *was* Yelena, the Flying Firebird!

'There she is!'

My moment of glory over, I look back up over my shoulder and see DI Shaw staring down from my bedroom window, her black eyes blazing. It's now that I recognize her corrupted soul – *she* was the dour-faced woman in the front row who refused to clap my performance.

'Stay exactly where you are!' she snarls.

Ignoring her, I sprint towards the fence and vault over to my neighbour's garden with startling ease. Feeling more and more like Yelena from the circus, I bound over the next fence and the next, working my way towards the street. As I reach the last garden, I notice its boundary wall is topped with broken glass. Recalling the Wall of Knives, I leap high into the air, tuck my legs in, and perform a tight somersault over the glinting points of glass. Clearing the danger by a hair's breadth, I land unharmed on the pavement in a low crouch.

The familiar rush of acrobatic daring courses through my veins and I can't help grinning at my old-found skill. Then my smile falters as a pair of white trainers plant themselves in front of me.

10

'Good to see you again, Genna,' says a smooth, snide voice.

I look up into the coal-black eyes of Damien. His lean chiselled face is even more marble-white than I remember. But he appears to have used his time in prison to weight train and bulk up. His arms are well defined and his hoodie is tight round his chest. He flicks his fringe of raven hair from his eyes and flashes me a smile as charming as a snake's. 'So, where are you going in such a hurry?'

'*Murderer!*' I roar, launching myself at him in a fit of rage. However, before I can get my hands on his throat, I'm grabbed from behind and my arms are pinned. I glance behind me to see the rest of his gang surrounding me. They all wear hoodies, their faces cast in shadow. But I recognize each of them. The blond-haired boy whose arm I broke in the crypt. The girl with the black widow spider tattoo on her neck. The muscular thug holding me, his nose bent crooked courtesy of Phoenix, who broke it for him twice. And the most lethal of the lot: the tall and powerful girl who wears knuckleduster rings and carries a steel pipe in her back pocket.

'Genna, you've had many parents before and they've all died,' says Damien unsympathetically. 'I don't know why you're so upset. You should be used to it by now.'

Once again the disturbing image of two bodies wrapped in blood-stained togas flashes before my eyes – and this time it makes sense. My mother and father from a past life, murdered by Hunters. My anger now doubles and I writhe in the iron grip of the thug. 'How come you're free?' I spit at Damien.

He grins. 'DI Shaw vouched for our good-behaviour inside . . . got us out early on a *rehabilitation* programme. So kind of her, don't you think?'

'I don't understand. None of you should be Hunters any more,' I say, my anger giving way to bewilderment. 'Phoenix killed Tanas. I saw him die right in front of my eyes.'

'That you did,' replies Damien. 'But you underestimated his power. Tanas is back and stronger than ever.'

I stop struggling. 'He's returned? In *this* lifetime? That's not possible.'

'Oh, but it is!' Damien can't hide his glee. 'You see, Tanas himself incarnated into another body.'

A wave of despair overcomes me at this revelation. Phoenix had thrust an obsidian blade straight through Tanas's chest and told me how this shard of black volcanic rock was my enemy's Achilles heel and that the Incarnate's soul would be too weak to return for at least a lifetime, if not more. That's the reason my Soul Protector left me unguarded – he'd believed his job was done for this life. *How wrong he was!*

Damien draws a six-inch-long green knife from his belt. I instantly recognize the lethal weapon, although the last time I saw it the blade was shattered into several pieces, so Mei's parents must have had it restored. Made of pure jade, its hilt carved with an icon of a jaguar crossed with a man, the four-thousand-year-old knife is the one Tanas needs to cut out my heart when performing the ceremony that will extinguish my soul forever.

Seeing the fear in my eyes, Damien advances on me. 'Poor Genna,' he sneers. 'There's no Phoenix around to protect you now.' He smirks, waving the repaired knife in my face. He licks his lips hungrily before barking an order to his gang. 'Hold her spreadeagled against the wall.'

The four other Hunters glance uneasily at one another.

'Shouldn't Tanas perform the ritual?' questions Knuckleduster uneasily. 'You know what our master thought about our attempt in the park.'

Damien shoots the girl an irritable look. 'We can't afford to let this First Ascendant's soul slip through our fingers again,' he growls. 'Besides, I think I deserve a little of his power. Now do as I say!'

Thug goes to pin me against the wall when a sharp voice shouts, 'Oi! Leave that girl alone!'

The policewoman from my house is pelting round the corner towards us, closely followed by another officer. DI Shaw is nowhere in sight. Taking advantage of the distraction, I twist myself free of Thug's grip and elbow him hard in the solar plexus. He gasps in pain and doubles over. I don't wait around for the other Hunters to react.

I run.

Over the pounding of my feet on the tarmac, I can hear the two police officers giving chase. I work my way back to the main street, hoping to lose them among the crowds of shoppers. But my pursuers are gaining on me fast. As I weave between the startled pedestrians, I barge straight into a woman with her shopping. Her bag rips open and tins of cat food go scattering across the pavement.

'Sorry!' I shout, running on. But the collision works in my favour as the policeman on my tail stumbles on a tin and goes sprawling to the ground.

'Genna, STOP!' orders the other officer, nimbly leaping over her colleague and continuing to give chase.

I daren't stop, though. I can't risk being taken into custody and put under DI Shaw's charge. My heart thudding hard, I power on up the street. Ahead of me is a busy junction. Just as the traffic lights turn green, I dart across the road. A horn blares as a car pulls out, narrowly missing me, then careers straight into the policewoman close on my heels. She tumbles over the bonnet and lands in a heap in the road.

I glance back, worried she's seriously hurt. But I see her moving, more bruised than broken, so don't hang around any longer. Damien and his Hunters are still on my trail. Fleeing down the opposite street, I duck into a building site where a block of flats is under construction and conceal myself behind a cement truck. I peer out cautiously as the two police officers stagger past, one clutching her side, the other limping badly.

A few moments later, Damien and his Hunters rush by.

Catching my breath and slowly counting to calm myself, I wait a full minute until I'm certain I've lost both the police and the Soul Hunters, then I emerge from my hiding place.

I've barely taken two steps, however, when the muscled thug appears at the site entrance. His craggy features still bear the faint red fern-like scars from the lightning strike that almost killed him in the stone circle. Wheezing and hunched over, he's nursing his stomach where I elbowed him earlier.

I stand stock-still hoping he won't notice me among the construction workers in their high-vis jackets. Then my mobile rings, loud and jaunty. Fumbling in my pocket, I cut the call and mute my phone.

But I'm too late.

11

Thug turns towards me and his lips twist into a grin as crooked as his nose. He whistles to alert the others, then shrugging off his injury he advances on me like a slow-moving bulldozer. While I may have defeated him once in the crypt, those samurai skills seem to have deserted me this time. For several seconds I stand like a wide-eyed defenceless deer. Thug is taller, bigger and stronger than me in every way.

Then I recall my most recent Glimmer . . .

This isn't about the size of your opponent. It's about the range and reach of your attack.

As Thug goes to grab me, I summon up Aarush's Kalari skills and jump high into the air. Imagining the Hunter's face to be the leather ball, I lash out with a flying kick. My foot connects and there's an eye-watering crunch. He crumples to the floor, clutching his broken nose and moaning, 'Ugh . . . not *again*!'

I land in a lion stance beside him. 'Well, as my guru once said, it's no good just tickling the nose of a warrior!'

But I don't have time to relish my victory. Damien and the rest of the Hunters appear at the entrance. I dash through the building site, hoping to lose them amid the chaos of construction all around. The cement truck is now unloading a slurry of concrete; a jackhammer thunders as loud as a machine gun somewhere nearby. A bright yellow bulldozer rumbles past. I try to cover my tracks within the dust cloud swirling in its wake. Behind me the Hunters are shouting to one another as they spread out to look for me.

'There she is!' yells Damien to the others as I duck beneath a crane lifting a girder towards the half-finished roof.

The blond-haired Hunter is on me in seconds. We race round the outside of the building and under a tower of scaffolding. Ahead, I notice the concrete path is glistening, as if it has just rained. With Blondie close on my heels, I once more draw upon Yelena's acrobatic prowess and leap for one of the scaffolding struts above my head. Swinging up and over, I spin round the strut to come down behind the Hunter, and I kick him hard in the back. He goes flying face-first into the wet concrete.

'Be thankful it isn't a Pit of Glass!' I say, laughing as he flounders in the hardening mix of gravel and cement.

Before the other Hunters can grab me, I swing to the next strut and haul myself up.

'Don't let her get away!' shouts Damien.

Climbing the scaffold, the two remaining Hunters scramble after me. For the first couple of floors I manage to keep one step ahead. Unfortunately for me, though, the girl with the spider on her neck lives up to her tattoo. Scaling the scaffold with remarkable speed, she catches up with me in a matter of seconds, seizes my ankle and yanks me off my feet. I shriek as I drop on to a wooden plank and almost plunge three storeys to the ground below. The near-fatal fall is a sharp reminder of how my former incarnation died. If I'm not careful, that will be my fate in this life too.

Focusing on surviving, I kick myself free of the Hunter's grip and clamber to my feet. Spider joins me on the plank. With a flick of her wrist, she produces a butterfly knife. Unarmed, I don't stand much of a chance against her. I back away as she advances, the plank wobbling dangerously beneath us. But, being blessed with Yelena's skill of balancing, that doesn't faze me. The same can't be said for the Hunter, however, who throws out her arms in an attempt to steady herself. I wobble the plank more. As her arms flail, I kick the girl in the chest and she tumbles off the scaffold. With a terrified scream, Spider plummets all the way to the ground . . . and lands in a skip of plasterboard, where she lies winded and writhing in pain.

In the meantime, Knuckleduster has caught up with me.

With the scaffold going nowhere but up, I clamber into the building through a hole in the brickwork. Inside, it's just a shell – all concrete walls and floor. Steel supports dot the open space like a metal forest. In the centre is a stairwell, but before I can get to it Knuckleduster jumps through another window and blocks my escape.

She pulls the steel pipe from her pocket. 'Payback time,' she snarls, the corners of her mouth curling into a vengeful grin. In the crypt I managed to knock her out with a spinning hook kick to the head. But on that occasion my martial art skills had the element of surprise – and even then she almost beat me. Now I'm faced with a wiser and more vindictive opponent. To make matters worse, my samurai fighting skills continue to elude me. I raise my hands into a hesitant fighting guard, but the stance feels unnatural and awkward. It's as if I have a mental block, a gap in my memory.

Knuckleduster girl seems to sense my uncertainty. Letting out a yell of fury, she swings her pipe at me. I duck. The steel clashes against a roof support. She brings the pipe down again and I jump aside. In a flurry of vicious swipes, she forces me to retreat. I duck, dodge and dive repeatedly, my gymnastic ability helping me to avoid most of her attacks . . . until she catches me across the arm. Her weapon leaves a stinging red welt. Then the pipe clips my leg and deadens my thigh. As I stumble over a pile of building materials, she hits me with a surprise uppercut. Her knuckleduster rings rock my jaw, stars burst before my eyes and I go sprawling to the deck.

'Now to tenderize the meat,' she says, raising the pipe above her head.

Out of the corner of my eye, I spot a twisted steel bar and in desperation snatch it up off the floor –

'Aarush, concentrate!' chides my guru as she strikes me with her otta *in yet another marma point on my ribs.*

'But I can barely see your attacks,' I complain, getting stiffly to my feet.

My guru fixes me with an unrelenting look. 'In order to be aware of your enemy's every movement, your whole body must become an eye,' she explains. 'Have no delay between mind and movement. Make your otta *an extension of your arm. Grow into it as if you were one and the same.'*

Imagining the weapon to be my arm and its rounded tip my finger, I take aim for the amsa *point on my guru's shoulder. However, as old as my guru is, she evades my thrust with the light-footed grace of a cat. In the same fluid motion she deflects my* otta *and disarms me, my wooden stick clattering to the dirt floor.*

'How did you do that?' I gasp, astonished at her skill and dexterity.

'Like an elephant's trunk, the otta *can curl round your opponent's weapon,' she explains. 'Use its unique shape to your advantage. Just as Lord Shiva himself witnessed an elephant combat a lion with its powerful trunk, you too can declaw an enemy –'*

The steel pipe arcs down towards me. Instinctively I block it with the twisted bar. The clang of the two weapons echoes round the empty building. The Hunter strikes again. Once more I deflect the attack. Rolling backwards to my feet, I hold the bar in a familiar reverse grip. Blows rain down. But I manage to fend off each and every thrust, swipe and sweep of the pipe. Knuckleduster becomes more and more frustrated and frenzied in her attacks. As she overreaches on a jab, I block her strike and with a deft twirl of my wrist disarm her of the pipe!

She howls in rage, thunderstruck at my sudden skill. Unable to defend herself, I thrust the tip of the bar into her chest, targeting the *hridaya* point. She lets out a pained gasp and collapses to the floor.

Although I didn't hit the point exactly, the strike is enough to put the Hunter out of action. Tossing the steel bar aside, I stagger over to the stairwell. By now Damien has also found his way into the building and is ascending the stairs. I hobble up to the next level and on to the roof. The city skyline is stretched out before me. A group of builders welding a girder into place turn to me, a look of consternation on their faces. 'Oi! What are you doing up here?' one of them shouts.

'Looking for a way down,' I reply. But there doesn't appear to be another staircase. Peering over the roof's edge, I'm greeted by a five-storey drop. A quick but lethal exit.

'Impressive acrobatic skills,' Damien remarks, ignoring the gruff protests of the builders as he strides towards me. 'Any more performances?'

With nowhere to go, I retreat to the very edge of the building and glance down over my shoulder at the drop. 'Just one . . .' I say, before leaping from the roof.

In the brief seconds that I'm tumbling through the air, I'm struck by an ominous flash of déjà vu. Just as Yelena plunged to her death from the trapeze, I find myself free-falling to the ground. Below, the building site becomes a circus ring; the upturned faces of the construction workers, my horrified audience.

I realize I could just let myself go. End it all in a swift fatal accident. Just like Yelena's tragic death, it would be a sure-fire way to escape Tanas's clutches . . . at least in this life. But, according to Phoenix, a violent or wrongful end can damage my soul and weaken the Light, and I've no intention of strengthening Tanas's hand. Besides, my survival instinct is too powerful for that.

As I plummet downwards, I reach out and grab hold of the girder ties hanging from the crane's hook. Gripping them as if they were Dmitry's outstretched arms, I swing across the building site like the trapeze artist I once was. The crane operator is so startled he lowers the hook in double-quick time. A metre or so from the ground, I let myself drop and land running. Glancing behind me as I flee the building site, I catch sight of Damien standing on the roof, glaring at me in stunned fury.

12

My heart pounding and my hands shaking, I board the Underground train and take a seat by the door. I still can't quite believe I jumped from the top of that building. The shocked expression on Damien's face at my reckless stunt must have matched my own look of astonishment. Even my incarnation as Yelena would surely have thought twice! Yet I timed my leap perfectly with the passing arm of the crane, my reflexes as instinctive as ever.

I allow the slightest gleam of hope to enter my heart. *Maybe, just maybe, I've a chance of keeping one step ahead of Damien and his Hunters . . .*

The tube train slows for the next stop, its doors swish open and a flurry of passengers get on and off. I remain in my seat, trying to avoid eye contact with anyone. While I've escaped Damien for the time being, I remind myself that Tanas's Watchers are everywhere. What if one becomes aware of my presence and alerts a Soul Hunter to my location?

Glancing furtively round the carriage, my old paranoia returns. *Any of these passengers could be a Watcher!*

Donning my baseball cap and sunglasses from my backpack, I feel like a fugitive as I change trains and hide my face from the security cameras dotted around the station. Within a matter of hours my life has once again been turned on its head. It was little more than a week ago that my counsellor, Dr Larsson, convinced me that my Glimmers weren't real, that Phoenix had supposedly gaslighted me with fantasies of Soul Hunters and First Ascendants. But it turns out that it's *all* true. Dangerously so.

I feel an odd sense of relief in discovering that I wasn't crazy. In fact, Dr Larsson had been the one manipulating my mind, even if his intentions had been good. Instead of listening to him, I should've been spending my time preparing for Tanas's return. Although his second incarnation in this life of mine was unforeseen, his eventual reincarnation in another was guaranteed. So, rather than rationalizing and explaining away my trauma over these past six months, I should have been acquiring the skills and knowledge that could protect me in those future encounters . . . as well as in my present life. If only I had done so, then I –

A sudden stab of guilt pierces my grieving heart. If *only* I had, then I may have been able to save my parents' lives; it's *my* fault they're dead. Just like Phoenix's mother was killed in an attempt to eliminate Phoenix, my parents were murdered in order to get to me. The sharp sting of bitter tears pricks my eyes and I clench my fists as a silent scream rises in my chest.

Suddenly my emotions threaten to overwhelm me: the grief at my parents' murder . . . shock at Tanas's resurrection . . . horror at Damien's release and relentless pursuit . . . guilt at my own failure . . . and fear that my soul is once more in the balance. Desperate not to draw attention to myself, I suppress the urge to cry out and take several deep breaths, counting slowly to ten to calm myself.

The storm within me subsides, and I realize my sessions with Dr Larsson weren't a total waste of time and money. But my distress is soon replaced by another troubling thought – the apparent loss of my samurai fighting ability. Phoenix assured me that once I'd experienced a Glimmer of a particular skill, that skill would be with me always. While the recent Kalari training and circus acrobatics are fresh in my mind, my samurai martial arts seem to have dwindled. *What if all my abilities slip away?* I barely managed to escape the Hunters this time. Next time I may not be so lucky.

The gleam of hope I held earlier in my heart now begins to fade. I rest my head wearily against the carriage window and watch as the underground stations pass by in a blur. Entering the dark tunnels, I lose track of time and place –

'We can't wait much longer,' I whisper. 'The train will be here soon!'

Like two sewer rats, we crouch tense and nervous behind a pile of debris where the ceiling has caved in. The U-Bahn platform is dimly lit and deserted. Old newspapers litter the floor and a faded sign for NORDBAHNHOF *hangs crookedly from the tiled wall.*

'This may be a ghost station,' Hans replies under his breath, 'but that doesn't mean it's entirely abandoned.'

He nods towards a walled booth at the far end of the platform, where a pair of dark eyes peer through a narrow slit in the brickwork. Before the Berlin Wall was built, this used to be a busy U-Bahn station linking East and West

Germany. Now it's a crypt haunted by phantom-like armed guards.

But the watchful eyes are drowsily closing.

'At last!' mutters Hans. The previous night he'd befriended the guard and plied him with drink, with the aim of exhausting him for his shift. With the guard now asleep, we scurry over to the barrier erected alongside the track. Under the greenish glow of the flickering fluorescent lights, Hans takes out a pair of pliers and furiously snips away at the tangle of barbed wire.

Feeling dangerously exposed on the platform, I shudder as a chill runs through me. Many before us have tried to escape East Germany and failed. Hans considered crossing over the Wall itself, but the combination of razor wire, landmines, attack dogs and shoot-to-kill patrols persuaded him not to. He's seen far too many perish along the 'death strip' to take such a risk with me and my soul. But the infamous Stasi officer Gerhart Wolf and his black-eyed henchmen have finally tracked us down to East Berlin. With nowhere left to run, the closed U-Bahn station offers our last hope of escape.

The old newspapers rustle like leaves on the platform and from the tunnel a rising whine tells us a train is approaching, its headlamps growing larger in the gloom.

'Hurry!' I hiss. The train is our ticket out of East Germany. I snatch a glance towards the bunker where the guard still dozes. But for how much longer?

Pulling the barbed wire aside, Hans makes a gap large enough for me to crawl through. He's right behind me as I leap down on to the track bed.

'Careful of the middle rail,' warns Hans. 'That's live.'

I nod, steeling myself for the most dangerous part of our escape plan. Lying flat on our backs on the track bed, we wait to catch our ride. The train trundles over us, mere centimetres from our faces. As soon as the last carriage passes, we jump to our feet and run after it.

All of a sudden an alarm goes off. The steel door to the underground bunker clangs open and the hung-over guard emerges, a gun in his hand.

'RUN!' shouts Hans as a shot echoes down the empty platform, a bullet ricocheting off the train's rear carriage.

I sprint hard, trying not to step on the live rail. The train enters the tunnel and begins to accelerate away. Chasing its red tail lights, I make a grab for the door handle. Hans hoists me up on to the back runner. Turning, I stretch out my hand to him, just as a second shot rings out. Hans stumbles and falls to his knees.

'NO!' I cry as the train continues to pull away.

'You're free, Erika!' he shouts back, the guard looming over him. 'Just never stop running –'

As the train disappears into the cool darkness, a third and final shot echoes down the tunnel –

My head jerks up as the doors open and a recorded voice announces, '*This is Heathrow Airport, Terminal Five. Change here for . . .*'

In a daze, I step off the train and allow myself to be carried along with the tide of other passengers. The Glimmer of escaping East Germany and seeing my Soul Protector sacrifice his life once again for mine brings home the deadly race I run. Hans told me to never stop running and it seems I never will. No place is safe and without my Protector at my side I feel doubly vulnerable. I have no shield. It's just me.

Keeping my head down, I tag on to a family loaded with suitcases, hoping people will think I'm another of their kids. As the children chat excitedly about their imminent holiday, I have to blink back the tears. I'm keenly aware that this is exactly what I should have been doing today with my own family. Instead, I'm on the run, alone and frightened.

Taking the escalator, we arrive on the departures level and I stop beneath a large screen displaying the upcoming flights. In my backpack I have our tickets to Barbados. The plane doesn't depart for another eight hours, but my uncle, aunt and my dear Papaya will hopefully be waiting for me at the other end. That's where I really want to go.

But it isn't even an option now. I can't put their lives at risk.

As I scan the other flights listed on the departures board, my mobile phone vibrates in my pocket, interrupting my search. It's Mei. I notice several missed calls from Prisha too.

'Gen!' cries Mei down the other end of the phone. 'Where are you? What's going on? Are you OK?'

'I-I'm fine,' I reply unsteadily, then wince from my still-aching jaw. 'At least . . . I'm still alive.'

'Well, that's a bonus!' says Mei with a forced laugh. She lowers her voice to a whisper. 'The police have been going nuts here. They questioned me for nearly an hour. They've been asking me why you ran. To be honest, I've no idea what to tell them. But you ought to know that that detective inspector thinks you're involved in your parents' deaths.'

'*What?*' I exclaim. 'That's ridiculous!'

'I know,' Mei reassures me. 'I said you were with me all night at Prisha's. But you running away like that has made you a suspect. So, what am I supposed to tell them?'

'You could tell them the truth, I suppose. That Soul Hunters are after me . . . but they won't believe you. They didn't believe me the last time.'

'Gen, listen to yourself,' says Mei cautiously. 'You have to admit, it does sound a little bit unbelievable.'

My hand tightens round my phone. 'Well, DI Shaw is framing me for murders *she* is guilty of! I know that's hard to believe, but it's true.'

'What do you mean?' asks Mei, shocked.

'She released Damien and his gang,' I explain. 'They were waiting for me. Damien had the jade knife. He must've been the one who burgled your house – and I've no doubt *he* killed my parents with that same knife. Which, in my mind, means DI Shaw is equally responsible for their deaths.'

'But why would she free Damien?'

'Because Tanas is back.'

On the other end of the line Mei falls silent a moment before continuing carefully, 'How can he be back? You told me he's dead.'

'Not any more, it seems.' I sigh wearily. 'That's why I've got to run. I've no other choice.'

'Gen, I'm worried about you,' says Mei, her voice edged with heartfelt concern. 'Where will you go? What's your plan?'

'I don't really have a plan,' I admit. 'I'm figuring it out as I go along –'

'*Last call for Flight* BA0209 *to Miami*,' interrupts a terminal announcement.

'Are you at an *airport*?' questions Mei.

'Yes.' I resume my scan of the departures board.

'Oh, Gen, don't flee the country! It'll only look worse,' Mei pleads. 'Come back to my house. We'll look after you. You'll be safe –'

'No, I'll only be safe with Phoenix,' I reply firmly.

'But you've no idea where he is!' cries Mei.

I spot the flight I'm looking for: a plane leaving in a little over an hour to Los Angeles.

'I'll find him,' I reply with determination, 'or else he'll find me.'

13

I take my seat on the plane by the window, stowing my backpack at my feet. An old, white-haired woman in a peony-pink cardigan sits herself down next to me, and I smile politely, then turn back to the window. I expect police cars to come charging across the tarmac at any minute to stop the flight. But none do. When the plane takes off, I'm finally able to breathe.

I managed to book the flight to Los Angeles at the last minute online, using my mum's credit card, as well as sort out the necessary travel authorization at the same time. With everything automated, it was a relatively easy process to pass through airport security. I even used my ticket to Barbados for that, rather than the LA one, in an effort to throw the police and Hunters off my trail. I'm not naive enough to think they won't eventually track me to Heathrow. But with any luck, when they get there and scour the airport for me, they'll be working on the assumption I've fled to Barbados. By my calculations this gives me a seven-hour head start. The only problem is the flight to LA is eleven and a half hours . . .

As the plane reaches cruising altitude and levels out, the adrenaline triggered by my frantic escape begins to dissipate and exhaustion seeps into my bruised and aching bones. I recline my seat to try to get some sleep. But every time I close my eyes I see Mum and Dad on the kitchen floor, lying in a pool of their own blood. I still can't believe they're actually dead. Despite knowing I've had many parents over my many lives, the pain of losing them feels just as raw and unbearable as if they were the first to die at the hands of Tanas and his Hunters.

'Are you all right, sweetie?' asks the old woman, hearing me stifle a sob.

I give a silent nod, too afraid to reply in case my grief bursts out in a flood of uncontrollable tears.

'First time travelling alone?' There's a soft Californian lilt to her voice, and again I nod. Her sun-weathered cheeks wrinkle into a sympathetic smile. 'I remember the first trip I made on my own. It sure was daunting, but in my experience travelling solo is the best way to meet interesting people. As I like to say, those you *meet* on the journey *make* the journey. I'm Rose, by the way,' she adds, offering her hand. 'What's your name, honey?'

I stare at the woman as a faint blue gleam enters her watery eyes. I immediately recognize the star-like shimmer for what it is. She's a Soul Sister. Not a Protector like Phoenix, but a good soul nonetheless – one who is on my side, even if she's not aware of it. *Think of them as angels on Earth*, Phoenix once told me after a favourable encounter with a trucker called Mitch. *Sometimes they turn up in just the right place at just the right time.*

Sensing I can trust Rose, I shake her hand and introduce myself.

'So, Genna, ever been to LA before?'

'No,' I reply, and suddenly I'm struck by the formidable task ahead of me. *How am I supposed to find Phoenix in a country as vast as the United States?*

'Well, in my experience it's always best to have a local contact in a new country, for when you happen to need a little help.' She gives me a sage look before searching in her handbag and fishing out a business card. 'If you ever need somewhere to stay, or a recommendation for a place to visit, then you just call me.'

'Thank you,' I say, pocketing the card as a flight attendant interrupts us to take our drinks order. I ask for a bottle of water and then, reassured by the presence of the Soul Sister at my side, I settle back into my seat. In an attempt to keep my mind off my grief, I scroll through the in-flight movies and randomly choose an action flick. The opening scene features the heroine escaping across the desert from a band of sabre-wielding bandits on camels. Watching her trek over the sun-baked dunes, I'm suddenly gripped by a real thirst. I sip some water, but my mouth remains parched. Worse than that, my lips begin to feel dry – even cracked – and my skin sore, as if sunburnt and sandblasted. I wonder if it's because of the air conditioning in the plane. So I drink more, draining the bottle, yet I still can't seem to quench my thirst –

'Water!' I rasp as I drag my sandalled feet through the oven-hot sand.

Amastan weakly passes me his goat-skin bladder. Lowering my veil, I raise the open stopper to my cracked lips . . . but barely a dribble runs out. I offer him the last drops. He refuses, despite being in need of water just as much as me, and insists that I drink what little remains.

'But what about you?' I croak.

His eyes, as deep blue as the indigo robes he wears, send me a look of resignation. Our camels are dead, our bladder is dry and the remorseless Saharan sun is rising fast towards its zenith. Amastan knows we're both living on borrowed time. Without water, there's only so far even a Tuareg of Amastan's renown can get.

But there is one small sliver of hope: my guide and protector knows of a salt mine midway along the trading route to Oualata. If we can make it there, we may just survive.

So we stagger on. The sun beats down, harsh as a hammer. I pull my veil back across my face, my dark skin already raw from the whip of the scorching desert winds. Our feet sink in the sand, making our going painfully slow. Then, as we crest a dune, a shimmer of water floats in the near distance. Praying it isn't a mirage, I glance at Amastan for confirmation.

He nods. 'I see it too, Sura. Maybe it's an oasis.'

Our pace quickens in spite of our exhaustion. The water gleams and ripples at our approach. But when we reach the edge of the lake, we discover it's bone dry. The sparkling glint was just salt crystals refracting the sunlight. I look around in desperation. There are no trees, nor any other shelter, nothing but sand and salt stretching out as far as the eye can see. Then, to our left, I spot a series of small dark mounds. Another mirage?

'Taghaza,' Amastan croaks.

We lurch towards the mine, our feet crunching over the dry flakes of salt. Like a mirror to the sun, the arid lake reflects the heat, baking us in an open furnace – but now salvation is tantalizingly close and we press on. We pass deep holes dug into the sand, where layer upon layer of salt slabs have been exposed and removed. Numerous cutting tools lay strewn across the barren ground.

Through the narrow gap in his tagelmust headscarf, Amastan surveys the desolate scene. 'The mine's been abandoned . . .' he mutters.

Before long we come across a human skeleton bleached white by the sun, lying in a shallow grave. More bones litter our path as we enter Taghaza itself. A mean and ugly village, consisting of meagre dwellings built from blocks of salt and roofed with stinking camel skin, we find it desolate and deserted. Many of the houses have been razed to the ground and the only life is a plague of flies that descend on us in a feverish buzz.

'What's happened here?' I ask, feebly swatting away the flies.

Amastan shakes his head in dismay. 'A raid, most likely.'

I squint against the glare of the sun. 'There's a well,' I point out hopefully.

We hurry over to the ruined hole in the ground beside a ragged rope tied to a rock. Hauling on it, Amastan pulls up a small bucket, which contains a thin slurry of liquid in the bottom. He takes a cautious a sip and immediately retches.

'It's more salt than water!' He gags. 'We may as well drink poison!'

Discarding the bucket, we slump down in the scant shade of a salt-built mosque, the only building left standing.

'What now?' I say despairingly. I pick up a large crystal of pure salt. It gleams in my palm like a jewel. This single crystal would be worth its weight in gold in Marrakech, but here in the middle of the desert it's worthless.

Amastan sighs. 'It's another ten nights on foot to Oualata. There's no water on the way and, without camels or supplies, we cannot hope to survive the journey. Only death awaits us in the desert.'

He takes out a leather tube from under his robes. 'With the strength we have left, we should bury this. We don't want Tanas getting his hands on it. And, who knows? Even out here, if you can find it in a future life, its precious contents may be of use to you.'

Rising stiffly to his feet, he enters the mosque. A few moments later he comes out with a large clay jar he's found. Stowing the leather tube inside the jar and sealing the top, he heads over to the well and ties the rope to it. 'Remember this Soul Jar in Taghaza,' he says to me gravely, lowering the jar into the depths of the dry well.

I gaze around me at the dead village, bleached bones and swarms of flies. 'I certainly won't forget the place,' I rasp.

Then out of the shimmering heat we see a figure in black robes crossing the salt lake towards us. Riding a camel, he heads a small caravan of six other black-clad bandits.

My eyes widen in horror. 'He's found us –'

I jerk awake. I feel a hand on my shoulder and open my eyes to see the wide, beaming smile of a flight attendant. The kind old woman has gone. 'We've landed,' she says brightly. 'Welcome to America!'

14

'Passport!' demands the immigration officer behind the desk. Her tight-lipped expression is the complete opposite of the sunny 'have-a-nice-day' demeanour of the American flight attendant on the plane.

I hand over my documents with a nervous smile.

The officer inspects my passport. Then her dark eyes scan my face with almost robotic precision. For a brief, heart-stopping moment I fear she's a Watcher. But the officer is merely doing her job; her naturally dark eyes don't have the cold and empty depths of an Incarnate's soul.

'Place your fingers on the scanner and look into the camera for me,' she orders.

Trying my utmost to stay calm, I do as instructed. But my fingers are noticeably trembling as I rest them on the scanner. Not only am I nervous about passing through immigration control, but my Saharan Glimmer has really shaken me. I feel doubly jet lagged: exhausted from the flight and from recalling my past life as Sura. *Why, after six months of nothing, am I suddenly experiencing so many flashbacks?*

The officer feeds my passport into her computer. The process seems to take an age. Her sharp eyes flick to the queue of passengers waiting to pass through border control. 'Where are your parents?' she asks.

'At home,' I reply, struggling to keep my voice steady.

She stares at me. 'They're happy about you travelling alone, at your age?'

I nod, a lump forming in my throat at the thought that I'll now always have to travel without my parents. 'I-I do it all the time,' I say. 'They've always encouraged me to be independent.'

Apparently satisfied with my answers, the immigration officer is about to hand me back my passport when she glances at her computer screen and a slight frown breaks across her impenetrable expression. She beckons over another officer, a bear-sized man with close-cropped curly black hair, a neatly trimmed beard and deep brown eyes. He too peers at the screen, then takes the passport from his colleague.

'Will you come with me, Ms Adams?' he says.

My chest tightens. 'Is there a problem?' I ask, shouldering my backpack.

'No, this is just standard procedure for minors travelling alone,' he replies, escorting me away from the rest of the incoming passengers. I've no option but to follow him along a short corridor and into a windowless room. He closes the door behind us.

'Please sit down,' he says, gesturing to a chair next to a grey desk with a computer terminal.

I try to get comfortable on the hard plastic seat. 'Will this take long?' I ask, noticing a CCTV camera in the corner of the room. 'I'm meeting a friend.'

'Depends,' he replies as he runs my documents through the computer for a second time. 'Truth is, your passport has been flagged. I need to find out why before I can admit you to the United States. Do you have any idea why it should have a watch on it?'

The small room suddenly feels hot and airless, its plain grey walls seeming to press in on me. It had been too much to hope that I'd make it through airport security unchallenged. The police back home must have informed US immigration of my status as a key suspect in a murder enquiry. Nonetheless, I shake my head, playing dumb.

The officer stabs at the keyboard, then furrows his brow. 'Darn computers,' he mutters. 'The screen's frozen again.'

While we wait for the computer to reboot, he nods at my backpack. 'May I take a look in your bag?' he says, his tone more an order than a question.

'Is that standard procedure too?' I question, clutching my backpack closer to me.

'It's best you cooperate, Ms Adams,' he says sternly. 'As a customs and border protection officer I have the right to inspect your baggage, with or without your permission. But I'd prefer it to be *with*.'

Reluctantly I hand over my backpack. He sifts through the contents, smiling wryly at my soft rabbit Coco, then raising an eyebrow at the thick envelope of US dollars. As he pulls out my clothes, Phoenix's Guardian Stone drops out on to the table. The officer examines the amulet curiously.

'Well, now. This is a *strange* piece of jewellery,' he murmurs, seeming almost mesmerized by the circular sky-blue ring veined with gold. He peers closely at the Egyptian symbols on the amulet's bail and, in a slightly dreamy voice, says, 'I swear I've seen it before.'

There's a knock on the door and a woman pokes her head round. 'The FBI are here. They want to see the girl.'

The officer's eyes widen in surprise. 'Really? That's one fast response. I've not even processed her yet.' He glances at me, then back at the amulet, seemingly deep in thought. 'Tell the agents I'll be with them in a minute. I need to finalize her visa documentation.'

As soon as the woman has gone, he turns to me, a grim expression on his rounded face. 'Well, Ms Adams, it appears you have a welcome party.'

My stomach tightens and I begin to perspire. My gaze flicks round the room, looking for a way of escape, but there's only one door, and the bear-sized officer is blocking it.

Noticing my rising panic, he rests a large and reassuring hand on my shoulder. 'OK. I guess a not-so-welcome party,' he says, a smile cracking his stern expression. That's when I notice his brown eyes are now shining with a distinctive blue corona. Turning his back to the room's CCTV camera, the officer appears captivated once more by the amulet as he whispers under his breath to me, 'I've the strangest feeling we've met before . . . Have we?'

I look deep into his eyes and get a flash of a . . .

. . . sickle-shaped bronze blade, the hiss of a snake, the glimpse of a bald-headed man in white robes, my blue amulet round his neck and a sceptre bearing the Egyptian symbol of ankh in his hand. His sandy-coloured face is taut with a strange mix of terror and hope –

The vision passes quickly. 'Quite possibly,' I reply.

The officer leans in, his voice still low. 'Well, I've no idea why, Genna, but I feel I owe you a debt. So listen carefully. You'll have to act fast. If you take the first corridor on your left, it leads to a locked door to the baggage area and from there to the terminal exit. The code is three-five-eight-two.' Then he raises his voice back to normal volume. 'I need to discuss your case with the FBI, Ms Adams. I won't be very long. I sense they're rather keen to meet you.'

Giving me a subtle wink, his eyes sparkling blue, he leaves the room . . . and the door ajar.

I stare after him, momentarily dumbstruck. Then without further hesitation I grab my bag, stuff my passport, money and clothes back into it, and dash over to the open door. Peering round the corner, I spot the officer, the amulet still clasped in his hand, talking to two people in dark suits and sunglasses. One is an athletic, stylish-looking woman with a mane of straight black hair and sharp angular cheekbones. Her arms are crossed and her foot taps with impatience. The other is a well-built man who looks like he's been carved from a slab of granite, all square-jawed, solid muscle and stony expression. He stands before the officer with a menacing stillness. Neither agent looks particularly friendly, and certainly not someone I would wish to meet.

'I appreciate you have an arrest warrant for the girl, Agent Lin, but I'm the guy who has jurisdiction at the border,' the officer is saying to the woman. He holds up a hand as the man mountain takes a step forward. 'Agent Haze, if you'd respectfully give me five minutes to finish –'

With the immigration officer distracting the two FBI agents, I slip out of the holding room and dart down the corridor on my left. I race along until I come to a door with a keypad. Stabbing in the code, I emerge into the busy baggage hall and head for the terminal exit. Everywhere I look, the place is swarming with airport security.

I keep my pace fast yet steady, trying to blend in with the other travellers, pass through customs unchecked and enter the arrivals hall, where the tight knot in my stomach begins to loosen. Then I spot a couple of suits in dark sunglasses standing outside a coffee shop and my gut clenches again. More FBI agents. I'm by no means free yet. As I pull my baseball cap low over my face, I accidentally bump into a girl with a nose ring and short spiky blond hair. I mumble an apology and follow the terminal directions to the taxi stand.

Weaving through the stream of passengers, I risk a glance back to check that the FBI agents aren't following me. That's when I notice the nose-ring girl for the second time. She's wearing a green beanie, a loose chequered shirt and ripped jeans. Her eyes are hidden behind a pair of round mirrored sunglasses, yet I get the distinct impression that as she casually waits in the arrivals hall she's looking in my direction.

A Watcher? A Hunter? Or am I just being paranoid?

Reminding myself that not everyone is a threat, I hurry on. But as I approach the glass doors to the lower concourse, I catch a glimpse of the green beanie and mirrored sunglasses in the reflection and my pulse quickens. The girl is definitely following me.

Once outside the air-conditioned terminal, the atmosphere is hot and choked with car fumes. I spot the long queue for the taxi rank and don't fancy waiting around, not with the FBI looking for me and a strange girl on my tail. Further along the concourse a shuttle bus is pulling up at a stop and without breaking my stride I head directly for it. But a man in a yellow high-vis bib steps into my path.

'Hey, do you need a ride, young lady?' he asks in an over-friendly tone.

'No thanks.' I reply, trying to step round him.

He grins, flashing a gold tooth. 'Best cab prices in the city,' he insists, his ebony eyes searching mine as he blocks my path. 'Best cabs too. Where you heading? Disneyland? Venice Beach? Universal Studios?'

Behind him, over his bony shoulder, I notice the last passengers boarding the shuttle. 'Thanks, but I'll take the bus –'

There's a sudden revving of an engine. The girl with the nose ring rushes up and shoves me hard. Crying out in alarm, I tumble into the path of an oncoming taxi. The yellow cab swerves and mounts the kerb – and hits the girl instead of me. She flips over the bonnet, striking the windscreen, then bounces off on to the pavement. I don't wait around to see if she's OK. I'm convinced this girl's a

Hunter. She's dangerous, anyway – why would she push me in front of a car if she wasn't? Scrambling to my feet, I barge past the man in the high-vis bib and dash for the bus, leaping on board just as the doors close.

15

I stare numbly at the waves rolling in from the gleaming Pacific Ocean, their white crests curling in perfect tubes as they approach the shoreline. Along the wide stretch of golden sand lie equally golden sunbathers basking in the last of the day's sun. Behind me, a steady stream of tourists meander along the boardwalk where street performers breakdance to heavy beats, sing through portable speakers, or drum up an audience to watch their tricks. One performer is getting the crowd to chant '*Hooba! Hooba!*' before he jumps barefoot on to a pile of broken glass; there's even a skateboarding dog.

Detached from the mayhem, I sit alone on a patch of sand. My bus journey ended at Venice Beach, the last stop, and I was happy enough to be dropped here. The shock of being pushed into the road has finally faded and now I'm only left with questions: *Who on earth was that girl – a Soul Hunter? Why did she try to kill me? And what about the FBI – are they my enemy too?*

I can't allow myself to get caught. If the authorities detain me, I'll more than likely be deported back to England . . . straight into the custody of DI Shaw, and from her into the clutches of Damien and his gang. Then my dramatic escape will have all been for nothing.

Squinting against the sun, I try to spot Phoenix among the tanned surfers catching waves or relaxing along the shore. My Protector said that he might hang out at the beach in LA. I've no idea where the best surfing spots are around here, but Venice Beach is famous enough and as good a place as any to start looking for him.

But after an hour of fruitless searching my hopes begin to wane, along with the setting sun. My bold plan only went as far as getting to LA; I hadn't thought much about how exactly I'd locate Phoenix. *I'll find him*, I'd said to Mei, but that confident boast is beginning to ring hollow and I fear the task I've set myself will be beyond me. Phoenix once told me that it's a combination of luck, deduction and fate that brings us together. A sensation like two magnets drawn to one another. The closer we get, the stronger the attraction. Yet if that's the case, then why don't I feel this irresistible magnetism?

Right now, all I feel is lost and unmoored. A compass with no bearing. *Do I just wait around for him to find me?* But in Phoenix's mind the threat against me is over for this life. *Why would he have any reason to look for me?*

As I watch a surfer wipe out on a wave, I realize I can't just rely on Phoenix finding me: I have to go looking for him. *But where to start?* I suppose I could camp out here on the beach in the hope that one day our paths cross. *But what if he isn't in Venice Beach at all? What if he surfs at another spot along the coast?* And all the while I'm watching and waiting, the FBI will be looking for me. Tanas's Soul Hunters too.

My time is running short.

I begin to despair at the near-insurmountable task ahead of me. It seemed such a good idea to run into Phoenix's arms. To feel safe and protected once more. But the hard reality is now hitting me: I've fled to a country I don't know and where I know no one, have no friends, and there's only the remotest chance of meeting my Soul Protector. All of a sudden I remember the business card Rose gave me on the plane. I touch my hand to my pocket to check it's still safe inside. Yes, I do have *one* friend. Perhaps I could call Rose, stay with her for the short term while I figure out a better plan.

Pulling out my mobile, I power it up and wait for a signal. Then I dial the number on the card. It rings three times before being answered. 'Hello, Rose speaking,' says a kindly and familiar voice.

'Hi there ... it's Genna,' I say hesitantly. 'The girl who sat next to you on the plane?'

'Oh hi, sweetie!' Rose replies. Her tone softens further. 'You OK?'

'Erm ... not really,' I admit. 'My accommodation has fallen through. You kindly offered if I ever needed somewhere to stay ...'

'Of course! You're very welcome,' says Rose, picking up on the desperation in my voice. 'I'll come get you. Where are you?'

I tell Rose my location and she promises to be with me shortly. I thank her and hang up. Then I realize what a fool

I've been. When I was last on the run, Phoenix warned me that phones could be traced and that I shouldn't contact anyone in case the line is being tapped. As my mobile pings with multiple texts and voicemails from Mei and Prisha, I immediately switch it off, even though that makes me feel guilty for ignoring my friends, and stuff the phone back in my bag.

I glance nervously around, paranoid. The beach is mostly empty of sunbathers now; there are only a few surfers left in the water, and the boardwalk is a little quieter than an hour ago. Bathed in a deep orange glow, Venice Beach appears to be taking a breather before the evening crowd descends. I turn back towards the ocean and wait nervously for Rose.

My mind wanders to my parents and an aching loneliness fills my heart. I miss them so much. A tear rolls down my cheek as I think of where the three of us should be right now, in Barbados with Papaya and the rest of the family, drinking fresh coconut juice and watching the sun set over the Caribbean Sea together. I've never felt so lost or far from home in my life.

The Californian sun gradually dips below the waves, a blood-red eye against the darkening horizon. It's a beautiful sight, but as I gaze around I start to notice that several of the people on the beach aren't watching the sunset. They're watching *me*. Silhouetted against the fiery sky, they stand motionless, staring ominously in my direction. Despite the warmth of the evening, my skin shivers suddenly into goosebumps and the hairs on my neck rise. Everywhere I look, there seem to be more and more of them. Each new

Watcher seems to trigger an awareness in the next blackened soul.

I suddenly feel dangerously exposed. Snatching up my backpack, I shake off the sand and head for the boardwalk.

The Watchers turn and follow me, their unhurried manner disturbing in its zombie-like calm.

My heart thudding harder in my chest, I reach the promenade and quicken my pace. The skateboarding dog is gone, but the man who was jumping on glass is still here.

At my approach, he chants in a low rasping voice, '*Hooba! Hooba! Hooba! Here comes the Light!*' His brown eyes pool into fathomless black holes as he grinds his bare feet into the pile of broken glass. I hear the shards crunch and crackle, then see the blood seep from his lacerated skin. Sickened, I hurry on. But he too follows, leaving a slippery trail of red behind him.

I break from a walk into a jog, then into a run. More Watchers appear, twitching to life among the groups of people strolling along the boardwalk, their eyes glazing over and clouding into darkness. Some merely point at me, while others turn and follow or shout out in strange dialects. When a few try to grab hold of me, I frantically fend them off, then flee across the road.

I'm barely halfway over when a black SUV screeches to a halt in front of me and a suited man in dark glasses clambers out. His intimidating bulk unsettles me almost as much as the Watchers. I recognize him as Agent Haze, the heavyset, square-jawed FBI agent who turned up at the airport. Behind the wheel sits his partner, her cold gaze fixed upon me.

'Stay where you are!' orders Agent Haze as he strides towards me, hand outstretched.

I glance around desperately. From all sides the Watchers are closing in, cutting off any hope of escape. I dash down the road and the agent immediately gives chase. My breathing ragged and my heart pounding, I realize I've no chance of outrunning him, so in an attempt to lose him, as well as the Watchers, I cut a sharp right into an alleyway . . . and come face to face with the spiky-haired girl with the nose ring, the girl who'd tried to push me under a taxi at the airport. The dying rays of the sun are reflected in her round mirrored glasses. She greets me with a lopsided smile that does nothing to ease my frayed nerves. A sleek silver car parked behind her blocks the alley's exit. I turn to go back the other way, but the FBI agent has already caught up with me.

I'm trapped!

16

'It's time to stop running, Genna,' says Agent Haze, entering the alley and advancing on me.

I back away, remembering that Hans told me to never stop running.

The agent's hand goes for his gun as I turn from him to escape the other way. The blond-haired girl pulls out her own gun – a Taser – then aims and fires. The Taser's darts whizz past, missing me by a fraction, and hit the FBI agent in the chest. He convulses and collapses to the ground, his muscles immobilized by the electric shock.

'Quick! Get in!' orders the girl, opening the door to the silver car. 'We've got about thirty seconds before he recovers.'

I hesitate, dumbstruck. *Do I trust this girl?* One moment she's trying to kill me, the next apparently to save me. 'D-did Rose send you?' I stutter.

'Who's Rose?' she demands impatiently. Before I can answer, the Watchers start clustering at the alley entrance. '*Come on!*' the girl urges.

The FBI agent is already coming back to his senses and I know I've got no choice. It might be a leap from the frying pan into the fire, but I jump into the strange girl's car. She limps round to the driver's side and climbs in behind the wheel. I throw her a dubious look. 'Can you drive?' I ask, suspecting she's not much older than me.

'Don't need to,' she replies, pressing the ignition button. The car boots up, its display screen flashes into life, and the electric engine, silent as a whisper, reverses us sharply out of the alley without the girl doing anything else.

However, the car's auto-drive isn't perfect. There's a blare of a horn and the screech of brakes as we almost collide with another vehicle. Through the front windscreen I spot Rose in a 1960s pink Cadillac, her shocked face almost as white as her permed hair. We stare at each other a moment, exchanging a brief look of recognition, before my car starts to pull away.

At the same time the tasered FBI agent lurches out of the alley and lunges at my door. I flinch away in fright as he hammers furiously on the window, but when he yanks on the door handle he roars in pain, letting go of the handle as if the car is on fire.

'Anti-theft device,' explains the spiky-haired girl with a smirk. 'Electro-stun door handles.'

The self-drive car accelerates away, leaving the frazzled agent behind. As it navigates itself through LA's back streets, nimbly avoiding the traffic, I stare silently, and equally stunned, at my rescuer. Reclining in her seat, her feet on the dashboard, she nonchalantly reloads her Taser.

The girl glances sidelong at me. 'So? You going to thank me or not?'

'For what?' I reply, bemused and angry. 'Pushing me in front of that taxi at the airport? Or abducting me from the street?'

'Hey! I can drop you off right now if that's your attitude!' she replies testily. 'But you won't last the night.'

'I almost didn't last the day, thanks to you,' I point out. 'Why did you try to kill me?'

The girl snorts. 'Kill you? If I wanted to do that, I could've just left you standing there.'

'What do you mean?' I ask.

She shakes her head in disbelief. Then in a slow deliberate voice, as if talking to an idiot, she explains, 'That guy with the gold tooth was distracting you in order that a Soul Hunter could run you over and capture you.' Wincing, she massages her leg. 'I kinda wish I'd let him do it now. Would've worked out far less painful for me!'

I sit bolt upright in my seat. 'You know about Soul Hunters? Who are you?' I demand.

'Name's Jude,' she replies, as she lowers her mirrored glasses to reveal eyes as starlit blue as Phoenix's.

'Oh! You're a Soul *Protector*?' I gasp.

Jude shakes her head. 'Not quite . . . I'm a Soul Warrior.'

I frown. 'What's the difference?'

'A Soul Warrior is a former Protector who no longer has an assigned First Ascendant to guard.' She offers me a thin strained smile. 'We're a bit like ronin – wandering samurai without a lord to protect.'

'So there are female Protectors too . . .' I remark, viewing my rescuer in a different light.

Jude gives me a look. 'Are you stuck in the eighteenth century? Female Soul Protectors are often the best bet for a First Ascendant's survival. We blend in more easily than male Protectors.'

'If that's the case,' I say as the car pulls on to the Santa Monica Freeway and merges seamlessly with the traffic, 'may I ask what happened to your First Ascendant?'

Jude turns her attention to the road, even though she's not driving. 'What's it to you? It's all in the past,' she mutters. 'Besides, I saved you, didn't I?'

'I guess so,' I say, her waspish reply warning me off the topic. 'I'm Genna, by the way.' Then I ask, 'What were you doing at the airport – and how did you know to find me on Venice Beach?'

'The shuttle bus only has five main stops. That was a simple process of elimination,' Jude explains. 'Plus, I've got a police scanner tuned into FBI frequencies loaded on to the system.' She taps the car's tablet screen and pulls up an app that looks like an old CB radio receiver. 'They located your mobile signal –' she stares at me from behind her glasses – 'so *please* tell me you've dumped the phone.'

With a sheepish look, I fish my mobile out of my bag.

Jude scowls at me. 'How have you *ever* survived this far on your own?' She snatches the phone from my grasp, opens her window and tosses it out.

'But I need to call Rose,' I protest as I watch it clatter across the freeway. 'Let her know I'm OK . . .' My voice trails away as a truck drives straight over the mobile, destroying it for good. I feel I'm losing all control over my own destiny. I had a plan – albeit a thin one – and now it's literally been thrown out of the window.

Once more I find my fate is in the hands of a total stranger.

A woman's voice crackles through the car's speakers. '*Attention all units, be on the lookout for a silver Tesla XR, heading east out of Venice Beach. Licence plate 8TRR943.*'

'We'd best not hang around,' says Jude grimly, tapping an icon on the screen to override the car's speed limiter. The vehicle accelerates away.

'You still haven't explained what you were doing at the airport,' I say, gripping slightly tighter to my seat as we dart through gaps in the traffic at breakneck speed.

'Sometimes, as a Soul Warrior, you just get a sense you're needed somewhere,' she replies, reclining her own seat and lacing her fingers behind her head, apparently at ease with the Tesla's manic auto-drive. 'It wasn't until I bumped into you that I knew why.'

I glance at her, my spirits lifting on hearing it was no coincidence that our paths crossed. Yet I'm also struck by a pang of disappointment. *If Jude was drawn to the airport, then why wasn't Phoenix?*

'Being a Soul Warrior,' I say, 'does that mean you know my Protector, Phoenix?'

An enigmatic smile briefly crosses her lips. 'I may have in former lives.'

Leaning forward, I ask hopefully, 'Do you know where he is now?'

'I'm not his babysitter!' she replies tartly. Then, seeing my crestfallen look, she adds, 'But Caleb should know.'

'Who's Caleb?'

'A Soul Seer.'

I immediately tense. 'No thanks,' I say. 'My last experience with a Soul Seer was almost fatal.'

Jude raises an eyebrow in question and I explain my deadly encounter with Tanas when he was impersonating the priest Gabriel.

'You don't have to worry,' Jude assures me. 'Caleb's the real deal. He's more connected to the Upper Realms and the past lives of others than any Soul Seer I've met before. He can offer you protection as well as guidance. For now, though, I'd recommend getting some rest.'

Jude closes her eyes and settles back as the car zips on to the San Bernardino Freeway and continues to head east.

Realizing I've no choice but to put my trust in this spiky-haired Soul Warrior, I gaze out of the windscreen at the haze of mountains in the distance. 'So where are we going?' I ask.

'Out of the city,' she replies. 'You saw how many Watchers are here. LA is literally swarming with Tanas's followers.'

17

As dusk begins to fall and my jet lag catches up with me, I struggle to keep my eyes open. Jude is already dozing, her Taser resting in her lap, her bare feet on the dashboard. Having left the sprawl of Los Angeles far behind, we continue to head east on autopilot, passing through the San Gabriel mountain range. With the thrum of the wheels on the highway lulling me to sleep, my thoughts drift . . .

'Phoenix, you have visitors,' announces the nurse as she unlocks the door and enters.

My gaze shifts groggily from the TV screen flickering in the corner of my tiny cell-like room to two figures in tailored suits and dark sunglasses. For a moment I fear they're Hunters. But I know that's impossible. Tanas is dead in this life. I stare vacantly at them, struggling to focus on their faces. But I don't recognize either of them, nor do I much care.

'I'm Agent Lin,' introduces the slim, dark-haired woman, flashing her badge. FBI. I guess that explains the sunglasses. 'And this is Agent Haze.' The stony-faced, heavyset man gives a curt nod in greeting.

I feel far too lethargic to respond. Quickly losing interest, I return my attention to the TV. A repeat of The Simpsons. *It's about all I can manage.*

I hear the nurse talking in a soft, apologetic whisper. 'The poor boy experiences vivid hallucinations,' she explains. 'He believes he's had multiple past lives, that he's a protector for some girl or other. He's tried to escape on a number of occasions. So, for his own good, we've had to sedate him.'

'Uh-huh, that's quite understandable,' Agent Lin replies. 'Will you give us a moment with him?'

The young nurse hesitates. 'Erm . . . I'm not supposed to leave you alone with the patient,' she replies.

'You needn't worry,' says Agent Haze with a reassuring smile as he guides her towards the door. 'We're trained professionals, like yourself. In fact, it's better if you give us some space to do our job. I'm sure you understand.'

'Of course . . .' says the nurse, reluctantly retreating from the room. 'But for the patient's well-being I need to limit your visit to ten minutes.'

'Sure, that's all the time we'll need,' says Agent Haze. As soon as he closes the door, I see him lean his ample bulk against the frame and the smile drop from his face. Even in my doped state, I sense something's wrong. I try to will myself to move, but my limbs fail to respond and I can only lie limp and listless on my narrow bed.

Switching off the TV, Agent Lin pulls out the plastic chair from under my small wooden desk, sits down and eyeballs me from behind her sunglasses. 'Phoenix Rivers?' she says, clicking her fingers in front of my glassy gaze.

I can barely react.

She lowers her voice. 'Do you know Genna Adams is in the US?'

Genna! *Her name cuts through the fog of my medication like a knife. My eyes flick to the agent's face, my focus instantly sharp and alert.*

'I thought that might get your attention,' comments Agent Lin with a smirk.

'Is she OK?' I slur, my tongue feeling too big for my mouth.

'Uh-huh. For the time being,' the agent replies, leaning back in the chair and crossing her arms. 'But she's in big trouble.'

I sit up straighter in bed, fighting the effects of the sedative. My brain has to work overtime just to string a sentence together. 'I knew it . . . I felt her presence was closer . . . What sort of trouble?'

'Her parents have been murdered,' reveals the agent, 'and Genna's a key suspect.'

'What?' A burst of adrenaline lifts the fog and my mind is suddenly clear. 'That's ridiculous! Genna's no murderer.'

'That's what we want to prove,' says the agent encouragingly. 'But we can't help her if we can't talk to her. Unfortunately, Genna's gone on the run.'

Fearing for my First Ascendant's safety, I look from Agent Lin to the stocky agent blocking the door. 'You've got to let me out of here!' I plead. 'I need to help her.'

'Sure,' replies the agent with an agreeable grin. 'But first we need to know if you've had any contact with her.'

I dully shake my head. 'Not since I left England . . .'

'Have you tried to get in contact?' presses Agent Lin.

'What do you think?' I reply fiercely, angered by their line of questioning. 'I've been locked away ever since I was deported back to the States. I don't get much opportunity for social calls!'

'Sorry to hear that,' replies Agent Lin with little attempt at sincerity. 'But I anticipate you'll have a visit soon.'

I stare at her in bewilderment. 'What makes you think Genna will come here?'

'Why else would she fly all the way to America?' questions the agent. 'Her remaining family live in Barbados. She even had a plane ticket to go there, yet she came to LA. We believe she's looking for you –'

I jerk awake. My head is throbbing from where it was pressed against the window.

'You OK? asks Jude, peering at me questioningly.

'Yeah, just had a strange dream, that's all.' I sit up stiffly and brush my tangle of brown hair from my face and rub my eyes. *A strange dream indeed.* Certainly not a Glimmer, that's for sure. This was present day and the FBI agent called me . . . *Phoenix*.

The whole experience was very odd. I felt drugged, almost as if I was hallucinating. But at the same time I could clearly sense my Soul Protector's distress on learning I was in America but he didn't know where. I felt his emotions as if they were my very own. Confused and concerned, I stare out of the window at the endless desert scrub. In front of us the dawn sun is rising on the horizon, the sky blazing a pure crystal blue. *Maybe*, I think, *the dream is just a reflection of my own desire to find Phoenix?*

Pushing these thoughts to the back of my mind, I ask, 'Where are we?'

'Mojave Desert.' Jude yawns, taking her feet off the dashboard and stretching.

'How much further to go?'

She glances at the satnav. 'We're nearly there.'

'Nearly *where*?' I demand, irritated. The car's satnav displays our route but not our destination.

'Haven,' mumbles Jude.

I look to her, waiting. When no explanation comes, I prompt, 'Care to tell me any more?'

'You'll see soon enough,' she replies evasively.

Without warning, the car pulls off the highway and down an unmarked road. Ahead in the near distance lies a saw-toothed mountain range; otherwise, we appear to be driving into the middle of nowhere. Then after several miles the tarmac abruptly ends and we arrive at a ghost town, comprising a dozen derelict buildings crumbling in the desert heat.

'Nice!' I say, my tone dripping with sarcasm. 'Certainly worth the trip!'

'This used to be a thriving iron mine until they shut it down at the end of the last century,' explains Jude. She puts her boots on and grasps the steering wheel. 'It's manual from here,' she says.

I raise an eyebrow. 'I thought you couldn't drive.'

'I said I didn't *need* to,' she replies, and accelerates down a dirt track, a dust cloud billowing in our wake. 'The thing is, we've entered a dead zone.' She nods to the car's display screen, where a red icon blinks a warning of no GPS. 'The high concentrations of iron ore in the surrounding rock block all signals. There's no mobile, Wi-Fi or even satellite in this area.'

As we head deeper into the desert, the steep arid slopes of the mountain range rise up higher around us, the dirt road becomes rougher and more potholed. Then, as we enter a narrow gully, the entrance to the old mine comes into view. The shaft is sealed with a solid metal barrier, and large red signs warn trespassers of DANGER and to KEEP OUT. Nonetheless, after a quick glance in her rear-view mirror, Jude drives straight towards the blocked entrance.

'What are you doing?' I exclaim, gripping my seat in panic.

Just as I think we're about to crash, however, the metal barrier rises and we shoot inside the mine. My heart in my throat, I look back and see the barrier seal itself shut behind us, blocking out the desert sun . . . along with any way in or out.

'An abandoned mine is the perfect front for Haven,' she explains, the roughly hewn tunnel walls flashing by in the car's headlights. 'Keeps it safe and unseen from prying eyes.'

'Is it underground?' I ask as Jude navigates through the warren of dark tunnels. But no sooner have I asked my question than I get my answer. Heading towards an apparent dead end, the rock face parts and we career back out into bright sunshine. Shading my eyes from the glare, I'm stunned into awed silence by the most astounding sight. Nestled in the basin of a hidden valley is a breathtaking complex of white marble buildings, all shimmering in the early-morning heat. Around the complex, along the valley's ridge, six huge pillars of red rock, hewn by time alone, rise in a monumental circle. And at its heart, gleaming like a jewel in the sun, glistens an immense glass pyramid.

'Welcome to Haven!' says Jude with a proud grin.

I continue to gaze in amazement as we draw closer. Haven looks like some New Age futuristic temple: ancient Greek white marble and an Egyptian-style pyramid combined with modern engineered glass and cutting-edge solar panels – past, present and future in a seamless blend. A high circular wall encloses the main complex, giving the impression of a lost fortified city.

'Why didn't you tell me?' I murmur, breathless. 'It's unbelievable!'

'Just wait till you see inside,' says Jude. She drives through a pair of automated gates into a large gravel courtyard dotted with Roman statues. We pull up beside a sweeping arc of stone steps that lead to a pillared entrance.

As I get out of the car, I'm aware of the temple-like calm of the place. A light breeze caresses a wind chime, making it tinkle softly, and birds twitter somewhere nearby in the branches of an olive tree. In its shade I spot a ginger cat curled up fast asleep on the ground. And, while the morning sun is hot on my skin, I'm aware of a warm tingling from within my limbs . . . I feel more at peace yet also more energized than I have in ages. My cares and worries seem to slip away, and a smile comes unbidden to my lips.

Jude looks at me. 'Haven has that effect on me too,' she says.

We ascend the steps to the pillars, where she opens the large wooden double doors and we enter a cool, airy entrance hall. The floor is polished white marble, the ceiling painted a light pastel blue like a cloudless sky. Cream leather sofas and armchairs furnish the stylish room and floor-to-ceiling windows overlook a Japanese water garden. However, I'm most struck by the number of cats roaming around the place. Some laze on the sofas, others bask in the sunshine or peer intently through the window at the birds swooping through the water garden or drinking from the pond. A pair of kittens tumble together on the hearth rug where their mother nurses two more of her litter.

'Caleb likes cats,' Jude explains, noticing the curiosity on my face. 'In fact, he worships them.' She points to a large ebony statue of a cat decorated with jewels and gold Egyptian symbols.

As I examine the statue, a sleek, sandy-coloured cat with wide ears and a cougar-like face jumps up on a nearby table and greets me with a friendly chirp. Putting down my backpack, I offer her my hand. She nuzzles into me, purring loudly.

'Ah, I see you've met Nefertiti already,' a deep, resonating voice says with a chuckle. 'And she clearly remembers you!'

Turning, I'm greeted by an elderly man in a dapper ivory-white suit and cravat. He has a noticeable limp and supports his walk with a slim wooden cane, its handle carved into a lion's head. And, like the lion, his white hair is combed back in a mane. His oval face is kind, wise and deeply wrinkled, as if time has etched every year of his life into his liver-spotted, tanned skin. But despite his evident great age his eyes appear ageless – so bright blue they're almost blinding. He smiles warmly at me.

I instinctively smile back, then frown in puzzlement. 'The cat *remembers* me?'

He nods. 'Look again and you may remember her,' he suggests with a shrewd wink.

Feeling the cat push lovingly against my hand, I gaze into her sparkling emerald-green eyes.

18

Purring contentedly, Nefertiti curls up in my lap as I sit cross-legged eating sweet dates in the shade of a sycamore tree. From here in the palace garden I can see the progress of my father's pyramid as it rises above the ground, its gleaming white blocks of polished limestone now piercing the cloudless blue sky like a knife. He tells me that, upon his death and burial within this tomb, the structure will help him – the great Pharaoh Hepuhotep – travel to the gods above and reach the afterlife.

I lower my gaze from the countless workers toiling under the hot sun to construct his pyramid and notice a knot of ants swarming over the remains of a date stone at my feet. I realize I must appear like a god to these ants . . . just as we must appear like ants to the gods. So if anything will catch the attention of Osiris, the King of the Dead, then surely it will be this magnificent pyramid built by my father.

'My Princess Tiaa, a thousand apologies for disturbing you,' says a bald-headed priest, bowing low as he approaches.

'Your presence is most welcome, Ankhu,' I say, smiling. I notice my guard, Raneb, shift slightly in the corner of the

garden. Partly hidden behind a bush, he'd been so still I'd almost forgotten he was there. In fact, anyone passing through the garden might mistake him for a statue.

Keeping his head bowed, Ankhu sets aside his priest's sceptre and kneels. 'I know you have a fondness for dates,' he says, presenting me with a small wicker basket topped with a lid. 'My brother's a trader and has just procured some of the finest fruits from across the Jordan river. Please accept this humble gift as a token of my devotion to you and your father.'

'Why, thank you,' I reply, delighted yet somewhat surprised. While Ankhu has been part of my father's retinue for as long as I can remember, this is the first time he's bestowed a gift on me. Perhaps he needs a favour, or does he wish me to have a quiet word in my father's ear? My father's vizier, Khafra, has warned me to be careful of such approaches, not only because of my status as the pharaoh's only child and natural successor to the throne, but because of my destiny as a First Ascendant.

As the priest delicately rests the basket at my feet, I notice his white robes are damp and sticking to his back, and his bald, sandy-coloured pate is beaded with sweat.

'Come sit with me in the shade,' I offer. 'Do share in your kind gift.'

He bows gratefully and picks up his ankh-headed sceptre. 'Your generosity of spirit is boundless, my princess, but sadly I must depart on official business,' he replies, already retreating down the path. 'Enjoy the dates.'

I observe him leave the garden with uncharacteristic haste. Yet I'm aware that all my father's advisers are under intense pressure to complete his pyramid before the next harvest. I'm glad that Ankhu's gift has been given freely; as he gave it without any expectation of a favour in return, I feel I can trust him more. Eyeing the basket, I wonder if I should wait for my handmaiden Sitre to return with fresh lemon water before I sample its delights. But I'm too tempted by the promise of such exquisite and rare dates. So I decide to try just one. As I draw the basket a little closer, Nefertiti tenses in my lap, her ears suddenly alert, her green eyes wide.

'Nefe, what's wrong?' I ask. I glance around the garden but see nothing strange. Stroking my cat to calm her, I lift the basket's lid and am about to put in my hand when Nefe leaps from my lap, spitting, her back arched, her tail raised. I flinch away too, for out of the basket rises the fanned head of a black cobra.

I sit dead still as the snake flicks out its forked tongue and sways before me, its dark, unblinking eyes mesmerizing in their malice. Nefe hisses louder, the hairs along her back rising. But, before she can pounce, the snake strikes, its venomous fangs seeking to pierce my bare golden skin!

A bronze blade sings in the air. Its sickle-shaped edge slices clean through the cobra's neck and I let out a shriek as its decapitated head lands in my lap.

My handmaiden runs out into the garden, the water jug she carries crashing to the ground. 'What's happened?' she cries.

Raneb stands over me, his blood-stained khopesh in his hand and his blue eyes blazing. He makes a stabbing sign to his heart in reply. Sitre gasps, 'An assassin!'

'Y-y-you mean Ankhu?' I splutter. Raneb nods.

'I just passed the priest,' says Sitre, and she dashes from the garden.

With a trembling hand, I go to brush the cobra's bodyless head from my lap, but Raneb grunts, signing firmly for me not to touch it. To my utter horror, the snake's black eyes swivel in their sockets and its forked tongue flicks out. The fiendish thing is still alive! *As it snaps its fangs, little Nefe bravely bats the cobra's head away with her paw before it can bite me. The snake's shiny body continues to writhe out of the basket. Raneb kicks it into the bushes, then drives the tip of his khopesh into the still-snapping head of the serpent. Skewered, it ceases biting the air.*

My whole body quivers with shock and my heart thuds hard in my chest. Purring loudly, Nefe rubs herself against my arm and tries to comfort me.

A moment later Sitre returns with Ankhu. 'I managed to stop him at the gates,' she says, forcing the priest to his knees. A trickle of blood runs from the man's mouth and he looks half-dazed. My handmaiden is strong and skilled in combat. I've often wondered why my father chose her to care for me, along with the mute Raneb. But now I understand – between them they are my shield and my sword.

'Here's the other snake to despatch!' she growls, and Raneb raises his khopesh to behead the priest.

Then, in that last vital moment, Ankhu looks up at me, pleading, his eyes a strange swirling mix of black, hazel and glimpses of blue.

'NO!' I command, holding up my hand.

His khopesh poised quivering in the air, Raneb stares at me in disbelief. Nonetheless he obeys and lowers the blade.

I meet the frightened gaze of the priest. 'You, Ankhu, have been a loyal servant of my father, the pharaoh, for many years,' I say. 'Why do you try to kill me now?'

The priest begins to sob, his whole body trembling. 'I-I-I didn't want to . . . but he told me to do it . . . He made me do it!'

'Who?' I ask. 'Who made you?'

'Apep, the Eater of Souls,' he cries, his eyes wide and unseeing, as if blinded by sheer terror.

Sitre snorts. 'Tanas, in other words.'

Nefe hisses at the mere mention of the Incarnate leader's name and presses her body closer to mine.

Ankhu nods nervously. 'He came to me in the form of a snake. Invaded my dreams. My thoughts. Believe me, my princess, I have battled so hard . . . but he said he would devour my soul if I didn't do his bidding!'

'He would devour your soul anyway,' says Sitre sourly.

'What I don't understand,' I say, 'is how killing me with a snake can serve Tanas's purpose.'

'Y-you wouldn't have died . . .' the priest stammers. 'Not immediately. You'd have succumbed to a heavy sleep . . . long enough for Apep to perform the ritual sacrifice –'

'Enough! I say we kill this Incarnate traitor now!' snarls Sitre.

'Then what?' I ask. 'He'll just return in the next life, his soul blacker, another dark disciple of Tanas.'

Sitre shrugs dismissively. 'He's a lost cause. The best we can do is eliminate him and protect you in this life.'

I shake my head firmly. 'My father says, where there is life, there is hope.'

'Not for him!*' Sitre argues, and she nods a silent command to Raneb, who is all too eager to put his khopesh to good use again.*

The priest throws himself down at my feet. 'Please forgive me, my princess –'

'Raneb, NO!' I order as he starts swinging the blade. Scowling, Raneb once more resists killing the man. 'Hope is seeing there is light in spite of the darkness,' I explain.

Lifting the priest's chin to meet my gaze, I say softly, 'Ankhu, I believe you still have good in your soul. I can see it. You can follow the Path of Light if you choose to.' Then, staring deep into his eyes, I give him a little of my Light.

Like a faint frosted breath from my soul, a white spectral shimmer passes between us. As fine as gossamer, it enters his pupils and the once-churning darkness slowly settles into a faint steady starlit gleam. A damaged soul brought back from the brink. The priest's face floods with gratitude, as if he's seeing the dawn for the first time in a year of unending nights. He bows before me, kissing my bare feet over and over again.

'My princess, I owe you an eternal life debt,' he vows. Then, taking a circular blue amulet veined with gold from round his neck, he offers it to me. 'I bless this Guardian Stone with my own soul so that it lends you protection against the Darkness.'

19

Nefertiti blinks and the Glimmer comes to an end. I reel from its intensity. Unlike a dream, the vision stays bright in my mind.

'Nefe, you saved my life!' I gasp, recalling how she first warned me of the cobra then batted away its snapping head.

I think I understand other things now too: why the immigration officer said he thought he'd seen the amulet before, and why he felt indebted to me, and where the Guardian Stone's protective power originally came from. I draw the cat into a loving hug. She tolerates it for a minute, before wriggling free and jumping down to seek a warm spot in the sun to groom herself.

'I'm glad you two are now reacquainted,' says the old man, his walking stick clicking on the marble floor as he hobbles up to me. 'Please allow me to reintroduce myself. I'm Caleb, and I must say it's an honour to be in your presence again, Princess Tiaa, if I may call you by that name.' He inclines his head respectfully.

'Er . . . I'd prefer Genna,' I reply. Then: 'Have *we* also met before?' I ask with a frown.

A good-natured smile plays upon his lips and his eyes twinkle. '*Many* times before.'

Looking the white-haired Soul Seer up and down, I remain unclear. 'I'm sorry,' I admit, 'but I don't recall you from my Glimmer. I'm certain the priest is the border guard who helped me earlier today – I guess his life debt is repaid – and Raneb must be Phoenix. So . . . are you Sitre?'

Jude snorts out a laugh.

I turn to her. 'What's so funny?'

She sits herself in an armchair and a silver-grey cat immediately jumps on to her lap. 'Your handmaiden Sitre, or Phoenix as you now call him, was your Soul Protector in that life.'

'How do you know?' I ask.

She peers over her mirrored sunglasses at me. 'Because *I* was Raneb.'

I do a double take. '*What?*' I exclaim. 'Why didn't you tell me that our soul paths have crossed before?'

Nonchalantly stroking the cat, Jude shrugs. 'Better if you remember for yourself.'

Scrutinizing her ice-blue eyes, I begin to recognize her soul, not only in Raneb but also in a previous Glimmer. 'You were the girl in the canoe who helped Necalli rescue me from the Tletl tribe?'

Jude nods. 'And I was with you in the Second World War – Harry's best mate.'

I get a flash of a lanky, thin-jawed, dark-haired soldier on a bunk bed in an air-raid shelter during the Blitz; he's clutching his broken arm while I tend to Harry's injured leg. '*George . . . Cooper?*' I say hesitantly.

Jude shoots me a roguish and at once familiar wink. 'The one and the same, luv!' she replies in a perfect east London accent.

I throw my hands up in exasperation. 'Why do I feel like a stranger at my own reunion?'

Chuckling, Caleb takes my arm and leads me to the windows overlooking the garden. 'As Shakespeare puts it: *All the world's a stage, and all the men and women merely players: they have their exits and their entrances; and one man in his time plays many parts*. Except, that is, for a First Ascendant like you, Genna. Your play is just one of many, and you will perform countless roles in those times, from queen to cook and king to beggar. The one thread that connects each part is your soul. But with so many parts you can't be expected to remember all the other players.'

'So who were you back then?' I ask.

'I was Khafra, the vizier to your pharaoh father,' he reveals with a wistful smile. 'Hepuhotep was one of the great First Ascendants, although he had a tendency to flaunt his Light. His pyramid was a prime example!'

'*You* have a pyramid,' I note, peering at the gleaming glass structure towering over the garden.

Caleb laughs. 'True, but at least mine is hidden within a protected valley and not on display for the whole world to see!'

'But why am I suddenly having so many Glimmers? In the last day or so alone, I've recalled four past lives. And that last one was seriously intense.'

'That's perfectly understandable. You've been under a lot of stress,' says Caleb. He lays a reassuring hand upon my shoulder. 'Experiencing a Glimmer can be like unlocking a door in your mind. Once you open one, even more appear.'

I think of the strange dream I had of Phoenix. *Was that a result of stress too? Or another door being unlocked in my mind?*

Caleb leads me out into the water garden and bright sunshine. 'Genna, due to the concentration of the Light here, you may well find that you experience even more Glimmers now you're in Haven.'

'Caleb,' calls Jude from her chair, 'you were right, by the way. About LA. The city was crawling with them.'

Despite the Soul Seer standing in the full glare of the sun, a shadow seems to fall across his face. The lines on his brow deepen into canyons. 'I feared as much. We'll talk later.'

With a brisk nod, Jude gently pushes the cat off her lap and leaves the room. I watch her disappear down a corridor with my bag.

Suspecting Caleb already knows about Tanas's return, I say, 'Is everything all right, though?'

Caleb puts on a cheery smile and replies, 'Now you're safely here, yes.'

'And what about Phoenix?' I ask eagerly. 'Do you know where my Soul Protector is? Jude said you might –'

'Hush. All in good time,' Caleb reassures me. 'Let's settle you into Haven first.' Turning from me, he heads off through the garden. 'Come, Genna,' he calls over his shoulder. 'I think you'll like it here. You'll soon feel less like a stranger.'

Although I'm impatient for answers, I nonetheless follow him. The desert sun is blazing hot, yet thankfully the trickling stream and teardrop pond cool the air around us. A cat perches at the water's edge intently watching a koi carp glide past inches from its nose.

Caleb chats away freely as we stroll along a winding gravel path, his cane tapping lightly with each step. 'This garden is an exact replica of the one I tended for Daimyo Takeda at his home in Kai province,' he says. 'I even had a cherry blossom tree imported from that very same region in Japan.' He waves his stick at a flourishing pink-white tree further along the path.

'It's beautiful,' I say, feeling immediately at home in such surroundings. My own Glimmer as the samurai Miyoko comes back to me and I recall meditating in just such a garden some five hundred years ago . . . *My hands cupped in my lap, my eyes closed, the sweet scent of cherry blossom in my nostrils, listening to the ripple of water and the soft tinkle of a wind chime as I focus on my breathing and clear my mind of all distraction, my katana always close at hand –*

Caleb stumbles slightly on the path and I catch him by the arm; the Glimmer vanishes, along with the tantalizing reminder of my samurai skills. 'Are you OK, Caleb?'

He nods, his face crinkling with a pained smile. 'An old war wound,' he explains.

'And which war was that? I ask without irony.

'The First World War,' he says. 'I was shot in the knee. The trauma of the injury carried over to this life, as they're sometimes wont to do. But that's the least of my ailments. Due to my Soul Sight, I'm electro-sensitive. Any magnetic field, Wi-Fi or radio signal disturbs my aura. Of course, that wasn't a problem in the past, but nowadays this modern, high-tech world gives me headaches, nausea and crippling pain if I'm exposed to it for too long.'

'Is that why you built Haven here? In a dead zone?' I say, remembering what Jude told me.

'Partly,' he replies. 'But there's a far greater reason for choosing this place.' He points to the six colossal pillars of red stone that dominate the valley. 'This is a powerful and ancient spiritual site. A natural stone circle of immense cosmic energy. The local Mojave people gave their blessing to build Haven here within its protection. We're on sacred ground.' He looks at me. 'You must have felt it yourself upon entering?'

At his words I once more become aware of the warm tingling in my limbs. 'Yes, it's like . . . it's strange, but it's like liquid sunshine from within.'

Caleb smiles. 'The stone circle is feeding your Light,' he explains. 'And that sensation will only grow stronger the longer you're here.'

'But what is this Light? Why am I carrying it and what am I supposed to do with it?' I ask. 'My Soul Protector, Phoenix, told me I'm a First Ascendant, but I still don't really understand what that means. Am I a god or something?'

Caleb chuckles. 'So many questions,' he says, guiding me along the path towards the glass pyramid. 'Perhaps it's easier just to show you.'

20

For a moment I'm almost blinded. Then my eyes adjust and it appears as if I'm standing inside a huge prism. The glass panels of the pyramid refract the golden sunlight, casting a multitude of rainbows over my head like a kaleidoscope. I feel dizzy and intoxicated by the sight, my skin tingling and my nerves buzzing as if a small electric current is running through me.

'This is the Sun Room,' Caleb announces proudly. He notices my wide-eyed expression. 'Don't be alarmed at any heightened sensations you may be experiencing. They're a natural consequence of bathing in the Light.'

'Why is the feeling so strong, though?' I ask as I rub my tingling hands together.

'The glass pyramid focuses and magnifies the sun's energy,' he explains. 'Combined with the power of the stone circle, you're absorbing the Light at a higher rate than normal. But you still really haven't experienced anything yet!'

Caleb leads me across the pyramid's white marble floor, its smooth surface polished to such a high sheen that it's like a mirror and gives the impression of walking in mid-air. I notice that Caleb's no longer limping, his cane left behind at the entrance, and I assume the Light has temporarily strengthened his knee. I remember when fighting Damien within Havenbury's stone circle that my own muscles felt strangely empowered and that Phoenix's life was even saved by its restorative effects. In fact, my injuries from yesterday's escape from Damien and his thugs at the building site have all but disappeared – the aches are miraculously gone and the bruises are fading before my very eyes.

Caleb stops beside a white marble pedestal in the centre of the room. Chest-high and octagonal-shaped, the altar is the only solid object in the whole pyramid. Its sides are engraved with mystical symbols and hieroglyphs. With my Egyptian Glimmer still fresh in my mind, I immediately recognize the protective Eye of Horus and the loop-headed ankh cross that represents life. Below these, there's a circular yin and yang sign, letters in ancient Arabic, and an unusual triple spiral that I haven't seen before. Mounted on top of the pedestal sits a large, clear crystal cut into the shape of a pyramid capstone. I catch my reflection in its shining surface and am taken aback at the blazing blue gleam to my eyes. I've never seen them so radiant and star-like!

'Genna, I intend to show you your deep past,' says Caleb in a reverential tone, his eyes even more brilliant than mine. 'Watch and learn as I guide you on this journey. I warn you, though: the experience can be quite intense. It'll be more of a Glare than a Glimmer.'

He runs his fingers along the top edge of the altar, as if it were a tablet screen, and the solar panels of the glass pyramid adjust to redirect the sun's rays. The kaleidoscope of rainbows coalesces into a single white beam that strikes the very tip of the crystal capstone. The clear jewel bursts into life and a miniature sun burns bright at its heart. So dazzling is its fire that I'm amazed I can even look at it without losing my sight.

'Are you ready? Place your hands upon the crystal,' instructs Caleb, who stands opposite me, his palms flat against one side.

Hesitantly I reach out, expecting the surface to be scorching hot, but discover to my surprise that it's cool to the touch. Then the hairs on the backs of my arms rise, and a second later a surge of energy floods my body. My heart pounds, my blood roars and my amber skin begins to glow from within. The sun inside the crystal expands until my vision is consumed entirely by its bright golden light . . .

Everything . . . is Light.

Glorious, blissful and infinitely peaceful.

The Light sings, swirls and soars. Flowing freely and forever –

'What is this Light?' I say, my voice echoing through time. My spirits lift like a feather borne high upon the warmest, softest breeze.

'Love, in its purest form,' comes back Caleb's reply from afar. 'The origin and essence of the Universe.'

All of a sudden a rip appears in the Light. Its shimmering curtain is torn apart by an explosion of Darkness. Particles of Light are flung into the furthest reaches of an ever-expanding void – a billion trillion sparks floating away in an endless sea of black –

Just as suddenly a great sadness seems to suffocate my heart. 'What just happened?'

'The birth of Tanas,' replies Caleb in a mournful voice.

All around, the Light is slowly dying, the sparks blinking out, one by one.

Eons of time pass, the Darkness spreads and the Universe grows colder.

Then glints of Light begin to reappear, shining bright and bold in the Darkness, and we are born –

'First Ascendants are not gods. They are carriers of the Light,' explains Caleb. 'Your soul is the essence of that First Light. And it is this essence that's reincarnated from life to life, body to body, in the same way that one candle can be used to ignite another before it is extinguished.'

'But am I . . . human?' I ask with some trepidation.

Caleb nods. 'You're as human as anyone on this planet. But you're also a spiritual being. You see more, know more and feel more. Your presence, along with that of other First Ascendants, brings much needed hope, love and Light to Humanity.'

I stand upon the hilltop, facing east across the Great Rift Valley. The night has been long and cold, but the promise of a new dawn shimmers on the horizon. A soft orange glow slowly pushes back night's black mantle. I take my mother's hand, then my twin sister's, who in turn takes my father's, and we raise them to the sky. Across the hilltop the rest of our Ascendant tribe do the same. We raise our hands together to greet the coming sun –

'I have a sister?' I murmur in astonishment. I think back to what I said to Mei about her being like the sister I never had and, for the first time, I understand the deep yearning in my heart for a sibling.

'You had a whole First Ascendant family,' Caleb says warmly, 'and together you harnessed the Light . . .'

We begin to chant our soft subtle spell, a chorus of birdsong accompanying our ceremony. The low rhythmic notes of hoopoes mix with the higher-pitched calls of cuckoos and kingfishers along the broad banks of the river, where hippos grunt and a knot of gazelles gather quietly to drink from its waters. A symphony of sound that sends the night into retreat. At last the great red disc of the sun crests the horizon, its golden rays spilling across the bountiful savannah. Elephants, zebra and wildebeest roam free. A herd of antelope stir as a lion prowls through the long grass. Flocks of birds take flight. Up on the hill we are bathed in the Light, and the Earth comes to life –

As the deeply ancient vision passes, Caleb's voice once more resounds in my head: 'By upholding the Light, you help protect humanity and all life on this planet from Tanas and his Darkness.'

My chest tightens to the point where I'm almost unable to breathe. 'Are you telling me that the fate of the world is in my hands?'

'You're not alone in this task,' Caleb assures me. 'All Ascendants share this duty.'

'Still, that's some responsibility,' I say, the idea weighing so heavily upon me that my body trembles at the very thought of defying Tanas. 'How are we supposed to uphold this Light?'

'Primarily by passing your soul's flame on to its next incarnation and thereby keeping the Light burning . . . and the Darkness at bay.'

Having confronted Tanas once already in this life, I know this is no easy task. My Light has been on the point of being snuffed out forever on more occasions than I'd care to remember. 'Does every soul carry the Light?' I ask, hoping the burden is spread wide.

'No, only those that were born of the First Light.'

'But do any other souls reincarnate like us?'

'Some,' responds Caleb. 'It depends on their journey, what stage they are at and what they still need to learn. Certain souls are very ancient, others are fresh and new. They're the ones that need the greatest protection and guidance. For those that have come after the First Light are sparks that can either be fanned into flames to help our purpose – like Soul Brothers and Sisters – or else be put out.'

'What do you mean, "put out"?'

'Their souls blackened and turned by Tanas to become Incarnates,' Caleb explains grimly. 'You see, Tanas lurks in the night claiming the souls of the lost. He feeds off their despair, drawing them in with false promises and making it easy for them to be enticed by the Darkness. So the more evil that is committed in the world, the stronger he becomes. And while his army of Watchers and Hunters continues to grow, the sparks die and our Light dwindles . . .'

A storm thunders in the heavens. Lightning cracks and rain cascades down in torrents. Out of the darkness an army of black-eyed warriors marches across the plain towards our settlement. We are unprepared and unprotected. Not even the first of the First among our tribe predicted that Tanas would be able to incarnate himself on Earth, or draw such numbers of followers to his evil cause.

As strong and mighty as a silverback gorilla, Tanas sits high up on a colossal tusked elephant. He wears a lion's skull on his shaved head and the pelt of a leopard on his back. His tattooed skin glistens with rain under the stark flashes of lightning and in his hand he clutches a long spear, its vicious spike carved from a human thigh bone.

The screams of Ascendant men, women and children fill the air as we try to flee his army of Incarnates. But they lay waste to our settlement and slaughter everyone in their path. Leading the charge, Tanas targets the brightest of the Ascendants, spearing them through the heart with his fiendish weapon and laughing cruelly as they die –

'W-was that Tanas's first attack?' I ask in a faltering voice, the sharp, icy fear of that moment as fresh and fierce as I felt it all those countless millennia ago.

'Yes. The first of many.'

I swallow hard, trying to suppress the instinctive urge to run, reminding myself it's only a Glimmer. 'But how did we ever survive?'

'Be patient, Genna, and you shall see . . .'

21

I stand amid the carnage, terror rooting me to the spot while my fellow Ascendants are murdered before my eyes. My mother and father scream for me to run, then they too are caught up in the massacre. Like bloodthirsty lions hunting down a pair of gazelles, the Incarnates pounce on their prey and tear my parents limb from limb. I feel their brutal deaths like a stake through my own heart, the Light of the world dimming as they are lost.

Then I see my twin sister, Lakeisha, cowering in our hut, trying to hide from the bloodbath. Tanas goads his elephant with the tip of his spear. The enraged beast rears up and knocks the hut down, pinning my sister beneath the wreckage. I have to get her out before she's trampled under foot. In an instant I'm by her side.

Her starry eyes are wide with pain. 'Tishala, I can't move my legs!' my sister gasps.

Clearing the debris, I discover she's trapped under a wooden beam. I grab hold of it . . . but it's too heavy. 'You'll have to lift too,' I tell her.

Lakeisha nods and begins to push with her hands. My teeth gritted, I strain with all my might as Tanas charges back our way. Seeing the elephant thundering ever closer, I let out a yell of fear and fury. At the last moment the beam shifts and my sister wriggles free.

'Lakeisha, run!' I scream.

The huge elephant is almost on top of us. Lakeisha hobbles away and I dash in the opposite direction, frantically waving my arms to draw Tanas's attention. The distraction works, but the large elephant is deceptively fast and before I know it a tusk has gored my side, flinging me through the air to land, broken and bleeding, in the mud.

Leaping from his mount, Tanas strides over to finish me off. I try to crawl away, but I slip and slide in the rain-soaked red earth. He looms over me, his bone spear raised high above his head. A flash of lightning illuminates his dark demonic face, revealing two bottomless pits for eyes, and a scream wells up in my throat at his empty soulless stare. I know all hope is gone. Around me, the Light is being extinguished flame by flame, soul by soul, and I'm next –

'I thought you said we survived!' I gasp, my body trembling from a primeval fear. My side throbs painfully as if it has been gored anew, and my skin is as goose-bumped and chilled as it was long ago on that fateful night. Even in the glaring brightness of the Sun Room, I can sense Tanas's dark shadow looming over me.

'Be patient, Genna. This Glare is not yet over,' Caleb assures me. 'The tide of battle is about to turn . . .'

As I lie defenceless at Tanas's feet, I glimpse a forest of burning torches moving from the east. A war cry sounds and a host of axe-wielding warriors charge out of the night.

Taken by surprise, the Incarnates are driven back and forced to fight these new invaders.

Tanas goes to spear me through the heart when an axe blade cleaves his weapon in half and a bare-chested warrior with braided black hair knocks him flying. Flipping back to his feet, Tanas roars in fury and advances. Undaunted, the warrior swings his axe to behead him. At the last second Tanas ducks, then smashes the shaft of his broken spear across his opponent's arm, knocking the axe from his grasp. The warrior responds with a barrage of punches and disarms Tanas of his broken spear. They fight hand to hand – brutal blows, the battle like a clash between two great lions – but Tanas's superior strength gets the better of the brave warrior. Tanas kicks him to the ground, then stamps on him so hard I hear ribs break.

Leaving the man gasping and writhing in pain, Tanas picks up the dropped axe and turns back to me. Unarmed, half his size and badly injured from the elephant's tusk, I've little hope of fending him off. But then I spot a gleam of white bone in the mud – the broken spear tip! I scramble towards it, but Tanas seizes my ankle and drags me away. He flings me against the remains of a stone wall, knocking all the air from my lungs, before laying me across it like a sacrificial goat.

'You can lose your head before your heart!' he growls, raising the axe.

Suddenly his pitch-black eye sockets widen and he grunts in pain. Keeling forward, Tanas collapses face-first into the mud, a gleam of white bone protruding from his back – the broken tip of his own spear – and there, standing victorious over his dead body, is the braided warrior. Rain drips down his blood-soaked face and he has his arm clasped round his injured chest, yet the warrior offers me his hand. I grasp it and he pulls me to my feet. In that moment our eyes lock and a spark of Light passes between us. His deep-brown eyes take on a blue starlit hue and I know that from now on and forever more we'll be connected –

My breath catches in my throat and my pulse quickens at the memory. 'So that's how I met my Soul Protector?' I say.

'Yes . . . the Hakala warrior tribe from the mountains came to your rescue,' explains Caleb. 'That fateful night each warrior who saved a First Ascendant became their Soul Protector and an eternal bond was forged between their souls.'

'But we lost so many,' I say, tears brimming in my eyes with an ancient grief as I recall those who died, my First mother and First father among them. Their deaths weigh even more heavily on my heart than those of my present-life parents and for a moment I feel ashamed that my grief can make such a distinction between them, but then I realize my First mother and father were part of me in a way my present-life parents could never be.

'In that lifetime, yes, many were lost,' says Caleb sadly. Then I sense a smile starting to spread across his lips. 'But Tanas underestimated the power of the Light. You see, Light is energy and, by nature's law, energy can never be destroyed; it can only change from one form to another. Those who died that night came back in another life to bond with the remaining warriors.'

'So Tanas failed?' I say, a bud of hope blossoming at the news that my First mother and father's souls survived.

'Oh, if only!' Caleb replies bitterly. 'No, Tanas *learned*! And eventually, after many lifetimes of trying, he returned, having discovered a way to break that unbreakable law –'

The bloodcurdling scream from within the palace sends a shudder through the row of slaves in the courtyard. Prior to that, the rhythmic chants of 'Ra-Ka! Ra-Ka! Ra-Ka!' were unsettling enough, but it's the dead silence after the victim's final scream that is most disturbing.

I stand with the other slaves, clasping my twin sister's hand tightly, wondering how we might escape. There are leather-armoured guards at every exit, and the Akkadian slave trader has his beady eye on all of us as he fingers the short, knotted whip in his belt and mops his brow from the intense heat baking the Sumerian city of Uruk.

A tall, thin man in a gold-embroidered white robe appears on the steps. Thick black curls poke out from beneath the solid gold band that crowns his head, and a long squared-off beard shrouds his thrusting chin and earthy complexion. With regal grace, he descends to the courtyard. As he draws closer, flecks of blood are clearly visible on the front of his once immaculate robe.

'W-w-was that slave not satisfactory either?' stutters the trader in a flurry of panic.

'Oh, he was most *satisfactory,' Saragon replies in an oily voice. The Lugal of Uruk city slowly makes his way along the row of slaves, carefully examining each in turn.*

The slave trader shuffles along beside him. 'I-I-I can assure you, O Great Lugal, that these slaves are personally chosen by me to be of the best quality. They're meant for long-term service, rather than ... ahem ... short-term duties.' His flabby cheeks and plump lips fold into an ingratiating yet fearful smile.

Saragon shoots the trader a sharp look. 'It's none of your business what I do with my property!'

'N-no, of course,' replies the slave trader, bowing low as the Lugal inspects the teeth of a muscled slave, peers closely at his rounded face, then dismisses him. 'I merely wish to give you total satisfaction with the slaves I procure for you.'

'Don't worry, Rimush, you've done a fine job in rounding up these specimens, but I'm quite choosy as to who will suit my particular needs ...'

He stops in front of my sister and me. With a long, bony finger, he lifts my sister's delicate chin. His narrow eyes, as hard and shiny as black opals, fix upon hers and a sinister smile slides across his thin lips when he sees their blue gleam. 'I'll have this one,' he declares.

My sister's face goes pale and she recoils from the man's touch. I grip her hand more tightly, preparing to make a suicidal dash for freedom. Our only hope may be through the palace, but that would be like entering the lion's den itself. I look pleadingly to the slave trader for mercy. He'd shown us small kindnesses on the long arduous trek across the desert to Uruk, favouring us over the other captives, knowing we'd gain him a high price at market.

Rimush clears his throat nervously. 'A thousand pardons, but I really can't sell her for such purposes,' he announces with as much firmness as he can muster.

Saragon raises a thick eyebrow. 'Ah, a slave trader with morals? Don't make me laugh, Rimush,' he scoffs. 'I pay you well, don't I?'

'Yes, double the going rate, but that's not the –'

'Then what do my "purposes" matter to you?' he sneers. 'I want her and I'll have her.'

Rimush swallows hard and wrings his hands. 'But these two come as a pair,' he says weakly.

Turning his gaze to my equally starlit eyes, Saragon grins. 'Ah yes. Of course they do.'

'And with eyes like that they're very expensive, mind you!' blabbers the slave trader. 'Couldn't I interest you in a more reasonable purchase? One that satisfies your needs, but at a better price?'

'NO!' barks Saragon. 'I'll take this one first,' he continues, indicating my sister. 'Keep a close watch on the other.' Then he seizes my twin's wrist and drags her away.

'Aya!' I cry, clinging desperately on to her, but I'm struck across the back of the head with a stick. Dazed, I drop to my knees and can only watch as my sister is hauled up the steps and into the forbidding palace –

My knees suddenly give way and I slump to the ground. Even my head rings like I've just been struck. Pain, anger, sadness and despair, along with a whole host of other emotions, overwhelm me.

'I think that's enough for today,' says Caleb quickly, taking his hands off the crystal capstone and breaking the connection. He comes round and helps me to stand. 'Gently now. I did warn you that it can be an intense experience.'

Despite the earlier rush of energy, my body now feels utterly drained. I lean against the altar for support as tears stream down my cheeks and my heart burns with grief. I look into Caleb's wrinkled, time-worn face. 'What happened to my sister?' I croak in desperation.

'My apologies, Genna. I don't always have control over what appears,' explains Caleb, his face strained. 'Some Glimmers surface unbidden. Maybe we can revisit that one another time.'

'But I want to know,' I begin, before my head reels and my legs buckle again.

Caleb holds me up by the waist. 'There's only so much you can take in on a first Glare,' he says gently. 'You'll burn out otherwise, and that's no good to anyone. Come away now to rest and recover.'

He guides me back towards the pyramid's entrance and then out into the garden. Settling me on a bench under the shade of the cherry blossom tree, he returns to the pyramid to collect his cane, his limp once more apparent. I listen to the trickle of the stream, trying to calm my emotions and the torrent of thoughts swirling in my head: the blessing and burden of the Light, the brutal shock of Tanas's first attack, the joy of bonding with my Soul Protector, the uncertain fate of my sister – the fact that I even *have* a sister . . .

Nefertiti appears from the bushes and rubs against my legs. Instinctively I pick her up and put her in my lap. As I stroke her soft fur, the storm in my mind gradually subsides, like it always seems to do in her presence.

Hearing the click of a walking stick upon the path, I turn to the approaching Caleb and ask, 'Why don't First

Ascendants remember any of this past when they're born? Surely it would help us prepare for Tanas?'

'Perhaps,' he acknowledges, sitting beside me on the bench, 'but your awareness would also draw his Hunters to you when you're at your most vulnerable. Besides, considering the emotions you've experienced just now, it's a kindness you don't recall all your previous incarnations. Don't you think life would be almost unbearable under the weight of so many memories? *That* is the burden of a Soul Seer like me.' He smiles wearily and pats my knee. 'I trust we have answered your questions, Genna, at least for the time being. Now, how would you like to meet some other First Ascendants?'

22

With a giddy mix of excitement and trepidation, I follow Caleb through an arched wooden gateway into a large rectangular courtyard. On all four sides, fluted marble columns line a covered walkway in the style of a Roman villa. This surrounds an area of lawn and a small yet well-tended orchard. Orange, lemon and apple trees, ripe with fruit, scent the air; terracotta pots brimming with flowers decorate a stretch of lush green grass; and a water fountain gently trickles in the centre of this apparent Garden of Eden. As I look more closely, I notice a dozen or so sea-blue doors set into the courtyard's sand-coloured walls, an open door revealing a small apartment behind; and beyond the courtyard, visible above the red-tiled roofline, rises a large dome structure studded with small, round stained-glass windows.

Gathered in the garden, along with one or two cats, a number of people are enjoying the morning sun. There's a white-haired old lady in a rocking chair reading to a young girl on her lap. Nearby, a mother with braided black hair relaxes on the grass, cradling her baby in her arms. A family of four sit round a wooden table eating breakfast outside their apartment. Elsewhere, two men, one bearded, the other in a wheelchair, play chess, and a younger man with straggly brown hair tends an orange tree. They all turn as one when Caleb and I enter and, on seeing me, their faces light up with smiles like rays of sunshine. The young girl jumps down from the old lady's lap, races over and embraces me in a hug. For a brief joyous moment I think this must be my sister . . . but when she looks up at me with her gleaming blue eyes and I peer into her soul, I can see it isn't her.

'My name's Tasha,' says the girl, beaming brightly at me. Her hair is ice-blond, her skin pale as snow, and her accent, if my ears are not mistaken, is Russian.

'*Privet, Tasha, ya Genna*,' I reply, the language flowing as easily from my lips as if I were still the acrobat Yelena.

'I know. We've been waiting for you,' she replies in Russian.

Tasha takes me by the hand and leads me into the centre of the garden. I'm immediately surrounded by these amiable blue-eyed folk who each greet me in turn. I meet Viviana, the hardy grandmother from Italy. Then it's Thabisa and her baby son, Kagiso, recently arrived from South Africa. Next are Mr and Mrs Jeong and their son Nam and daughter Song, originally from South Korea but now settled in the USA. Then there are the two chess players: the bearded and gruff Santiago from Cuba and the cheerful upbeat Mick from New Zealand. And, finally, the long-haired, fruit-picking Fabian from the Netherlands, who hands me a fresh orange as a welcome gift. Like old friends reuniting, we hug, kiss and cry with joy. Each embrace is a warm fire in my heart.

Despite only recently meeting these people, I feel at ease, as if I were among my closest family. I look around, wondering where my First parents and sister are, whether they too have managed to survive the countless generations of Tanas's genocide . . . then an unexpected stab of grief hits me as I'm reminded of my present-life parents, now dead and gone. While they may not have been First Ascendants, I realize they still meant the world to me in this life. The image of them lying butchered on the kitchen floor causes me to draw in a hitching sob and bitter tears sting my eyes.

'*Stai bene, mia cara?*' asks Viviana, putting her arm round me.

'Yes, I'm fine,' I reply, quickly wiping away a tear with the back of my hand. 'Just . . . overwhelmed.'

She smiles warmly. '*Ah, certamente!*'

I glance round the courtyard, noting all the doors. There are many more apartments than people. I turn to Caleb hopefully. 'Are there more to come?' I ask, recalling the large and thriving tribe we once were.

Although he nods and grins, there's an unmistakable sadness in his smile. 'Yes . . . there are more Ascendants out there in the world. In fact, we're expecting a couple to join us this afternoon,' he replies. Then the bittersweet smile fades from his lips and he looks noticeably older. 'But there's no denying that the Light is becoming ever more diminished –'

Without warning, Caleb lets out an agonized cry and collapses.

'Caleb! Are you ill?' I reach for his hand. 'Is it your kn–'

Then I too am struck by the most gut-wrenching pain and drop to the ground beside him. I struggle to breathe, a fire burning in my belly as if I've been shot at point-blank range. Through eyes screwed up in agony, I see . . .

a shrouded figure floating before me . . . I can't make out their face but I sense it to be Tanas . . . then I catch a glimpse of a ceiling lined with pipes, a hospital gurney and the blood-smeared blade of a surgical scalpel . . . Fevered chants of 'Ra-Ka! Ra-Ka! Ra-Ka!' resound in my ears, the ritual of the soul sacrifice at once familiar and frightening . . . Watchers in ghostly white cloaks encircle me . . . A bitter taste taints my mouth and a cloying, aniseed scent in the air makes me nauseous . . .

'Tell me where Haven is and I'll free you of this pain,' promises a warped voice. 'Otherwise you'll suffer eternal banishment, like your Soul Protector . . .'

'Never!' comes my spluttered reply . . .

'So be it!' hisses the voice. There's a flash of steel and pain flares as the scalpel cuts through my body and my soul, the sickening sensation of separation tearing my very self apart –

I let go of Caleb's hand and the intense vision vanishes. The world around me dims and I feel an emptiness within my heart, like part of me is missing and will be lost forever.

'Are you all right?' asks Fabian, helping me to my feet.

'I think so,' I reply weakly. As I shake my throbbing head clear and rub my aching belly, I try to convince myself that what I just saw was a flashback to the church crypt. But I know it wasn't. And it wasn't me on the gurney either. In fact, the most disturbing thing about the Glimmer is that it wasn't from the past at all.

Just like the dream I had of Phoenix, it's happening right now.

In fact, doubled over on the ground beside me, Caleb still appears to be experiencing this present-life Glimmer. He's moaning, as if praying for an end to the pain. By holding his hand I must have somehow connected to whatever he's seeing and feeling – although that doesn't explain how I previously dreamed of Phoenix. *So did I somehow 'connect' to my Soul Protector?*

Eventually the groans stop and Caleb looks up. A sheen of sweat glistens on his brow and his eyes are noticeably dimmer. 'We've lost Saul . . .' he gasps, 'and his Protector, Maddy, is gone too . . .'

'NO!' wails Thabisa, clutching her baby closer to her chest.

Santiago goes to comfort her in his great bear-like arms. 'That's not possible!' he barks. 'Caleb, you told us Tanas had passed from this life.'

'That I did,' replies the weary Soul Seer as Fabian hands him his cane and helps him stand. 'Like you, I felt the Darkness lift some six months ago.'

'Then how can Saul's Light have been lost?' questions Jintao Jeong angrily. He holds his wife Sun-Hi's hand tight and wraps a protective arm round his children.

Caleb grasps the lion-headed hilt of his cane, his knuckles turning white as he struggles to support himself and appear strong for everyone. 'I'm afraid to say, his Watchers have returned,' he admits. 'Over the past few weeks my visions have been growing darker and more ominous. I didn't want to give them credence, but this morning Jude confirmed that she's sighted a horde of them in LA. I can only assume Tanas's Hunters have been revived too.'

'How can that be?' questions Mick sharply. 'With no Tanas, there are no Watchers, no Hunters and, therefore, no ritual sacrifices.'

'Tanas is back,' I say flatly, surprised that Caleb has only recently suspected this. Everyone falls silent, the previously joyful atmosphere of the garden now as solemn as a funeral. 'I've seen his Hunters with my own eyes,' I continue. 'Fought them off with my own hands.'

Tasha's willowy body gives an involuntary shudder and she clings to Viviana, burying her pale face in the folds of the old woman's floral dress. Fabian bows his head and Thabisa's baby son begins to cry. Caleb suddenly looks very tired and very old. With the help of his cane, he goes over to a stone bench and sits down heavily. 'My nightmares are true then,' he says with a sigh.

'I don't understand how he's back,' I go on. 'My Soul Protector, Phoenix, killed him in this life – killed him with an obsidian blade. He said that should keep Tanas at bay for at least a lifetime or two.'

Caleb rests his chin on the top of his cane. 'Well, maybe Tanas isn't as vulnerable to obsidian as we believed. Even so, his return seems too sudden, the rise of his Hunters too swift.'

'Couldn't he have simply been reborn?' suggests Fabian.

'Of course he could,' says Caleb. 'But even if he reincarnated immediately following his death, he'd still be too young to exert any influence or summon his Hunters.'

'I don't believe Tanas has been reborn,' I say. 'One of his Soul Hunters, Damien, boasted that his master *incarnated* himself into another body.'

Caleb looks up at me, his eyes sharp. 'What are you saying, Genna? That Tanas returned into an already-living body?'

I nod.

'That's unprecedented! Tell me, how *exactly* did Tanas die?'

The First Ascendants listen closely as I recount Tanas's attempt to destroy my soul and how Phoenix saved my life. When I finish, Caleb distractedly taps his cane on the ground, pondering a moment. 'You say Tanas died in a church,' he says. 'Was there anything unusual about this church?'

'Yes. Tanas had deconsecrated it with dark magic,' I explain. 'Black candles . . . spells . . . ancient runes . . . inverted crosses . . . He even drew a pentagram on the floor.'

Caleb straightens up and studies me intently. 'And did Tanas happen to die *within* this pentagram?'

I nod.

The Soul Seer raps his stick on the earth. 'Ah! *That* explains it,' he declares, rising to his feet and pacing the lawn with renewed vigour. 'You see, the power of the pentagram could have maintained a link between his soul and the physical world. A bridge by which he could return. It's feasible that Tanas incarnated himself into a different body on the very cusp of death, a body whose soul channel was still open. In theory, he could have taken over that soul, consumed it and occupied the body.' He shakes his head in amazement. 'But such an attempt carries a great deal of risk: if the body had died *as he was transmigrating*, his own soul could have been lost between the physical and spiritual realms for eternity.'

'Shame it didn't die!' spits Santiago.

'*Il male non muore mai*,' mutters Viviana as she tenderly strokes Tasha's blond hair in an effort to comfort the girl.

'Sorry?' I ask, not understanding her Italian.

With a grave look at each First Ascendant in turn, Viviana repeats in accented English, 'Evil never dies.'

23

'I need to find Phoenix,' I tell Caleb as my fellow First Ascendants disperse. Each will need to come to terms with Saul's death and Tanas's unexpected return.

'Don't worry, Genna. You're perfectly safe here,' assures Caleb, taking my arm and walking me across the lawn.

'I'd feel safer with Phoenix by my side,' I say. 'He can protect me from Tanas, like he's done in this life and all my previous lives.'

Caleb nods sympathetically. 'I appreciate your desire to be with your Soul Protector, but it's best you stay within Haven and not go searching for him. You saw for yourself how many Watchers are out there. Trust that Phoenix will find you. Besides, you have Jude here. She's more than capable as a Warrior.'

'That may be true,' I say, recalling Jude's sword skills as the mute bodyguard Raneb. 'But what about Phoenix? Where is he? Is he even aware Tanas is back?'

Caleb gently pats my arm. 'Don't fret now. Phoenix can look after himself, and you and your Light are safe here. That's all that matters.'

I frown, perplexed by the Soul Seer's apparent disregard for the danger. 'But what's to stop Tanas or his Hunters finding this place?' I persist. 'I glimpsed that vision of Saul's death too. You and I both know Tanas is searching for Haven.'

'And he'll never find it,' Caleb replies with surprising certainty. 'I've been very careful to conceal this sanctuary. Moreover, we're on sacred ground. No Soul Hunter can enter this valley without prejudicing their soul.'

'But Tanas managed to enter a sanctified church, where he killed your fellow Soul Seer Gabriel and sacrificed his soul,' I grimly remind him.

Caleb's shoulders slump and his head drops. 'Yes, I felt my friend's passing like a knife to my heart. That was indeed a dark day.' He looks me gravely in the eye. 'Which is why I've put precautions in place. Haven isn't on any map. Its entrance is concealed within an abandoned mine. Overhead, a holographic shield has been installed. And by virtue of the dead zone this place isn't detectable from the ground or the sky. In this valley, Genna, we're hidden from the world.'

'But is that enough?' I question. 'Just because we're not on a map, it doesn't mean Tanas can't find us.'

'Genna, you need to be led to Haven by someone who has been here before,' he reveals. 'That is the key to entering the valley. Our combined Light cloaks our presence here. Like a sea mist hiding a ship, Haven is effectively invisible to the Incarnates.'

He comes to a stop outside one of the sea-blue doors in the south-west corner of the courtyard. 'Ah, here we are.

This is your apartment,' he announces brightly. 'I'll leave you to get settled, then we can catch up later. In the meantime, rest and recover. You've had a long and fraught journey.' Bidding me farewell, he limps off to speak with the others.

Hoping his confidence in Haven's security isn't misplaced, I enter my small yet neat apartment. My backpack is already on the bed, and fresh clothes have been laid out. There's a chilled bottle of water waiting for me on the sideboard. Nefe is there too, curled up beside my pillow. I give her a cuddle, her deep purr reassuringly familiar after all the uncertainty and worry of the last few days. After I've drunk my fill of water, I unpack my meagre belongings, take a much-needed shower and change into denim shorts, black Converse trainers and a cream T-shirt. When I emerge again, blinking in the bright light, I discover breakfast has been set for me on a small round table – fresh fruit, yogurt, granola, bread and orange juice. I tuck in hungrily.

The past forty-eight hours have been a nightmarish blur. How I wish I could talk things over with Mei and Prisha, but I know I can't risk contacting them in case I give away Haven's location. Anyhow, I've no phone and there's no signal. What must my friends be thinking? I fled the scene of my own parents' murder and became an international fugitive, wanted by not only the police in England but the FBI in America. And I told Mei that the Incarnates are back. She'll think I've lost it again, that the brutal death of my parents has triggered another breakdown . . .

For a moment I wonder if I *am* having a breakdown. *Is this all in my head?* Then I look out across the courtyard where Viviana is comforting Tasha in the rocking chair;

Thabisa is feeding little Kagiso; Jintao and his family are having their breakfast; and Santiago and Mick are seated in the shade of an olive tree, deep in discussion; and I realize that all this feels more real than anything in my life. There's an undeniable, unspoken connection between us, a brightness that seems magnified by our combined presences and a sense of something else too . . . a sense of homecoming.

Despite the months I've spent in therapy being convinced otherwise, I know this to be my reality.

I am a First Ascendant, and always have been.

The trauma I suffered as a result of Damien's first attack and Tanas's attempt to ritually sacrifice me now gains some perspective. While those violent events are still distressing for me, I no longer question the reason for them, or feel such a helpless victim. My soul's purpose strengthens me and my shared experience with my fellow First Ascendants fortifies my resolve. I'm not alone in my suffering or my journey. I'm surrounded by people who understand me and what I've gone through.

Dr Larsson was right about one thing, though. I've shifted from victim to survivor, and given time I hope to become a thriver.

Still, I cannot help but question what the future holds. Having barely mourned the loss of my present-life parents, have I now gained my *true* family? Is Haven to be my permanent home? As beautiful and peaceful as it is, I can imagine it could quickly become a gilded cage. Am I to be trapped here for the rest of my life, hiding from Tanas and his Hunters? And how does that serve the Light, beyond keeping my soul safe from a ritual sacrifice? I still have these and many more questions for Caleb. And, whatever he says about how safe I am in Haven, I'd feel safer if Phoenix was here at my side.

Fabian strolls up to me as I take a sip of juice. 'The oranges were picked this morning from the garden,' he says.

'No wonder it tastes so good,' I reply, smiling and inviting him to join me at the table. 'So, tell me, how long have you been here?'

'In Haven? I guess a year now.'

I peer at him over the rim of my glass. 'And have you been beyond the walls in that time?'

Fabian shakes his head. 'No, far too dangerous. I barely made it here alive in the first place!'

As he pours himself a juice, I notice his hands are trembling. 'What happened?'

He takes a gulp before explaining. 'I was backpacking through Europe when Tanas and his Hunters caught up with me in Paris. They took me down into the city's catacombs to perform their ritual. It's a horrific place – the passageways are lined with the skulls and bones of those unfortunate souls killed during the French Revolution's Reign of Terror. I thought I was going to join them!'

A chill runs down my spine as I recall my own Glimmer of that time: the heavy *thunk* of the guillotine blade, Marie Antoinette's head tumbling into a basket, then myself being dragged up the steps of the scaffold to face the same gruesome fate. I wonder grimly if my former bones are among those in the catacombs. 'How did you escape?' I ask, breathless.

Fabian takes another unsteady sip of juice before continuing. 'I've my Soul Protector, Mateo, to thank for that. He rescued me from that labyrinth of death, then helped me to reach Haven.'

'Is Mateo here too?' I enquire hopefully.

Swallowing hard, Fabian's shimmering eyes well up. 'No, he didn't make it. He sacrificed himself for me.'

I reach out and clasp Fabian's hand. 'I'm so sorry. You must be devastated.'

'Don't be sorry,' replies Fabian, forcing a smile back on his lean face. 'Mateo's soul lives on. I'll see him again in another life – assuming I make it to the next life . . .' His smile slumps into a look of dread. 'Tanas must be getting stronger if he can incarnate himself straight into a living body.'

Nodding gravely, I glance round the courtyard at the other Ascendants, all still grieving Saul and Maddy's loss, and wonder what their stories are. Then I'm struck by a troubling thought. 'With Tanas back, aren't we endangering our souls by being in the same place?'

Fabian shakes his head. 'Caleb says that, together, our Light is brighter and stronger, and that our combined power acts as a form of protective shield against the Incarnates. He's convinced that we're safer in Haven than we would be spread out across the world – and after what I went through, I believe him.'

'Well, let's hope he's right,' I say, not entirely sharing that conviction. Finishing my orange juice, I rise to my feet with purpose. 'Do you know where I'll find Jude?'

Fabian points to the domed building beyond the courtyard. 'Knowing her, she's probably in the Glimmer Dome.'

24

Haven proves to be far larger than I first thought. Leaving the courtyard, I cross a paved plaza and enter a glass atrium into the next building. Despite its high-tech office appearance, the atrium has the Zen-like calm of a temple. The air is cool and carries the soft scent of spiced incense; tall stems of bamboo stand lush and green against its chalk-white walls, and an artificial waterfall flows freely into a pond, its gentle burble echoing through the open space.

There appears to be no one around, so I head down a corridor in what I hope is the direction of the Glimmer Dome. I pass a number of rooms including a lounge, a dining area, a small lecture hall, and a well-equipped gym where a woman of Amazonian proportions is bench-pressing a heavy stack of weights. In an adjacent exercise zone, a martial arts class is in progress: a bald-headed black man with the muscles of an ox is teaching a brutal takedown method to four students – a young dark-haired girl, two men (twins by the look of their matching straw-blond hair, ridged noses and rock-solid jawlines) and an older woman with a jagged scar across her pale right cheek. But Jude isn't among them. In the middle of demonstrating the takedown, the instructor looks at me through the porthole in the door. His stare is intimidating and I quickly move on.

Further along, I come to a dormitory block with windows overlooking a training ground. I pause to watch a small group of people in combat fatigues tackling a fitness assault course – but none of them sport Jude's spiky hair or green beanie. Reaching a junction at the end of the corridor, I wonder which way to turn. Then I spot a young lad with bushy eyebrows and wiry black hair in a nearby room. Dressed in a smart blue polo shirt and chinos, he's sat at a computer desk peering intently through a pair of square-framed glasses at a laptop screen and fiddling with the wires of a slim, mirrored tube. I knock on the door and he glances up from his work.

'Hey, you must be Genna!' he says, greeting me with a gap-toothed smile. 'Jude said she'd rescued a First Ascendant.' Rising from his desk, he lays a hand upon his heart and inclines his head. '*As-salaam 'alaykum*. My name's Tarek.'

'*Wa 'alaykum as-salaam*,' I reply, surprising myself at how natural my Arabic is, before recalling my Saharan Glimmer on the plane as the Berber girl Sura. 'Are you a . . . Soul Protector?' I ask, noting the starlit gleam to his brown eyes.

He gives me a regretful look. 'Not any more. I lost my Ascendant to Tanas during the American Civil War. A stroke of bad luck. I was hit by a mortar during the Battle of Gettysburg and lost a leg, so I was unable to give chase and protect my charge. But, believe me, I tried!'

'I'm sure you did,' I say kindly. 'It seems we've lost many First Ascendants over time . . . along with their Soul Protectors.'

Tarek nods solemnly. 'Too many. Hence I've been a Warrior ever since; although, to be honest –' his gaze drops to his laptop – 'I'm more of a keyboard warrior in this life.'

'I thought we were in a dead zone,' I say, noticing he's online. 'Isn't Caleb hyper-sensitive to computers and such stuff?'

'Yes, but this room's an electronic isolation chamber, a Faraday cage,' Tarek explains, casting his hand around at the fine metal mesh lining the walls and windows. 'The mesh prevents any electromagnetic waves escaping that may adversely affect him. We need to stay connected to the outside world so, even though there's no Wi-Fi, the internet is fibre-wired in and heavily firewalled to prevent hackers.'

I nod at the slim, mirrored capsule on his desk. 'And what's that?'

'Oh, just a little project I'm working on,' he says bashfully, pushing his glasses up his nose. 'A Light grenade.'

I give him a questioning look.

'It's like a standard flash-bang used by SWAT teams,' he explains, picking up the tube, 'except I'm attempting to use energy captured in the Sun Room to power an immense burst of Light. My hope is that the Light stored in this device will stun Hunters, if not temporarily blind them, without affecting Ascendants or Protectors.'

'Sounds neat!' I say. 'Does it work?'

'No idea,' he admits with a sigh. 'I haven't field-tested it yet. So, are you just taking a stroll? Or are you looking for someone?'

'Jude, if she's around,' I reply. 'I was told she might be in the Glimmer Dome.'

Tarek grins. 'She basically lives there!' He shuts down his laptop and pockets the Light grenade. 'Come with me – I'll show you the way.'

As I follow Tarek round the corner and down another corridor, I hear the muffled retort of a gunshot and instinctively tense. 'What was that?' I say, readying myself to run.

'Don't worry,' he replies as more shots go off. 'It's just the firing range.' He points to a door with a red light above it and a sign warning: CAUTION – FIRING IN PROGRESS. Through the range's observation window, I see a girl with copper-red hair emptying a clip into a target, every round hitting its mark.

'As Warriors and Protectors, we train in multiple skills,' Tarek explains. 'Firearms, defensive driving, martial arts – basically anything that might help us now or in a future life. I've been focusing on cyberwarfare and hacking techniques,' he tells me as we continue along the corridor. 'The future's only going to become more and more digital and we need to be at the cutting edge if we're going to stay one step ahead of the Incarnates.'

'So how many Soul Protectors and Warriors are there here?' I ask.

'Within Haven at present, there are nine Protectors and fifteen Warriors,' Tarek replies proudly.

'Is that *all*?' I almost stop in my tracks. Having seen with my own eyes Tanas's ever-growing army of Watchers and Hunters, I wonder how such a small number of us can ever hope to fend off the Incarnates.

'There are some more around the world – at least a dozen that I'm aware of,' says Tarek. He notices my uneasiness. 'Don't look so disheartened, Genna. Granted, our numbers may have dwindled, but we're still a force to be reckoned with,' he reassures me.

I think of Phoenix and his prowess in a fight. If the other Protectors and Warriors possess even half his skills and bravery, then Tarek has good reason to believe we can resist Tanas. Still, it seems a very uneven battle to me.

Heading outside through a back door, my attention is caught by the sight of an aircraft hangar, where a sleek white cockpit is just visible through a gap in the doors. 'Hey, is that a private jet?' I ask, incredulous.

Tarek nods. 'The newest hybrid-electric. Pretty swish, eh? There isn't much that's not at our disposal.'

I stare at Tarek. 'But all this must cost a fortune! Where does the money come from?'

'There's profit in the past,' he explains with a wry smile. 'Caleb has always used his knowledge and insights to invest wisely, in this life and in previous lives. He set up a trust fund for Ascendants. That's how he became a billionaire and was able to build Haven.'

We stop at the base of the domed building that I first spotted from the courtyard. 'Here we are,' Tarek announces, gesturing for me to go in first. 'The Glimmer Dome!'

We enter a short, darkened hallway leading to a pair of heavy wooden doors. Pushing them open, I step inside and gasp with amazement. Whatever I was expecting, it certainly wasn't this.

The immense circular room is a cross between a museum and a martial arts dojo. In the muted light I can make out five levels with wide landings running round a central open space. Housed in the middle is a square wooden platform carpeted with tatami mats. On each of the levels are artefacts from different ages and civilizations, going back millennia – stone tablets from ancient Egypt; wooden spears and bows from the Amazon; a rack of swords comprising straight-bladed rapiers all the way up to curved scimitars; a display of firearms from muskets to sub-machine guns; leatherbound books; African clay pots; antique framed paintings; marble statues; gold and silver jewellery; a long rail of period clothes; a magnificent collection of armour ... It's as if all the rarest, most unusual and most lethal treasures have been plucked from every major museum from around the world and deposited here.

Standing in the centre of the room, alone upon the raised platform, is Jude. Her eyes are closed, her hands clasped round an old oak staff. She's spotlit by shafts of the red, blue and green light that shine through the small stained-glass rose windows in the domed roof, high above our heads.

'What's she doing?' I whisper to Tarek.

'Glimmering,' he replies.

As I shoot him a puzzled look, Jude's eyelids start to flutter, her body trembles and her grip tightens on the oak staff. A moment later her eyes snap open, their starlit gleam bright and dazzling. She twirls the staff in her hand, expertly executing a series of strikes, blocks and thrusts. The staff whistles through the air as she leaps, turns and glides across the mat battling an imaginary enemy. When she spots Tarek and me in the doorway, she stops mid-strike, the staff quivering. Her brow is slick with sweat and she's panting hard.

'All right, Genna?' she calls, leaning casually on her staff. 'Missing me already?'

'That was impressive,' I say. 'How long have you been training for?'

Jude purses her lips. 'As a Shaolin monk? Maybe twenty years,' she replies. 'In this life . . . perhaps two minutes.'

'So that's a Touchstone?' I ask, gesturing at the staff, realizing she's just transferred her skills from a past incarnation.

Jude laughs. '*Everything* in here is a potential Touchstone.'

I gaze around in awe at the vast array of objects on display, at the sheer number of possible past lives that could be tapped into, and the multitude of skills that could be re-acquired.

'Caleb has been collecting artefacts all his life,' Tarek explains. 'These objects are to help us arm and prepare to protect you and the other First Ascendants from Tanas and his Hunters.'

'No wonder that you can become so skilled,' I say. Then it dawns on me that a millennium and more of knowledge is at my very fingertips. I wander over to a display cabinet and peer inside at a collection of knives. Each one is labelled.

There's a gleaming Viking seax ... a rusted Bronze Age dagger ... a German trench knife from the First World War ... a sixteenth-century Italian stiletto blade ... and a beautifully decorated, ivory-handled jambiya from Yemen. With a thrill of anticipation, I open the cabinet and select the jambiya.

'Erm ... that's technically not allowed,' pipes up Tarek as I clasp the handle tightly and –

Nothing happens.

With a frown of disappointment, I carry the weapon up to the platform and stand beside Jude. I draw the blade and hold it above my head in a warrior pose.

Still nothing happens.

In frustration I resheathe the blade and turn to Jude. 'I thought you said this was a Touchstone,' I say accusingly.

'A *potential* Touchstone,' she replies, twirling her staff nonchalantly before returning it to the rack. 'Not everything in the Dome will trigger a Glimmer – and, of those that do, only a handful may contain a relevant skill or fragment of knowledge that could prove useful in our fight against the Incarnates.'

I put the knife back in its display cabinet and with renewed determination set out to find a Touchstone that *will* trigger a Glimmer.

25

'Are you sure this is a good idea?' I hear Tarek whisper to Jude as I climb a spiral staircase to the first landing. 'Shouldn't we stop her?'

'Don't worry,' I tell them as I try on a knight's visored helmet from the fifteenth century. 'I've done this before.'

The iron armour is heavy and claustrophobic. Through the visor I can see Tarek and Jude talking heatedly. Though their conversation is muffled by the helmet, I make out Jude saying, 'One Glimmer isn't going to hurt.' I wonder what she means by that, but, since I'm not experiencing one anyway, I take the helmet off.

They watch me pick up several objects in quick succession, then Jude suggests, 'Why don't you let fate find it for you?'

Much to Tarek's consternation, I continue to browse through the artefacts, passing over an antique pocket watch, a battered bronze shield and a gleaming silver goblet, until I'm drawn to a flat, slender hairpin. '*Fāzān*, brass, Ming dynasty, circa fourteen hundreds,' I read. The pin's metal is dull, its flower design plain and uninspiring, but I feel compelled to pick it up –

The round-faced official gloats through the iron bars at me, his thin drooping moustache framing a triumphant smile. 'So, at last we capture the elusive Lihua!'

I stare back in stony silence, my chin still stinging from where he ripped off my false beard. Unfortunately, my male disguise hadn't been enough to fool the sharp-eyed Pingyao city official. Behind him stand the two muscle-bound guards who'd escorted me from the northern gate to the city prison, their iron-studded clubs hanging menacingly from their leather belts.

'Your thieving days are over,' declares the official with glee. Then he leans closer to the bars and lowers his voice: 'As will be your Light!'

I let out a shocked gasp as his narrow eyes pool into those of a Watcher. I'd hoped my arrest was merely a consequence of my nocturnal crimes and not my essence as a First Ascendant.

'Oh yes, Lihua. I know who you really *are,' he whispers under his breath so the guards don't hear him. 'And I've sent a message to the Forbidden City, letting Him know I've captured you.' His gloating grin broadens. 'How I'll be rewarded!' The official struts away, his guards in tow, leaving me locked in the dank dark cell.*

I curse and kick out in frustration at the jail's solid stone wall. I knew I was pushing my luck stealing from the city's over-zealous tax collector, but there were families in desperate need of money and I was certain I'd covered my tracks. Shen is going to be furious that I took such a risk. My Protector already disapproves enough of my chosen occupation.

Still, it has its advantages . . . whatever the official thinks, I've no intention of being here when Tanas and his Hunters turn up. Removing my black rounded wangjin cap, I tug out the fāzān hidden within my topknot and my long black tresses tumble down over my shoulders, instantly transforming me back into the woman I am. I reach through the bars and begin to work the lock. With practised ease, I insert the thin tip of my hairpin into the keyhole and carefully lift each tumbler pin in turn. There's a satisfying click as the lock opens and the cell door swings wide –

'Any luck?' calls Jude from below.

'Yes!' I reply, studying the brass hairpin in my hand with mild alarm. 'I've just discovered I was a thief during the Ming dynasty in China.'

Jude laughs. 'Hey, I was once a galley slave, so think yourself fortunate!'

'So, is this how you train as Soul Protectors and Warriors?' I ask, making my way back down the spiral staircase. 'Selecting objects at random until you find a useful skill?'

'More or less,' replies Jude. 'It's a quick and effective way to build up our capabilities. There are lifetimes of experience in this Dome. The more you learn, the less likely it is you'll repeat the mistakes of the past.' I notice her jaw tighten, and sense there's more to this statement than she's letting on, although I can guess what sort of 'mistake' she's referring to, considering she's now a Warrior rather than a Protector.

'Glimmering can be very demanding,' warns Tarek seriously, 'and there's a limit to how much one can absorb. Isn't there, Jude?' He gives her a pointed look.

'I know my limits,' Jude replies testily.

'Which is why the Dome is meant *only* for Protectors and Warriors,' continues Tarek, now looking at me.

I frown. 'And why not First Ascendants? Surely we need to enhance our skills too?'

Tarek shifts awkwardly under my questioning gaze. 'It would break with long-established tradition,' he explains.

'Would it? And what tradition is that, exactly?'

'That Soul Protectors *protect* First Ascendants,' booms a voice behind me. 'Just as we've done from the very first battle.'

Startled, I turn to see a powerhouse of a man stride into the Dome, who I instantly recognize as the martial arts instructor I saw earlier. Dressed in combat trousers and a khaki T-shirt stretched so tight across his chest that it looks sprayed on, he gives the impression of having been literally forged in war.

'Meet Goggins,' Jude whispers under her breath. 'Chief Protector.'

Goggins marches on to the platform and comes to a sharp halt in front of me. 'Like the samurai warriors for their emperor, we fight so you Ascendants don't have to.'

I think back to my battle in the building site with Damien and his gang. 'It doesn't always work out like that,' I say with a nervous laugh.

Goggins doesn't laugh. In fact, he looks like a man who never laughs.

Trying not to quake under his glare, I say, 'I don't mean to sound ungrateful, but how's this tradition working out for us? I mean, given that we're now so few in number, wouldn't it be wise if we First Ascendants trained in here too? Wouldn't that help increase our chance of survival?'

'Caleb believes that First Ascendants need to keep their Light as pure and untainted by violence as possible,' says Goggins. 'And I agree.'

'But I'd have thought that keeping the Light burning would be more important,' I point out, 'however fierce the flame becomes.'

The Chief Protector looks me up and down. 'Are you *sure* you're a First Ascendant?' he asks. 'You've got the guts of a Warrior. Who's your Soul Protector?'

'Phoenix,' I reply.

He cocks an eyebrow. 'Ah, you mean Asani.'

This first mention of Phoenix's original name, his *soul name* from the time we first bonded, stirs a deep memory in me of the young warrior with braided hair –

'No, Tishala, swing the axe like this,' instructs Asani, standing behind me and guiding my arm.

The axe is heavy in my grip, the movement unnatural. I'm still recovering from my goring by Tanas's elephant, but Asani is keen for me to learn his tribe's fighting art in case we're ever attacked again.

Taking another swing, I hit the trunk of the baobab tree with all my strength. Chunks of bark go flying.

'Excellent!' praises Asani, grinning broadly. Wielding the axe, I feel a giddy rush within me, a sense of power over my own destiny that I've never experienced before.

'WHAT are you doing?' barks Zuberi, Asani's chief, suddenly emerging from the bushes and striding towards us.

Asani drops to one knee while I try unsuccessfully to hide the axe behind my back. We both know that Ascendants have been forbidden from learning skills of violence in case it taints our souls – because killing would diminish the Light. But my Soul Protector holds a different opinion, believing I should be able to defend my own Light.

'I was teaching Tishala how to chop down a tree,' Asani replies.

Zuberi eyes the massively wide trunk of the baobab. It's obvious he doesn't believe Asani. 'Wouldn't a smaller tree be more suitable for such a lesson?'

Asani looks up at his chief. 'But you taught me, as a warrior, that one must be prepared for every size of opponent,' he says innocently.

Zuberi scowls. 'I also taught you that the bigger they are, the harder they fall.' His stony eyes swivel towards me. 'Be careful, Tishala, that in your eagerness to learn, the tree doesn't fall on top of you –'

The brief Glimmer passes and I discover Goggins smirking at me. 'I should've known!' he's saying. 'Asani's one of my most resourceful and rebellious Protectors.'

26

'LET ME OUT!' My fists ache from pounding on the locked door. The room is small, dark and claustrophobic. I keep hammering.

A large face with heavy jowls and a stubbled chin appears at the small, reinforced window. 'Quieten down,' warns the security guard, his soft tone threatening.

'Lissten to me! You have to let me out!' I implore. My voice is slurred, my tongue like cotton wool from the sedative. 'Genna'sss in trouble!'

The guard remains impassive.

'I'm helping the FBI with her case,' I insist.

'Of course you are, Phoenix,' says the guard, his lip curling in mockery. 'Now quieten down or I'll be forced to take measures.' His face recedes into the gloom.

I kick at the door in frustration. 'WILL. SOMEONE. LET. ME. OUT?'

After a minute of this repeated kicking, the guard's glowering face reappears. 'I warned you!' he growls.

Then, just as I'd hoped, I hear a whirring click as the electronic lock disengages. As soon as the door opens, I shoulder-barge the guard aside and dash out into the corridor. But he grabs me by the scruff of the neck and drags me back inside. It was hoping too much to think I'd get away that easily. I cling to the door frame, at the same time packing the lock with the wet toilet tissue I was holding hidden in my hand. A moment later, a dour-faced, heavyset nurse appears and raps my knuckles hard with her clipboard.

'Tut, tut, Phoenix,' says the nurse in a mock-disappointed tone. 'We've talked about your little escapades before.'

Gritting my teeth against the pain, I continue to wrestle with the guard. In the struggle I rip off his identity badge, tearing his shirt.

'You little punk!' spits the guard. Overpowering me with his sheer weight, he pins me to the bed while the nurse Velcroes restraints to my wrists and ankles, then secures one across my chest. But I've got what I need, so I submit to the restraints.

'Shall I administer more medication, Phoenix?' asks the nurse, her icy tone more a threat than a question.

I shake my head, feigning defeat. My mind is almost as numb as my tongue so I can't risk being doped any more than I already am.

'Good,' says the nurse with a razor-thin smile. 'Then we shall see you in the morning.'

The door swings shut and I'm left alone in the darkness of my cell-like room. When I'm sure both nurse and guard are gone, I open my hand holding the guard's badge, its logo of a green and yellow palm tree faintly visible in the gloom. Teasing open the badge's pin, I put it to work on the clasp. I've been tied up enough times in my many lives to be able to escape these bindings. Quickly freeing myself, I tiptoe over to the door and peek through the window. The corridor appears deserted. Tentatively I pull at the door. To my relief, it eases open, the thick wad of toilet tissue that blocked the lock now dropping to the ground. My plan worked! I'm out of here –

But my blood turns cold as a shadow steps in front of me. I stumble back in shock. No . . . no . . . it can't be –

I wake sweating, heart pounding. *Was that a nightmare? A Glimmer?* Once again it was as if I was experiencing everything from my Soul Protector's perspective. I could feel his anger, his frustration, his determination to escape, and his shock and horror at seeing . . . I try to recall the ominous shadow in the corridor, but the image fades from my mind. It's like grasping at smoke; the harder I try to reach for it, the further it retreats.

I sit up in bed and rub my eyes. The morning sun is pushing through the wooden blinds of my small courtyard apartment. Nefe is curled up asleep at my feet. She stirs, stretches and yawns as I throw back the covers and head for a shower. Even as the sting of cold water sharpens my mind, I can't shake off the feeling that Phoenix is in grave danger. This is the second vision I've had from the perspective of my Soul Protector, and they're occurring in present time. What I've experienced *has* to be more than just a dream. I need to speak with Caleb.

After throwing on my clothes and pinning back my hair, I head out into the courtyard. All appears normal and calm. Viviana is in her rocking chair, sipping an espresso. The hungry cries of the waking Kagiso are soon placated by his mother in their corner apartment. As I cross the lawn, I wave to Song, who is laying the table for her family's breakfast. But the others have yet to emerge.

'Where can I find Caleb?' I ask Viviana.

Pursing her lips thoughtfully, she replies, 'At this time of the morning he'll likely be meditating in the Tea Room.'

Thanking her, I leave the courtyard and make my way back through the Japanese water garden and into Haven's main entrance hall, where I find the normally dozing cats alert and watchful. For a moment I wonder what has spooked them, then I hear raised voices coming from the Tea Room further along the corridor.

'Caleb, we must prepare to fight!'

'No. Our best chance of survival is to stay hidden.'

'We cannot hide forever.' Goggins again – I recognize his booming voice. 'If Jude's report is accurate then it's only a matter of time before one of Tanas's Watchers finds us.'

'I assure you Haven is safe –'

As the argument continues, I creep stealthily up to the door and hover just out of sight in the corridor. Caleb, dressed in a Japanese robe of white silk, is sitting cross-legged before a low wooden table. A small clay teapot, bamboo whisk, a scoop and set of ceramic tea bowls are carefully laid out. Goggins' bowl looks untouched and remains full. He stands before Caleb, arms crossed, muscles tense under his khaki T-shirt, his expression set hard as stone.

'If his Watchers are growing in such numbers,' Goggins finally says, 'Tanas will surely recruit more Hunters from their ranks. We must take the battle to him before his army becomes too strong.'

'It already is too strong,' Caleb replies. 'Don't you recall what happened the last time we confronted Tanas?'

'Of course I do,' grunts Goggins, 'and we both know who's to blame for that! But being always on the defence puts us on the back foot.'

'While taking offensive action exposes the First Ascendants to unnecessary risk.'

'They're always at risk!' snaps Goggins.

'Yes, and it is your job to protect them,' Caleb replies calmly. 'Not abandon them for the sake of a futile battle.'

'No battle is futile if –' Goggins suddenly stops and turns sharply towards the door.

I pull back, pressing myself against the wall and hold my breath. There's a rumbling purr by my feet and I feel a soft, insistent rub against my legs. Nefe is threading her body round me, pleading hunger.

'There you are, Nefe!' I say with forced loudness, picking her up before appearing in the doorway. 'Oh, morning!' I call, as if I'm surprised to see Caleb and Goggins inside the room.

The Chief Protector narrows his eyes in suspicion, but Caleb puts on a cheery smile.

'Good morning, Genna! How did you sleep?'

'Not that well, to be honest,' I reply, putting Nefe down and entering the room. The floor is laid with tatami mats and one of the cream walls is decorated with a hanging scroll of a heron etched in black ink. In an alcove, I spot an arrangement of blossoming yellow flowers. Opposite me, a large circular window looks out on to a secluded Zen garden dotted with rocks. 'I was woken by a Glimmer,' I explain. 'At least I think it was, but it was very strange.'

Caleb gestures for me to join him at the table. 'Do tell us about it,' he says.

I sit down, cross-legged, and he pours me a cup of steaming sencha tea. When I take a sip, I experience a sense of déjà vu, the bitter taste recalling a similar moment I had as the samurai Miyoko some five hundred years ago in a teahouse in Kyoto. I savour another draught and feel strengthened by Miyoko's spirit, which somehow seems to be infused within the tea itself. With my courage fortified, I recount my two visions of Phoenix and his apparent failed attempt to escape. All the while, Goggins remains standing by the window but Caleb listens attentively. When I finish, Caleb drinks a measured sip of sencha, before saying, 'It would appear you have a soul link with Phoenix.'

'A soul link?' I murmur. *No wonder I always feel so close to my Protector, so connected.*

Caleb leans forward and studies me more intently, staring fixedly into my gleaming eyes as if he's searching for something. 'Normally only Soul Seers have the ability to tap into another's experiences . . .' The wrinkles on his lined face deepen, then his eyes widen, as if he's found what he's looking for yet doesn't quite believe it. 'Well, this is most unusual . . .'

'If it is a soul link, then Phoenix is in trouble,' I say urgently. 'We need to help him.'

Caleb's expression hardens and he breaks off from his intense stare. 'That's out of the question,' he says firmly. 'With Tanas back, it's too dangerous for anybody to leave Haven.'

'But he's my Soul Protector,' I protest.

'Genna, you can't risk your Light for anyone, not even your Protector,' states Caleb with finality.

'Then send someone else,' I insist, and I turn to Goggins. 'Phoenix must be worth rescuing, especially when so few Protectors are left.'

Goggins stares through the window at a miniature torii gate in the stone garden, as impassive as the rocks that surround it. Finally he replies, 'But how many Warriors would you have me risk for one Protector? How many Ascendants should I leave unguarded while we go looking for him?' He glances sidelong at me. 'You've provided scant information on his whereabouts; meanwhile, Caleb has informed me that Tanas's Watchers are everywhere.'

'But –'

He holds up a hand, cutting me off. 'I concur with Caleb in this instance. It's simply too great a risk to launch a rescue mission. After the recent deaths of Saul and Maddy, we can't afford any further, unnecessary losses.'

My fingers tighten round my tea bowl, threatening to break its delicate porcelain. 'I thought you were the one who wanted to take the fight to Tanas, to go on the offensive.'

Goggins glares at me. 'A-ha! So you *were* listening in.'

'Yes,' I admit, meeting his fierce gaze. 'I was. And what if it was *me* out there, instead of Phoenix?'

'That's different,' replies Caleb. 'You carry the Light.'

I almost drop my tea, shocked by the Soul Seer's cold-hearted distinction between Ascendant and Protector. 'So, what? We simply abandon him?' I gasp.

'Phoenix can handle himself,' retorts Goggins brusquely. 'Genna, you are to stay here in Haven. Caleb, we'll resume our discussion later.' He nods curtly and leaves the room, bringing our conversation about Phoenix's fate to a sudden close.

With dismay I finally understand that neither of them will be persuaded. On every count my own safety and the protection of the Light outweigh the well-being of my Protector.

'Would you like more tea?' asks Caleb.

'No, thank you,' I reply tersely, getting to my feet. 'I've already had more than I can stomach.'

27

I leave the Tea Room and Caleb to his meditation. However, rather than returning to the courtyard to join my fellow First Ascendants for breakfast, I head out of the main doors, down the sweep of steps and on to the driveway. I'm simply too furious at Caleb and Goggins to be sociable. The fact that they both regard me and my Light as too precious to even bother trying to save Phoenix doesn't sit well with me at all. As far as I'm concerned, if I do have a soul link with my Protector, then he is more a part of me than I ever realized and therefore just as precious. I can't simply leave him to his fate.

I look around. There's no one to stop me leaving by the front gate, but I'll need transport if I'm to get anywhere fast. Jude's Tesla is no longer on the driveway, but its tyre tracks are still clearly visible in the gravel, so I follow them to a set of garages at the rear. Spotting the car among a fleet of electric vehicles, I stride over defiantly and go to open the driver's door. As soon as I touch the handle, though, I receive a painful electric shock. Yelping, I shake the pins and needles from my injured hand.

'*Ana'āsif!*' says a deeply apologetic voice. Startled, I turn sharply to discover Tarek sitting at a workbench, his laptop open in front of him, a cup of coffee to one side. He yawns widely and runs a hand through his wiry hair. He looks as if he's been up all night or risen very early in the morning.

'I haven't turned off the anti-theft device yet,' he explains, adjusting his glasses and refocusing on the computer screen. 'I was just running a systems check –' he taps away at the keyboard – 'to ensure the cars are perfectly tuned. I always like to, especially after they've been out on a run.' A soft ping sounds from the computer and he smiles to himself. 'Ah, all good.'

'Do you have the key to this?' I ask casually, nodding at the Tesla.

'Sure,' says Tarek, waving to a key fob on the bench. Then he glances up abruptly and frowns. 'Why?'

'So I can find Phoenix,' I reply. 'My Soul Protector's in danger and I need to rescue him.'

Tarek blinks behind his glasses in surprise. 'That's different! I've never heard of a First Ascendant saving a Protector before.'

I stare at him, bewildered. 'But why on earth wouldn't I?'

His mouth opens halfway, and for a second he seems at a loss for an answer. 'Well . . .' he finally says, 'it's just that *we're* the ones who usually do the saving, not you.'

'Perhaps it's time for a change, then,' I reply, grabbing the key fob off the bench. 'After all, we're all in this fight together, aren't we?'

With that, I turn to open the car door, only to be confronted by Jude leaning nonchalantly against it, arms crossed. She's sporting a pair of denim dungarees, her spiky blond hair poking out from under a baseball cap worn back to front, her round shades perched on top. 'That's very admirable of you, Genna, but do you even know where Phoenix is?'

'Not exactly . . . I've a *feeling* though,' I reply, putting a hand to my heart. Inside my chest, that strange, indefinable magnetism has returned. It seems the recent soul link has strengthened my connection to Phoenix. 'I know he's in a hospital somewhere.'

'Well, *that* narrows it down,' says Jude sarcastically. 'Which state shall we start in? Texas? Montana?'

I clench my fists in frustration. 'Why's everyone so opposed to me helping my Soul Protector?'

'Because the Light comes first,' replies Jude matter-of-factly.

'Yeah, and without my Soul Protector, my Light is at risk – in this life and every life that follows,' I argue. 'So, by saving Phoenix, we're protecting the Light.'

She stares at me, momentarily stumped, but she's still unwilling to budge from the driver's door.

'Jude, you were the one who said that, as a Soul Warrior, you sometimes get a sense you're needed somewhere – and that sense led you to me,' I remind her. 'Well, now I have a sense that's leading me to Phoenix.'

As she considers this, Tarek interjects. 'Sorry, Genna, no one's allowed to leave Haven without Caleb's or Goggins' permission.'

'I know that,' I reply tetchily. 'But I'm going anyway. Caleb and Goggins may not want to risk anything to save Phoenix, but Phoenix would risk *everything* to save me. So I'm going to do the same for him. You can come with me and protect me . . . or I go alone.'

Jude unfolds her arms and looks me in the eye. 'You're certain you can find him?'

I nod.

'Then I'm driving,' she says, taking the keys from me and opening the door.

Too stunned to argue back, I rush round to the other side of the car. As we clamber in, Tarek hurriedly packs up his laptop. 'Hang on, I'm coming too,' he says.

'Are you sure?' questions Jude, glancing over her shoulder at him. 'Goggins won't like it.'

Tarek gives a shrug, then jumps into the back seat. 'Two Warriors are better than one, especially when it comes to an unauthorized and reckless rescue mission. Besides, I can't be a keyboard warrior all this life, can I?'

Leaving the sanctuary of Haven, we soon cross the state frontier into Arizona and I direct Jude down the highways and byways, following wherever my instinct leads me. But, despite my initial confidence, I quickly realize that Phoenix was right when he said that finding each other was a combination of luck, deduction and fate. My internal compass is present but not precise in its direction and the feeling within me takes us on a number of wrong turns and down several dead ends along the way. With each false destination, Jude becomes increasingly frustrated and Tarek more and more agitated that a Watcher will spot me and alert Tanas's Soul Hunters.

'Have either of you considered this could be a trap?' mutters Tarek, peering anxiously out of the back window at the stream of passing pedestrians.

'How can it be?' I question, my eyes scanning the streets for any road signs to a hospital. It's taken us most of the day, but my internal compass has finally led us to the state capital, Phoenix. The irony that we'll find my Protector in his namesake city is not lost on me, and the unlikely coincidence makes me question whether I really know what I'm doing or am simply guessing.

'If Tanas is involved, a trap is *always* a possibility,' Tarek replies, biting his lower lip as he toys anxiously with his Light grenade.

I frown. 'But there's no way he could know I'm soul-linked to Phoenix,' I say. 'They've no idea we're coming. Besides, maybe it's the FBI we should be worried about. They want to arrest me and send me back to England! We need to turn right at these lights, Jude.'

'What about the shadow you – I mean, Phoenix – saw?' she asks, steering us right, as directed.

I shake my head. 'I don't know who that was. It might just have been a nurse or a security guard or even a hallucination. Phoenix was heavily doped with sedatives. I was amazed he could even function! All I know is he was intent on escaping but somebody stopped him. Someone who put the fear of God in him.'

'Sounds like an Incarnate to me,' says Tarek.

'Well, if it is, then that's another reason why he needs our help,' I argue, directing Jude to go left at the next junction.

We enter the car park of a shopping mall. It's closed down and empty – another dead end. Jude sighs and circles round, looking for the exit. 'Well, if you don't locate Phoenix soon, we're heading back to Haven,' she announces.

'No! We have to keep looking,' I insist as she pulls back out on to the main road. 'Phoenix is close. I can *feel* it.'

'You've been saying that all day,' Jude replies wearily. 'We can't keep driving around on this wild goose chase. I'm with Tarek on this; it could be a trap. Anyhow, you're too exposed out here.'

As we approach another set of traffic lights, I spot a road sign with the logo of a green and yellow palm tree. Suddenly I experience a flashback to my soul link with Phoenix: *a glimpse of a palm tree logo, his hand grabbing the guard's badge, the shirt tearing –*

'Go right here!' I cry to Jude.

She has to yank hard on the steering wheel to make the turn. We follow the road for another half mile or so, my impatience growing, until we come to a large complex of buildings fenced off from the street.

'This is it!' I say excitedly as Jude drives slowly past the entrance to the hospital. I immediately recognize the palm tree logo on the signboard announcing WELCOME TO ARIZONA VALLEY SPRINGS SECURE BEHAVIORAL CENTER.

'You certain about this?' asks Jude, pulling up at the kerb.

'Absolutely,' I reply, the tug in my chest stronger than ever. I can almost feel Phoenix's heartbeat alongside mine, although that might just be my excitement at being so close to my Soul Protector again.

'This isn't a hospital,' Tarek points out. 'It's a mental health facility, and a secure one at that.'

We peer up at the high metal fence encircling the complex. 'Looks more like a prison to me,' says Jude.

Tarek nods to the closed gates. 'And it seems visiting hours are over.'

'We're not here to visit,' I say determinedly. 'We're here to break Phoenix out.'

28

We decide to wait until dusk falls and the staff car park empties before we make our rescue attempt. In the meantime, Tarek has hacked into the centre's computer system. To my relief, he confirms Phoenix is registered there as a patient. Allowing myself the smallest of smiles, I imagine the joy of our imminent reunion: I can almost picture the look of surprise and elation on Phoenix's face when he sees me. Having been forced apart, the thought of being with my Protector again after so many months and such a frantic escape to America is not only uplifting, it also gives me the last bit of courage and determination I need to go through with our daredevil plan.

'According to their files, he's being held in the acute stabilization wing on the east side,' Tarek says, turning his laptop to show us a map of the building. 'He should be in here, room B12. Night security guards patrol the corridors and there's a nurses' station at the end of each wing.'

'What's our best way in?' asks Jude.

'Unless you want to make a scene with the guard on reception, I'd suggest the service door on the south-east side,' says Tarek. 'I've disabled the alarm.'

'OK, let's go,' orders Jude, climbing out and heading round to the boot of the car. Popping it open, she pulls out a small backpack and a loaded Taser from a weapons box. As she slips the gun into her pocket, along with some plastic wrist ties, she sees me looking at her. 'Always pays to be prepared,' she says in response to my unspoken question, and she hands me a black hooded jacket, gloves and a face mask. 'Here, put these on. We don't want to be identified.'

As I put them on, it dawns on me that we'll likely be arrested if we fail tonight. But, since I'm already on the run for the suspected murder of my own parents, I guess being charged with breaking and entering is the least of my worries. Still, my heart pounds a little harder at the prospect of extricating Phoenix from a secure mental health facility.

Tarek looks in the boot for his own jacket, but Jude puts a hand on his shoulder and shakes her head. 'Tarek, you stay here.'

His face falls. 'But –'

'I need you to keep an eye on the security cameras,' she explains, 'and be ready if we need to make a quick getaway.'

He sighs as Jude hands him the keys. 'At least I get to drive the car, I suppose,' he says grudgingly. Pocketing the keys, he delves into the boot and opens a small briefcase containing a comms set. He passes each of us a discreet earpiece. 'So we can stay in touch.'

Jude and I fit the tiny devices into our ears as Tarek takes the comms set and settles himself into the front seat of the car with his laptop. 'I'll follow your progress on the security cams, and temporarily block each feed the security guard can see as you go,' he explains, his voice coming clearly through my earpiece. 'Good luck!'

With a thumbs up, we leave him, cross the road and make our way round to the south-east side of the complex. The night is clear, a crescent moon hanging in the sky, and the air is warm and close. My breathing is loud behind my face mask. We keep to the shadows as we skirt the boundary. The security fence is even higher close up and, for a moment, I wonder how we're ever going to get in. Then I'm struck by a curious thought: *It's no higher than a trapeze*. Impatient to free Phoenix, I scale the fence with the nimble agility of Yelena, swing my legs over and drop down to the other side.

'Nice move!' whispers Jude in the darkness, then she speaks into her earpiece: 'Hey, Tarek, can you open the rear gate?'

A moment later, a small gate in the fence buzzes open and Jude strolls through, a smug grin on her lips.

'Nice move,' I repeat drily, feeling a bit ridiculous. 'If I'd known there was a gate . . .'

Crouching low, we both dash over to the main building, dodging a security guard patrolling the site. We find the service door easily. 'Tarek, buzz this one too, will you?' says Jude quietly into her mic.

'I've tried,' he replies, 'but it must be manually locked.'

We both check the door and see the keyhole below the handle.

'Now what? We don't have a key,' Jude mutters as I notice the sweep of the guard's torchlight in the distance. 'Any other way in?'

'Give me a moment,' says Tarek, and we hear the faint tap of a keyboard.

As we wait for him to respond, I examine the lock. It's a standard pin tumbler. Instinctively, as if I were still Lihua the thief, I tug a couple of hairpins from my hair, bend one into an L-shape and straighten the other into a pick, then I set to work on the lock.

'Whatever you're doing, hurry up!' urges Jude. 'The guard's coming this way.'

Applying tension to the tumbler with the L-shaped wrench, I use the pick to lift each of the lock's pins in turn. I hear a soft click as the first pin disengages and smile to myself at my old-found skill. But I can also hear the approaching footsteps of the security guard. My fingers trembling, I seek out the next seized pin, then the next, and the next . . . A few seconds later, there's another satisfying click and the door pops open.

The beam of the guard's torch spotlights the wall and starts sweeping towards us. 'Who's there?' calls a gruff voice.

A second ahead of the beam, we silently slip into the building and quickly close the service door behind us. My heart in my mouth, I lean against the door and let out a relieved breath. This time I'm the one sporting a smug grin. 'Guess my breaking-and-entering days aren't over!' I whisper, now deeply grateful for my Glimmer as Lihua.

Just then Tarek's voice sounds in our earpieces. 'I've found another option –'

'Don't worry,' interrupts Jude. 'We're already in.'

Looking around, we find ourselves in a gloomy corridor, a whiff of disinfectant tainting the air. There's a heavy, unsettling quiet, broken only by the occasional muted cry or moan of a patient coming from behind the rows of locked doors. I almost leap out of my skin when I spot a ghoulish face in one of the wire-meshed windows – a bone-pale young woman is staring wide-eyed and wordless at us. I put a finger to my lips, willing her to remain silent. She copies my actions and giggles nervously from behind the glass. Her eyes strike me as very dark, although that may just be the lack of light. Much to our relief, she doesn't raise the alarm.

'I've got you on camera,' says Tarek. 'I'll track your movements.'

We creep along, following his directions. The nurses' station is, thankfully, empty. 'The next corridor's all clear too,' Tarek informs us. 'Turn left at the end; Phoenix's room is the fifth door on the right.'

As we make our way along the east wing, a security guard suddenly emerges from a staff toilet. He's still buckling his belt when he looks up. 'Hey! What the –'

But he doesn't get to finish the sentence. Jude draws her Taser and fires. The guard convulses and collapses to the floor in a jibbering heap. Before he can recover, Jude pulls a pair of plastic ties from her pocket and together we secure his wrists behind his back and shackle his ankles. Then Jude takes a handkerchief from the guard's pocket and stuffs it into his mouth.

'Help me drag him back into the toilet,' she says, grunting with the effort to lift him.

As I grip the man's arms, I recognize his heavy jowls and stubbled chin. He's the one who restrained Phoenix. Once inside, I drop him on the tiled floor, a little too heavily, and he groans from behind his gag. We're back out into the corridor in seconds, shutting the door on the guard's pained protests.

'We'd better hurry,' says Jude. 'It won't be long before someone notices he's disappeared.'

My nerves now on a razor's edge, we run to room B12. Phoenix's door is locked.

'Tarek, can you open it?' I ask urgently. But there's no response. 'Tarek? Can you hear me?'

Jude tries too and gets no answer either. Just the hiss of static. 'Dammit. We've lost reception,' she mutters.

I examine the lock but to my dismay Lihua's lockpicking skills will be no help here. The door can only be opened with an electronic key card. 'Jude, what are we going to do?' A touch of desperation enters my voice at this last hurdle.

She clicks her fingers. 'The guard!' she says, and races back to the toilet. Moments later, she returns with his key card.

'Good thinking!' I whisper as she swipes it through the slot. The lock whirrs and the deadbolt slides across. Tentatively I push the door open and enter the cell-like room. In the semi-darkness I can just make out the silhouette of a boy lying across the bed. My heart swells on seeing him. '*Phoenix?*' I hiss, taking off my mask. 'It's Genna!'

As he sits up, the moonlight shimmering faintly through the barred window falls across his pale, lean face. He greets me with a fiendish grin. 'Good to see you again, Genna,' says Damien.

29

My knees almost give way beneath me and I stumble back against the wall. '*You!* But how did you g-get here?'

Damien looks faintly amused. 'British Airways. Business class, in fact.'

'You know that's not what I meant!' I reply furiously. 'What have you done with Phoenix?'

'Nothing . . .' he says, casually inspecting a fingernail. 'At least, not yet.'

Enraged, I clench both fists and launch myself at him. Attacking more with fury than skill, I throw a wild punch. He deftly evades it, jabs me in the stomach, then pins me against the wall. His forearm presses hard across my throat, and I fight for breath. Damien leans in close, his black pooling eyes peering intently into mine. For the briefest of moments I glimpse a faint blue gleam in their depths, like the glint of a coin at the bottom of a well, my Light reflected in his Darkness. Drawn ever deeper, I begin to feel a strange connection, an entwining of souls, like two vines wrapping round each other . . . Then Damien looks away, breaking the spell.

'I admire your spirit, Genna, but we don't have time for this,' he snarls. 'Everyone's waiting for you.'

As I try to make sense of what just occurred between us, he directs my gaze towards the door where three of his Soul Hunters are clustered in the corridor. Thug, his nose bandaged from our last encounter, restrains a squirming Jude in his powerful grip, his hand clamped across her mouth. Spider holds Jude's Taser, the weapon reloaded now and aimed at me. Beside her skulks Knuckleduster, her dark eyes narrowed into a livid glare. Damien pushes me towards the door and into her eager clutches. Her nails dig painfully into my skin as she yanks my arms behind my back and fastens a plastic tie round my wrists.

'I see you've brought company,' Damien says, giving Jude a derisive look up and down. 'A so-called Soul Warrior. Fat lot of good she did guarding you, Genna. No wonder she's a *failed* Protector.'

The muzzled Jude glares back at him with a fierce loathing, her blazing eyes rimmed with tears. She says something in reply, but her words are muffled by Thug's beefy hand.

'I want to see Phoenix!' I demand angrily.

'Why, of course,' Damien replies, the slyest of smiles sliding across his pale lips. 'After all, you've come such a long way.'

He beckons his Hunters to follow and we're manhandled along the corridor to a set of double doors. Swiping a key card through the lock, Damien leads us down a stairwell into the bowels of the building and I begin to wonder how he and his Hunters can roam so freely about the facility. Stopping in front of a heavy wooden door marked MAINTENANCE ONLY, Damien swipes the key card again and we enter the basement. The air is dank and cold and reeks of wet rags and mouse droppings. A pile of mops, buckets and disinfectant has been dumped near the doorway. Overhead, the high ceiling is veined with rusting utility pipes that recede into the gloom. Only a feeble strip light near the entrance is working and that flickers and buzzes incessantly like an electrified mosquito.

What's most haunting about the place, though, is the gathering that's taking place in the far depths of the basement. Dressed in white hospital robes, their heads bowed, a mob of patients form a ghostly semicircle round the far end wall. They each hold a black candle, the flames flickering in the semi-darkness, the hot wax dripping over their fingers and on to the bare concrete floor. In unison they're reciting in a low, unsettling murmur: '*Ra-Ka, Ra-Ka, Ra-Ka . . .*'

As we approach, the chanting stops and they part to allow us through. Their dark pooling eyes follow our procession with a hunger and frenzied intensity that makes my skin crawl. Among them I spot the bone-pale young woman from earlier; she puts a finger to her lips and lets out another tremulous giggle. The full horror of our predicament now hits me – this isn't just a mental health facility. It's Tanas's lair!

Then we reach the centre of their gathering – and my world falls apart.

'*Phoenix!*' I gasp. My Soul Protector is laid out on a hospital gurney, his arms and legs restrained by Velcro straps. Set against the wall a large metal trolley has been transformed into a makeshift altar with an array of surgical instruments carefully arranged round a pair of tall black candles and a crudely carved wooden statue with cat-like eyes and pointed fangs. I've seen this idol before and I shudder at the memory of the gruesome godhead – a grim reconstruction of the ancient deity honoured by the Tletl tribe some five thousand years ago. On the floor beneath Phoenix's gurney there's another chillingly familiar symbol: an upside-down pentagram scrawled in black ink. Within its lines are dark stains of dried blood and for one heartbreaking moment I think we're too late . . .

Then Phoenix stirs. Although heavily sedated he appears to be unharmed. But that's when I grasp whose blood it really is on the floor. For I recognize the criss-cross of pipes on the ceiling from the soul link I shared with Caleb. This is where Saul and Maddy were killed, ritually slaughtered by Tanas himself.

'*Genna?*' groans Phoenix, woozily lifting his head to get a better look. His dull eyes widen in alarm. 'NO! The Hunters – they caught you!'

Damien laughs coldly. 'Not exactly, Phoenix. She came here of her own free will . . . to rescue *you*, would you believe!'

'*Whaaa?*' he slurs.

'You see, she and this so-called Soul Warrior thought they could break you out of here,' Damien explains as he circles the gurney, 'but actually they were walking straight into a trap!'

Phoenix's unfocused gaze wavers from me to Jude. There's a flicker of recognition. 'Jude, you idiot!' he cries, his anger cutting through his haze. 'What were you thinking?'

'Don't blame Jude,' say Damien. 'It's your connection to Genna that drew her here.'

Phoenix falls silent, the weight of the Hunter's words slowly sinking in. His head lolls to one side and he gazes at me. 'You should never have come for me,' he murmurs, his blue eyes welling with grief and guilt.

'But I'm soul-linked to you,' I reply, tears running down my own cheeks. 'I *had* to . . .'

Savouring our distress, Damien claps his hands together and rubs them in satisfaction. 'Well, now that we're all happily reunited, we can begin,' he says. 'Hunters, prepare for our first sacrifice!'

'Shouldn't we wait for –'

Damien cuts Spider off with a scowl. 'Do as I say.'

Ignoring the uncertain looks from the rest of his gang, Damien pulls his hood up over his head, turns to the altar and raises his hands to the godhead in tribute. 'All praise, Ra-Ka!'

The congregation of Incarnate patients resume their incantation, swaying from side to side as if in a trance, their vacant stares horrifying in their chilling emptiness. Knuckleduster pulls me over to the altar and forces me to face Phoenix on the gurney.

'I want you to have the best view,' she hisses in my ear. 'I want you to watch as his very soul is torn from him and obliterated *forever*.'

Feeling both sick and furious, I try to wrench myself free of her grip, but she merely digs her nails in deeper and seizes a handful of my hair, jerking my head back. '*Watch*,' she snarls.

Meanwhile Thug drags Jude to the other end of the gurney, ensuring she can witness the ritual too. 'You'll be next,' he gloats, his voice thick through his bandaged nose. Jude glowers at him like a wild cat, subdued only by the Taser trained on her by Spider.

From the makeshift altar Damien picks up a surgical scalpel, its keen blade glinting in the flickering candlelight. Turning to the gurney, he places its sharpened tip at the base of Phoenix's throat. Sedated and shackled, Phoenix can only lie there and accept his fate.

'No, no – don't,' I beg, a surge of desperation welling up in me. 'Damien, *please* don't.'

With a vengeful glance in my direction, Damien slices straight down Phoenix's chest. I screw my eyes shut, unable to watch. But I hear no pained scream from Phoenix. *Is he too sedated to feel anything?* Tentatively opening my eyes, I let out a sob of relief. Damien has merely cut Phoenix's T-shirt in half to expose his chest.

Damien smirks at me. 'I need a clean strike with the jade knife, you see,' he explains gleefully.

Turning back to the altar, he holds his left hand over a metal bowl into which hot black wax drips from the fanged mouth of the godhead. With a quick flick of the scalpel, he cuts his palm and lets his own blood trickle into the mix.

'*Ruq haq maar farad ur rouhk ta obesesh!*' he murmurs, reciting the archaic hex learned by rote from his master to seal the spell. Then he sets the scalpel aside, picks up the bowl and returns to the immobile Phoenix. Cradling his lolling head, Damien forces him to drink the pungent potion. I grimace, feeling nauseous myself as I recall the scalding bitter taste of the concoction in my own throat, how it enfeebled me and made me vulnerable to Tanas's powers. Phoenix screams and arches his back as the toxic mix worms its way through his veins. He writhes in agony against his restraints, then collapses limp and sweating on to the gurney once more.

'*Rura, rkumaa, raar ard ruhrd . . .*' intones Damien.

As he recites the ancient ritual that will separate Phoenix's soul from his body and send it into oblivion, the congregation begin to extinguish their candles, one by one. As the basement dims into deeper darkness, I start to weep. I know there's no coming back once the ceremony is complete. With my hands bound behind my back and Knuckleduster keeping a tight grip on me, I'm powerless to save my Protector.

The blue gleam of his eyes is fading, turning darker with each passing second.

'Your life with mine, as always,' I cry, trying to catch Phoenix's bleary-eyed, desolate stare.

'*Yess, as alwayssss*,' he slurs with a sad, lop-sided smile. But we both know this will be our final and forever parting.

'How sweet,' Damien mutters scathingly. 'Now we've got our goodbyes out of the way, let's finish this once and for all!'

Picking up the Guatemalan jade knife, the one stolen from Mei's home, he approaches the gurney and raises the blade over Phoenix's bare chest. The chanting of the patients grows louder and more insistent, a thudding heartbeat of '*Ra-Ka! Ra-Ka! Ra-Ka!*'

There are only a few candles left to snuff out before the darkness will be total. The Incarnates start stamping their bare feet on the floor as the ritual reaches its climax and Damien roars, '*Uur ra uhrdar bourkad, RA-KA!*'

All of a sudden the basement door bursts open and a flood of light spills back in.

'STOP RIGHT THERE!'

30

'Put the knife down!' orders Agent Haze, his gun trained on Damien. As he advances, with Agent Lin covering him from behind, the patients step fearfully aside to allow them through.

Reluctantly, Damien lowers the jade knife and places it on the gurney. My sense of relief at seeing the two federal agents is only surpassed by my joy that Phoenix's life has been spared at the very last moment. I shouldn't have been so distrustful of the FBI after all – their intervention has saved not only Phoenix, but Jude's and my life as well.

'Thank goodness you've come!' I say breathlessly. 'They wer–'

'Shut up!' snaps Agent Haze, turning the glare of his mirrored glasses on me.

I recoil instantly, his brusqueness stunning me into silence. Still, I suppose he's got a right to be angry. I did run away the last time we met – and Jude even tasered him – so he's bound to be peeved. All that matters now though is that the two FBI agents arrest Damien and his gang and get us out of here –

But my relief turns to shuddering horror as, around me, the congregation begin prostrating themselves on the floor and bowing to the two agents. Even Damien's gang of Soul Hunters drop to one knee at their approach.

'I trust you weren't attempting the ritual by yourself, Damien!' snarls Agent Haze.

'It's only a Protector,' Damien replies petulantly. 'As a most loyal servant, surely I could be granted that small privilege?'

Agent Haze backhands Damien across the jaw. 'How dare you presume to usurp the Darkness!'

My mind reels and I feel sick with bewilderment. It takes a full thirty seconds for the terrible truth to finally sink in: Agent Haze is an Incarnate! Not only that but, judging by the servile reaction of the congregation, he's their leader.

This must be Tanas!

The ground beneath me seems to drop away. Damien wasn't lying when he said Tanas had incarnated into a new body, as this one is noticeably stronger and more powerful than that of Gabriel, the old balding priest I'd encountered in the deconsecrated church six months ago. Dwarfed by his granite-hard physique, I begin to despair of our chances – our enemy is more formidable than ever!

'I give you my word, I wasn't being presumptuous,' Damien assures him, bowing his head obediently as the blood drips from his split lip. 'I only wish to hasten our cause, to deal swiftly with those who hamper our destruction of the Light.'

'That's still no reason to start the ritual without us!' scolds Tanas. 'For your impatience you must suffer the consequences.'

Damien looks up imploringly, his black eyes blazing not with anger but fear. 'But I've captured a First Ascendant, a Protector *and* a Warrior. Surely that deserves –'

'*Deserves? You* do not decide what you deserve.'

As Tanas rebukes Damien for his insubordination, Knuckleduster remains on bended knee, her head bowed low in an effort to avoid Tanas's wrath. Hoping she doesn't look up, I blindly reach behind me towards the altar. *There!* My fingers brush against the cool steel handle of the scalpel. Secretly I work the blade into position and start cutting at the plastic tie binding my wrists.

I glance over, first at Jude, who's eyeing the Taser in Spider's hand, then at Phoenix, who stares blankly at the ceiling. Stupefied by both the hospital sedative and the ritual potion, he remains insensible to what's going on. It occurs to me that the odds of all three of us escaping the basement alive are slim at best.

Then I feel a ping of plastic and my hands are free. Gripping the scalpel tightly in my sweaty palm, I glance at Jude and surreptitiously show her the blade. She gives the briefest of nods. We both know what must be done to end this.

I steel myself for our desperate do-or-die attack.

On Jude's next nod, I dash forward as she twists herself free of Thug and elbows him hard in the face. Before anyone can stop her, Jude snatches the Taser from Spider's grasp and fires the weapon at Tanas. At the same time, drawing on all my anger and grief, I rush to plunge the scalpel into his dark heart.

But Knuckleduster is quick to react. She seizes me by my hair and yanks me back before I can land the mortal blow. Crashing into the gurney, I wrestle with the powerful Hunter for control of the blade. She twists my wrist, forcing me to let go. Meanwhile Tanas has shaken off the shock of the Taser and is raising his own gun to shoot Jude. But Jude, fending off Spider with a kick, manages to deliver another long burst from the Taser. This time, despite his colossal size and strength, Tanas succumbs to the fifty-thousand-volt shock. Convulsing, he drops his gun, topples forward and lands heavily across Phoenix on the gurney.

I notice Damien doesn't rush to his master's aid. No doubt content to let his Hunters subdue us first, he watches with a detached, almost amused expression as Knuckleduster rotates my arm almost to breaking point. Gritting my teeth against the pain, I try to resist –

'Aarush, the bamboo that bends is stronger than the oak that resists,' counsels my guru as she wraps me in yet another excruciating armlock. Once more her strength defies her age and, however hard I struggle, I'm unable to break out of her hold.

With my face pressed against the dirt floor of the kalari, I splutter my complaint: 'But you've tied me up in knots!'

'So? What do you think all the stretching and jumping exercises are for?' she chides, applying more pressure to the lock. 'Become supple like a reed, flow like water, roll like a wave –'

Heeding my guru's advice from centuries ago, I call on Aarush's Kalari skills and roll out of the armlock, flipping myself over and free of Knuckleduster's grip. Then I strike a marma point at the base of her throat. She chokes and I front-kick her into the surrounding mob of black-eyed patients baying for our blood.

I realize that our best chance of survival is to kill Tanas in order to break his hold over his followers. As I'm searching desperately for the dropped scalpel, which *has* to be here somewhere in the darkness, the stunned Tanas suddenly slides off the gurney on to the floor. The room goes still. The Incarnate leader's black eyes are blank and unblinking . . . fresh blood blossoms on his shirt . . . the green handle of the jade knife protruding from his mortally wounded chest.

Phoenix gives me a groggy smile. One of his restraints is cut through and his hand free. 'Did I get him?' he asks weakly.

I nod, numb with astonishment that my Protector was even able to hold the knife in his drugged state.

The gathering of Watchers and Hunters stand motionless, watching their leader bleed to death before their eyes.

As Tanas's life ebbs away, I feel no remorse, no pleasure, no satisfaction, merely relief that this evil soul will be banished yet again from this lifetime. That some form of justice has been delivered as penance for the murder of my parents. When he splutters his last breath, I turn to Jude with a hopeful expression. Once more we have defeated Tanas –

But Jude isn't celebrating. She's looking round apprehensively at the congregation of patients. It's only then that I notice that none of them is turning back to their former self. Every eye remains as black and fathomless as ever. Damien and his Hunters haven't reverted either.

Stepping forward, Agent Lin tugs the jade knife from Agent Haze's chest. 'That was a bold attempt, Genna. But you got the wrong man – or perhaps I should say . . . *woman*.'

31

I look Agent Lin up and down, taking in her tailored blue suit, her sheen of arrow-straight black hair and her angular jawline and cheekbones. She's the epitome of the high-achieving, law-abiding enforcement officer.

'*You're* Tanas?' I splutter, as she lays the jade knife carefully down upon the altar.

With a scythe-like smile, Agent Lin takes off her glasses to reveal two pools of swirling darkness for eyes. I flinch away in horror.

'You seem surprised,' she says, laughing at my shock. 'Admittedly, in the past I've favoured being male simply for the advantage of strength. But, as poor Agent Haze has just proven, a man makes for a more obvious target. Besides –' Tanas glances down, admiring her own athletic physique – 'I couldn't have wished for a more capable body to incarnate into. Apart from the bullet wound that almost killed her, Agent Alex Lin kept herself in good shape. And being an FBI agent to boot has even greater advantages. I've access to all sorts of people, places and resources I could only have dreamed of as a priest. Turns out that you and your Protector did me a favour by killing me the first time.'

'Then let me do you another favour!' says Jude, snatching up Agent Haze's dropped gun.

But before she can pull the trigger, Damien has seized her arm, pulling the gun off target. A deafening blast echoes round the basement and a bullet ricochets off the wall. I duck as shards of brick go flying in all directions. Jude tries to get in a second shot, but, with military precision, Damien disarms her of the weapon and turns the barrel on her.

'Nice try, Spiky,' he sneers. 'Have you forgotten I trained in Krav Maga martial arts in a former life?'

Faced with getting her head blown off, Jude reluctantly surrenders and submits to the brutal grip of Thug behind her. She winces as he puts her into an excruciating armlock. Knuckleduster grabs me too, ensuring I can't attempt any more surprise attacks either.

Tanas brushes a speck of brick dust from her shoulder. 'You've just redeemed yourself, Damien,' she says, offering him a cold thin smile that appears more threatening than thankful. 'While your hunger for the Darkness is understandable, do *not* overstep the mark again. I need not remind you of the pact you made for your soul.'

'How can I forget?' replies Damien, bowing his head. 'You are my lord and master.'

Tanas narrows her eyes. 'I'm pleased you know your place. Now, since Agent Haze will no longer be joining us, you may take his place at my side.'

Damien glances up sharply, a grin on his lips. 'An honour indeed, O Great One,' he murmurs. Slipping the gun into his waistband, he steps over the agent's corpse and joins Tanas at the altar.

'Haze's death is regrettable, yet a mere inconvenience,' Tanas goes on, waving to two patients to take the body away. 'We can more than make up for his loss by extinguishing Genna's Light. But first, let us finish what you started.'

As Tanas approaches the gurney, I exchange a desperate look with Jude. Reflected in her eyes is the same resignation, the same burden of defeat, but also a flash of anger at me. I don't blame her for resenting me for our failed mission. It's my fault. I was the one who brought her here; I was the one who wouldn't listen to Caleb and Goggins. I realize now – too late, of course – that they were right. The risk I made us take to rescue my Protector has proven too great and costly. Not only will Phoenix's soul be obliterated forever, but Jude, myself and my Light will be destroyed too.

Blinking away tears of shame and regret, I gaze at Phoenix lying helpless on the gurney and curse my deluded overconfidence. I'm no Protector! I should never have pretended I could be. Yet, despite everything, I know that if I was faced with the same choice again, I'd make the same decision. Phoenix is my Soul Protector. He's saved my life over and over. I owed it to him to try and save his.

None of that matters now, though. With Tanas preparing to complete the ritual sacrifice, I know that Phoenix and I have reached the end of our souls' journey together. The thought of being separated forever fills me with dread, almost as much as the terror of what lies ahead for my own soul when it too is torn apart and destroyed by the Darkness.

Leaning over the gurney, Tanas runs a hand through Phoenix's locks of chestnut-brown hair, almost caressing him as a mother might a sick son. 'Ah, Phoenix. You thought you could destroy me once with an obsidian blade,' she says in an ominously soothing tone. 'How wrong you were!'

Seizing a clump of hair, she wrenches Phoenix's head back, causing his eyes to flare in pain. Phoenix's free arm shoots up to throttle Tanas, but Damien quickly pins him down.

'You have blighted me in too many lives,' spits Tanas, her upper lip curling into an ugly snarl. 'But I assure you, Phoenix, this is your very last.'

On her command, the host of Incarnate patients rise to their feet and resume their low, hypnotic chant of '*Ra-Ka! Ra-Ka! Ra-Ka!*'

Letting Phoenix's head drop, Tanas picks up the jade knife, still wet with Agent Haze's blood, and recommences the ritual incantation: '*Rura, rkumaa, raar ard ruhrd . . .*'

With each line uttered, the last vestiges of hope are stripped from my heart. Then from nowhere I suddenly remember Tarek. In all the confusion and conflict, I'd forgotten he was watching our backs. Surely he's witnessed what's happened to us on the centre's security cameras, heard our shouts and cries over the earpiece?

'*Tarek?*' I whisper. But I get no reply. Just static. The basement is no better for signal than the corridor above. Yet even as I try to get in contact, I question what one Warrior can do against a whole host of Incarnates. Even if Tarek did manage to alert Haven, any back-up would be hours away. Still, he may have the resources to –

The basement door opens again and I look up expectantly, praying for a last-minute rescue. Forced to stop mid-incantation, Tanas glares at the new arrivals. But her anger at the untimely interruption soon dissipates as the blond-haired Hunter roughly shoves a sorry-looking Tarek into the room.

'Ah! A latecomer to the party,' smirks Tanas, gloating over yet another capture.

On seeing Tarek bruised and bloodied, all the fight goes out of Jude and she stops resisting Thug's armlock. My own hopes dashed, I sag, defeated, in Knuckleduster's talon-like grip. My mission to save Phoenix is not only a failure; it's a tragic failure for which I blame only myself.

'I'm so sorry, Tarek,' I mumble as he's dragged over beside me. His glasses are cracked and his shirt ripped; his right cheek is swollen and blood oozes from a badly split lip.

'No, don't apologize,' Tarek replies, wincing from his injuries. 'He jumped me in the car. I was so focused on the laptop I didn't see him coming.'

'It's all my fault,' I say, almost too ashamed to look at him. 'I should've listened to you. You were right – this was a trap.'

'Yes, and you fell into it!' Tanas cries with a gleeful laugh. She licks her lips, her tongue flicking out like a serpent's. 'Two Warriors, a Protector *and* an Ascendant. This promises to be a long, dark night of sacrifice.'

Tarek glances up at her, a crafty look in his eyes. 'Are you so sure about that?'

Tanas frowns, then her dark eyes widen in alarm as Tarek pulls a slim metal tube from his pocket. I recognize the device straight away. The Light grenade clatters to the floor and rolls until it stops at Tanas's feet. She dives for cover behind the altar, as does Damien; the patients all cower in fright. The Hunters grab Tarek, Jude and me and use us as impromptu shields.

Several tense seconds pass . . . and nothing happens.

Tarek curses. 'Damn! It didn't work –'

Damien starts laughing and gets back to his feet. Tanas emerges too, her face like thunder. 'No one makes me look like a foo–'

There's a sudden deafening blast as the Light grenade explodes, blazing as brightly as the sun. The Incarnates howl in terror and agony as the Light burns into their retinas. Flooded with a dazzling radiance, the basement turns from night to day in an instant. Yet the intense glare doesn't seem to hurt my own eyes – in fact, I see more clearly than ever.

'Quick!' urges Tarek. 'The grenade won't last long.'

As the Incarnates reel from the extended flash, I rush over to the gurney and rip off the restraints. Phoenix, revived by the burst of concentrated Light, sits up.

'Can you walk?' I ask, slinging his arm over my shoulder.

'I'll crawl if I have to,' he replies as the grenade begins to fizzle out like a spent firework.

'Get him out of here! I'll get Tanas!' orders Jude. On the floor, glinting bright, is the scalpel. She snatches it up.

'Save your master!' shouts Damien to the cowering throng, his eyes screwed shut against the Light.

Still dazzled, the Hunters lash out wildly, striking anything in range. The Incarnate patients surge forward like blind rats, swarming over us and shielding Tanas with their bodies.

Knocked over in the chaos, Jude loses her grip of the scalpel and has to abandon her attempt to assassinate Tanas. She joins me and Tarek as we struggle to keep Phoenix on his feet. Together we battle our way through the remaining horde of patients, their fingers clawing at us and their teeth snapping. Pushing ahead, Jude punches and kicks a path through them to the door.

'GO!' orders Jude as we enter the stairwell. 'I'll hold them off.'

The sightless Incarnates lurch after us. Jude grabs a janitor's mop and breaks off the end. Spinning it like a staff, she beats back the tide of patients. Her skills as a Shaolin monk prove their worth as she jabs, thrusts and strikes at each advancing Incarnate in turn.

Bearing Phoenix's weight between us, Tarek and I help him up the stairs. But on reaching the ground-floor landing, we're confronted by a locked fire door. 'How are we going to get out?' Tarek cries, pulling futilely on the handle.

'Keep going up,' I say.

'But that'll only lead to the roof, and we'll be trap–'

We flinch as a gunshot echoes up the stairwell, followed by a pained scream.

'*Jude?*' I call out fearfully.

From below, the sound of pounding footsteps grows louder. Jude appears, blood seeping from a flesh wound to her arm. 'Damien's taking pot-shots!' she yells. 'No time to hang around.'

Swiping the guard's key card through the lock, she kicks open the door and we dash along the corridor towards the main reception. Behind us Damien and his Hunters stumble half-blind and disorientated from the stairwell. As Jude swipes the key card for the exit, Damien takes another wild shot. The bullet hits the door frame and splinters fly everywhere. Even in his doped state, Phoenix instinctively tries to shield me.

'I'm the one saving you this time, remember?' I say as I hustle him through the doorway after the others.

Ignoring the startled security guard at the reception desk, we stagger out into the car park and over to the main gates. Jude inserts the key card again and the gates start to slowly open. Too slowly. Before we've been able to squeeze through, Damien and his Hunters have burst from the building like a pack of attack dogs. They chase after us as we push ourselves through the gap and sprint over to the waiting Tesla. The doors open automatically and Jude jumps into the driving seat while I help Phoenix into the back. As Tarek clambers into the passenger seat next to Jude, Damien charges out through the gates, gun in hand. He fires off several rounds, the thud of bullets peppering the car's bodywork. Jude floors the accelerator. The rear window shatters, but we're already speeding away into the night.

32

We're driving along the empty desert highway under a canopy of stars when Phoenix leans his head out of the window and sticks two fingers down his throat. He vomits up black bile, emptying his stomach of the ritual potion.

I gently put a hand on his back as he heaves again. 'Are you OK?' I ask softly.

'Better for getting rid of that poison,' he sighs, pulling his head back in. 'But how about you?'

'I'm fine,' I reply, handing him some water.

He drains the bottle. The combination of the Light grenade and the purging of the potion seems to have re-energized him a little, and the starlit gleam to his eyes is slowly returning. Relieved, I smile warmly at my Protector. 'I'm so glad we found you in time,' I say, and go to embrace him.

But Phoenix holds me at arm's length. 'What the hell do you think you were doing, Genna?' he scolds, looking me in the eyes as if I'm crazy.

'I-I-I came to save you,' I stammer, confounded by his reaction.

'That was *stupid*!' he says, shaking me in barely restrained fury. 'You could've been killed!'

I flinch, his harsh words stinging me to my very core. He begins checking my body over for injuries.

'Hey! I said I'm fine!' I snap, brushing him off. I glare at him. 'I can't believe I've come all this way, risked my life for you, only to be told off like a little child!'

'That's because you're acting like a child,' he replies testily. 'I would've thought after what we've already been through in this life, you'd have more sense than to walk straight into a trap!' Before I can respond, Phoenix turns his temper on Jude in the front seat. 'And what were *you* thinking, risking Genna's soul like that?'

'She was determined to come find you,' Jude replies stiffly, as Tarek tries to bandage the wound on her arm while she drives. 'I had no choice –'

'Pah, course you did!' Phoenix retorts scornfully. 'You know the rules!'

Jude glares at him in the rear-view mirror. 'Yeah? Who are *you* to talk about the rules?'

'OK, but at least my Ascendant's still alive!' he shoots back.

Jude goes tight-lipped and stares fixedly on the road ahead, her eyes glassy. Phoenix appears to regret this last comment and for several long minutes no one speaks. There's just the sound of the desert wind whistling through the shattered rear windscreen.

'What were we supposed to do?' says Tarek eventually, tying off Jude's bandage and looking sourly over his shoulder at Phoenix. 'Let Genna go off alone? Imprison her in Haven?'

'Yes! If that's what it would've taken,' says Phoenix through clenched teeth. 'I can't believe Caleb and Goggins allowed you all to leave.'

'They didn't,' I say brusquely, stunned by my Protector's reaction. 'And Jude and Tarek aren't to blame either. I was determined to rescue you, no matter what.'

Phoenix looks at me despairingly. 'Genna, you *can't* risk your soul like that! Didn't Caleb explain? Don't you understand how important you are?'

'He did. But *you're* important to me,' I reply, my voice quivering with emotion. 'You're my Soul Protector. I need you –'

'If you were in Haven, there was no need for me. You were safe,' interrupts Phoenix. 'Your Light is *all* that matters.'

My heart hardens at his words and I have to blink back the tears that threaten to come. 'So, you only care about the Light . . . not me.'

Sighing heavily, Phoenix runs his hands through his hair and wearily shakes his head. 'You misunderstand, Genna,' he says. He glances up, his expression softening. 'Your soul and the Light are one and the same. *You* are the Light. That's why you must be protected above all else.'

'But what about you?' I ask. 'As my Soul Protector, aren't you equally important?'

'No,' says Phoenix bluntly. 'I vowed to protect your soul. That is my duty and, if necessary, my sacrifice.'

'Well, I think differently,' I reply, crossing my arms and daring him to challenge me. '*Your life with mine, as always.* Isn't that what we say? So a little appreciation might be nice. Because if Tanas had sacrificed you, our souls would never reunite again. Not in this life, nor in any of our future lives. I'd be alone. My soul unprotected. And what would become of my precious Light then?'

'A Warrior would step in,' replies Phoenix. 'Jude, in fact. She's guarded you before, and admirably too.' His gaze flicks to Jude in the front seat, but she stubbornly refuses to make eye contact. Phoenix turns back to me. 'Genna, you need to understand that Tanas had no intention of sacrificing me. At least not until she'd captured you. I was the bait and you took it.'

'And I'd take it every time,' I say defiantly.

Phoenix shakes his head. 'You can't let Tanas – or, for that matter, Damien – manipulate you like that! Now they know they can get to you through me. That's a weakness. One that we can't afford to have.'

'And I can't afford to lose you,' I say with finality. I turn away from him and stare out of the window, determined not to show my Protector how much he truly means to me. The desert scrub whips past and a faded road sign for Route 95 is briefly illuminated in the car's bright headlights before disappearing back into the darkness.

After a moment's silence, Phoenix tenderly and tentatively takes my hand. 'Genna, I'm sorry,' he says, the anger in his voice gone. 'I do understand your reasons; they're the same reasons you are so important to me. And why I'm so upset that you put yourself at such risk. I can't afford to lose you either.'

Despite my determination to resist, I feel my heart thaw at his words. Still, I stare out of the window, observing his reflection in the glass and the look of devotion on his face.

'I *am* truly grateful – to you, and to Jude and Tarek – for rescuing me,' he goes on. 'But don't you remember what happened the last time? How dangerous it is to put me before your own survival?'

I mutely shake my head.

'Surely you recall the Glimmer when we were Cheyenne?' he prompts, squeezing my hand. 'When we were riding across the Great Plains and one of Tanas's Hunters shot me off my horse?'

My memory of that life stirs as I watch the arid rust-coloured sand of the Mojave Desert flit by, the mountains in the far distance rearing up like shadows of sleeping giants against the horizon –

The horses' hooves thud in the dry red earth, pounding ever closer as I pull Hiamovi to his feet. The bullet wound in his side gushes like a stream and my own horse whinnies in agony from where she was shot in the flank.

'I said . . . ride on, Waynoka,' groans Hiamovi, gritting his teeth against the pain.

'I know,' I mutter as I stagger under his weight and make for the cover of the hills. 'But I vowed to be bound to you in life and death.'

'But not . . . in the death . . . Tanas promises,' grunts Hiamovi, limping alongside me.

As we stumble across the plain, the white-hatted US marshal and his posse ride up and encircle us. Then one of the black-eyed bounty hunters lassoes Hiamovi and me, tightening the rope round our chests and yanking us off our feet. Whooping and hollering, the bounty hunters drag us behind their steeds, the rough ground raking our bare skin raw. After several hundred brutal yards, we come to a stop beneath a crooked tree.

'Yes, sir – time for a lynching!' says the dark-eyed US marshal, spitting a wad of tobacco on to the ground. 'Let's see these worms squirm before we snuff out their Light!'

Securing a lasso round each of our necks and throwing the ends over a thick branch, they haul us into the air. The marshal takes out a small black leather-bound book from his pocket and begins to mutter a strange incantation. Legs kicking frantically, I fight for breath as my throat is crushed by the coarse rope. Hiamovi pulls weakly at his own noose, rivulets of blood dripping from his lacerated skin into the rust-coloured dirt –

I gasp for air, my hand instinctively going to my throat. I can still feel the pressure on my windpipe. Turning to Phoenix, I ask, 'If Tanas and his Hunters had us at their mercy then, why are we here now?'

'Our tribe came to our rescue,' explains Phoenix. 'But only in the nick of time. Otherwise we'd have both been ritually sacrificed that day. That's why you *can't* put me before you. If we hadn't been bound to one another, you might have obeyed me and ridden on when I was shot.'

I shake my head. 'Whether we were together or not, I'd still have rescued you.'

'And that's the chink in our armour,' insists Phoenix. 'That's the vulnerability Tanas will always exploit. Just as he's done again in this life.'

I swallow hard, the tightness in my throat fading. 'But if I hadn't turned back, you wouldn't be here today . . . and nor would I.'

Phoenix softens at my words. 'Then I guess we need each other,' he says, at last opening up his arms to me. 'Just promise not to take such a risk for me again.'

'I can't promise that,' I reply, sinking into his embrace. 'But I do promise to come better armed next time!'

Phoenix laughs and shakes his head at my continued stubbornness.

'Sorry, I don't mean to break up the happy reunion,' says Jude tetchily, 'but we've got a problem.'

'What?' asks Phoenix, his body instantly tense and alert.

A high-pitched bleeping sound is coming from the dashboard and Jude nods to a red warning light flashing on the car's display. Seconds later the screen blanks out, the alarm cuts off and the vehicle's headlamps fail entirely.

We drift in silence through the darkness.

'Dead battery!' mutters Jude. Wrestling with the steering wheel, she brings the car to an unsteady stop at the verge.

Tarek flips open his laptop and tries to reboot the car's computer system, but with no success. 'A bullet must have damaged one of the fuel cells,' he suggests.

'So what now?' I ask, glancing anxiously out of the shattered rear window at the dark and desolate road behind us.

'We walk,' says Phoenix. 'We may have escaped this far, but Tanas will be on our trail. And she'll use every resource at her disposal. We need to get to Haven . . . before she gets to us.'

33

After the air-conditioned interior of the car, the desert air feels warm and still. The night sky is an ocean of stars, the moon a silver disc. We gather what few supplies we have: Jude's small backpack, an emergency medical kit, a couple of torches, and a single bottle of water. Noticing the blood already seeping through the hastily wrapped bandage round Jude's arm, I insist on redressing her wound, my past life skills as a wartime nurse once more proving their worth as I apply pressure and stop the bleeding.

Impressed, Tarek takes note of my technique. 'I wish you'd been around when my leg got blown off in the Civil War!' he jokes.

As soon as I've finished tying off Jude's bandage, we're ready to start walking. Straight away, Phoenix strides off into the desert.

'It'll be easier if we follow the road,' Jude points out. She nods along the highway, wincing slightly as she shoulders her backpack.

'But more risky,' Phoenix argues, stopping and glancing back over his shoulder. 'One of Tanas's Watchers could easily pick us up. We should cut across the desert.'

'That'll take more time,' counters Jude. 'Time we can ill afford. Besides, we could get lost.'

'I grew up in Arizona,' Phoenix reminds her in an irritated tone. 'I know where we are and I know which direction to head in for Haven.'

Jude sighs heavily. 'Then you'll obviously know we're not equipped for crossing a desert.'

'This isn't the Sahara!' snorts Phoenix.

'Nor is it a beach with a bar open twenty-four seven!' shoots back Jude. 'We've only got *one* bottle of water between us, in case you've forgotten. We could die of dehydration out here!'

As they continue to bicker, Tarek rolls his eyes at me, as if Jude and Phoenix's disagreements are a familiar occurrence.

'Listen,' I interrupt. 'The longer you two argue, the more likely Tanas will catch us up.' I peer uneasily into the darkness for approaching cars. 'Tarek, what do *you* think we should do?'

Tarek shifts awkwardly on the balls of his feet and adjusts his broken glasses. 'Erm . . . you both make a fair point. For speed, I'd favour the road –' Jude smirks triumphantly at Phoenix – 'but with nowhere to hide we'd be sitting ducks.' Now it's Phoenix's turn to assume a self-satisfied look.

'Then we take the desert route,' I say, making a decision for everyone, my trust in Phoenix's judgement overruling Jude's common sense.

'Fine,' says Jude curtly, 'but don't blame me if this doesn't work out.'

Abandoning the car by the side of the road, we set off into the night, our feet crunching on the bone-dry earth.

Phoenix is just ahead of me, leading the way through the arid scrub of thorny bushes and spiky cacti, with Tarek and a disgruntled Jude trailing behind.

'So what's with you and Jude?' I ask Phoenix quietly as we hike under the star-studded sky. 'You seem to have a history.'

Phoenix snorts a hollow laugh. 'Yeah, a *long* history.'

He walks on for several paces in silence, his face turned away from me, fixed on the path ahead. 'I assume you were both in the same warrior tribe, the Hakala?' I prompt. 'The one that originally saved me and my fellow First Ascendants?'

Phoenix pauses and I draw level with him. He raises an eyebrow. 'You remember that far back?'

I nod. 'Caleb showed me. During a Glare in the Sun Room.'

His brow furrows as if a deep memory has just resurfaced. 'That was a dark night. Never seen a storm like it. But every Hakalan warrior felt a calling. A sense that if we did not intervene in your battle, the sun would never rise again.' His blue eyes turn to me, gleaming as bright as the stars overhead. 'None of us realized that we were saving the Light. It was only afterwards, when each of our souls connected to yours, that we fully comprehended the magnitude of our commitment. That we would be forever bound to one another, souls entwined.'

My hand finds his in the darkness. 'Well, I'm glad it was you, *Asani*, who saved me that night.'

Phoenix blinks in surprise at my use of his soul name, then he smiles, the same knowing, worldly-wise grin he's worn through the centuries. And for the briefest of moments his face appears to morph into that of the braided warrior:

broad-cheeked, strong-jawed and smooth-skinned, as if his features were hewn from the heart of an ebony tree.

'It was fate that I became your Soul Protector, Tishala,' he says, using my soul name and squeezing my hand in return. 'And fate that has brought us together again. Look!' He points to something far overhead –

'You see that star, Tishala,' whispers Asani as we sit close together on the brow of the hill, a warm breeze wrapping itself round us like a blanket and the soft chirp of crickets lulling us into each other's arms.

I gaze up at the night sky that glitters like an ocean over the Rift Valley. 'Which star?' I ask, breathless.

'That bright one to the north.' He draws me closer and points. 'Wherever you are, in whatever incarnation, look to that star and know that I am with you. Your life with mine, as always –'

'Our star!' I gasp. I feel my pulse quicken and our connection deepen. The constant star in the heavens linking that very first life as Tishala and Asani to this one as Genna and Phoenix. While our souls may have journeyed far through time, I realize we are still where we always were. Together.

I look into Phoenix's face, his weary yet determined features softened by the moonlight. 'Your life with mine . . .'

'As always,' he replies, completing the phrase and affirming our eternal bond.

For a while, we walk on in silence, at peace with each other, the steady scrunching of our footsteps and Jude and Tarek's whispered conversation the only sounds. Then Phoenix says, 'I heard about your parents. I'm truly sorry.'

The stars in the sky suddenly blur and I have to blink away tears. The unanticipated reminder of my loss threatens to burst the dam in my heart. 'Thank you . . .' I reply, my throat tightening and my voice faltering, 'I-I-I miss them s-so much.'

He gently clasps my shoulder as I heave a sob. 'Don't despair,' he says softly. 'You'll be reunited one day, of that I'm sure.'

I wipe away my tears with the back of my hand. 'You think I really will? But they weren't First Ascendants.'

'No, and that might be their saving. The Hunters who killed them wouldn't have bothered with ritual sacrifice,' he explains. 'So their souls wouldn't be prevented from reincarnating. Granted, they may not be your parents in another life, or even look the same, but you'll recognize them nonetheless. And they'll show you kindness, even though they won't remember you as their daughter.'

The weight of grief in my heart lightens at his words. 'Thank you. That makes things a little easier to bear,' I reply with a bittersweet smile. While the loss of my parents still leaves an aching emptiness within me, it's comforting to know that I may meet them again in a future life.

As we crest a rise, Phoenix suddenly bears left.

'Do you really know where you're going?' I ask. To me, the desert seems the same barren wasteland in all directions.

'More or less,' he replies, glancing up at the sky. 'Haven is west of here. So we follow Mintaka,' he says, pointing to the furthest star on the right in Orion's belt. Phoenix's confidence at navigating the desert reminds me of Amastan and the time he taught me how to find my way across the Sahara. Looking up, I begin to get my bearings. I can identify the planet Venus, and there's Sirius – the brightest star in the sky. And now I can pick out the constellation of Cassiopeia, reliably pointing the way to Polaris in the north. I recall too the importance of smell in the desert, especially of distant camp fires, and how moonlight is better than torchlight for finding one's way in the hours of darkness.

We keep walking through the night, Phoenix determined to put as much distance between us and the broken-down car as possible before daylight breaks and we lose the cover of that darkness. But gradually the horizon brightens and the dawn sun chases the stars away. With no shade or shelter, the desert quickly heats up and our exertions soon leave us sweaty, thirsty and tired. We share the bottle of water but between the four of us it doesn't quench our thirst for long.

'See? I told you we should've gone by road,' Jude mutters irritably as Tarek drains the last few drops. 'At least we could've bought some supplies at the first town we came to.'

'We'll reach Haven before we die of thirst,' replies Phoenix calmly.

Wiping her brow of sweat, Jude scowls. 'According to my estimates, we've still got at least a day's trek ahead of us.'

'So we'll find water on the way,' says Phoenix.

'You kidding? *Where?*' questions Jude, waving her hand around. Surrounding us is nothing but sand, scrub and arid hills. A heat haze shimmers in the distance and I'm painfully reminded of my time as Sura in the Saharan desert. Her agonizing thirst in the salt mines of Taghaza isn't an experience I'd be keen to repeat. My throat feels sore just at the thought of it.

'Don't fret. I was once a Tuareg,' reminds Phoenix. 'I know where to source water in a desert. In the meantime, put this in your mouth,' he suggests, picking up a smooth, rounded pebble from the ground.

Jude peers sceptically at it. 'That won't stop dehydration,' she says dismissively.

'No,' replies Phoenix, 'but it'll shut you up, so you won't lose any more moisture from your blabbering –'

'Hush! Do you hear that?' says Tarek, interrupting their escalating argument.

'What?' asks Phoenix, turning to him.

'A buzzing. Like a mosquito . . .'

Frowning, Phoenix listens hard. As do I and the others. The desert is eerily quiet, just the occasional chirp of an insect. I begin to think Tarek's imagined the noise. But then I become aware of a distant whirring, which grows steadily louder. Squinting against the sun, we peer into the bright blue sky, searching for the source of the buzzing.

'Drone!' cries Tarek, pointing to a small black dot skimming high above the desert.

'You think it's Tanas?' I say, feeling dangerously exposed on such open ground.

'Probably,' replies Jude. 'A drone would be the quickest way to hunt us down.'

'Come on!' says Phoenix, breaking into a run. 'We need to find cover.'

We dash across the rough and stony terrain, our feet churning up dust. The buzzing seems to chase us.

'Over there!' says Phoenix, pointing to a crevice in a small rocky outcrop.

Dropping to our hands and knees, we scramble into the narrow gap. Panting hard, I lie still and listen for the approaching drone. My heart thumps hard in my chest, my breathing becomes ragged. The buzzing of the drone grows louder, drawing ever closer . . . I exchange an anxious look with Phoenix. For several impossibly long seconds the drone hovers above our hiding place. Then we hear it move off and disappear into the distance, the desert falling mercifully quiet once more.

'Do you think it spotted us?' I whisper.

'No way of knowing,' says Tarek, cautiously peeking up at the now-empty sky. 'I didn't like the way it hovered over us. A high-res camera could easily pick up our tracks . . .'

'We need to keep moving while we can,' says Phoenix.

One by one the others clamber out of the refuge, back into the blazing sun. As I follow them, the last to crawl from the gap, my foot disturbs a rock behind me and I hear a harsh rattling noise. I look back over my shoulder, peering into the crevice, and stop dead still. A sandy-coloured, diamond-backed rattlesnake unfurls itself from behind the dislodged rock. Its beaded tail quivers threateningly and its forked tongue flicks in and out, tasting the dry air.

A deep-rooted fear from my distant past paralyses me and I have a flashback to the garden in Egypt and the cobra rising from the wicker basket, recalling how it tried to sink its fangs into me. That time, Nefe had warned me and Raneb deprived it of its head.

But this time I'm not so lucky. Before I can break its mesmerizing spell and scramble away, the rattlesnake strikes.

34

The searing pain is instant, venom burning through my veins like wildfire. As the rattlesnake rears up to strike again, Phoenix drags me clear, all the while Jude and Tarek are shouting and hurling rocks at the scaly serpent. Frightened, it slithers into the darkest recesses of the crevice and disappears.

I lie panting and in pain on the hot stony ground.

Phoenix examines me hastily. 'Did it bite you?'

Nodding, I pull up my trouser leg. Two small puncture wounds mark my calf, blood seeping from the holes. The skin is already turning red and swollen.

Phoenix turns to Jude and Tarek, who stand over me, their faces taut with alarm. 'Did either of you get a good look at the snake?'

'Yeah,' says Tarek, taking the medical kit from Jude's rucksack. 'Sandy-yellow and brown, with diamonds down its back.'

Phoenix swears under his breath. 'A Mojave rattlesnake.'

'Is that bad?' I ask as the sharp stinging in my leg creeps upwards.

Jude rolls her eyes to the heavens. 'Kind of. It's only one of the world's most venomous snakes!' she mutters.

'*What?*' I cry, my heart racing.

'Thanks, Jude,' mutters Phoenix sarcastically. 'That's a *great* help. Go ahead – panic the patient, why don't you?' He rests a hand on my shoulder and looks me in the eyes. 'Genna, you need to stay calm. Or the poison will spread faster through your system.'

I nod and try to slow my breathing. But the pain is intensifying with each passing second.

Kneeling down beside me, Tarek examines the wound. 'The fangs went deep,' he observes.

'What have you got in that med kit?' asks Phoenix.

'All the usual stuff,' he replies, sifting through the bag. 'Antiseptic wipes, plasters, saline solution, bandages –'

'Wrap those round her leg now,' Phoenix instructs.

'You shouldn't use a tourniquet on a snake bite,' says Jude firmly.

'I know. I learned that the hard way in the Amazon jungle in a previous life,' Phoenix replies, holding my leg straight. 'But we need to apply pressure to restrict the venom's flow if we can.'

I grit my teeth as Tarek wraps the bandage tightly round my calf and thigh and ties it off. 'Without anti-venom, there isn't any more I can do,' he explains with an apologetic smile.

'Then we need to get Genna to a hospital, as quickly as possible,' says Phoenix.

'No problem,' says Jude, pointing into the empty desert. 'There's one just round the corner.'

'Your sarcasm isn't helping,' snaps Phoenix, glaring at her. 'But you *can* help me carry Genna. We'll make for the nearest road and flag down a car.'

Tarek joins the other two and they hoist me into the air. As I'm borne along under the unforgiving steel-blue sky, my head begins to throb and sweat beads across my brow. But it isn't from the desert heat. Rather, I feel as if I'm burning up from inside.

'*Thirsty*,' I gasp, but there's nothing they can do. We've no water.

The three of them stagger on. But the combination of the heat from the sun, our lack of water and my dead weight soon wear out my bearers. Exhausted, they lay me on the ground. My heart is now pounding and my breath is coming in short rasps. I try to sit up and feel immediately dizzy and sick. My skin is becoming strangely numb. I'm aware enough to realize that, despite the compression bandage, the venom is coursing through my veins and attacking my nervous system. I collapse back into the sand.

Tarek puts a hand to my forehead and checks my pulse. 'She's feverish,' he confirms, 'and her heartbeat's rapid.'

'We've got – to keep going,' insists Phoenix, panting hard.

'No!' Jude overrules him. 'We're only making things worse for Genna by moving her.'

'Then one of us has to run ahead and find help,' says Phoenix.

'I'll go,' volunteers Tarek without hesitation, already standing up and turning away. He runs off into the distance, heading west.

As soon as he's out of earshot, Jude rounds on Phoenix. '*This is all your fault, Phoenix!*' she snaps, stabbing a finger at him.

'How's it *my* fault?' he shoots back as I lie writhing in agony on the parched earth. 'You were the one who let Genna leave Haven in the first place!'

'Well, if we'd gone by the road, we wouldn't be in this situation!'

'Snakes are everywhere in this desert – it's just bad luck!'

As they continue arguing, my vision begins to blur and the figures of Phoenix and Jude warp before my eyes –

'More like a stupid decision,' counters Jude. 'How come when I lost my First Ascendant everyone blamed *me*, but for you it's just plain bad luck?'

'You lost your Ascendant to Tanas –' their raised voices become distant and muffled in my ears – 'I'm *not* losing Genna . . . not now, not ever.'

Their words swirl in my head – 'Phoenix . . . she's dying . . . a *snake bite* . . . both know how poisonous . . . for her soul . . . for the Light . . . as if Tanas's own blood is in her veins . . .'

My thoughts become confused, my mind disorientated, and I no longer want to try to make sense of what they're saying. The sky above me darkens, the ground ripples, and out of the heat haze an ominous silhouette appears. Small at first, it grows steadily larger. I know I should warn the others, who are still arguing, but my face has gone numb, my tongue loose and heavy, and I can no longer speak. The black shadow relentlessly draws nearer until it looms over me and blocks out the sun entirely . . .

The world is plunged into Darkness. Overhead, the sky roils like a turbulent ocean. Seething thunderclouds flash with forked lightning. The air is thick with smoke that stings the eyes and chokes the throat. I stand, cold, alone and shivering, upon a desolate hillside. Next to me is a dead and withered tree, its crooked trunk white as bleached bone. Perched at the end of a splintered leafless branch rests a large black crow, the glinting beads of its eyes watching me. The scorched land that stretches out around the hill is shrouded in permanent shadow, the sun no longer rising, its life-giving rays banished beyond the horizon. In the valley far below I can make out legions of people toiling in the barren ruined earth –

I splutter and cough as a hot, bitter liquid is poured down my throat. Through a whirl of acrid woodsmoke, a grotesque face with sunken eyes, a hooked beak for a nose and black-and-red feathers sprouting from its crown shifts in and out of focus. The figure mumbles some mystic words and I cry out as a sharp pain stings my leg before it goes numb –

The crow caws loudly and with a great flap of its dark shiny wings it takes off from the branch. It circles overhead three times, then swoops into the valley. I shudder as it gives another harsh caw, beckoning me. I feel a strange compulsion to follow the clamouring bird down the hill and through the fields of slaves. It leads me to a huge plaza in which thousands of subjects are upon their knees, bowing and praying to an immense statue of a fearsome god with a snarling mouth and snake-like eyes that are as black as pitch.

Still the eerie crow guides me onwards, through the chanting crowd to a fortress of volcanic rock, its crenellated towers rising up like jagged mountains on either side of me.

At the base of a long flight of steps, hideous jaguar-masked guards stand to attention, as rigid and straight as the spiked spears in their hands. Passing uneasily between them, I climb the stairway and enter the fortress –

The heat is almost unbearable. Bathed in sweat, I feel as if I'm in a furnace. Scalding steam billows around me. Through the pungent clouds of mist, the strange beaked figure reappears and once more speaks in strange tongues. I hear a harsh rattling and flinch away, fearing another snake attack –

Gliding along a dark corridor, the crow leads me into a cavernous room with a polished stone-clad floor, tall marble columns and a high vaulted ceiling. With a piercing screech, the bird swoops down and alights neatly on the back of a throne shaped like the head of a massive black cobra. Beneath its hooklike fangs reclines an unnaturally long-limbed and cadaverous Tanas, flanked by his black-eyed Soul Hunters. At my approach, a cruel scythe-like smile curls the corners of his thin, pale lips.

'The last of the Light,' he sneers, stroking a serpent curled in his lap. 'How dull and diminished it is.'

'You won't win,' I say defiantly. 'I am protected.'

'Oh, but I've already won,' he says, his cold laughter echoing hollowly around the vast throne room. 'Did you not witness my kingdom? And, as for your protection, that is no more . . .' He clicks his fingers and two jaguar-masked guards drag in a limp and broken body.

'Phoenix!' I cry as they throw him unceremoniously to the floor. He lies there, unmoving, his body scarred by a tapestry of bruises, welts and deep cuts.

'His suffering was a true delight,' reveals Tanas with relish. 'I fed off it for many nights.'

'Phoenix!' I wail again, falling to my knees beside my lifeless Protector.

Tanas narrows his fathomless eyes and fixes his deathly gaze upon me. 'And now to destroy you . . . and the last Light of Humanity for eternity!'

At his command, his Soul Hunters rise as one and advance on me. Scrambling to my feet, I flee from the fortress as the heavy beat of drums thunders from the battlements –

The pounding in my head grows louder and my eyes open wide in terror as a tall figure in feathers and furs draped over its inked skin dances round my stiff and aching body. Yelping and hollering, it strikes a hide-covered drum, each *thump* and *thud* resounding through me, vibrating within the very marrow of my bones. My whole being resonates with its energy – then the drumming suddenly stops and the figure stands stone-still over me, its eyes gleaming –

I kneel upon the hill, weeping at the pain and suffering of the enslaved people. Mourning the death of humanity. Grieving for the loss of my Soul Protector and of the Light. With my death, Tanas's victory will be complete. The world and all that's beyond the world will be his and his alone. He rules with an iron fist, his power and pleasure derived directly from the agony and torment of his subjects. There is no hope. All is Darkness.

The Soul Hunters surround the hill and, murmuring an incantation, stealthily ascend towards me. I look around for a way of escape but there is none. Then in the dirt I spot something gleaming. My fingers dig into the barren black earth and I uncover two shards of rock – one smooth, hard and flint-like, the other rough and glittering like gold. Buried beneath them is a small pile of dry tinder. Not much . . . certainly not enough to make a fire.

Hearing an ominous flap of wings, I turn to see the creepy crow has returned and settled again on the crooked branch of the dead tree. But its reappearance has given me an idea. Hurrying over, I snap off the end of the brittle branch and with trembling hands break it into pieces of kindling. Then desperately striking rock against rock, I strive to create a spark. Over and over I hit the rocks together until my fingers bleed and my nails are black with bruises.

I'm almost on the point of giving up when, at last, a spark flies and lands amid the tinder. With a gentle breath, I fan it into a red glow . . . and then into a tiny faltering flame. The Hunters' advance falters as the kindling catches light . . . The flicker of flame grows into a fire and in turn swells into a blaze.

With a great roar of fury, Tanas bursts from his fortress and commands an icy wind to blow out the Light . . . But more sparks are born. They float up like tiny stars into the night sky, pushing back the Darkness –

35

A shaft of soft sunlight filters through a narrow gap in the canvas doorway. Outside, birds chirrup a dawn chorus, while here inside the sounds are gently muted, as if the world is wrapped in cotton wool. A curl of smoke rises from the ashes of a small fire in the centre of the dome-shaped dwelling in which I find myself. My shelter is built from a sturdy framework of branches tied together and covered in thick animal hide that I recognize from my former Cheyenne life as being a *wickiup*. A handful of smooth, rounded stones are piled beside the fire and a wooden drum and leather-handled rattle sit near the doorway. The air is tinged with the pungent aroma of herbs and woodsmoke. Through the haze, a mask with a menacing hooked beak and a furious sprouting of black-and-red feathers seems to peer at me.

Cautiously examining myself, I discover that I'm lying on a diamond-patterned wool rug that's been placed on the bare ground. My lower left leg is wrapped in long pale green leaves, but I no longer feel any pain. My throbbing headache is gone, the burning fever quenched and the venom in my veins seems purged. My lungs are clear and I breathe freely and easily, as if I've been inhaling crisp mountain air. It's as if my whole body feels cleansed.

Sitting up, I almost jump out of my skin when I spot a bare-chested, elderly man perched cross-legged in the shadows. His tanned and weathered skin is tattooed with bold lines of blue ink and round his face, which is wrinkled like old shoe leather, his black hair falls in a curtain past his broad shoulders. His earth-brown eyes gaze off unseeing into the far distance. For a moment I wonder whether he's a wooden totem, then his vacant stare regains focus and he turns to look at me.

'You are healed,' he declares in a hushed and husky tone.

I shrink back from him. 'Wh-who are you?' I stutter.

He raises a thick bushy eyebrow. 'The question is, who are *you*?'

'Genna,' I reply.

He shakes his head. 'I didn't ask you your name, for that can change,' he says. 'In this life alone, I've been known by many names: Hobelia, Cairook, Black Crow . . . You can call me John if you wish, though I do prefer my present Mojave name, Empote. No, Genna, I asked you to tell me *who* you are.'

His brown eyes lock with mine and he peers directly into me as if searching my soul. Returning his unwavering gaze, I notice an indigo hue ebb and flow in his irises, like the waves of the deepest and purest ocean. Whoever this man is, he appears to be a Soul Brother of the rarest sort.

'I'm a First Ascendant,' I reply, trusting my instincts to be open with him. 'Born of the Light and a Soul Carrier of the Light.'

'That you are,' Empote says, nodding. 'Yet you are so much more. For it's my humble belief that you are the one spoken of in the Soul Prophecy.'

'The *what*?' I ask, confused.

'The Soul Prophecy,' he repeats. 'There have been many versions in many languages over the many lives lived, but they all tell the same story . . .' In a reverential tone, he then says, as if he's reciting some ancient truth:

'For each Soul born of the Light shall
carry their burden bright;
But like day follows night, so shall night follow day.
The Darkness that once was will be once again,
For it's the Light that casts a shadow and the Shadow
that casts out the Light.

With every Soul extinguished or
swallowed by the Dark,
The Incarnate Lord steps closer to fulfilling
his cruel cold heart.
But one Soul shines brighter and
bolder than the rest;
This one must ignite the spark when
put to the Darkest test.'

'What is that? What are you talking about?' I ask, bewildered.

Breaking off from his intense gaze, Empote picks up a slender smoking pipe with a funnel, packs it with shredded brown leaves and lights its tip. He blows out and a cloud of rich tobacco smoke drifts through the air. 'Your vision,' he replies.

I flinch in shock. 'You saw what I saw? Are you a Soul Seer?'

He gently shakes his head. 'No, I don't have the sight. I'm – for want of a better term – a Soul Healer.'

I glance down at my leg. 'My snake bite . . . you healed it?'

Sucking on his pipe, he nods. 'To tell you the truth, it was a close call. By the time I reached you and your friends, you were on the border between this life and the next. The venom had almost run its course; its poison had started to weaken and pollute your very soul. But, sensing you had more to give this life, I drew you back.'

Tentatively I peel off the leaves wrapped round my leg and discover that the swelling and redness has gone. Even the puncture wounds have miraculously healed.

'The poultice of plantain leaves reduced the swelling and acted as an antitoxin,' Empote explains matter-of-factly. He points to the pile of rounded stones by the fire. 'The sweat bath helped purge you of the snake's venom.' He then directs my gaze to a clump of dried herbs hanging above his head: 'The burning of wild sage and the inhalation of its smoke purified your body and soul. The drumming and my chants drove away any malignant spirits that were attached to you. Lastly and mostly importantly, the bitter tea you drank contained black cohosh. This sacred herb not only neutralizes the venom, it induces visions and a trance state.'

'So what I saw was a . . . *Glimmer*?' I ask hesitantly, a shudder running through me at the nightmarish memory.

'No,' he replies solemnly. 'Glimmers are purely of the past. You experienced what we the Mojave call *su'mach*, a dream.'

I breathe a huge sigh of relief. 'So it wasn't real? Thank goodness!'

'No, I didn't say that,' he corrects me. '*Su'mach* are viewed by the Mojave as immensely important and sources of great wisdom. While the dreamer can travel to the deep past, they can also acquire spiritual guidance, mystical insights and even foresee the future. The person who experiences such a vision is considered *su'mach a'hot* – gifted.'

I shift uneasily on the woollen rug. 'Are you saying that what I dreamed is the future?'

Empote draws heavily on his pipe. 'Such visions are often deeply symbolic,' he replies through the haze of smoke curling from his lips. 'Your *su'mach* is one possible future. In it you were shown what Tanas's kingdom will be like if he conquers the Light. Darkness smothering the land. The night sky starless and suffocating. Humanity enslaved.'

My blood chills at the prospect. 'How do you know all this?' I challenge him. 'If you're not a Soul Seer, how could you witness my vision?'

He leans towards me, his voice soft and low. 'In order to heal effectively, I too must enter a trance state. My soul has the ability to transform into my guardian spirit and thereby enter your *su'mach*.'

I study his lined, leathery face, trying to spot any hint of deception in his guileless expression, wondering if this is truly possible. Then my eye catches sight of the beaked mask near the doorway and I'm struck by the truth. 'You were the crow!'

He smiles enigmatically. 'And I believe *you* are the one foretold in the Soul Prophecy. The one Light that shines brighter than all the others, and that will light the Darkness when no other can provide the spark. For even in the darkest moment of your dream, you managed to ignite a fire. Therefore, I believe you – *and only you* – can ultimately defeat Tanas and banish his dark soul forever.'

Stunned by his revelation, I shake my head vigorously. 'With the greatest respect, Empote, you must be wrong. I can't be this saviour you talk of.'

He raises both eyebrows at my protest. 'Why ever not?'

'Because I'm no Soul Protector like Phoenix, nor Warrior like Jude,' I argue. 'I may well be a First Ascendant, but, as I understand from Caleb, my purpose is to keep the Light burning, not fight the Darkness.'

Empote puts down his pipe and looks intently at me. 'The only way to defeat the Darkness is to confront it with Light!'

Unnerved by his prediction, I stand up, suddenly desperate to escape the *wickiup*. 'I'm truly grateful to you for saving my life, Empote, but there seems to be some sort of misunderstanding,' I say, backing away from him towards the exit. 'I want to find my friends now, please. Can you kindly tell me where they are?'

With a sage nod, Empote points a gnarled finger at the doorway just as Phoenix strides in.

'Thank heaven, you're alive!' he says, embracing me so hard I can feel his heart beating. He pulls back and looks me in the eye, his concerned gaze edged with guilt. 'I've been so worried. You've been unconscious a whole day and night. For a while we didn't think you'd pull through . . .' He trails off and turns to the healer. 'Thank you, Empote. You've performed a miracle!'

Nonchalantly waving away the praise, Empote replies, 'No. The miracle is in your arms.'

Phoenix cocks his head and looks at me. 'What does that mean?'

But, before I can reply, Jude bursts in on us. 'We have to leave, *now*!' she says, a fraught look on her face. 'Tarek's just spotted two more drones in the sky. Tanas must have found us.'

Phoenix looks cautiously out of the *wickiup* and curses. 'We'll never escape on foot. Not with those drones overhead.'

Empote clears his throat. 'If I may, I can help you,' he says.

'You've got horses we can borrow?' Phoenix asks hopefully.

Empote grins. 'No, not horses. Something even better. A pickup truck!'

36

'Can't this truck go any faster?' asks Jude, peering up anxiously at the cloudless blue sky, searching for the drones.

'Not unless we're going downhill,' Empote replies with a wry smile. 'Besides, it's best we stick to the speed limit to avoid drawing any unnecessary attention to ourselves.'

All five of us are crammed into the front of his rusting and creaking pickup. The cab smells of warm leather, hot oil and stale tobacco, and the vehicle is so old it still boasts a radio cassette player. Empote drives with one hand loosely on the wheel, his other arm hanging out of the window. The warm desert wind ruffles his mane of black hair as he squints at the sand-blasted highway ahead of us.

Every so often Phoenix glances back through the rear window, checking for any cars that may be following us, while Tarek and Jude keep an eye on the skies. It was Tarek who'd come across the Mojave healer in the desert and told him of my plight. Since the chances of their paths crossing in such an empty and unforgiving wasteland were close to zero, I suspect Empote was already on his way to my rescue, his soul intuition guiding him, just as Phoenix and Jude had been drawn to me before.

'I see one!' cries Tarek, pointing to the north. I sit tense and silent between Empote and Phoenix, as Jude leans out of the side window to track the drone's flight path. I notice that her injured arm is no longer bandaged, that too healed by Empote, no doubt.

'No, it was just a plane, by the sound of it,' says Jude, and we all settle back into our seats. 'I think we've lost the two drones for now,' she adds.

'If that's the case, then it's safe to head to Haven,' instructs Phoenix. Empote pulls off the highway and down an unmarked dirt track, driving towards a familiar range of saw-toothed mountains in the distance. 'But we can't afford to drop our guard,' reminds Phoenix, looking back towards the highway. 'Tanas doesn't give up that easily.'

As the others keep surveying the sky, I turn to Empote. 'I guess you know where you're going?' I say.

'Of course,' he replies, nimbly navigating the bumps and ruts in the road. 'I'm a Mojave. This is our land. In fact, I'm the one who persuaded the elders to allow Caleb to build Haven within one of our most sacred and secret sites. They understood the protection it affords and, moreover, the importance of protecting the Light.'

Turning the wheel hard, Empote joins a potholed tarmac road and heads north. After a mile or so, a small, isolated town comes into view on the horizon.

'Have you always been a Soul Healer?' I ask.

Empote nods. 'No matter the life I've been born into, I've been a healer of one sort or another. Some centuries that's been a blessing, other times a curse.' He gives a regretful shake of his head. 'People are often afraid of what they don't understand. Among the Mojave I'm a respected medicine man, but during the time of the Spanish Inquisition I was persecuted and burned alive as a witch.'

My skin suddenly feels hot, the faint whiff of engine oil in the cabin turning to the acrid stench of burned hair and charred wood. Through the open window I hear far-off tortured screams carried on the wind and wonder for a moment if the radio is on and out of tune. Then I catch a glimpse of flames reflected in the windscreen and of a grey-haired woman tied to a stake surrounded by a pile of blazing wood.

'*I remember!*' I gasp in horror.

Empote casts me a grave and consoling look. 'Then that must be *your* Glimmer of that dark period,' he says solemnly as we approach the outskirts of the abandoned mining town. 'For our souls have only met in this lifetime.'

'Maybe I was too late to save you,' I say, shaking off the disturbing vision.

'And maybe we weren't destined to meet until now,' Empote replies with a sanguine smile. 'It's not enough to be in the right place at the right time. One has to be the *right person* in the right place at the right time. Probably you weren't ready, and perhaps –' he lowers his voice to almost a whisper – 'perhaps I wasn't ready to recognize you for who I believe you are.'

'What are you two talking about?' asks Phoenix, turning back from his vigilant watch through the rear window.

'The Soul Prophecy,' Empote replies.

Jude pulls her head back into the cab, her hair messed up by the wind into a flurry of candyfloss. 'You believe in that fairy tale, old man?' she says with a smirk.

Empote glances meaningfully at me. 'Absolutely.'

Jude gives a pitying shake of her head. 'Then you're not as wise as I thought you were. The Soul Prophecy is a made-up story to give us hope in what is otherwise a hopeless battle.'

Phoenix's jaw falls open. 'Jude! Is that *really* what you think? That our battle is hopeless?'

'Well, we're not exactly winning, are we?' replies Jude.

'No, maybe we're not yet, but that attitude won't help our cause,' argues Phoenix fiercely.

Jude returns his glare. 'Nor will believing in fake prophecies!'

The cabin falls silent, except for the rush of the wind and the rumbling of the tyres on the rough tarmac. I sit between Empote and the others, feeling uncomfortably like an uninvited guest at a private party. *Am I the only one who didn't know about the Soul Prophecy?* I wonder. *Why hasn't Caleb, or Phoenix for that matter, mentioned it before?*

We pass through the ghost town, its crumbling sun-bleached buildings as unwelcoming as ever.

'Hope is also the only thing stronger than fear,' declares Empote, 'so it's crucial to keep hope in your heart. The Soul Prophecy is no myth: it's the truth.'

'We've been given false promises before,' says Tarek, 'and with tragic consequences. What makes you so convinced it's true now?'

I look to Empote, surprised to learn there have been previous proclamations, and I wonder what went wrong in the past. I find myself questioning the Mojave's judgement even more.

Empote turns in his seat to reply. 'Because –' he begins.

Suddenly an object drops from the sky and crash-lands in front of the truck. Empote hits the brake hard and we skid to a shuddering stop.

'What the hell was that?' yells Phoenix.

We all peer at the small impact crater in the road. 'A missile of some sort?' I ask, fearful.

'Whatever it was, it missed us,' observes Jude.

Tarek gets out of the truck and cautiously inspects the wreckage on the ground. He comes back looking grim, a tiny broken camera in his hand. 'It's a drone,' he informs us. 'The GPS transmitter must've failed when it entered the dead zone.'

Dread creeps over me as the camera's shattered lens seems to stare at me, triumphant and gloating.

'Dammit! That means Tanas is on our trail,' says Jude, punching the dashboard in frustration.

'Then we'd better get back to Haven. *Fast!*' orders Phoenix.

37

'YOU DISOBEYED A DIRECT ORDER!' roars Goggins, his face as thunderous as his voice. The cats lounging in Haven's entrance hall are so startled they scatter for cover or flee the room altogether. 'You've put yourselves at risk! You've put Haven at risk! And you've put THE VERY LIGHT ITSELF AT RISK!'

I stand stunned and shamefaced in the storm of the Chief Protector's fury. Phoenix, Jude and Tarek are also dumbstruck by this brutal dressing-down. Goggins now glares at us, his silent rage somehow fiercer and more unsettling than his shouts.

'I-I'm sorry,' I venture. 'It isn't the others' fault. I'm the one –'

'*SORRY?*' snaps Goggins, the veins in his muscled neck bulging. 'You tell me a drone has followed you back, and all you can say is *sorry*? Of course it's their fault! They should know better. What's the point of all their training, in this life and past lives, if they're going to make such reckless decisions and stupid mistakes?'

'Goggins, what's done is done,' says Caleb calmly. 'Genna is safe, Jude and Tarek are unharmed, and Phoenix has been rescued.' Despite his placatory tone, I notice Caleb's bony fingers are clasped so tightly round the top of his cane that its lion's head is in danger of snapping clean off. He's clearly just as concerned as Goggins.

'So you say, but at what cost?' Goggins mutters through clenched teeth. He turns his seething glare upon Phoenix. 'And for what gain? Tell me that, eh?'

'It's good to see you too, Father,' replies Phoenix with a strained smile.

I do a double take. *Father?* I know from the police report DI Shaw once showed me that Phoenix's mother was from Córdoba in Mexico and died in a car crash, while his father was registered as 'Unknown'. But I struggle to see any resemblance between the man mountain that is Goggins and my lean Soul Protector.

'Not in this life,' explains Phoenix, noticing my questioning look. 'Goggins is my first father, my Soul Father. You may remember him as Zuberi, chief of the Hakalan tribe.'

I have a flashback to that deeply ancient Glimmer of Asani teaching me how to wield an axe and of Zuberi's glowering disapproval. The chief's expression hasn't appeared to change one bit over the countless millennia in between.

'And that's why I'm so bitterly disappointed,' growls Goggins. 'As my Soul Son, you *shouldn't* make such careless errors that allow drones to follow you. And now Haven and every First Ascendant sheltered here is in jeopardy!'

The enormity of our blunder and the stupidity of my own foolhardy rescue mission finally hit home. I hang my head in remorse. 'I didn't mean to endanger my fellow First Ascendants,' I plead, 'only to save my Protector.'

'I get that,' snarls Goggins. 'But you've ended up squandering everyone else's safety in the process!'

Empote, who's been standing to one side, clears his throat. 'I accept some damage has been done, but it isn't quite the catastrophe you fear. I can cover our tracks, then take a long drive through the desert to lead any Hunters astray. The drone only gets Tanas and her Hunters to the mining town, anyhow.'

'Thank you, Empote,' says Caleb, hobbling over and embracing the Soul Healer. 'Your help is a godsend, as ever. You've brought back Genna, safe and sound, and that's what matters in the end.'

As they embrace, I notice Empote whisper something in Caleb's ear. Caleb's gleaming blue eyes widen a little and momentarily flick my way. A short intense discussion follows, and it isn't hard for me to guess that they're talking about the Soul Prophecy. Caleb gives an almost imperceptible shake of his head, then Empote nods and smiles. But Caleb doesn't return his smile; he only looks more troubled than ever. With a final earnest handshake, Caleb bids Empote farewell. 'Take care, old friend. Keep your wits about you,' he says aloud.

'You too,' replies the healer. Then with a pointed look he adds, 'Have faith in yourself. This time it's different.'

Stepping outside, Phoenix, Jude, Tarek and I bid Empote a hurried goodbye. I thank him once more for his healing, feeling a deep, almost grand-daughterly attachment to him. He clasps me by the shoulders, his big hands cradling me as if I were a young sapling he was about to plant.

'Be the Light that helps others to see,' he whispers to me. 'Look within yourself to ignite the spark!' With those parting words, he clambers into his battered pickup truck and drives off, Haven's inner gates closing fast behind him.

'Phoenix, Jude, Tarek, you three come with me!' orders Goggins fiercely, already striding off in the direction of the Glimmer Dome. 'We've got some damage control to attend to.'

'You all right?' Phoenix asks me, seeing my far-off stare.

I nod. 'Just worried about Empote,' I say, telling him only a half-truth. Of course I'm concerned for Empote. He's taking such a risk on our behalf, but it's the burden of the healer's belief that weighs most heavily on my mind – that I'm the one foretold in the Soul Prophecy.

Phoenix searches my guarded gaze, clearly sensing there's more to my answer. 'Don't worry. He'll be fine. And don't beat yourself up about what Goggins said. Your intentions were good. It's exactly what I'd have done in your posi–'

'NOW, PHOENIX!' barks Goggins, gesturing impatiently for him to follow.

Phoenix offers me as hearty a smile as he can muster. 'I'll catch up with you later,' he promises, squeezing my hand affectionately. As Phoenix hurries to join the others, Tarek gives me a wave and Jude an unreadable yet decidedly cool look. I wave back, then I step inside Haven's entrance hall and make my way through to the water garden.

I find Caleb pensively watching the koi carp in the pond, just like one of his cats would do. He doesn't look up as I approach.

'Did you know that if you put a koi carp in a fish bowl it'll only grow to around three inches,' he says absently. 'But in a large pond or lake, where it's free to move, the same koi will grow to its full size of twenty inches or more.'

'No, I didn't know that,' I reply, somewhat bemused at his remark. 'Listen, Caleb, I'm sorry –'

'I just wonder what their size would be in an ocean,' he goes on, seeming not to hear me. 'Of course, the seawater would likely kill them since they're freshwater fish . . .'

Trailing off, he continues to stare into the pond, his gaze tracking a particularly large golden carp.

'Caleb, have I really put Haven in danger?' I ask, guilt weighing heavily on me.

Without meeting my eye, he replies, 'As I said before, one needs to be led here to enter the valley and fortunately, thanks to the dead zone, the drone fell short.' He scatters a handful of fish food into the pond and observes the carp eagerly feeding on the pellets. 'With any luck, Haven should remain hidden from Incarnate eyes. Still, regrettably your little venture has significantly increased our risk of discovery.'

The disappointment in his voice is more painful than Goggins' furious outburst. I've not only let Caleb down but everyone in Haven. A tense silence falls over us as we stand beside the pond, watching the hungry mouths of the carp gobble up their food.

After a minute or so, I ask tentatively, 'Did, er . . . did Empote say anything to you . . . about me?'

Caleb glances up as if startled. 'Sorry, Genna? I'm a little distracted,' he says with a brief, tense smile. 'If you'll excuse me, I need to meditate on our situation.' Tossing the last of the fish food into the water, he limps stiffly away, his cane tapping along the path until he disappears round the corner in the direction of the glass pyramid.

I remain by the pond, uncertain how to read Caleb's reaction. Was he just still angry with me about the rescue? Or was he trying to avoid talking about the Soul Prophecy? Whatever the reason, he appeared strangely agitated and – dare I say? – even *scared.*

38

Feeling desperately in need of a shower and some rest, I head through the Zen garden, into the courtyard and over towards my apartment. Santiago, Mick and Jintao are huddled round a table, deep in conversation. They stop and turn as I enter. I offer a hesitant wave in greeting, but Santiago scowls and Mick mutters something to him, while Jintao responds with a cool look. Saddened by this frosty response, I follow the covered walkway round to my apartment. On reaching the door, I hear a friendly mew and am greeted by Nefertiti, who rubs against my leg and begins purring loudly.

'Hello, Nefe. At least you're giving me a warm welcome,' I say, picking her up and stroking her gently.

'Oh, don't fret about them, *mia cara*,' soothes a lilting, richly accented voice. 'Or about Goggins.'

I look round to discover Viviana reclining in her rocking chair under the olive tree outside her apartment. My cheeks burning, I mumble, 'You heard him? From *here*?'

Viviana arches a thin pencilled eyebrow. 'It's difficult not to, with Goggins. Always he's shouting at someone or other,' she says, excusing his behaviour with a wave of her hand. 'Indeed, I don't think he's happy unless his voice is raised to at least a hundred decibels.' She sighs heavily, a frown deepening the careworn wrinkles on her brow. 'But we must remember, the Chief Protector has such a great burden upon his shoulders.' She pats the stool next to her. 'Come, *mia cara*, join me in the shade.'

I sit down next to her. Without hesitation, Nefertiti jumps up and settles on my lap.

'We've all been very worried about you,' admits Viviana.

'Really?' I question, snatching a quick look across at Santiago and the others, whose expressions haven't lightened. 'The others seem more angry than relieved.'

'Oh, *men*!' she tuts. 'Granted, some of us were upset at the risk you took with your Light, but now we're just glad you're safe. That's the truth.' She graces me with a grandmotherly smile of care and love.

'I didn't mean to worry everyone,' I insist, a knot of the guilt twisting my stomach. 'But I *had* to rescue my Protector. Phoenix is the only one who can keep my soul safe.'

'Yes, yes. I understand, *mia cara*,' she says, gently patting my knee. 'What you've done is admirable . . . if a little foolish. If my Goggins were in trouble, I'd certainly feel compelled to save him. But what's an eighty-year-old woman with arthritis going to do?' She shrugs.

I blink in surprise. '*Goggins* is your Soul Protector?' I find it hard to envisage a more mismatched pairing.

'For my sins, yes!' she chuckles. 'I was living quite peacefully in my remote little chalet, high in the Italian Alps, until *he* turned up!' She puffs out her cheeks in apparent annoyance. 'But unknown to me a pack of Soul Hunters was slowly closing in. One morning I awoke to find my *villetta* surrounded. I thought my end had come.' Viviana shakes her head woefully at the memory, then the corners of her mouth curl into an artful grin. 'But like a bull in a china shop, as you say, Goggins appeared – and if my old *villetta* wasn't a ruin before, it certainly was after that!'

She laughs ruefully.

'What? He destroyed your *home*?' I say, astonished.

'Goggins is not one for subtlety. He's more of a hammer than a scalpel!' She gives a weary roll of her eyes. 'And yet, while I may complain, I wouldn't wish for any other Protector for my soul. He's saved me on so many occasions, sacrificed so much over our countless lifetimes together, that I can forgive his somewhat brusque and brutal ways. I have to remind myself he only has my best interests at heart. In fact, he has *all* our interests at heart.'

Recognizing that I hold similar feelings to these for Phoenix, I'm about to agree with Viviana when a flurry of ice-blond hair throws herself down beside my chair. 'Genna, *vy vernulis*!' cries Tasha. She hugs my knees tightly, dislodging Nefertiti, who leaps off my lap with a disgruntled *meow*.

'Yes, I'm back, Tasha,' I reply, returning the girl's eager embrace, glad someone other than my cat is happy at my return.

'I heard you were bitten by a *snake*!' she says, breathless, her crystal-blue eyes wide in horrified amazement. 'What happened? How did you survive?'

'Don't worry, I'm fine now,' I assure her, before recounting my experience with Empote and his remarkable healing powers. I'm careful, however, to leave out my vision and what it apparently reveals about me and the Soul Prophecy.

When Tasha begins to pepper me with questions about Phoenix's rescue, Viviana gently interrupts, 'Tasha, *mia bambina*, Genna is very tired and probably hungry too. Be a good girl and ask Fabian to make her something to eat.'

Nodding obediently, Tasha dashes off on her errand. But not before she's whispered in my ear, '*Whatever the others say, I think you're very brave!*'

As I watch the blond-haired bundle of energy dance off through the orchard, I remark to Viviana, 'She's certainly a bright soul.'

'That she is . . .' says Viviana, her wrinkled face creasing with affection for the girl. 'All the more amazing considering the hard start she had to this life.'

I turn to Viviana. 'What do you mean?'

Rocking back in her chair, Viviana knits her arthritic fingers together and prepares to explain. 'The poor child Wakened early,' she says, 'and was under threat from the Incarnates long before she was ready.'

'Are any of us ever ready?' I question, thinking of my own Wakening at Mei's parents' exhibition at the museum and that first terrifying encounter with Damien.

'No, I guess not!' agrees Viviana with a humourless laugh. 'But Tasha was barely eight years old when a black-eyed Russian Security Service agent visited her family without warning.'

My jaw drops open in shock and pity. I can't imagine how I'd have coped at such a young age. 'Poor Tasha! How did she ever survive?' I ask.

'In truth, it's a miracle she did,' admits Viviana. 'From what little she's been willing to tell me, she was forced to flee her home and hide on the cold, bitter streets of Moscow. At some point she sought shelter with the Bratva, the Russian mafia. However, they turned out to be almost as dangerous as the Incarnates themselves, so she found herself on the run from both the FSB Hunter and the Bratva.'

'She did that *alone*?' I say, aghast. 'She was only eight! Where was her Protector?'

'Desperately looking for her.' Viviana's rheumy eyes narrow. 'Just as the FSB Hunter was – and it was he who found Tasha first.'

'So how come Tasha's still alive?' I ask.

Viviana gently shakes her head as if mystified herself. 'Somehow she managed to escape on to the frozen Moskva river. But the ice cracked beneath her feet and she fell into the icy water. That might have been the end for little Tasha had the Hunter not pulled her to safety –'

'He *saved* her?'

A grimace darkens Viviana's face. 'Yes, but only so that Tanas would be able to perform his unholy ritual.' A smile then curls the corner of Viviana's cracked lips. 'But Tasha's Protector wasn't too far behind, thankfully, and caught up with them at the river. There was a vicious battle. Tasha's Protector, despite being gravely wounded, managed to kick the FSB Hunter into the water, where he drowned!'

'That *was* a last-minute rescue,' I remark. 'Thank heavens. Who's Tasha's Protector?'

'Clara,' reveals Viviana. 'You may have seen her around here. She has a scar across her cheek, a rather permanent reminder of that particular encounter.'

I nod, remembering the older woman I'd seen training in the gym when I first arrived at Haven. 'Well, however tough Tasha's Wakening was, she seems to have an even tougher Protector!'

'We're all blessed with our Protectors,' agrees Viviana, 'and we all have our own stories to tell.' She thrusts her chin in the direction of Santiago and the others. 'Santiago is what you would call a *traditional* man,' she explains with a wry smile. 'He's still getting over the fact that he was saved from an Incarnate ambush by a fifteen-year-old girl wielding a Glock 17 pistol!'

Recalling the sharpshooter on the firing range, I ask, 'Does she have red hair?'

Viviana nods. 'That's right. Lena, from Poland.'

'What about Mick?'

'Tragically, he lost his Protector to Tanas in a previous lifetime. He now relies on a Warrior. Likewise, so does Thabisa and her son Kagiso. In fact, Tarek is Thabisa's Warrior. But it's a fact that the bond between Ascendant and Warrior is never as strong as it is with your Protector. That's why I understand your need to save Phoenix.'

'Thank you,' I reply, heartened. At that moment Tasha darts back across the lawn and presents me with a bowl of steaming fresh pasta.

'*Spasibo*,' I say, thanking her in Russian, the language coming easily to my lips. As I tuck appreciatively into my food, the other First Ascendants wander over to check I'm

OK. Fabian joins us from the kitchen; Sun-Hi and her children come with a jug of freshly squeezed lemonade; Thabisa and her son offer a bunch of flowers picked from the garden; and even Santiago and the others gather round eventually. My misadventure is apparently forgiven in the relief of my safe return.

As we chat and laugh, the feeling of togetherness is once again strong, and I feel reassured. There is a sense of family – but in that same moment I also experience a pang of longing for my mum and dad, and my home in Clapham, and I wonder how Mia and Prisha are coping with my continued disappearance. I miss my friends and the opportunity to talk openly with them about what I'm going through. While I've known Viviana and the other First Ascendants in previous lives, and we share a close bond through the Light we all carry, nothing comes close to having a best friend to confide in and rely on. I guess that's another reason why I was so determined to rescue Phoenix. He's not only my Soul Protector; he's my most trusted friend and truest companion in this life and my previous lives.

Once I've finished my meal, my exhaustion finally catches up with me and I make my excuses. But before I head into my apartment for some rest, I turn again to Viviana. 'Have you heard about the Soul Prophecy?' I ask her quietly.

She gives me a curious look. 'Of course. Why do you ask?'

'Empote mentioned it to me,' I reply, trying my best to sound casual, 'and I'd never heard of it before – at least not in this lifetime.'

'Ah, I see,' says Viviana, rocking gently back in her chair. 'Caleb is the best one to talk to about the Prophecy.'

'I tried, but he seemed reluctant to tell me anything about it,' I explain.

'That's understandable,' mutters Viviana, her bony hands clenching the arms of her chair.

I frown, intrigued by her reaction. 'Do *you* believe in the Prophecy, Viviana?'

She stops rocking and her eyes become glassy. 'I did once.'

'Once?' I ask. 'Why not now?'

'I –' she swallows hard – 'I lost my Soul Daughter because of it . . .' A tear runs down her wrinkled cheek and she wipes it away with a trembling hand. 'Sorry, I still find it too painful to talk about.' Rising stiffly from her rocking chair, Viviana hobbles away across the courtyard. Tasha runs after her and gently takes her hand.

As they disappear into the shade of the fruit trees, I begin to understand their deep connection to one another. Tasha's loss of her family in this life and Viviana's in one from her past have brought them together, each one filling a hole in the other's heart.

Sadness overwhelms my own heart as I think about the passing of my present-life parents and I wonder once more where my Soul family are . . .

39

The crow caws loudly, warning of approaching Soul Hunters. The forest around me is pitch dark, the diseased trees bent and twisted. Through the leafless canopy, the sky swirls with black clouds and pulses of lightning. A roll of thunder rumbles overhead as cold rain begins to fall upon the leaf-strewn ground.

I kneel in a small clearing, alone and shivering. In my fist I clasp a box of matches. A meagre pile of kindling is stacked before me. From the forest I hear the brittle crack of a dead branch, the crunch of decaying leaves, the pad of stealthy footsteps drawing ever nearer.

With a trembling hand, I take out a match and try to light it. The head snaps off. I fumble with another match, dropping it on the wet ground. The third match fails to light. As does the next . . . and the next . . .

In a panic I empty the box into my hand just as a jagged fork of lightning strikes a tree and illuminates the forest. A startled cry escapes my lips . . . a circle of hooded Hunters surrounds me, their cruel faces shrouded in shadow, their black eyes glinting. Behind them, swinging slowly in the wind, I see my fellow First Ascendants, each hanging by their neck from a twisted bough. Tasha is among them, her head lolling, her blue eyes open but unseeing.

Crushed with grief, I tear my eyes away and stare in dismay at what's left in my hand . . . one solitary match.

The crow squawks its final warning before taking flight into the seething black sky. Borne by the wind whistling through the trees, Tanas's harsh voice breathes into my ear.

'I'm coming for your soul –'

I wake, my heart pounding, brow slick with sweat. Outside my bedroom, the birds in the olive tree are in commotion, shrieking in alarm. With a flutter of wings, they scatter into the cloudless blue sky – leaving Nefe clinging halfway up the tree trunk, disgruntled at being denied her afternoon snack.

Rubbing my eyes in an effort to erase the disturbing image of Tasha hanging from a noose, I wonder if I've just experienced another *su'mach*. I pray it was merely a nightmare.

As I begin to collect my thoughts, I'm conscious that the question of the Soul Prophecy remains unanswered. Viviana's revelation that her Soul Daughter died as a result of it only deepens the mystery and increases the urgency of my need to know the truth. Pulling on a pair of fresh jeans and a top from my pack, I resolve to seek out Caleb and put the matter to rest. It's one thing to discover I'm a First Ascendant charged with carrying the Light of Humanity, but quite another to be considered the one person who can defeat Tanas, especially when it seems some other soul has already tried – and failed.

Leaving Nefe a bowl of dry food (which she turns her nose up at), I cross the lawn and head towards the glass pyramid. I'm not sure how long I've been asleep but the sun is high in the sky now. I hope Caleb will still be there, meditating. Quietly and respectfully I enter the vast prism-like room. Sunlight arcs in rainbows over my head, its rays reflected in the polished marble floor like an infinity mirror. The familiar and welcome tingle of the Light courses through my body and, as I relish the invigorating sensation, my fears and concerns ebb away and are replaced by a reassuring buzz of warm energy.

'Caleb?' My voice rebounds off the glass solar panels and echoes into silence.

The white marble pedestal stands unoccupied in the centre of the room. I cast a look around as I walk over to it; the pyramid appears to be deserted. The crystal capstone atop the pedestal gleams in the bright sunlight and tentatively I reach out to touch its surface, wondering if this may be able to reveal the answers I seek. I'm left disappointed when nothing happens.

Taking my hand away, I accidentally brush against the leading edge of the pedestal. In response, a circular sun icon with a golden eye at its centre softly illuminates. I press it. With a soft whirr, the solar panels align themselves and a shaft of blinding white light strikes the tip of the capstone. The crystal blazes once more like a miniature supernova and I –

– drop to my knees and can only watch as my twin sister is hauled up the steps into the forbidding palace.

'Aya!' I moan, clasping my throbbing head. My hand comes away slick with fresh blood where the guard hit me

with his stick. I attempt to rise, my knees weak, my vision blurred. The palace guard goes to strike me again.

'Enough! Don't damage her any more!' Rimush snaps at him. 'Your Lugal will be most displeased.'

As the guard grudgingly backs down, the slave trader takes my arm and helps me to my feet. Quickly regaining my senses, I shake off his sweaty grip and snatch the short, knotted whip out from under his leather belt.

'Arwia, stop!' gasps Rimush, his piggy eyes widening in alarm. 'Don't make matters worse for yourself.'

Fearing more for my sister's life than my own, I ignore his warning and, with a flick of the whip, I lash the palace guard in the face. He howls in pain, his hands go to his blinded eyes, and he drops his stick. I pick up the weapon and turn back to Rimush, raising it to give him a beating too. The slave trader cowers before me, his trembling hands raised over his bald head.

'No, have mercy!' he begs, the bully turned coward in the blink of an eye.

'Tssk, you're not even worth wasting my energy on,' I say, spitting on him.

Witnessing my bold stand, the other slaves take courage at my defiance and as one rise up to fight for their freedom. The guards within the courtyard are quickly overwhelmed and I'm given a clear path into the palace. Armed with both whip and stick, I dash up the steps, through a pair of huge, metal-studded wooden doors and into an empty entrance hall. I race along a corridor that's lit by oil lamps, following the sound of my sister's screams, until I come out into a vast chamber.

Here, under the flickering light of more oil lamps, a black-cloaked congregation is in the middle of a monotonous chant – 'Ra-Ka! Ra-Ka! Ra-Ka!' – while they bow in unison before a towering statue of Nergal, the gruesome lion-headed Sumerian god of plague and war. At the statue's base stands Saragon, the Incarnate leader, tall and proud in his blood-stained white robes, his golden headband gleaming in the lamplight. Aya lies before him on a wide marble altar, her limbs pinned by four gold-masked acolytes. She struggles, but futilely, as Saragon pours a steaming liquid down her throat. Then he begins to utter a strange incantation: 'Rura, rkumaa, raar ard ruhrd . . .'

Never before have I witnessed such a ritual, not in this life nor in our previous ones, but Saragon's warped words fill me with the utmost dread. As he raises a gold dagger aloft in both hands, I share my sister's overwhelming panic; feel her terror and the pain of the scalding potion in her stomach; sense even her gradual paralysis as the potion somehow seeps into my own limbs as well as hers.

Fighting against the numbing sensation, I charge into the chamber intent on rescuing her, but in my haste I run straight into the guard standing sentry at the doorway, a long spear tipped with a burnished copper spike in his grasp. As he turns to confront me, I strike his head hard with my stick. He collapses in a heap and, discarding my stick and whip, I grab his spear before it clatters to the marble floor. Then, striding boldly forward, I launch the weapon with all my strength at Saragon. It flies true through the air, whistling over the heads of the black-cloaked congregation.

The Lugal glances up, a surprised scowl on his bearded face as the spear shoots towards him. But at the last second he deftly evades its deadly tip and catches the wooden shaft in mid-air. I stare, aghast.

His cold mocking laughter echoes round the now-silent chamber. Then he snaps the spear in half across his knee. 'Guards, seize her!'

I try to run but a muscled sentry grabs me from behind.

Saragon raises the glinting dagger over Aya once more and looks at me. 'Well,' he gloats, 'now you can watch as I tear out your twin's heart and destroy her soul for eternity!'

'F-for eternity?' I exclaim, meeting my sister's drugged and despairing gaze.

'Yes! The Light of Humanity will be extinguished soul by soul.' A scythe-like smile cuts across Saragon's lips. 'Bring the girl closer so she can witness my dark power first hand.'

But the guard doesn't obey the command. Instead he pulls me back towards the corridor.

'I said, BRING HER TO ME!' Saragon thunders.

Still the guard retreats, forcibly taking me with him. I manage to glance over my shoulder at my captor. His eyes sparkle like stars. 'Asani?' I gasp, recognizing his soul.

'Bashaa to you in this life,' my Soul Protector replies as the black-cloaked congregation turns on us both. With us in danger of being surrounded and our escape route cut off, Bashaa thrusts his spear into a large clay jar by the wall, cracking it open. Oil spills out across the marble floor, making it slick and treacherous. But that's only half his plan. He kicks over a burning lamp, the flame igniting the oil and

turning the floor into an inferno. The blaze pushes back the Incarnate congregation, but also separates me from my sister.

'NO!' I cry as Bashaa drags me away. 'What about Aya?'

'I am your *Soul Protector, first and foremost,' he replies, holding me tightly as I frantically try to break free. 'I can't save you both.'*

Through the flames I lock eyes with my twin, our connection eternal and undying . . . or so I thought. With a final invocation of 'RA-KA!', Saragon buries the gold dagger in my sister's chest. She screams and I scream, our soul-shattering shrieks resounding through the chamber like a cyclone. Aya's body and soul are rent from each other and I feel an agonizing wrench deep within me, as if my own heart is being torn from my *chest too. Unimaginable pain rips through me. I reach out in desperation to my sister.*

She calls out my soul name: 'TISHALA!' The starlit gleam in her eyes blazes briefly, before fading all too fast. Then, like a blade of ice, Saragon's spell severs our connected souls. It cleaves through the core of my very being, my very Light, and the world around me darkens –

40

'Genna! Speak to me! Are you OK?'

Opening my eyes, I discover Caleb kneeling beside me on the floor of the Sun Room, his mane of white hair slightly dishevelled and his cane discarded to one side as if abandoned in a hurry. I'm lying sprawled at the foot of the marble pedestal, its crystal capstone emitting a muted glow but no longer burning with its previous intensity. Despite the warming presence of the Light within the glass pyramid, I feel chilled to the bone, my heart hollowed out, as if my soul has somehow shrunk.

'Tanas . . . killed . . . my sister,' I mutter, my chest so tight I struggle to say the words. 'Destroyed . . . her soul . . .'

With a sorrowful sigh, Caleb bows his head. 'Yes, he did.'

I sit up, tears blurring my vision. 'Why did her death hurt so much?' I ask, clasping my still-aching heart. 'It felt like I was dying too.'

'You were, in a way,' Caleb replies. 'You see, Aya wasn't just your sister in that life, or the lives before that. She was your Soul Twin.'

I blink away my tears. 'My *Soul Twin*?'

Caleb nods and helps me to my feet. 'When you were first born as Tishala, a carrier of the Light, you had an identical twin – Lakeisha.'

As he says this, I remember her as clearly as if she was standing right before me. Her oval, dark-skinned face, fresh and smooth like a pebble from the river. Her short black hair, braided and adorned with coloured beads. Her sapphire-blue eyes bright, beaming and endearingly innocent. Her smile wide and ever joyful, her laugh like the trickle of a stream. My heart warms at my vibrant memory of her, of our lives together and entwined. Not just as Lakeisha . . . but as the fair-skinned Aya . . . and all of a sudden I realize *she* was also the girl with long, flowing hair and white shimmering robes who I'd seen during my intense Glimmer in the stone circle with Phoenix near Andover. The memories start coming thick and fast . . . The two of us playing by a stream together and trying to catch a frog . . . collecting honey in the Amazonian jungle and getting stung for our efforts . . . hunting a gazelle across the open savannah, then being chased by a hungry lion . . . hiding in a snowy Himalayan cave as Soul Hunters passed close by . . . But now I know these memories are all ancient, all from before her death at Tanas's hand.

'You were formed from the same spark of Light,' Caleb explains, running a finger along the edge of the pedestal and causing the soft glow within the crystal to coalesce into a single tiny particle. It hovers in the centre of the capstone, bright as a star at night. 'In essence, you shared each other's soul.'

With another touch of his finger, the spark divides in two. 'What she felt, you felt. What you experienced, she experienced.'

As the two sparks orbit one another, I begin to understand my deep connection to my twin – the shared Light that bound us together like gravity.

'In breaking this unique and powerful soul bond, Tanas caused excruciating pain to both you and your sister,' says Caleb with a grim expression. Then he looks at me, the slightest of smiles turning up the corners of his wrinkled mouth. 'However, like splitting the atom, he also released an immense burst of energy. This means *you*, Genna, carry more Light than the other First Ascendants. Your sister may have been killed by Tanas, her soul destroyed for eternity, but at her death she passed on some of her Light to you.'

I give Caleb a questioning look. 'Do you mean I'm different to the others?'

Caleb nods. 'Yes. You shine brighter.'

As I let this sink in, I think about what Empote told me: *But one Soul shines brighter and bolder than the rest.* My heart begins to pound a little harder and I force myself to take a steadying breath before saying, 'Empote thinks I'm the one foretold in the Soul Prophecy.'

'I know he does,' Caleb replies, his expression impassive.

'And so . . . what do *you* think?' I ask hesitantly, scared of what his answer might be.

Once more he peers into my eyes as if searching for something. A struggle plays out across his aged face, then he says, 'I can't tell.'

'What do you mean, you can't tell?' I say, confused by his response. 'Are you saying that you won't tell me, or that you don't know? There's a difference.'

Caleb drops his gaze to the two sparks circling one another within the capstone and falls silent.

'You're a Soul Seer!' I exclaim in frustration. 'Surely you of all people should know!'

'I've been proved wrong before,' he admits ruefully.

I try to meet his eye. 'How so?'

But the Soul Seer continues to stare fixedly at the capstone, his jaw tense, his brow furrowed. 'It doesn't matter!' he replies through clenched teeth. 'What's done is done. I'm not even sure I believe in the Prophecy any more!'

'OK,' I reply gently, taken aback by his uncharacteristic anger. 'Still, Soul Prophecy or not, Tanas *has* to be destroyed. Surely it's our only hope if the Light of Humanity is to be saved.'

'No. It isn't.' Caleb shakes his head firmly. 'We can hide and thereby protect the Light.'

'But for how much longer?' I argue, thinking of how our numbers have been whittled down over the centuries.

'For as long as we have to!' he replies sharply. 'Whatever happens, I will not risk your soul or your Light ever again – or the souls of *any* of the remaining First Ascendants!'

With that, Caleb picks up his cane and walks determinedly out of the pyramid.

As his footsteps echo away, I stand alone with my thoughts, a storm of emotions brewing in me. Added to my rage at Tanas for killing my Soul Twin Lakeisha and extinguishing her Light there's bewilderment as to where her Protector was in her time of need. There's still the raw grief over the murder of my present-life parents and at the same time concern for the unknown fate of my Soul Mother and Father. There's the shock too of Caleb's confession that he's made a mistake interpreting the Soul Prophecy in the past . . . and a frustration boiling over into fury at our apparent powerlessness in the face of the relentless Incarnates.

Caught up in these chaotic thoughts, I clench my fists and want to let out a scream so loud that it'll shatter the glass panes in the pyramid.

Gradually, though, the turmoil subsides. At least I now understand why Caleb is so cautious, so over-protective of his charges. Haven is his means of keeping the surviving First Ascendants and their souls safe.

It's also his way of avoiding the final and inevitable battle between the Darkness and the Light.

But now that I can recall my Soul Twin and how she died, I will no longer allow Tanas and his Hunters to pick us off, one by one, until the Light is ultimately extinguished. Soul Prophecy or not, I am determined to make a stand. To stop Tanas, once and for all, and end his reign of terror.

No longer will I run. No longer will I hide. No longer will I be the hunted!

41

My resolve hardened, I leave the Sun Room to look for Phoenix. He's the one person who understands me best and will stand by my side, no matter how great the danger. I just need to convince him of my plan.

Crossing the plaza, I enter the glass atrium and discover the Protectors' quarters are abuzz with activity. Clara, Tasha's Protector, is addressing a group of four Warriors, including the Scandinavian twins I'd seen in Goggins' martial arts class the day I arrived. Today they look like a couple of ranch hands, kitted out in matching denim jeans, checked shirts and rawhide cowboy hats perched atop their tangles of straw-blond hair. I briefly wonder if these two Warriors have the same connection I had with my Soul Twin, or they just happen to be born together in this life.

'Goggins wants a round-the-clock patrol of the perimeter,' Clara is telling the group. 'Report *any* unusual activity, however insignificant.'

As the four Warriors march off to begin their sentry duty, I approach Clara, a tall, willowy woman with a bob of black hair streaked grey. Her cheekbones are well-defined, her starlit eyes wide and cat-like, and her skin porcelain smooth, lending her the poise and looks of a former model. But when she turns towards me, I see for the first time the full extent of the vicious scar the FSB Hunter inflicted on her, a jagged red line that runs from her right eye to the tip of her pointed chin.

'You must be Genna,' she says with a lopsided grin. 'The cause of all this excitement.'

I smile awkwardly, embarrassed by her dig at me. 'I'm sorry –'

'I'm sure you are,' she says curtly, cutting me off. 'But nothing we do or say can change the past.'

Feeling my cheeks flush hot, I bow my head in shame.

'However,' Clara continues, 'everything we do *now* changes the future. So whatever the fallout from your little expedition, I want you to know I think Phoenix is fortunate to have you as his First Ascendant. Our strength lies in our loyalty to one another.'

I glance up, surprised. 'Thanks,' I say, reassured that I did the right thing by my Protector and that someone else thinks so too. 'Do you know where Phoenix is?' I ask.

'Training ground,' she replies, pointing down the atrium's main corridor. 'At least that's where I saw him last.'

'Thank you,' I say, and hurry away. I pass the lecture hall where Goggins is briefing another group of Protectors and Warriors. From the volume of his voice, it's evident he's still in a foul mood. I duck under the door's small window, not wishing to become the target of his wrath a second time. At the end of the corridor I see Tarek hunkered down in his shielded computer room. Through the mesh-lined window, I spot him analysing the feed from several surveillance cameras positioned around Haven, the abandoned mining town and the surrounding mountain range. From a quick glance there doesn't appear to be any sign of Tanas or her Hunters and I allow myself a little hope that Empote has been successful and has led the Incarnates on a false trail away from Haven.

Then I bump into the red-haired Lena carrying an assault rifle that looks three times too big for her. 'Wow, that's some weapon!' I remark.

Lena grins like a mother with a newborn baby. 'An FN Scar 17S,' she says proudly, patting the barrel. 'A high-end adaptive automatic rifle, weighing only three point one nine kilograms. Shoots over six hundred rounds per minute, with an effective firing range of up to nine hundred metres!'

I nod and try to look suitably impressed. 'You certainly know a lot about guns,' I say.

'I was a sniper in the US Special Forces,' she explains. 'In a former life, obviously.'

'Obviously,' I reply with a good-humoured smirk.

'Well, I'd best strip and clean her,' says Lena, opening the door to the firing range. 'We might need her firepower sooner than we think.'

Spread out on a long table in the range are several other high-calibre weapons, varying from pistols to rifles to what looks like a grenade launcher. Reassured by the sheer amount of firepower Lena clearly considers necessary to defend Haven, yet unsettled by it too, I wish her good luck and head outside to the training ground.

At first glance Phoenix isn't anywhere to be seen and I wonder if he might be in the Glimmer Dome. Then I spot him by the aircraft hangar with Jude. They're talking intently, almost nose to nose, their eyes locked. Then to my surprise they embrace. As I watch them wrapped in each other's arms, my stomach plunges like a lead weight and my throat feels tight and constricted. Phoenix has been evasive about his past history with Jude . . . now I know why. *She* must've been the reason he didn't get in contact with me when he first returned to the States. Feeling as if I've been punched in the gut, I turn and head back towards the main building.

However, as I'm opening the door to the rear entrance, I hear Phoenix shout, 'Genna!'

I hesitate, halfway across the threshold, wondering if I should pretend I haven't heard him. But his footsteps rapidly approach. 'Genna!' he calls again.

'Oh . . . hi,' I say weakly as he runs up to me. I notice Jude slink off into the hangar and disappear.

'Were you looking for me?' Phoenix asks with an over-bright smile.

'Hm, yes, I was –' I reply, turning away so he doesn't catch the wounded look on my face – 'but it doesn't matter now.'

He reaches out and gently rests a hand on my shoulder. 'You OK?'

'Yeah . . . fine,' I say, trying hard to suppress my hurt feelings. I tell myself I've no reason to be jealous. Phoenix has always maintained that he's my Protector, first and foremost. But I feel that our closeness, the link between our souls, is something special . . . or at least I hoped it was.

'Are you still upset about what Goggins said?' he asks. 'Because you don't –'

'No, it isn't that,' I say, and, deciding to press on with the reason I came looking for him in the first place, I start to explain. 'I've just had a Glimmer in the Sun Room and learned about my twin sister, Lakeisha. How Tanas ritually k-killed –' my voice hitches as my grief and anger rise once more – 'how Tanas killed her. I felt our souls being *ripped* apart, her Light extinguished! The pain was like nothing I've ever experienced before –'

'My precious Genna,' he says, moving to draw me into his arms and comfort me. 'That's one Glimmer you *don't* want to recall.'

For a moment I almost surrender to his strength and protection. But then I step away, straightening to look him in the eye.

'I need your help,' I tell him firmly.

'Sure . . . anything for you,' he replies, a touch taken aback.

'I want you to train me as a Soul Warrior.'

Phoenix blinks. 'But you're a First Ascendant . . .'

'I'm well aware of that!' I reply, crossing my arms. 'But I need to be able to fight Tanas and his Hunters. I want you to guide me through my past lives, find the Touchstones in the Glimmer Dome that will migrate the necessary skills to me – anything that could help me in our battle against the Incarnates.'

Phoenix's eyes narrow. 'Is this Genna talking, or Miyoko-san?' he says. 'Why are you suddenly so keen to take the fight to Tanas?'

'Because he killed my Soul Twin!' I exclaim, my tone suddenly fierce. 'And my parents, and countless First Ascendants and Protectors, and he'll go on killing us and obliterating our souls until we put a stop to him.'

Phoenix holds up a hand to placate my fury. 'I appreciate your reasons, Genna,' he says cautiously, 'but Goggins and Caleb won't like the idea. It puts you directly in harm's way.'

'I'm in harm's way whatever happens,' I argue. 'You once told me I had a warrior spirit. *You* were the one who reminded me of my past life as a samurai, a time when as Miyoko I hardly needed your protection at all.'

'That's not the point, Genna. I want to protect you,' he says ardently. 'It's my duty.'

'I get that,' I say, softening slightly. 'But that shouldn't be a reason for me not to fight for myself – for the Light. Besides, *you* set me on this path in the first place. The Asani I knew was only too keen to teach me how to wield an axe!'

Phoenix fixes me with his starlit gaze, a questioning look in his eyes. 'Ever since your healing in the desert you've been different. What happened to you in the *wickiup*?'

'Nothing,' I reply with an over-casual shrug.

But he continues to stare at me as if searching my soul. 'What's Empote said to you? Does this have anything to do with the Prophecy?'

I hold his gaze a moment longer, then cave in. 'OK . . .' I admit. 'I had a *su'mach*. And now Empote believes I'm the one foretold in the Soul Prophecy.'

'Are you?' counters Phoenix, his expression earnest and expectant.

'How am I supposed to know?' I say irritably. 'Even Caleb doesn't know that! Or at least he won't commit to an answer.'

Phoenix goes quiet, apparently pondering this. Eventually he says, 'While I'm in no position to proclaim anyone as the one promised by the Soul Prophecy, I do know I believe in *you*. I've always suspected there's something special about your soul. That's why I need to protect it at all costs.'

'So you'll train me to fight?'

Phoenix nods and grins craftily. 'I believe I've been training you in all the lives we've had for this moment,' he replies. 'It was just a matter of waiting until your soul was ready.'

42

I stand with Phoenix on the raised tatami-matted platform in the centre of the Glimmer Dome's vast circular chamber. The room has the soft silence of a library and the untold promise of a secret museum. Beams of muted sunlight shine down through the roof's stained-glass windows, haloing us in an almost mystical glow.

'So, where do you want to start?' asks Phoenix.

My eager gaze flits across the five levels brimming with artefacts from all the ages until my eye is caught by a pair of samurai swords on a stand. 'With those,' I say, grinning.

Phoenix ascends the spiral staircase to the first floor and collects the two swords. Slipping one into his belt, he returns to the platform and presents the other to me with a ceremonial bow.

I weigh the katana in my hand, the five-hundred-year-old weapon feeling strange yet vaguely familiar at the same time. 'Phoenix, you said that once I'd experienced a Glimmer I'd always remember that particular skill in this life. But my samurai abilities seem to have faded.'

'That can happen,' admits Phoenix. 'Like any skill, you need to keep practising . . . or else revisit the Glimmer to refresh your mind. Of course, the level of skill depends on when and where in a past life you drop into during the Glimmer.'

He unsheathes his sword and assumes a fighting stance. Mirroring his actions, I draw my own blade. 'So, what now?' I ask, feeling awkward as we face each other on the dais as if for a duel.

'*Saisho no chi ni*, Miyoko-san,' he replies.

The mention of my samurai name stirs a memory deep within me –

'To first blood,' announces my bald-headed sensei, who sits cross-legged upon a zabuton cushion set on a wooden dais at the far end of the dojo. His long wispy beard hangs in a curtain from his chin, a waterfall of white against the black silk kimono wrapped tightly round his wiry frame.

I glance over at my elderly teacher in astonishment. 'You want us to cut *each other?'*

My sensei gives a small yet undeniable nod of his head. 'Just as one cannot learn to swim on dry land, one cannot expect to wield a samurai sword effectively without duelling for real.'

I turn back to my sparring partner, Takeo, a stocky young samurai with a square jaw and wide nose, his sleek black hair tied into a topknot. As a wandering ronin, he'd offered his services to my father and for the past year had dedicated himself to training alongside me. We've fought many times before with wooden bokken, with bo staffs, with tonfa, with fists and feet . . . but never with the intention of actually hurting one another.

'I'll hold back,' I promise him under my breath as we bow.

'Don't,' he replies, drawing his sword and taking up a fighting stance. 'The ninja Tora Tsume won't with you.'

Steeling myself for the duel ahead, I unsheathe my own katana. It gleams like liquid silver in my hand, its blade so sharp that it seems to cut the eye by merely looking at it. I fear that I may seriously injure my friend if I'm not careful.

But Takeo doesn't appear to have any such qualms. With unforgiving speed, he launches straight into an attack, the tip of his blade almost slicing through my ivory-white gi. I deflect his sword with my own blade and retaliate with a thrust to his stomach. Deftly evading my attack, he kicks me against a pillar and swings round to cut off my head. I'm stunned by the ferocity of his fighting and only at the last second do I manage to duck, his blade embedding itself in the wooden pillar where my head had been a moment before.

'Takeo!' I cry. 'You're supposed to protect me, not kill me!'

'You ducked,' he says matter-of-factly, tugging his katana free.

A soft chuckle emanates from my sensei. 'Miyoko-san, your friend is now your enemy,' he reminds me. 'Don't let your emotions cloud your warrior mind. Even the slightest hesitation in your attack could be your undoing.'

Heeding my sensei's advice, I suppress my feelings for Takeo and imagine him to be Tora Tsume, the black-eyed ninja who haunts my every step. I let loose with a series of flowing cuts, lightning-quick slashes and piercing thrusts.

Forced to retreat, Takeo dodges, ducks and deflects each attack. Our swords clash, the steel singing out through the dojo. My sensei nods with approval at the skilful battle, all his countless hours of instruction proving their worth. As Takeo tries to disarm me with a twist of his blade, I counter his move, my own blade flicking upwards, the kissaki catching him under the chin –

Phoenix dabs at a thin line of blood that seeps from a fresh cut to his face.

Guiltily I lower my katana, horrified to discover that I've injured my Protector. 'Sorry! I didn't mean to –'

'Don't,' he says, grinning as he echoes his previous incarnation's words. 'I'd be disappointed if you didn't beat me again.'

'Again?' I pant, out of breath.

Glancing at my katana, I notice Phoenix's blood smeared on the blade and it dawns on me why my pulse is racing so fast. *We were fighting for real!*

'Are you saying we *shared* that Glimmer?' I ask, incredulous.

'Yes, we've just duelled,' Phoenix explains, sheathing his sword. 'By glimmering in the Dome, we can relive the moment from a previous life in this life and thereby reinforce our skills.'

With a sharp twist of my wrist, I flick his blood from my blade – *chiburi* – and in one fluid motion resheathe my sword – *nōtō*. In these simple yet instinctive actions, I realize Miyoko's martial art skills are once more a part of me, as if I'd trained all my present life, the sword now feeling like an extension of my own arm.

'It worked!' I exclaim. 'I *know* kenjutsu.'

Phoenix nods. 'And you'll soon know so much more, Genna,' he says encouragingly. 'It's just a matter of recalling the Glimmers.'

Taking the katana from me, he returns the swords to their display stand. 'Are you up for another?' he calls down from the first level.

'Absolutely,' I reply. Searching the Glimmer Dome, my gaze falls this time on what looks to be a wooden bow with a rounded gourd attached to one end. Although it appears to be a musical instrument rather than a weapon, for some reason I feel drawn to it. 'That one,' I say, pointing.

'The berimbau?' he replies with a wistful smile. 'Good choice.'

He joins me on the platform. Holding the instrument in one hand and a stick and shaker in the other, he begins to strike the string, beating out an insistent rhythm and sounding a simple yet compelling tune. He then begins to chant a Portuguese ballad –

'Nem tudo que reluz é ouro,
Nem tudo que balança cai . . .'

I sway and shift my feet in time to the corrido song, mirroring my opponent's movements. We kick up dust from the bare patch of ground on which my small band of escaped slaves and I practise our daily capoeira. Our quilombo village may be located deep in the Brazilian jungle, but as fugitives we're all keenly aware that the colonial bush captains are always on the hunt for us – we're never completely safe. Hence our morning martial art training.

Standing in a circular roda around us, my fellow capoeiristas clap and sing as I cartwheel out of the way of Gana's sweeping leg attack. Lithe and loose as an anaconda, he whirls in with a high kick and I duck low, spinning round to strike him in the head with my instep. As he bends away like the bow of the berimbau, I hear a warning cry and those in the roda immediately scatter into the jungle.

Gana and I cease our mock fight, but we are too late to flee; a unit of armed colonial soldiers charge into our quilombo from all directions. Leading the ambush is a black-eyed capitães-do-mato on horseback, his uniform stained and muddy from weeks scouring the jungle.

'Maria!' shouts the bush captain with a triumphant grin.

'I don't answer to my slave name!' I say, spitting on to the ground. Then standing tall and proud, I declare, 'My true name is Sabina.'

'Well . . . Sabina, there's nowhere you can hide that I won't find you!' he replies.

'You haven't caught me yet,' I shoot back defiantly.

'Oh, but from where I'm sitting I already have,' declares the captain smugly as his soldiers rapidly encircle us both.

'Then you come and get me,' I goad.

He nods a command to his soldiers and they close in. Gana and I begin to sway, keeping ourselves in constant motion to avoid becoming an easy target. As the soldiers surge forward, I become a whirling dervish, spinning, leaping and lashing out with my feet. So too does Gana. Executing an aú batido, *I perform a half-cartwheel and catch the nearest soldier by surprise with a kick to the face. The next one is treated to an* armada pulada, *my spinning aerial kick breaking his jaw. The third is swept off his feet with a* corta capim, *cutting him down like a blade of grass before he even gets close. The fourth soldier is more nimble than the others. He leaps over my leg reap . . . but it was a planned feint on my part. Dropping down to my hands, I arch my other leg over my back and attack with the* escorpião, *my foot striking the soldier's neck like the sting of a scorpion's tail. He crumples to the ground as –*

I discover myself performing a one-handed handstand in the middle of the Dome's platform.

'Impressive!' says Phoenix, setting aside the berimbau.

With a twirl of my legs, I flip back to my feet. 'Well, that's something I didn't learn in gymnastics class,' I say breathlessly, exhilarated by my rediscovered ability.

'Capoeira may look like an acrobatic dance, but in truth it's a deceptively effective martial art,' explains Phoenix. 'As you've just glimmered, a skilled capoeirista is capable of fighting off multiple opponents at once. In fact, I remember one Portuguese soldier complaining that it takes a whole platoon to capture a single quilombo warrior!'

'Well, I certainly feel like I could defeat an army!' I say with a grin, and on impulse I perform an *aú sem mão*, cartwheeling without hands. But, as I land, my knees go weak and I crumple to the floor. All of a sudden my body feels sapped of energy and a wave of dizziness washes over me. 'Wh-what's happening to me?' I gasp.

Phoenix is at my side in a moment, his arms cradling me. 'Genna, you have just taken on a lifetime of training,' he explains. 'You're bound to feel fatigued. That's why you shouldn't glimmer too much in one session. You can easily overload yourself.' He examines my drained face and checks my pulse. 'We should call it quits for today.'

'No, I'm fine,' I insist, shrugging off my exhaustion and getting to my feet with renewed determination. 'Tanas and her Hunters could attack at any time. I *must* be ready.'

43

'You're going to burn out,' Phoenix warns as I collapse to all fours on the platform for the third time in a row. My brow is slick with sweat, my hair matted, my muscles aching. I've lost track of time, the multiple Glimmers distorting my perception. A few hours . . . a whole day . . . or several lifetimes may have passed since we began our session in the dome. All I know is that it feels like I've run a dozen marathons back to back.

Peeling off the *zodog*, I hand Phoenix the collarless blue short-sleeved jacket that triggered my Glimmer as Buri, a Mongolian warrior skilled in the ancient art of Bökh. I'd been wrestling another man at a Naadam festival on the steppe, competing in honour of Genghis Khan himself. The lengthy bout had been going in my favour until my foot slipped on the dewy grass and my opponent had surged forward like an angry ox. Driving me off balance, he buried me head first into the hard ground with a valley drop throw. The shame of that defeat still flushes hot in my cheeks, yet I also recall the immense skill, stamina and strength required to wrestle like a true Mongolian warrior.

However, not all the Glimmers today have proven as useful. While a small round *paricha* shield gave me a welcome reminder of my training with my elderly and sharp-witted guru in Kalari, a promising iron longsword disappointingly revealed me to be a lowly squire to a medieval Germanic knight, my duties restricted to carrying said sword, polishing his armour and taking care of his flatulent horse! A curved *koummya* dagger from the thirteenth century prompted a brief and brutal flashback of my mugging and murder in the maze-like alleyways of the medina in Marrakech. And a gladiator's trident was one of several weapons that failed to trigger any Glimmer at all.

After a while, on Phoenix's suggestion, we moved on to more innocuous Touchstones. Among these, a conical straw hat reminded me of the intense heat I endured harvesting rice as a paddy farmer in Northern Thailand some eight centuries ago. Then a tankard from the early Tudor period gave me a Glimmer of my miserable time as a serving wench in an English coaching inn, while a battered rolling pin took me back to my busy life as a cook in the stifling kitchens of the castle of Charles the Bald, the ninth-century king of West Francia. Although none of those Glimmers will be particularly helpful to me in a fight, at least I can add threshing rice, pouring a pint of beer and baking bread to my skill set.

'Let's get some rest,' suggests Phoenix, hanging up the *zodog* on the clothes rail alongside army uniforms, vintage dresses and fur-lined jackets I've yet to try on. 'We can continue again tomorrow.'

The light in the Glimmer Dome is weakening as the sun begins its descent through the desert sky. Rainbow-coloured beams slant in at an angle through the stained-glass windows, leaving one side of the dome in shadow.

'One last Glimmer,' I insist. As shattered as I am, I'm addicted to the adrenaline rush of experiencing a past life, of remembering a forgotten skill, of rediscovering former knowledge. But most enticing is the fact that I'm learning more about who I truly am. Each life recalled is another piece of the puzzle, another layer of my eternal soul.

Phoenix assesses my condition as I struggle back to my feet. 'Either you're a glutton for punishment or you have a rare ability to absorb Glimmers. I don't know any Protector or Warrior who'd be able to keep going for as long as you have. Two, maybe three Glimmers a day at most is the usual limit.'

'I could keep this up all night,' I say, swaying slightly.

He gives me a sceptical look, yet nonetheless relents. 'So, what Touchstone takes your eye this time?'

'You choose,' I reply.

Phoenix's gaze sweeps over the vast array of artefacts on the various levels, passing over gleaming swords, racks of armour, antique guns, ornate sceptres, gold coins, metal-studded shields and countless other objects recovered from the wide sweep of history. Eventually his gaze fixes on something on the fifth level and he grins to himself. As he climbs the spiral staircase, I wonder with growing anticipation which weapon has caught his eye.

But on returning to the platform all he appears to be carrying is a slim, folded-up fan. He opens it with a flourish of his wrist, revealing a magnificent flaming phoenix entwined with a Chinese red dragon upon a golden background.

'A taijishan from the late Song dynasty,' he announces in an excited tone. 'The dragon represents the masculine yang, and the phoenix the feminine yin. Together they symbolize harmony and balance, and are considered to bring good luck.'

'A fan?' I say, somewhat underwhelmed by his choice. 'It's beautiful . . . but how will this help me fight Tanas?'

An amused look plays in Phoenix's eyes. 'You asked me the very same question last time . . .' he reminds me, holding the fan up in front of my face. The dragon and phoenix shimmer in the fading light and seemingly out of nowhere a warm breeze, scented with the sweet fragrance of peach blossom, ruffles my hair. As he lowers the fan –

– a fist comes flying at me. I barely have time to duck when I hear a snap like the wings of a great bird. Startled by the noise, I lose focus and the iron-edged fan, now a slim yet sturdy rod, strikes me hard on my head.

'Ow!' I yelp, my skull ringing as blossom petals fall around me.

Then there's another sharp crack and the dragon and phoenix flash before my eyes. My gaze is instinctually drawn to them – and I'm rewarded by an unseen kick to the shin.

'Argggh!' I yell, hopping on one leg and trying not to lose my balance on the uneven paving of the temple's courtyard. 'Stop, Feiyen, stop! This isn't in the spirit of harmony!'

Feiyen closes the fan with a snap, a playful grin on her slender face, her eyes glinting with mischief. 'See, Yuán? A fan isn't merely a shade for the sun or to cool the air, or even to conceal one's expression. In taiji, it can be used to hide attacks, startle an opponent, distract them, and even become a weapon itself –'

I rub my throbbing head and blink; Feiyen's soft features revert to Phoenix's defined cheeks and strong jawline before my very eyes. 'I guess I've learned my lesson twice,' I say, noticing that Phoenix is holding the taijishan high over his head in a fighting stance.

'As the boy Yuán, you always underestimated the fan as a weapon,' he says, lowering his guard. 'But, as we trained together at the Purple Cloud Temple in the Wudang mountains, you came to appreciate the subtle yet powerful martial art of taiji.' He wafts the golden fan like a butterfly across my face and I feel a chill ripple along my skin, my breath misting in front of me –

The thin mountain air is cool and fresh, the snow settling like wisps of cloud upon the temple's curved roof as we prepare for our pushing hands practice of tuishou. *Rooting myself with a low, wide stance, I raise my hands into a guard and face Feiyen. With our wrists lightly touching, we rock smoothly back and forth.*

Our arms entwined and undulating like waves, I watch her carefully, looking for signs of an attack as well as any opportunity to unbalance her. But I soon lose myself in her gentle rhythm, mesmerized by her graceful frame. Without warning, she shoves me hard with an explosive release of fajin *and I land squarely on my back in the snow.*

'Don't use your eyes,' she chides, her breath fogging in the chill air. 'Listen for my intention with your body. Feel my energy!'

My cheeks red with embarrassment rather than cold, I dust off the snow and take up position again. As we recommence our slow circular dance of pushing hands, I try to sense her flow of energy, her jin.

Feiyen steps nearer, closing the space between us. The icy air around me seems to warm and I begin to wonder if I'm feeling her jin *or if it's just that I'm so close to her . . . All of a sudden she twists her shoulder into me, knocking me off balance, and I'm sent skidding across the courtyard on my backside.*

'Don't lose your centre, Yuán,' she chides. 'Be like a reed. Remember: the soft and pliable will defeat the hard and strong.'

'But how can I predict your attacks?' I ask, dusting the snow off myself yet again. 'They happen so fast and with such power.'

'You must give yourself up entirely to follow the other,' she explains, helping me to my feet. 'Then you will sense my intent.'

Nodding, I assume my wide-footed stance and imagine myself to be a reed in the wind. Rooted yet supple. Once more our wrists touch and I feel an unmistakable tingle pass between us. Feiyen smiles and I wonder if she feels it too. Following her flow, I surrender myself to her movements and slowly begin to sense each push before it comes, each subtle shift in her balance . . . even the rise of fajin, *swelling like a wave within her . . .*

I meet her attack, yielding yet not losing my balance. With a deft twist of my body, I redirect her energy away and let it exhaust itself before I come back with my own forceful push of hands.

'Hǎo shēnshǒu!' *praises Feiyen with a smile, as she now leans away from my attack.*

Our bodies fall back into sync and we seem to become one. In the ebb and flow of our sparring, I feel our energies entwine. Yin meeting yang. The increasing warmth between us is undeniable, the snow no longer feeling cold as we sway ever closer –

44

Phoenix and I stop, no more than a breath apart from each other. Our eyes are locked, our bodies a mirror image. The moment seems to stretch forever. We stand as still as a pair of Greek statues, wrapped in each other's arms, the fading light in the dome reflecting softly in our starlit eyes. My brain seems to have been hijacked by my emotions. A heady cocktail of feelings that makes my pulse race and my skin flush hot. As I continue to hold my breath, I'm overcome by the strongest sense of déjà vu, that we've been in this situation before. Not just in the courtyard of the Purple Cloud Temple back in twelfth-century China, but many, many times in our numerous past lives together.

We remain entwined. For a moment I question whether Yuán's yearning for Feiyen has transferred to me along with the lessons in taiji. I'd be lying to myself if I didn't admit that my feelings for Phoenix are the same. If anything, my feelings are even stronger in this present life. A brief Glimmer flashes before my eyes . . . *walking hand in hand with him on a golden beach, the sun warming our bare skin as we wade out to a secluded rock in the blue waters of the Pacific Ocean* . . . It seems whichever way round our yin and yang happen to be, our souls are forever entwined. Abandoning all caution, I decide to make the first move and lean in.

But Phoenix pulls away. 'I-I can't,' he stutters, a conflicted look in his eyes.

My heart thuds to a stop, his rejection stinging. I peer into his sapphire-blue eyes, sensing the struggle going on in his soul. 'Is it because of Jude?' I ask, already knowing the answer.

He frowns. 'What do you mean?'

I disentangle myself from him. 'Don't worry,' I say, trying hard to keep my tone even and detached, 'I saw you in the aircraft hangar. It's obvious you two have a history together and . . . from what I can gather, a future.'

Phoenix stares in puzzlement at me, apparently dumbfounded by the idea. Then he laughs. 'What? You think me and Jude are an item?'

I nod, swallowing hard on the truth as if it were a stone, and blink away the tears that threaten to come.

'Heaven forbid!' he exclaims with a nauseated grimace. 'She's my *sister*.'

'Your sister?' I gasp. 'But you don't look like her at all.'

'No, not in this life,' Phoenix explains. 'She's my First Sister, from our time in the Hakalan tribe.'

My jaw drops. 'Why didn't you tell me before?' I say, their constant bickering now beginning to make some sense.

Phoenix shrugs. 'Well . . . we haven't exactly had time to chat since you rescued me.'

I give him a reproachful look. 'We had more than enough time on our night hike across the desert,' I point out.

'OK. I guess so . . .' Phoenix admits, 'but I really didn't want to get into it then, not with Jude right behind me. Our relationship is *complicated*, to say the least.'

'Like the relationship with your Soul Father, Goggins?' I ask.

'No, that one's relatively straightforward,' replies Phoenix, a scowl darkening his mood. 'He's always mad at me, whatever life we meet in.'

'And why's that?'

'Because I'm still alive,' he says, his tone strangely flat.

I frown, bewildered by his reasoning. 'Isn't that a good thing?' I offer. 'Especially for a Soul Protector.'

'Not in his eyes,' explains Phoenix through gritted teeth. 'Not when he lost his first-born son – my First Brother Jabali – to Tanas. I think he'd rather it had been me.'

My hand flies to my mouth in shock. 'Oh, I'm so sorry.' I notice the pain of rejection in his eyes. 'I didn't know you had a brother . . . I don't recall him in any of my Glimmers.'

'It's OK, it was all a long time ago,' says Phoenix sadly. He sits down on the edge of the platform, sets the fan to one side and stares off into the now-gloomy recesses of the dome.

I join him and we sit for a moment in silence, our legs dangling over the edge. Then Phoenix continues, 'Ever since Jabali's passing, my Soul Father's been angry. I guess it's what fuels him. Keeps him going over the countless millennia to fight for First Ascendant souls and battle Tanas and his Hunters.'

As Phoenix gazes bitterly at the lengthening shadows, I remember what Viviana told me about Goggins: *He's more of a hammer than a scalpel . . . I have to remind myself he only has my best interests at heart.* I lay my hand gently on Phoenix's. 'He's probably just afraid of losing you too,' I suggest.

'Well, he has a funny way of showing it,' mutters Phoenix, his eyes filling.

We lapse back into silence. As we sit side by side, hand in hand, I think of the loving and close relationship I had with my father in this life and realize how blessed I've been. Then I wonder if Phoenix's difficult and tense relationship with his father may have something to do with his reluctance to open his heart to me. I pick up the taijishan and gently spread its spines, revealing the dragon and phoenix bound in their eternal dance. Twirling the fan in my fingers, I ask, 'If Jude isn't the reason for you holding back with me, what is?'

Still stubbornly staring off into the thickening gloom, he replies, 'Because kissing you would be . . . a mistake.'

I snap the fan shut. 'What?' This answer has stung me more than the idea he might have been with Jude. 'How on earth could it be a *mistake*?'

Phoenix turns to me, his expression strangely impassive, formal like a soldier on guard. 'Because my duty is to protect you, first and foremost.'

'Yes, I *know* that. You've told me that before,' I say, exasperated. 'But don't you *want* to kiss me?'

'No – I mean yes – of course I do –' he replies, suddenly flustered, 'but it complicates matters. I'm here to protect you, not fall in love with you . . .'

'What about Fiji then?' I say, reminding him of the tranquil life I'd glimmered of us long ago on an island off the Fijian coast.

'Fiji was different! Besides, you were betrothed to the son of the chief of the next village,' he replies, his tone evasive.

I give him a look. 'From what I remember, that didn't concern you when we were on Sunset Rock.'

A smile plays on his lips. 'OK, I admit it – there have been lives when we've been close . . . too close.' He shakes his head, clearly disappointed with himself. 'But just as a bodyguard should never get involved with their principal, so a Soul Protector should not cross that line with a First Ascendant.'

'The two of us being together in Fiji didn't seem to affect how well you protected me,' I argue. 'In fact, I felt safer.'

Phoenix looks at me. There's anger in his eyes, but not at me. Rather, at himself. 'We were lucky then,' he explains. 'The island was remote enough in those days that the Hunters never found you. But there've been other times we weren't so fortunate. You already know how close Tanas came to ritually killing you as a Cheyenne. If I hadn't been asleep at your side that morning, I might have spotted him and his bounty hunters in time for us to escape. That's why I'll no longer compromise my role as your Protector. I *can't* jeopardize your soul like that again.'

'Well, that's your view,' I say, opening up the fan once more and looking at the exquisitely painted image of the entwined dragon and phoenix, 'but I see our bond as our strength.'

With the gentlest of touches, Phoenix turns my face towards his, his anger at himself melting into a deep tenderness for me. 'Believe me, Genna,' he whispers, the struggle once more playing out in his eyes, 'I'd rather love you and die in this life than live a hundred lifetimes without loving you –'

'Then why don't you?' I plead.

I feel his fingers run through my hair and for a moment I believe –

'WHAT ARE YOU TWO DOING?' bawls a furious voice.

45

Startled, we both jump to our feet as Goggins strides into the Glimmer Dome, his face like thunder. Caleb limps in behind him, his lion-headed cane clicking on the floor, his wrinkled brow furrowed and his blue eyes glaring.

'Chatting,' Phoenix replies as I flick the fan shut and surreptitiously slip it into my back pocket.

Goggins eyes him sternly. 'You know the rules. The Glimmer Dome is only for Protectors and Warriors. Were you both glimmering?'

'Yes . . .' admits Phoenix, 'but Genna is different.'

'How so?' demands Goggins, placing his ham-sized fists on his hips and squaring up to Phoenix.

'She can absorb multiple Glimmers, far more than any Protector or Warrior is capable of,' he explains proudly.

'That's no reason to risk tainting her Light,' interjects Caleb, noting with a worried look my strained expression. But my pain has nothing to do with being exhausted from glimmering and more to do with being interrupted at an inopportune time.

'But Genna shines brighter than the other First Ascendants,' Phoenix argues. 'Empote sees this. Even *I* can see her aura in this life . . .' He gestures with his hand up and down my body. I examine myself but can't see what he means. '*But one Soul shines brighter and bolder than the rest; this one must ignite the spark when put to the Darkest test –*'

'Yes, all right. You don't need to recite the Prophecy to me!' snaps Caleb. 'Phoenix, you are jeopardizing Genna's Light by teaching her such things. Genna is *not* to come in here again.'

'But what if Genna is that *one true soul* foretold in the Prophecy?' persists Phoenix. 'Surely she should gain as much knowledge and as many skills as she can if we're to stand any chance of defeating Tanas? In all our incarnations together, Genna's shown herself to be special. Uniquely talented. That's why I've always tried to guide, encourage and train her. In fact, I believe –'

'SILENCE!' shouts Goggins, glaring at him. 'You've done more than enough damage as it is.'

'But what if –'

'Please! No more talk of the Prophecy,' Caleb interjects firmly. 'I forbid you to spread such rumours!'

Fuming, Phoenix assumes a tight-lipped scowl.

'But, Caleb . . .' I begin hesitantly, 'even you have said my soul shines brighter. Not that I want to be the one in the Prophecy,' I add quickly. 'But why are you so unwilling to even consider the possibility?'

'I'll show you why,' says Caleb, going over to a display stand. He rummages around in the darkness before returning with a string of prayer beads. He holds them out to me. 'Take this Touchstone and you shall see . . .'

'Can you see them yet, Kendra?' asks Alhwin, peering into the sea mist billowing like dragon's breath off the

chilly Northumbrian coast. His callused hands are clenched tightly round the pitchfork he took from his father's farm.

I shake my head in mute answer to my Protector, my blond tresses hanging in a veil over my shimmering eyes and hiding my fearful expression. My bare feet sink into the wet sand as I hold the burning torch aloft, its flames trembling almost as much as me.

'I heard these black-eyed Norsemen laid ruin to the priory on Lindisfarne,' growls the nobleman Oswald, his sword and shield at the ready. 'They spilt the monks' blood like wine on the altars and trampled their bodies underfoot like dung in the streets!'

'You need not fear the Incarnates in this life,' says our priest, Geraint the Soul Seer, as he fingers his polished prayer beads. 'For the one foretold in the Prophecy is among us.'

He nods towards Mercia, a young girl with albino-white hair and eyes as bright as stars. Surrounded by Soul Protectors and First Ascendants, she stands upon the rise, her bare arms wide and waiting for the Incarnates' coming. She too holds a flaming torch, blessed by Geraint himself, and chants a soft prayer as melodious as the dawn calls of a song thrush.

'These devils shall not bring their Darkness upon us any more,' Geraint promises. 'For she is the soul to ignite the spark!'

Out of the mist a sinister silhouette emerges, its body low to the water, its spindly limbs stretched out like spider's legs. The creak of oars and their rhythmic swash in the waves grow louder. Then a carved dragon's head pierces the mist and the Viking longship beaches on the shoreline.

As its oars are stowed, we all tense up in nervous anticipation. After century upon century of running and hiding, we are making a stand against Tanas and his Hunters.

The longship rocks ever so slightly, shifting in the sand. Then a thunderous battle cry resounds as a hundred black-eyed, axe-wielding Vikings leap from the vessel and charge up the beach towards us.

'NOW!' shouts Geraint. 'Ignite the spark!'

Mercia throws her hallowed torch to the ground. I do the same, along with every other First Ascendant. The oil-and-wood-filled trenches hidden under the sand burst into flame. The blaze roars up, consuming the invaders: the consecrated fire prepared in a painstaking ritual to burn away their inherent darkness, cleanse their souls and guide them back to the Light. We watch in hope and horror as the axe-wielding figures flail in the flames. Their bloodcurdling screams fill the air –

But these are no screams of pain.

They're howls of fury!

Charging out of the inferno, their bearskin cloaks ablaze, the Incarnate invaders are untouched by the consecrated flames. Baying like wolves and foaming at the mouth, they storm up the beach and set on us in a fit of frenzied violence.

'Defend your Ascendants!' yells Oswald as our plan, so carefully laid, fails before it has even truly begun.

Axes swinging, the Viking horde set about slaughtering us like lambs. Oswald's shield is shattered in a single blow. Ducking a lethal swipe to his head, Alhwin jabs his pitchfork into a shield-maiden's stomach, but her chain mail blocks the wooden prongs and he's kicked brutally in the chest for his efforts.

Her long braids alight with flames, the fearsome shield-maiden now lashes out at me. With a merciless punch to my jaw, she splits my lip and knocks me to the ground. Then sitting astride my body, she raises her hook-bladed axe to cleave me in half. I make a desperate grab for its handle. As I try to wrestle the weapon from my attacker's grasp, I glimpse a mountain-sized Viking stride up to Mercia. His fur cloak is a ball of fire and he brandishes an axe so large it looks like it could fell a tree in one strike. The scythe-like blade glints in the blaze, revealing a swathe of occult runes etched into the iron.

Mercia holds up her pale hands in virtuous defiance, her sea-blue eyes blazing bright as the sun. 'I AM THE PROPHECY!' *she declares.* 'I AM THE LIGHT!'

Calling upon all her soul's energy, she focuses her beaming gaze upon the Viking. Her skin of translucent alabaster shines with a divine radiance, her gleaming white hair aglow, as if her whole being was comprised of pure Light. 'I AM THE SPARK THAT WILL DEFEAT THE DARKNESS!'

The Viking throws up his arms to shield his black eyes from the glare and staggers back in pain . . . but already Mercia's Light is fading all too quickly, allowing the Viking to regain his strength. Releasing a cold bitter laugh, the Incarnate leader invokes an archaic spell of his own and with a swipe of his mighty bewitched axe he decapitates Mercia where she stands.

'NO!' cries Geraint, a moment before he too loses his head. His body crumples into the sand, his string of prayer beads crushed under the Viking warrior's feet.

Overcome with despair, I feel the strength in my arms drain away. The shield-maiden wrenches the axe handle from my weakened grip and brings the blade down –

But before she can land the killing blow, a pitchfork comes crashing over her head. Stunned, the shield-maiden collapses on top of me. Then Alhwin is there, his face smeared with blood and taut with terror. He drags her off me. 'We must flee for our souls!' he shouts. 'Hurry, Kendra!'

As he grabs my hand and pulls me to my feet, I snatch up Geraint's string of prayer beads and –

– stare at them in horrified shock. The Glimmer of the Viking slaughter is so intense that I can still smell the stench of burning oil in the air, hear the cries of the butchered First Ascendants, and even taste the blood on my lips from where the shield-maiden landed her punch.

I look up from the beads to Caleb. 'These were *yours*,' I murmur.

He nods, shame colouring his cheeks. 'Because of my misjudgement in interpreting the Soul Prophecy, the First Ascendants were almost wiped out. Many Protectors lost not only their lives that night, but their souls too.'

'I was barely given a chance to fight!' Goggins mutters bitterly, grinding his fist into his palm.

'You were the nobleman, Oswald,' I say, the realization sinking in. 'But what I don't understand is how the Incarnates survived the hallowed flames. The fire trap was supposed to stop them, purify their souls, wasn't it?'

'Berserkers!' Goggins spits. 'Only too late did we discover the Incarnates weren't merely bloodthirsty Vikings in that life. They were the most vicious and formidable warriors of their kind. Rumour had told of the Berserkers' invulnerability to steel and fire, yet no one truly believed in those stories . . . until then.'

Caleb takes back the prayer beads from me. 'So, Genna, now you understand why we must hide. Why we are safest in Haven. And why we can't rely on the Soul Prophecy to save us.'

46

'It was stupid of us to risk tainting my Light,' I mutter as Phoenix and I leave the Glimmer Dome and make our way across the empty training ground. The sun is low in the evening sky, wrapping us in the first shadows of dusk. My earlier thrill at glimmering past life skills has now been marred by the recollection of our failed stand against Tanas all those centuries ago.

'No, I don't think it was stupid,' replies Phoenix. 'You need to be able to defend yourself. Especially if there's the possibility you're the Light told of in the Soul Prophecy.'

I turn on him sharply. 'How can you even entertain the idea of the Prophecy after what happened last time? Just like Caleb was wrong about Mercia, Empote is wrong about me.'

Phoenix narrows his eyes. 'Do you *really* believe that?'

I shrug wearily. 'I don't know what to believe any more. But there's every chance we're doing more harm than good to my Light.'

As we head towards the main building, what I thought was Caleb's heavy-handed approach to protecting First Ascendants now makes total sense, while my eagerness to avenge my sister's death seems foolhardy in light of our crushing defeat at the hands of the Incarnate Berserkers. Disheartened, I resign myself to Caleb's will.

'I guess we're stuck here for the rest of this life,' I conclude with a sigh.

I gaze morosely around at the fortified complex, and the Ascendants' courtyard begins to take on the oppressive air of a prison block. The Glimmer Dome, once grand and mysterious, is this evening more a mound of inaccessible dead history than an exciting doorway to past incarnations. The glass pyramid still gleams jewel-like in the evening light but it has lost much of its awe-inspiring sparkle. And the six sacred pillars ringing the valley ridge stand like stone sentinels on guard duty, their shadows lengthening with the setting sun. Even the boundary walls appear to shrink inwards. Haven suddenly feels all too small.

'It isn't a bad place to be,' Phoenix replies with forced cheeriness. 'It's secure, and at least we'll be together.'

'Yeah,' I say, glancing sidelong at him, 'but are we ... *together*?'

He answers with the smallest shake of his head. 'As long as Tanas is around,' he replies, his tone serious, 'we have to set those feelings aside, Genna, if your Light is to survive.'

'Ah ... the Light,' I say without enthusiasm, watching the sun drop towards the valley ridge.

As precious and divine as the Light is, it's starting to feel like a curse. Not only am I pursued by a ruthless and evil entity, but I'm denied the affection of someone I consider to be my soulmate. *What good is the Light without love?* I wonder.

I look longingly at Phoenix. He makes an attempt at a conciliatory smile, then breaks away from my gaze, the moment between us clearly having passed. Phoenix appears to have made up his mind. It doesn't make it any easier for me to quell my feelings for him, especially when he says one thing out loud but his eyes seem to say another.

We walk on in silence, each consumed by our own thoughts.

As we pass the hangar, I'm reminded of Jude. 'So . . .' I say, keen to move on to another topic, 'you didn't finish telling me why your relationship with Jude is complicated.'

Phoenix kicks at a loose stone. 'As you've witnessed for yourself, she and I tend to see things differently. In most lives we argue and fight tooth and nail. But when you spotted us in the hangar, we were making up, for the first time in I don't know how many lives.'

I raise an eyebrow, curious. 'What brought that on?'

He shrugs. 'In part I was thanking her for helping rescue me . . . and for finding you when I couldn't.'

'*That* wasn't your fault,' I point out. 'You were locked up!'

'I know. But it *was* my fault for leaving you unguarded, and Jude made sure to remind me of that,' he replies guiltily.

'Why's that any business of hers?' I ask.

Phoenix sighs. 'An old score to settle. You see, after Jude lost her First Ascendant to Tanas, I distanced myself from her as much as I could. I found it hard to forgive her for her mistake of not being there when her Ascendant needed her most. Our Soul Father even disowned her for a while. Ever since, Jude's been trying to prove her worth as a Warrior, to regain my respect and our father's approval. That's why she tends to be so waspish and hard on herself.'

A wave of sympathy for Jude rolls through me, my previous feelings of irritation now seeming petty. 'I can't even imagine how tough it must be to lose a First Ascendant,' I admit. 'Whose Protector was she?'

Phoenix hesitates, then turns to me with a deeply regretful look. 'Your Soul Twin's.'

I stop dead in my tracks. '*What?*' I gasp, staring at Phoenix. My sympathy for Jude evaporates in an instant as a surge of anger and grief wells up in me. 'Jude was *Aya*'s Soul Protector?'

Phoenix goes to take my hand. 'Please, don't be angry at her –'

'Angry? Why should I feel angry?' I mutter, battling to control my torrent of emotions. 'I'm outraged! She only failed to protect my *sister*!'

'I know that it must come as a shock but –'

'A *shock*?' I cry in disbelief, clenching both my fists to keep from screaming. 'I was there! I saw Aya die. I *felt* her die. I tried to save my sister that day. But you stopped me!'

'My priority had to be *your* safety, Genna,' explains Phoenix defensively. 'As I said at the time, I'm *your* Soul Protector, first and foremost. I couldn't save you both.'

'Then where was Jude?' I demand bitterly.

Phoenix lowers his gaze. 'It's not my place to say. You really need to speak with her –'

'Don't worry. I will!' I growl through clenched teeth.

At that moment the doors to the main complex fly open and Jude strides out in our direction.

'Hey! I want to talk to you!' I say, struggling to keep my tone even as I march furiously towards her.

'I need to talk to you too,' replies Jude, the gravest look on her face. 'Tanas has found us!'

47

We crowd into the lecture hall, where the screen shows a live feed from Haven's surveillance cameras. Under a blood-red sky a convoy of vehicles is gathered in the dusty streets of the abandoned mining town. At the front are sleek black SUVs, and, although unmarked, their tinted windows and uniform look scream FBI. Behind this frontline is a haphazard and equally threatening cluster of pickup trucks, four-by-fours, mini-vans and even an Arizona State police car.

'I count at least forty vehicles,' says Clara, her cat-like eyes narrowed as she studies the screen. 'I reckon we're looking at nearly two hundred Incarnates.'

'*Two hundred!*' gasps Thabisa, clutching her baby to her chest.

'Tanas has certainly been busy recruiting,' remarks Jude drily.

I shoot a scathing look in her direction, but it has nothing to do with her comment. I'm still wrestling with the bombshell that she was my Soul Twin's Protector – and that she failed in that duty. *Where was she in Aya's time of need? What was she doing to incur such disdain from her father and anger from Phoenix? How can I trust her to protect me – or any First Ascendant, for that matter?* But I'm forced to put aside these feelings in light of the immediate threat.

'We're outnumbered five to one!' points out Santiago with a defeated shake of his head.

'That may be so,' grunts Goggins, muscled arms crossed and jaw set in a fiercely determined expression. 'But every Protector and Warrior here is worth at least five of their Hunters.' His tone is confident, perhaps overly so, for I notice some of the Warriors in the room exchange doubtful looks. The odds are definitely stacked against us.

Tarek zooms in on the convoy as Tanas steps out of the lead SUV. Dressed in what looks like tactical assault gear, she takes off a pair of dark aviator-style glasses and scans the empty desert terrain. The tension in the lecture hall ramps up as every pair of eyes follow the black-haired, lean and lethal FBI agent on the screen.

'*Is that Tanas?*' Tasha whispers to me.

I nod, a chill running down my spine, icy fear mixing with a cold thread of guilt that *I'm* the one responsible for leading the Incarnate leader to Haven's doorstep.

We watch as Tanas crouches close to the ground, sifts through the wreckage of the drone, then examines the direction of the tyre tracks in the dirt. Standing up, she signals to the other Incarnates with a sharp circle of her hand. Then, slipping her glasses back on, she climbs into her SUV and drives off at high speed. Like a herd of stampeding buffalo, the convoy races along the track after her, leaving a billowing dust cloud in its wake.

A murmur of disquiet ripples round the room. 'We should flee while we can,' says Fabian, already heading towards the door.

'NO!' says Goggins firmly. 'That's exactly what Tanas hopes for. If we're flushed out by fear, we'll easily be picked off. We stay put, we stay safe.'

'But what's to say we're safe here any longer?' pipes up Nam, Mr Jeong's young son, which triggers a heated discussion among the Ascendants over whether to stay or flee.

'No one need panic,' assures Caleb, stepping on to the speaker's podium and holding up a hand for quiet. 'Haven can't be found unless one has been led to it.'

'What about the drone?' Mick questions from his wheelchair. 'Didn't that lead them to Haven?'

'No, only as far as the mining town,' Caleb replies. 'So with any luck Tanas will follow the false trail left by Empote. Tarek, what's their progress so far?'

Tarek switches to another camera angle, giving us a long-distance view of the Incarnates. We watch with bated breath as Tanas approaches the point where Empote's false trail begins. For a moment the convoy pauses.

'She's taking the bait,' says Clara gleefully.

But then, to our dismay, Tanas ignores Empote's tyre tracks and instead drives on towards the mine. Our hopes plunge and again I feel the weight of guilt like a millstone round my neck.

'Tanas knows where we are!' cries Sun-Hi, her eyes wide and terrified. She gathers her children protectively in her arms.

Jintao turns on me with a fierce look. 'This is *all* Genna's fault!' he declares.

'You're right,' agrees Santiago. 'If Genna hadn't gone on her reckless rescue mission, Tanas wouldn't be here now!'

Several more Ascendants and Warriors murmur their agreement and turn on me too.

Phoenix steps in to my defence. 'Don't blame Genna,' he says. 'If you wish to blame someone, blame me.'

'No, we won't be blaming anyone!' scolds Viviana, giving Santiago, Jintao and the others a reproachful look. 'If Genna hadn't saved Phoenix, we'd have lost another Soul Protector. And there are few enough as it is –'

'Yes, and we'll be even fewer soon!' snaps Santiago, glowering at me. Shame colours my cheeks and I feel a burning regret at my actions. An argument breaks out as fear and frustration give way to anger and resentment. I stand in the midst of the storm, my guilt growing as Tanas and her convoy draw ever closer. I should have listened to Caleb and Goggins – protected the Light rather than risk everything to save my Protector. But if I had, Phoenix wouldn't be here now at my side to defend me. I feel deeply conflicted. *Was it selfish of me to think of him over the safety of the others?* My intentions were good, but the consequences have proven tragic.

With so many raised voices battling to be heard, even Caleb cannot bring order to the room. I'm aware of him hoarsely calling out for calm.

'SILENCE!' bawls Goggins, bringing the squabbling to an abrupt stop. 'Our fight is with Tanas, not each other.'

Suitably chastised, everyone gazes shamefaced at the floor.

'This is exactly what Tanas would want us to do,' observes Caleb, his wrinkled hands clasping the lectern as if he were a captain holding on to the bridge of a sinking ship. 'Discontent and disagreement sow the seeds of our destruction. They diminish our Light. We *must* remain united. The closer we stand by one another, the brighter the Light.'

A mutter of assent is followed by a mumble of apology. No matter what anyone says, I know it was my decision to save Phoenix that set us on the path to our current crisis.

I vow to myself that somehow I will make up for my mistake.

Everyone turns their attention back to the screen. The convoy has now reached the mine entrance and Tanas and her Hunters are climbing out of their vehicles. I recognize Damien by his slick of raven-black hair. He sports a thick padded assault jacket and a pair of dark glasses, matching those worn by his master. He's surrounded by his motley gang – Thug, Spider, Blondie and Knuckleduster – all kitted out in the same gear.

But there's someone else with them. They haul him out from the back of Tanas's SUV. Bloodied and bruised, his hands tied behind his back, the elderly man sways so weakly on his feet that Thug has to hold him up.

'*Empote!*' I gasp, horrified.

Caleb's face goes pale and he leans against the podium's lectern for strength. 'Oh, my dear friend, no . . .'

My fellow First Ascendants express their own despair at his capture, either crying out or sinking into an anguished silence. Thabisa slumps down in one of the chairs and begins to weep; Viviana glares fiercely at the screen, her arthritic hands clenched in her lap. Goggins lashes out, punching the wall and leaving a fist-sized dent.

'E-even if the Incarnates manage to enter the mine,' stutters Caleb, struggling to maintain his composure, 'they'll get lost in the maze of shafts and passageways and give up . . .'

But the Incarnates don't even bother with the sealed mine entrance. Arming themselves with an array of weapons and lugging a large box of explosives, they begin to climb the steep barren slopes of the mountainside. The radio on Clara's hip bursts into life and the twin Warriors on patrol call in, confirming the Incarnates' ascent. Clara orders their immediate return inside Haven's gates.

'We're doomed!' cries Fabian, cradling his head in his hands.

His words set off a chain reaction among the First Ascendants and once more Goggins is forced to call the room to order so that Caleb can be heard.

'Haven's safety isn't compromised,' insists the Soul Seer, having rallied himself from the shock of his friend's capture. 'Remember: no Incarnate can enter this sacred valley without prejudicing their soul! The stone circle remains unbroken as it has done for milliennia.'

'In the meantime, we must prepare, but not panic,' says Goggins, his tone reassuringly calm. 'Gather any essential belongings and travel documents in the unlikely event of us being forced to evacuate Haven. We'll rendezvous at the garage. You know the drill.'

On his command, the Protectors start escorting their Ascendants back to their apartments and the Warriors head off to take up defensive positions around Haven. As Phoenix walks ahead of me, Jude falls in line behind. I glance irritably at her. 'Phoenix is my Protector,' I say coolly. 'I don't need you.'

She gives me a perplexed and indignant look. 'Goggins has ordered me to protect you too.'

I want to say something about my sister, confront her about what happened, but now isn't the time. 'Fine,' I reply stiffly, and walk on.

We head outside into Haven's central plaza. The capstone of the glass pyramid glints like a beacon with the last rays of the setting sun. The six sacred stone pillars upon the valley ridge are now such a dark ochre that the rocks themselves look to be bleeding. Then the sun dips below the mountains, the pillars fall into shadow and, in a portentous sign, the tip of the pyramid ceases to shine.

Hurrying across the plaza and entering the garden courtyard, I find Nefe by my apartment door, alert and watchful. Acknowledging her with a quick stroke, I dash inside and hastily stuff my passport and money into my pockets. Just as I'm throwing Coco and a spare change of clothes into my backpack, I hear Nefe hiss and spit. Turning, I see her tail is raised and bushy. I race outside to rejoin Phoenix and the others in the courtyard, where I find them staring up at the valley ridgeline. Around the rim stand the army of Incarnates silhouetted against the darkening sky. I immediately spot Tanas, along with Damien and his gang on the nearest ridge, close to one of the stone pillars. They have forced Empote to his knees beside it, his head bowed.

'Why are they just standing there?' asks Tasha, clinging on to Viviana's hand.

'They can't see Haven,' Viviana explains. 'Our combined Light cloaks our presence, along with the holographic shield. All they see is an empty valley in shadow.'

But then a voice echoes down to us from high upon the ridge. '*I know you're somewhere down there!*' shouts Tanas. '*I can feel it. And, believe me, we* will *find you.*'

She orders one of her Hunters to descend the slope. I take hold of Phoenix's hand, clasping it tightly as we watch the Hunter pick a path through the rocks. Despite Viviana's assurance, my heart thuds harder with every step the Incarnate takes towards us. We may be invisible, but we're not undetectable. Once on the valley floor, the Hunter need only reach out to touch Haven's walls . . . Then I notice the red-headed Lena is set up on the roof of Haven's entrance hall, her assault rifle trained on the approaching Hunter. But before she has a chance to pull the trigger, the Incarnate suddenly stiffens and twitches, loses his footing and collapses to the ground. None of the other Incarnates go to help him. They leave him to writhe like a tortured insect in the dirt.

'*A sacred site!*' Tanas shouts in a gloating voice. '*All the proof I need.*'

My hand goes slack in Phoenix's, our hopes of remaining hidden crushed by the sacrifice of a single Incarnate. Viviana draws Tasha closer to her and mumbles a desperate prayer, while the rest of us look on in grim, tense silence as Tanas pulls something green and gleaming from her belt.

The jade knife!

Standing over Empote, she seizes a handful of his hair and wrenches his head back. With an incantation that carries across the valley like the cawing of a crow, she slices the blade across Empote's throat. I gasp, clutching my own throat as if the savage cut had been inflicted upon me. Every First Ascendant seems to feel it too, Tasha letting out a soft cry, Santiago wincing and Viviana dropping to her knees. A sharp spike of pain penetrates my soul and the Light within me dims.

While Damien holds up the dying Empote, Tanas cups her hands beneath the flow of blood. Then reciting an occult spell she smears the nearest stone pillar with the gore, inscribing ancient runes and symbols on the rock face. In a final act of the gruesome ritual, she drinks a long draught of Empote's blood before Damien and his gang toss his lifeless body down the slope.

A moment later a thunderous explosion rocks the valley. The detonation is so huge the ground beneath our feet trembles. Then one of the far pillars crumbles and topples over, dust billowing from the blast in a huge red cloud. There's a flicker of an electrical grid in the sky as the holographic shield fails and the stone circle is broken.

Raising her blood-soaked hands to the coming night, Tanas shrieks, 'NOW I SEE YOU!'

48

With the ground deconsecrated by Empote's ritual murder and the sacred circle destroyed, the last of Haven's outer defences falls. The valley that was once our hidden shelter is now laid bare and becomes a trap of our own making.

As red dust rains down upon us, I turn to Phoenix in panic. 'What do we do now?' I scream.

He takes my hand. 'We run! As we always have –'

The sharp *crack* of a gunshot rings out and reverberates round the valley. I flinch but I know the bullet isn't meant for me. High upon the ridge Tanas is blown off her feet and lands in a heap upon the stony ground. The Incarnate horde stare in stunned silence at their fallen leader, while we gaze on in hopeful disbelief.

From the roof of Haven's entrance hall comes the soft click of an assault rifle being reloaded and, in the gathering red-tinged gloom of dusk, Lena gives a thumbs up to Goggins. He finishes steadying Viviana on her feet, then looks over towards the flame-haired Protector.

'Sharp shooting, Lena!' he bellows with a wide, white-toothed grin – the first and only time I can remember the Chief Protector ever smiling.

But our sense of triumph is short-lived. Standing up and dusting herself off, Tanas appears to rise from the dead.

'Well, that's a nice welcome!' she shouts sarcastically, inspecting the hole in her black jacket exactly where her heart is. 'But I've learned to take the necessary precautions when turning up uninvited to a party.'

Phoenix scowls with annoyance. 'Bulletproof vest!' he mutters under his breath.

I curse at how easily Tanas has cheated death yet again. Frustration and anger well up in me. *Will we never be rid of this evil?*

'And now for my gift of greeting to you!' Tanas shouts, signalling with her hand.

A second later there's a *whoosh* overhead and the roof to Haven's entrance hall explodes in a ball of fire as a rocket-propelled grenade strikes its target. We dive to the ground, covering our heads as debris rains down on us and another missile blasts a hole in Haven's outer wall. Explosion after explosion assault the perimeter. Then, as the dust settles once more, a fearsome battle cry sounds and the Incarnates charge down the slope towards us.

Ears ringing, I stagger to my feet with Phoenix. My first thought is of Lena, and I turn to where the entrance hall used to be. It's a smoking ruin, of course. Lena would have been obliterated in a flash. No time to process that now – Jude has her Taser at the ready. Then I spot Tarek with Thabisa and baby Kagiso – Tarek has a couple of Light grenades clipped to his belt. Santiago is standing, mute and in shock, gazing numbly at the decimated roof where his

Protector had been moments before. Mick is tugging on his arm, imploring him to leave.

'*FOLLOW ME!*' roars Goggins, bearing Viviana in his huge arms, a pistol in his hand.

We rush out of the courtyard, into the plaza and over towards the garage housing Haven's fleet of electric cars. But the Incarnates are quick to spot our escape plan. From the ridge another grenade rockets down and destroys the garage, triggering a series of blasts as each car's cell battery detonates in quick succession. We're knocked off our feet by the multiple explosions –

Bombs continue to rain down, the night sky flashing with anti-aircraft fire. The cries of the wounded fill the air, along with the crackle of flames and the crumbling of buildings as the Blitzkrieg pounds London into a nightmarish hell.

I lie in the rubble, pinned beneath a pile of bricks, blood trickling from a cut to my forehead. Harry, his army uniform torn and coated with brick dust, is sprawled in the street alongside his best mate, George, who clutches his arm and groans in agony.

'Harry!' I shout, noticing a shard of metal piercing his thigh.

Weakly he raises his head and coughs up dust. 'Mary . . .' he croaks.

'Thank the Light you're alive!' I say, pushing away the bricks and crawling over to him. I tear off a strip of my nurse's uniform and tie a makeshift tourniquet round his thigh. Then through the smoke and flames I spot shadows moving . . . on the hunt. 'Harry, they're coming!'

'Genna, get up!' begs Phoenix, pulling insistently on my arm. 'They're coming!'

Blood trickles from a cut on my brow and for a moment I'm totally disorientated, convinced that I'm still in my Glimmer from the Second World War. Then blinking away the blood I see the wave of Incarnates swarming into Haven.

'All our defences have been breached!' rasps Phoenix as I take his outstretched hand.

Swaying on my feet, I survey the devastation. A veil of darkness is descending on the valley but the carnage is brightly lit by the flames from the burning cars. Ascendants and Protectors alike lie dazed and bleeding on the ground. Jude is still out cold from the blast. One of the twin Warriors is dead, and his brother rises in fury, a pistol in each hand. He starts shooting from the hip, and three Hunters go down – but there are simply too many for him to stop their advance. When his guns click empty, he is jumped on by a pair of Hunters brandishing heavy clubs.

'Watch out, Genna!' cries Phoenix, pushing me aside and disarming an Incarnate of a butcher's knife before throwing her hard to the ground.

Shaking off my bomb-blasted daze, I turn to confront our enemy. It appears that Tanas has recruited a motley army of FBI agents, truck drivers, farmhands, police officers, construction workers, soldiers, gangsters and gun-toting survivalists to her sinister cause. Their unnatural, dark-pooling eyes are the only thing they all have in common.

As the Incarnates rush towards us, Phoenix shouts, 'Remember your Glimmer as Sabina!'

'*Claro!*' I reply in Portuguese, and we both drop into the low, shifting stance of capoeiristas. Back to back and in constant motion, we become a frustrating target for the approaching mob. As they attempt to attack, we launch into a blistering series of whirling kicks and strikes. I cut one down with a *corta capim*, and knock out another with a *martelo em pé*. Phoenix floors a soldier with a devastating *meia lua de compasso*, the spinning reserve kick catching the Incarnate totally off guard and breaking his jaw. Like a frenzied spider, we take on multiple opponents at once. But as effective as we are, there are only two of us yet the Incarnates keep coming, and I know there's only so long we can keep up this frenetic pace.

Goggins shouts a rallying cry, ordering the Warriors to form a defensive circle round the dazed First Ascendants. Caleb stands at the centre, calling upon the Light to save and protect us. As Clara corrals Tasha to safety, a bare-chested Hunter with a skull tattoo attempts to grab the young girl. Without a second thought, Clara shoots him between the eyes. Viviana stays close to Goggins, safe in his formidable shadow. But Fabian isn't so fortunate. He's snatched away by two Incarnates after Zaine, his Warrior, is hit in the head with a baseball bat. They don't kill the First Ascendant there and then, however. Instead they bear him away to Tanas, who waits at the ruined entrance gates to Haven with Damien and his gang and a sinister group of Incarnate High Priests in hooded cloaks. As soon as Fabian is on his knees, they begin their evil ritual with a chant of '*Ra-Ka! Ra-Ka! Ra-Ka!*' – and Tanas plunges the jade knife into Fabian's heart.

Instantly I'm crippled by a stabbing pain deep within me and I collapse to the ground. I feel the Light dim once more as Fabian's soul is ripped from him and extinguished forever.

'They're picking us off, one by one!' cries Santiago, trying to stop Mick being hauled from his wheelchair by a couple of black-eyed farmhands. Two Warriors rush to their aid but are outnumbered and overwhelmed. Elsewhere, despite Tarek's furious defence, Thabisa and her son are captured and carried away towards Tanas. In desperation Tarek tosses a Light grenade. The blinding flash stuns the Incarnates fighting nearby and they writhe on the floor, reeling from its effects. While Tarek grabs Thabisa and her son out of their clutches, Clara leads a group of Warriors to finish off the Hunters.

Still reeling from the loss of Fabian's soul, I'm barely back on my feet when a heavyset Incarnate grabs me by the hair and starts dragging me away like a sack of bricks. I yell to Phoenix but my Soul Protector is caught up in a three-way fight. I see him knock down one of his attackers in an effort to reach me, but the other two pounce on him.

'*Genna!*' he cries as he disappears beneath a barrage of blows.

Legs kicking and arms flailing, I tear at my assailant's hand where he's holding my hair, but his grip is as strong as steel. Relentlessly he hauls me towards Tanas and her eager circle of High Priests. Damien is there among them, welcoming me with open arms. I've almost given up hope when the Incarnate abductor convulses and collapses to the ground beside me.

Confused but grateful, I scramble away and look up to discover Jude, a spent Taser gun in her hand. She offers to help me up. I know she just saved me, but I'm still too angry about Aya to accept her proffered hand and get to my feet myself. I mumble a begrudging thanks.

'All part of the service,' she quips, before an FBI agent in dark glasses jumps her and she's lost in the maelstrom of fighting.

Tanas roars her fury at my last-minute rescue and sends two Incarnates to retrieve me. But a second Light grenade goes off, stunning them mid-stride. With a safe path cleared by the grenade, I dash back to the ever-diminishing group of Warriors and Protectors.

My fellow First Ascendants are now reduced to nine.

'Where's Nam?' I ask Sun-Hi, who clutches Song desperately to her chest, her daughter wide-eyed and weak with terror.

'He's been taken!' she cries, pointing towards Haven's blasted gates.

I look beyond the circle and see the young lad being forced to his knees before Tanas. I turn to the Warrior nearest me. 'We have to save him!' I yell, but she's caught in a furious fight for her own life.

I search frantically for Phoenix and find Tarek instead. 'Light grenade?' I ask in desperate hope.

Tarek shakes his head. 'I'm all out!' he replies as he retreats with Thabisa and Kagiso in the face of the Incarnates' brutal attack.

Powerless to break through their ranks on my own, I can only watch as Tanas thrusts the jade knife into Nam's young chest and rips his soul from him. 'NO!' I scream, feeling yet another agonizing wound within my own soul and the Light of Humanity fade a little more.

'FALL BACK!' Goggins is bellowing as our resistance crumbles under the relentless onslaught. Bloodied and limping, the Chief Protector leads the retreat to the pyramid – our last and only sanctuary.

49

With victory in her grasp, Tanas commands the remaining ranks of Incarnates to attack, turning our ordered retreat into a desperate fight for survival.

Somehow Phoenix battles his way back to my side, leaving his two attackers writhing in pain on the ground. 'Thank the Light you're OK,' he says, a nasty cut now marring his cheek.

'It was Jude who saved me,' I grudgingly admit, glad to have my true Protector once more as my shield.

'Looks like I owe her yet again,' he says, fending off an Incarnate with an elbow strike. 'Where is she?'

'I don't know,' I reply. Then I feel a twinge of guilt at how cold I am to her fate. I glance around and spot Damien and his gang striding through Haven's ruined gates. Dark glasses glinting in the flames, they move quickly to cut us off.

'I can't see Jude,' I say. 'But I do see Damien! Look – over there,' I warn Phoenix as we retreat rapidly through the haze of smoke and red dust.

'Follow me,' orders Phoenix, changing course in the direction of the Glimmer Dome.

'But the pyramid's the other way,' I say, worried that we're leaving our fellow Ascendants and Protectors behind.

'We won't make it before Damien intercepts us,' Phoenix replies. 'Besides, there are no weapons in there.'

With Damien and his gang hot on our heels, we split from the others and race across the training ground and into the Glimmer Dome. The chamber is dark and quiet as a grave; the muffled silence is eerie compared to the frantic noise of the battle outside. The flicker of flames from the still-burning garage casts a wavering ghostly light through the stained-glass windows in the roof.

'If we're going to stand any chance of surviving this night,' says Phoenix, leading me on to the Glimmer platform, 'we need to fight to our advantage. Arm ourselves from the past!'

I wait on the platform as he dashes up the spiral staircase, two steps at a time. Suddenly the doors crash open and Damien and his gang march in.

'Well, this is a fine collection!' declares Damien, lifting his dark glasses to peer round at the numerous artefacts on display. He casually picks up a white Ming dynasty vase decorated with blue lotus flowers and gives it an admiring glance. 'Someone certainly likes to hoard relics of the past. But I'm afraid there's no future in it. At least not for you, Genna.'

He drops the priceless object and it shatters into a hundred pieces. 'Oops, butterfingers!' he says, grinning.

'You don't have much respect for the past,' I remark, attempting to buy time for Phoenix.

'Oh, I wouldn't say that,' Damien replies, toying with a seventeenth-century Italian rapier. 'There's much to be learned from one's previous lives . . . as you well know.'

While he goes on to examine a Viking round shield, I'm keenly aware that his gang are stealthily surrounding the platform, picking up weapons of their own choosing along the way. To my alarm, I fear they're able to glimmer past life skills too. Thug lugs a heavy mace-and-chain, the spiked ball at the end particularly brutal. Blondie finds a pair of nunchaku. Spider acquires for herself a rather lethal set of throwing knives. And Knuckleduster, sporting her duster rings as ever, complements them with a gladiator's trident.

'Now – where's your Protector got to *this* time?' asks Damien breezily. 'I have to say, he appears somewhat neglectful of his –'

'Up here, Damien!' calls Phoenix from the first-floor landing. Armed with an antique longbow, he draws back on the string and lets loose an arrow. It flies true and straight through the air, whistling over my head directly towards the Soul Hunter. But Damien grabs the Viking shield from the display and there's a sharp splintering as the arrow pierces the aged wood.

'Impressive shot!' Damien shouts from behind the safety of the shield. 'Next time I'll put an apple on my head.'

Infuriated, Phoenix goes to string another arrow, but Spider throws a slim stiletto blade at him. The knife pierces Phoenix's shoulder, forcing him to drop the bow.

'Finish him off!' orders Damien, tossing aside the shield.

Spider mounts the outside of the spiral staircase and swings up to the first floor. She rushes at Phoenix with a long curved knife that I immediately recognize as the beautiful ivory-handled jambiya that failed to give me a Glimmer. Judging by the arc of vicious swipes she makes with its lethal blade, it's all too evident that Spider's *very* familiar with the weapon from a past life.

With a gasp of pain, Phoenix tugs the stiletto from his shoulder. He tries to defend himself with it, but the slim blade is no match for the jambiya and Spider knows it. Grinning, she launches into a merciless attack.

As Phoenix retreats under the onslaught, Damien throws me a pitying look. 'It would seem your Protector is preoccupied at the moment,' he says. 'So why not make this easy on yourself and come quietly? Save us all this painful fighting, hmm?'

'It's only going to be painful for you!' I reply. Emboldened by my recent influx of Glimmers, I assume a taiji fighting stance – my hands up in a guard, my weight on my back foot and my front leg bent and primed to kick.

'Suit yourself,' says Damien. He nods at his three other Hunters. 'Be *gentle* with her. Tanas needs her alive – or at least breathing – to complete the ritual.'

Thug clambers on to the platform, swinging the mace-and-chain around like it's a cat's toy. Blondie leaps up with the nimbleness of a ninja, his nunchaku whirring. And Knuckleduster mounts the steps, trident in hand, as if she was a gladiator entering the Colosseum.

I stand in the middle of the three armed Hunters, trying to calm my pounding heart and ready myself for the fight to come. Above me the singing of knives tells of the fierce battle still underway between Phoenix and Spider.

I've no choice. Without my Protector at my side, I'll have to rely on the multiple past life skills I've glimmered if I'm to survive.

Thug lumbers forward first. As he tries to swat me like a fly with his mace-and-chain, I become the acrobat Yelena and backflip out of the way. The spiked ball thuds into the floor, shredding the tatami mat. Blondie now swipes at my head with his nunchaku. As if I'm performing the most deadly circus routine of my life, I duck and roll, then I leap into the air and somersault over Knuckleduster's trident.

Before I can recover my breath, Thug comes at me again, swinging hard with his mace-and-chain. Recalling Feiyen's teaching at the Purple Cloud Temple, that the soft and pliable will defeat the hard and strong, I bend backwards like a reed. The spiked ball skims over me and embeds itself in one of the Dome's wooden pillars. Thug struggles to free his weapon. I charge at him like Buri the Mongolian warrior. Despite the Hunter's overwhelming size, I manage to drive him off balance. Next, remembering how I was defeated in the Bökh wrestling match, I seize the thug's belt, twist my hips and with a valley drop throw send him over the edge of the platform. He crashes head first to the parquet floor and flops unconscious.

But I'm given no time to relish my victory. While my back is turned, Blondie, quick on the attack, strikes me from behind with the hard handle of his nunchaku. My skull rings like a temple bell and stars burst before my eyes. I stagger across the platform and almost topple forward into Knuckleduster's thrusting trident . . . but my instinct as a gymnast saves me as I tuck into a roll and spring back to my feet. *Never would I have imagined that gym lessons at school would one day help me in a fight for my life!*

Still stunned, I sway at the edge of the platform. Blondie comes at me again, his nunchaku a blur of spinning sticks. For a moment I'm at a loss for what to do, but then I remember the taijishan in my back pocket. Pulling out the fan, I block the nunchaku with the fan's iron edge. Blondie is taken off guard by this unanticipated defence. With a flick of my wrist, I open the fan. His attention is so caught by the flash of the red dragon and flaming phoenix he doesn't see my fist as I hook-punch him hard in the jaw, dislodging his dark glasses. Then I snap the fan shut and, using it like an *otta*, I jab its iron tip into the centre of his chest, targeting the *hridaya* marma point that my Kalari guru had once used against Aarush. His pooling eyes widen in pain and he gasps for breath. Falling to his knees, Blondie drops his nunchaku and clasps his chest.

Two down. I turn to the last Hunter.

'You're not pulling that trick on me, not after last time!' Knuckleduster snarls, stabbing with her trident. I try to spin out of the way, but the prongs catch my arm and rip the taijishan from my hand.

Nursing my injured arm, we circle one another like two gladiators in a pit. Without the iron fan, I've only my agility as a capoeirista to rely on. Bobbing and swaying away from each thrust and jab, I glance up to the first floor in the hope that Phoenix has overcome Spider and can come to my aid. But he's still engaged in the knife fight. The Incarnate's dark jacket is ripped and torn in places, and to my dismay I see that Phoenix is lacerated with multiple cuts from the jambiya, more in need of help than I am.

Knuckleduster stabs for my chest. At the last second, I manage to twist away, but one of the prongs scores a bloody line across my ribs. I barely dodge another thrust, and I know I have to end this battle fast before she harpoons me like a fish. Running out of options and tiring with every duck and dive, I try to think what Sabina would do in this desperate situation. A flash of inspiration comes, letting me recall her favourite move.

As Knuckleduster thrusts her trident once again, I slip to one side, drop to both hands and arch my right leg over my back like the stinger of a scorpion. The *escorpião* kick is so unexpected it strikes the Hunter square in the face. She keels backwards, landing like a felled tree upon the tatami mat.

Flooded with a rush of adrenaline, I grin at my surprise victory.

'Well, that's all rather embarrassing,' says Damien, looking round in disgust at his defeated Hunters. 'But I suppose if you want a job done well, you have to do it yourself.'

He picks up the Italian rapier, its sliver of blade glinting like a needle, and mounts the platform in a single bound. I consider grabbing the trident to fend him off but I've no past experience in wielding that heavy weapon. Besides, I'm focused now on going to Phoenix's aid.

Then I hear a cry of pain and glance up. Phoenix slumps over the rail. Spider is skewered to the back wall by two knives: the stiletto blade through one shoulder and the jambiya through the other.

'Catch!' shouts Phoenix. Injured as he is, he somehow manages to throw me a samurai sword. I catch it by the handle and at once feel Miyoko's strength and skill infuse my body.

'To first blood!' he groans before sliding unconscious to the floor.

Damien grins maliciously. 'Oh dear. It appears your Protector has failed you.'

'You're wrong!' I reply fiercely, unsheathing the katana to reveal its long curving blade. 'He's taught me to protect myself.'

50

We face one another on the platform, samurai versus fencer, katana against rapier. Damien stands tall, his sword held lightly in one hand, his other arm raised behind for balance. I sink low into my kenjutsu stance, gripping my katana with both hands. My blade gleams like a beam of light in front of me.

'Are you ready to finish that duel, Tora Tsume?' I challenge, my ferocity fuelled by my anguish for Phoenix.

Whipping his rapier through the air, Damien laughs. 'I admire your sense of humour, Genna. But don't you recall how that fight ended for you?'

'And don't *you* remember how our fight in the crypt ended for *you*?' I retort, tightening my grip on my steel.

Damien scowls. 'Our fight isn't over until one of us is dead forever,' he sneers. 'And tonight your soul will meet its end.'

He lunges at me, the rapier moving so fast I barely see it. I shift to one side, but still feel a sharp sting on my forearm. Blood beads from the puncture wound.

'First blood!' brags Damien with a smirk.

Infuriated, I cut down with my katana, slashing across his body – but Damien quickly pulls back out of range.

Then he executes another lightning-quick thrust and the sharpened tip of his rapier pierces me a second time. He retreats to a safe distance once more.

'It's been a while since I've used one of these,' he says, admiring his slender weapon. 'But I must say I like it!'

He comes at me again, jabbing and whipping the blade in a flurry of attacks. I feel as if I'm being stung by a swarm of wasps. I deflect, parry and slash back at him. But as skilful as I am and as lethal as the katana is, his nimbleness, speed and reach give him the edge. I wince as the tip of his blade cuts a line across my cheek.

'Miyoko-san, I'm disappointed in you,' Damien teases. 'At least give me a duel worthy of a samurai!'

Enraged, I attack again. Calling upon every ounce of Miyoko's skill, I retaliate with a stream of flowing cuts and swift slices, driving Damien back to the edge of the platform. Outside, the sounds of battle still rage, the chants of '*Ra-Ka! Ra-Ka! Ra-Ka!*' growing ever louder. All of a sudden I'm struck by a familiar stab of pain to my soul, hitting me like a double punch. I cry out and drop to one knee, giving Damien the chance to escape my onslaught.

'The Light is fading, Genna,' Damien taunts as I struggle back to my feet. 'The Darkness is coming.'

'Hope is seeing there is light . . . in spite of the darkness,' I reply, suppressing the pain in my soul and raising my sword once more.

'Fine words,' he says, 'but you appear to be blind to your inevitable defeat!'

He launches into another blistering attack.

I'm finding it harder to defend myself and his moves are too fast for me to see and counter. My rage and despair rise with every stinging wound he inflicts upon me –

Don't let your emotions cloud your warrior mind.

My sensei's words resound in my head and I force myself to calm my breathing and regain my composure. In so doing, I now hear my Kalari guru's voice quiet in my ear. *In order to be aware of your enemy's every movement, your whole body must become an eye.*

As I continue to battle Damien, I try to focus on his every movement, his every shift in balance and his every twitch of muscle. Listening for his intention with my body, just as Feiyen had taught me in taiji, I start to sense his attacks, *hear* his energy. Before he's even thrust his rapier, I cut across with my katana, catching his blade at the hilt. Then with a deft twist of my wrist I disarm him and flick my sword upwards. His rapier clatters to the floor as my katana slices the tip of his chin.

'Is that more worthy?' I ask, pressing the blade to his neck.

He angrily wipes away the blood from his chin. 'Death is only the beginning, Genna,' he sneers. 'Kill me and I'll be back in the next life. But I assure you: *you* won't!'

At that moment the double doors burst open and a pack of Incarnates charge in. Seizing upon the distraction, Damien backflips away from my blade like the ninja Tora Tsume to land on the floor among them.

'You missed your chance, Genna,' he says with a gloating laugh.

I grip my katana tighter, trying to steady my nerves as the pack advance on me. I know I've little chance against such odds. Nonetheless, I steel myself for the battle to come.

Then I hear a voice behind me. 'Genna, this way!'

Jude is helping a bleeding but conscious Phoenix down the spiral staircase, a bag of weapons slung across her shoulder and her bo staff in her free hand. They make for the rear of the dome and, as the Incarnates rush to the platform, I dash after them. Hidden in a recess there's a door flush to the wall that I'd never seen before. Jude presses a thumb to a discreet scanner and the door slides open. As soon as we're through, the door shuts behind us and locks itself. The Incarnates hammer furiously on the other side.

'They can knock all they want,' says Jude with a grin, 'but that door's four inches of reinforced steel!'

'Where are we?' I ask, relieved at our narrow escape. I peer down a stairwell leading to a narrow passageway that's dimly lit with strip lights.

'Service tunnels,' Jude explains. 'They link all the main buildings. That's how I got to you both without them seeing me.'

As I lower my guard and sheathe my sword, Jude dumps the bag of assorted weapons at her feet and Phoenix slumps against the wall.

I grimace at the patchwork of wounds on his chest and arms. 'Are you OK?'

He nods. 'Just a few scratches,' he says with a pained smile. 'I'll live. I'm just glad you're alive. Sorry for fail–'

I put a finger to his lips, silencing his apology. 'No, don't even think it. If it wasn't for you, I'd never have glimmered so many skills. You've shown me how to protect myself. Reminded me how to wield a sword. That's as important as you being my shield.'

'From what I saw you don't need a shield –' remarks Jude over the continued thuds of the infuriated Incarnates – 'although we might need a miracle to escape Tanas completely.'

I glance at the Soul Warrior. Her left cheek is bruised, and she has cuts on her arms and her knuckles are raw. She's clearly fought hard to reach us. 'It's a miracle you turned up when you did,' I say gratefully, 'otherwise Phoenix and I would now either be dead or else captured.'

I'm only too aware that this is the second time Jude's saved me today; the fourth in total if I include her rescues at the airport and Venice Beach. And then there was the time she cut off the cobra's head as Raneb . . . I'm starting to feel somewhat ashamed of my hostility towards her earlier. Still, I can't bring myself to forgive her for failing to protect Aya, my Soul Twin. If she'd only shown this much diligence and daring in that fateful life, then my sister might still be alive and at my side today.

'Did the others make it to the pyramid?' asks Phoenix, getting stiffly to his feet.

Jude looks grim. 'Some, yes. But not all.'

Almost too afraid to ask, I whisper, 'Who have we lost?'

'It would be better to come and see who we *didn't* lose,' says Jude, avoiding my troubled gaze and picking up the bag. 'Let's just hope these weapons are enough for all of us.'

51

'Genna!' cries Tarek as we emerge from the concealed opening in the polished marble floor of the pyramid. His wiry hair is a mess, his glasses cracked and bent, and there's a smear of dried blood running from his forehead and down one side of his face. He hurries over to help Jude and me with Phoenix.

'By the Light, what happened to *you*?' gasps Tarek, gaping wide-eyed at Phoenix's multiple knife wounds.

'We had a run-in with Damien and his gang,' I explain, easing Phoenix to the floor.

'I'm fine,' groans Phoenix, wincing as he waves us off. 'Honestly, it's not as painful as it looks.'

'I sure hope so!' replies Tarek.

Unconvinced by Phoenix's bravado, I grab a first-aid kit from a pile of hastily gathered gear and begin to patch up the worst of his injuries. With Tarek's help, I rapidly stem the bleeding and bandage the most serious cuts, my skills as a wartime nurse once again proving their worth.

'And what about you?' says Tarek, nodding at the nasty gash across my ribs from Knuckleduster's trident.

Only now do I become aware of how much I hurt. Apart from the cut to my ribs, there's the bruise to the back of my head, the slice across my cheek and the multiple stings from Damien's rapier. 'Best patch me up too,' I say.

While Tarek tends to my injuries, I gaze round numbly at the handful of survivors in the Sun Room. Santiago is slumped on the floor, his head in his hands. Thabisa cradles a crying Kagiso, trying in vain to soothe him. Tasha, her ice-blond hair wild and her blue eyes darting around nervously, clasps the wrinkled yet firm hand of Viviana, who upon seeing me gives a relieved tired smile. A bloodied Goggins stands guard beside them. But Clara is nowhere to be seen. Nor are Mick, Jintao or his daughter Song. A lone Sun-Hi weeps in the arms of her Protector Blake. Of the Warriors, apart from Tarek and Jude, there appears to be only a couple left: Kohsoom, the young Thai girl who I'd first come across in Goggins' martial arts class, the weight-lifting Zara from Brazil, and a blond-haired, bearded Norwegian called Steinar who has the physique of Thor and the defeated look of a broken man.

My spirits lift momentarily, however, when I spot Caleb. He's kneeling beside the central altar, his head bowed in apparent prayer. Leaving Phoenix in Tarek's care, I head over to the Soul Seer. Goggins nods at me as I pass, and I notice his eyes are rimmed red with smoke or . . . *are those tears*? That's when it really hits me. Our situation must be truly dire if even the Chief Protector is crying.

At that moment Tasha dashes into my arms and buries her head in my chest. 'C-Clara's gone – *forever*,' she wails. I hold her trembling body tight and gently stroke her hair as she sobs. 'She held off the Incarnates – so I could enter the p-pyramid – but Tanas got her – and k-k-killed her . . . *in front of us*!'

I turn my attention to the barricaded door. Tanas is standing outside with her cohort of hooded high priests, all wearing dark glasses as if the night is too bright for them. Clara's body lies at their feet. Sickened, I look away and spot an aggrieved and glowering Damien rejoining his master; the remainder of his gang, bar Spider, follow some distance behind him, limping and nursing their multiple injuries. Surrounding the pyramid in an unruly mob are the rest of the surviving Incarnates. They hammer incessantly on the windows. One of them even tries to shoot us through the glass, but the bullet ricochets off and kills him instead.

Goggins grunts a humourless laugh. 'Haven't they learned yet? The glass is bullet- and bombproof!'

Leaving the devastated Tasha with Viviana, I head over to the altar. 'Caleb?' I say softly.

He looks up despondently. For a moment he seems not to recognize me, then his whole face lifts with joy. '*Thank the Light you're safe!*' he exclaims, clambering to his feet. 'I lost my soul link to you when Jintao and Song were both sacrificed. For a while, I believed you were gone too.'

He grasps me with both hands, his grip unduly firm on my arms as if afraid to let me go again.

'We went to get weapons,' I explain. 'From the dome.'

'We don't need weapons,' he says, gazing at me with an almost devout reverence. '*You're* our weapon!'

I return his stare, perplexed and increasingly concerned by the maddened gleam in his eyes. 'What do you mean?'

Caleb straightens himself up and clears his throat. 'HOPE IS NOT LOST!' he announces to the room. 'For the one foretold in the Soul Prophecy is among us!'

He takes my hand and raises it to the sky. A stunned silence falls over those in the Sun Room, only the banging on the glass from the frustrated Incarnates intruding on the shock announcement. The weight of everyone's gaze upon me seems to crush the air from my lungs and for a moment I, too, am left speechless.

Then I turn sharply to Caleb. '*I thought you said you didn't know!*' I hiss under my breath.

'Well, I do now,' replies the Soul Seer with a sanguine smile. 'In fact, I first saw the truth during our tea ceremony when I discovered you could soul-link with others.'

I frown at him, recalling the strange look he gave me when he peered into my eyes. 'You've known since *then*?'

Caleb shrugs. 'I knew, but I didn't dare trust my instincts.'

'So why should we trust your judgement this time, Caleb?' calls out Santiago, casting a sceptical look in my direction. I turn back to Caleb, equally doubting his judgement. I certainly don't feel like the chosen one. *What if he's wrong – again?*

Caleb steps boldly forward. 'Because it was Empote who proclaimed her first. He witnessed Genna's *su'mach*. He saw her defeat the Dark!'

'I didn't defea–' I begin.

'We all know Genna's soul shines brighter and bolder than the rest because of her Soul Twin,' Caleb goes on fervently, and a few of the Ascendants nod in agreement, including Viviana. 'Her Protector, Phoenix, has been secretly training her in the Glimmer Dome. Genna is not only a First Ascendant – she's now a Soul Warrior too!'

A murmur of astonishment ripples round the Ascendants and Protectors and their focus turns to Phoenix, who gives a simple nod.

'Even so, that doesn't necessarily mean Genna's *the one*,' counters Santiago.

Caleb urges me forward as if presenting me as some prize fighter. 'Through my soul link I witnessed how Genna fought the Hunters in the Glimmer Dome,' he reveals. 'Only the one true soul could defeat such a number of powerful Incarnates single-handedly. She wields the Light like a weapon!'

'*That* I'd like to see,' mutters Goggins, although his tone is more curious than hostile.

Without prompting, Tasha jumps up excitedly. 'I believe Genna's the one mentioned in the Soul Prophecy!'

A hesitant smile hides my panic at her enthusiasm. The situation is quickly getting out of my control. 'Tasha, your faith in me is appreciated, but it may be misplaced –'

'I don't think it is,' states Phoenix, rising to his feet too. 'I believe in you, Genna. I always have.'

'Me too,' says Thabisa, her little son Kagiso all of a sudden settling into a quiet gurgle as if also in agreement.

My continued objections go unheard as Sun-Hi and her Protector add to the growing chorus of approval. Viviana stays silent, though, her wrinkled face etched with an unresolved grief, while Jude and Santiago's expressions remain as unconvinced as mine. To me, it seems I am another false saviour, that Caleb's pronouncement is merely a last-ditch attempt to bolster our morale. But the certainty in his gleaming eyes is undeniable. I just wish I felt the same way. My determination to stop Tanas is as strong as ever, but to do so with everyone's fate in my hands – and with no idea of how to do it – well, it seems reckless . . . even suicidal.

Noticing my hesitancy, Phoenix limps over. 'Genna, I saw for myself what you're capable of. You have a gift and the Light burns bright in you.'

I turn away from the expectant gazes of my fellow Ascendants and whisper urgently to him. '*But what if, like Mercia, I'm* not *the one foretold in the Prophecy? Caleb was wrong once before.*'

He meets my question with a look of unwavering confidence. 'I'm convinced you are. Remember what Empote said in his truck – *Hope is the only thing stronger than fear*. Whether you believe you're the one true soul or not, you've given everyone renewed hope, and that may just be enough to help us survive this.'

'Then what am I supposed to do?' I ask him, my tone almost pleading.

Phoenix takes my hand in his and holds it tight. 'Ignite the spark when put to the Darkest test.'

'But I've no idea *how* to focus my Light!' I protest. 'Not in the way Mercia did against the Berserkers –'

'Tanas is up to something,' interrupts Steinar in his gruff voice.

We look towards the door and see that two large canisters have been placed by the entrance and the Incarnates are in the process of spraying their contents over the strengthened glass.

'Don't be alarmed. This pyramid is built as a safe room,' explains Goggins. 'They'd need a battering ram to get through that door.'

The glass begins to mist over and a frost forms.

'I don't think they intend to use a battering ram,' says Tarek, peering curiously at the misted door. 'Those canisters contain liquid nitrogen. Tanas is attempting to freeze the glass to weaken it.'

'Jude, start handing out those weapons,' orders Goggins, checking the empty magazine of his pistol and discarding the weapon in frustration. 'Protectors and Warriors, save your Ascendants! And, Genna . . . if you are the one in the Soul Prophecy, then now is the time to prove it!'

52

I stand motionless amid the panic, trying to summon up my Light. As Jude distributes the few weapons Phoenix managed to retrieve from the Glimmer Dome, I think of Mercia, how she called upon her soul's energy until she was literally ablaze.

'*I am the Prophecy . . . I am the Light . . .*' I mutter to myself, staring hard at my hands. 'I *am the spark that will defeat the darkness . . . I am the Prophecy . . . I am the Light . . .*'

I chant the mantra over and over again, hoping that this will somehow unlock my supposed powers. Phoenix stands close by my side, a Roman gladius sword in his hand. Jude is on my other side armed with her bo staff. The rest of the Soul Protectors and Warriors take up position around their Ascendants, all of whom are looking expectantly in my direction. Outside the pyramid the Incarnates fall quiet, their silence more disturbing than their previous howls and hammering on the glass.

As the glazed doors to the entrance finally freeze solid, Phoenix turns to me. 'Any revelations yet?'

I give the smallest shake of my head, aware I'm being watched by everyone, and resume my mantra with even more urgency. After several rushed repetitions with no effect, I become desperate. It seems I don't have it within me to summon the Light. Then Empote's last words come back to me – *Look within yourself to ignite the spark.*

I begin to think of everything I've done. Every life I've lived. Everything I've lost. My friends . . . my parents . . . my sister –

All of a sudden I get a flashback to the ancient stone circle near Andover and my intense Glimmer of a young girl with golden flowing hair and a divine light shining from within her as if her very heart was a miniature sun . . . my sister could channel the Light!

What she felt, you felt. What you experienced, she experienced.

Closing my eyes, I try to tap into my twin's ability, recalling the way she opened herself up to the universe, letting the Light flow through her like a river. As I recite the mantra, my skin seems to take on a warmer glow. I chant faster and louder, noticing the radiance growing within me each time. A tangible heat begins to emanate from the palms of my hands, like embers in a fire.

'That's it!' gasps Caleb. 'You're harnessing the Light!'

With each recital of the mantra, the sensation intensifies until I can almost envisage the Light shining in beams out of my palms –

A sharp bang resounds through the pyramid, startling me. I open my eyes, expecting to see the Incarnates surging through the doorway.

'Don't worry, Genna,' says Phoenix, adjusting his grip on his gladius. 'The glass held.'

'For now,' mutters Jude, her bo staff at the ready.

'If the pyramid is breached,' announces Goggins, 'retreat to the tunnels.'

A second bone-shuddering thud echoes round the pyramid and an ominous crack spiders across one of the doors. The glass continues to hold, but the sudden noise is enough to break my concentration. The power of the Light passes from me and the glow quickly fades from my skin.

I grimly recall how Mercia's Light faded too, allowing Tanas to regain his strength and overcome her. With dismay, I realize I can't harness the Light in the way my sister did, and certainly not for long enough to wield it as a weapon.

Caleb and the others continue to watch me with bated breath, willing me to resume the mantra. But I look back at them searchingly, less sure than ever I'm the one foretold in the Soul Prophecy. Still, I've vowed to make amends for drawing Tanas here, so I'm determined not to give up. Not yet, anyway. I'll have to think of something else.

I look up through the pyramid's glass panels in hope of some divine inspiration. Night has fallen. The sky appears blacker than ever, the stars few and far between. Even the moon has all but disappeared, its crescent like a razor cut of fading light against the suffocating night. The inky sky reminds me of my two *su'mach*. In those dreams I had a flint and pyrite and a box of matches. *But how am I supposed to light a spark now?* I ask myself. I have nothing to start a fire with and my own inner Light wouldn't be enough to ignite a match.

I need something bigger, something to gather and focus the Light.

'What's Tanas up to now?' grumbles Steinar, his eyes narrowing as he tracks the silhouette of an Incarnate laying something at the base of the door.

'While the glass should withstand freezing,' says Tarek, his brow creased and troubled, 'if rapidly reheated it could well go into thermal shock and shatter.'

'Prepare yourselves!' orders Goggins, hefting a teardrop-shaped Maori war club in his massive hand.

Phoenix glances at me. 'It's now or never, Genna!'

Caleb sees the desperation in my eyes. 'Have faith! For you are the One!'

Have faith . . . I think of Caleb praying and my gaze falls on the altar's crystal capstone. Once more I hear Empote's voice in my head: *The only way to defeat the Darkness is to confront it with Light.*

I turn to Tarek. 'Does this pyramid store the Light?' I ask.

He nods. 'We use the solar energy to power Haven.'

'Is there any way to reverse the flow?'

His troubled brow creases further. 'Technically . . .'

'Then do it!' I say urgently.

Tarek stares at me, uncomprehending. 'But such a release of energy could be catastrophic.'

'Exactly,' I reply.

A crafty grin spreads across Tarek's face. 'Genius! It would be like –'

Suddenly there's an explosion that almost throws us off our feet, the ground trembles and a fireball engulfs the pyramid. The glass doors shatter with an ear-splitting crack.

As we regain our senses, Tarek dashes over to the altar, swipes a finger across the display and begins to type furiously. Goggins and his band of Protectors and Warriors form a defensive wall against Tanas and her Incarnates, who charge through the billowing smoke and debris, fanning out and surrounding us in a matter of seconds.

Tanas quickly sweeps her gaze over the pitiful display of resistance. 'The last of the Light,' she gloats. 'How dim and diminished you are.'

'You'll *never* extinguish the Light!' snarls Goggins as he points the Maori club at her. 'Not on my watch.'

Tanas smirks. 'Oh, how the dog barks, yet its teeth are all but pulled.'

I glance anxiously over my shoulder. Tarek's fingers are still flying over the console at the altar, his head bent in concentration. '*How much longer?*' I whisper, his feverish activity blocked from Tanas's view by Phoenix, Jude and myself.

'*Nearly there!*' he replies, a bead of sweat running down his brow.

Caleb bravely steps forward. 'We don't fear you, Tanas,' he says. 'For the Light will always shine through the Darkness . . . and the Darkness is at its end.'

Tanas chuckles softly. 'Old man, you appear to be somewhat confused. It's the Darkness that consumes the Light! And from where I'm standing, the night is already upon us.'

She gestures with her hand to the pitch-black sky.

'That's where you're wrong, Tanas,' asserts Caleb, striking his cane on the marble floor in defiance. 'For the one foretold in the Soul Prophecy will end the night and bring about a new dawn!'

Tanas raises a slim eyebrow from behind her glasses. 'And who might "the one" be *this* time?' she sneers.

With a triumphant expression on his wizened face, Caleb turns towards me. 'Genna . . . our Soul Saviour!'

Tanas looks over at me and laughs. 'Her? Yet another false hope. Caleb, when will you learn? This schoolgirl saviour of yours is nothing but a candle in the wind. One puff from me –' Tanas clicks her fingers – 'and her feeble flame will be snuffed out!'

'You couldn't do it last time,' Phoenix taunts her. 'In fact, *you* were the one snuffed out!'

Tanas scowls at him. 'You may have killed me once in this life. But I've come back stronger!'

Phoenix raises his gladius. 'Then I'll just keep cutting you down until you never come back.'

Tanas runs her eyes over his many knife wounds and bandages. 'It appears one of my Hunters has left her mark on you. We should really finish her handiwork.'

As she ridicules Phoenix's injuries, I notice Damien peering curiously past us at Tarek. I step forward and block his view. 'I defeated your Hunters, Tanas,' I declare, drawing my katana, 'and I will defeat *you*!'

'Oh, bold talk from a peace-loving First Ascendant,' Tanas replies snidely. 'When did you become so assertive? I thought you Ascendants always hid behind your Protectors.'

'They may be our shields,' I reply, 'but that doesn't mean we can't carry a sword. And this one will run you through!'

'Will it now?' Her patience suddenly at an end, Tanas snarls, 'Incarnates! Snuff out her Light . . . for eternity!'

With a roar, the Incarnates surge forward.

'Fall back to the tunnel!' Goggins orders.

'We must give Tarek more time,' I cry, fending off an Incarnate wielding an axe. 'It's our only hope.'

'I thought *you* were our only hope,' Goggins replies. He swings his club wildly, stunning three Incarnates in a single blow.

'Just hold them back a little longer,' I plead as I deflect a sword strike aimed at Tarek's back.

Phoenix's gladius flashes like a lightning strike, while Jude's bo staff becomes a blur, knocking down anyone who steps too close. Steinar, Kohsoom and the other Protectors battle ferociously against the relentless onslaught, trying to forge a safe path to the service tunnel entrance.

'*Tarek!*' I cry as the tide of Hunters breaks through our defences.

'Just – another – second . . . There! Done!' he shouts. On the altar the circular sun-and-eye icon lights up, pulsating softly.

'Then what are you waiting for?' I reply, kicking at a Hunter coming at me with a baseball bat. 'LIGHT IT!'

But, before he can, Tarek is knocked backwards by Thug's sledgehammer of a fist and falls to the floor. Goggins and the few remaining Warriors are battling in an ever-tighter circle round the last of the Ascendants. Caleb has even drawn a hidden blade from inside his cane and is valiantly staving off any attacker who ventures too close. But there are simply too many of them. In the chaos Knuckleduster manages to snatch Tasha and carries her away, kicking and screaming, to Tanas. Immediately the hooded host of demonic priests commence their chanting – '*RA-KA! RA-KA! RA-KA!*' – and Tanas begins the sickening ritual to sacrifice Tasha's life and soul.

'*Tasha!*' I cry as I dive for the altar and hit the sun icon. The capstone flares with Light. Burning brighter than a supernova, it pours out beams in all directions, the shafts of Light reflecting off the pyramid's glass panels and creating a blinding intricate web. The intensity grows so white-hot that the air itself shimmers and I feel my whole body crackle with energy. Even my samurai sword appears to glow from within as if freshly forged. Then the capstone overloads and detonates in a last burst of incandescent Light, blasting out the pyramid's panels and pushing back the night.

53

I hear a crunch of glass and cautiously open my eyes: Phoenix's grinning and glittering face greets me.

'When I said, "ignite the spark", that isn't exactly what I had in mind,' he says, helping me to my feet. 'But it sure as heck worked!'

Shell-shocked, I gaze round at the devastation. Only the pyramid's frame remains. A carpet of powdered glass fans out in every direction, glistening like snow. Tanas and all the Incarnates lie, lifeless, on the ground. Goggins is gently picking glass fragments out of Viviana's white hair, while Kohsoom checks on a bewildered Tasha; Steinar carefully helps Thabisa see to her surprisingly calm baby; close by, Santiago and Sun-Hi are picking themselves up and brushing themselves down.

Everyone appears to be fine. In fact, their skin is literally radiating with the Light and any injuries are all but gone. I'm most relieved to see that Phoenix's painful collection of cuts and bruises have either healed over or disappeared entirely.

Jude leans casually on her bo staff. 'So . . . anyone care to explain what just happened?'

With an appreciative whistle, Tarek examines the obliterated altar. 'We just let off one *epic* Light grenade!' he says in an awestruck voice. 'Although, to be honest, it was more like a Light bomb. At that intensity, the blast had every chance of killing us too.'

'Well, that's comforting to know,' replies Jude drily. 'Still, I'm glad I'm not an Incarnate.' She taps Thug with her foot and gets no response. None of the other Incarnates is moving either. Damien lies beside his master, his dark glasses cracked, his body motionless.

'It's over!' I sigh, dropping my katana and sinking with relief into Phoenix's arms. 'It's *really* over this time, isn't it?'

Phoenix gazes deep into my eyes, into my soul. 'Yes, I believe it is,' he says with the first truly carefree smile I've seen since I've known him. 'Your life with mine, as always?'

A warmth radiates through my heart, and I know this feeling has nothing to do with the Light. '*Always*,' I reply, sensing the barriers that have held him back before are no longer there.

As Phoenix leans in, I hear an insistent *meow* and glance down. Nefertiti, her sandy-coloured fur sparkling with powdered glass, rubs against my leg, demanding my attention. I look at Phoenix and roll my eyes. *Great timing, Nefe!* I think, but nonetheless I pick the loyal cat up and dust off her coat. 'How did you ever survive?' I ask her, stroking her fur. She purrs loudly in response.

'I guess she has nine lives,' chuckles Phoenix, giving Nefe's ear a friendly scratch.

'I think we *all* have nine lives – if not a lot more!' says Tarek with a glance at the handful of healed and softly haloed survivors.

His joke breaks the tension and I laugh out loud. My happiness ripples round everyone, and soon we're all laughing, even Goggins. The feeling is joyous after so many days and nights of running, fleeing and fighting. I can't believe that barely a week ago I was celebrating Prisha's birthday with Mei, talking about seeing the Rushes live and getting excited about my holiday in Barbados. To think that I had dismissed my true nature as a First Ascendant, explaining away my Glimmers as mere figments of my imagination!

In reality, I am more than I ever dreamed or imagined possible.

I have conquered Tanas. I have defeated the Darkness. I have saved the Light.

A wave of relief floods through me as I realize I've more than made up for putting Haven at risk in going to save my Protector. The magnitude of what I am and what I've done with the help of my fellow Ascendants and Protectors starts to sink in . . .

As does my awareness of the repercussions of my actions.

My elation fades as I look round at the litter of lifeless bodies amid the debris of the explosion. So much death and destruction. In his fallen, pitiful state, Damien once more appears like the teenage boy he once was. Raven-haired and pale, his face lean and youthful, he isn't very different from some of the boys in my school.

'What about the Hunters? And these other Incarnates?' I ask Caleb hesitantly. 'Are they all . . . dead?'

Caleb slides his slender sword back into his lion-headed cane. Kneeling down, he examines an Incarnate sprawled at his feet. The man's eyes are blank and unseeing. 'Such an intense burst of the Light will have obliterated the Darkness in their souls,' he explains. 'And with so little left of their true selves, I'm afraid it will have taken their lives along with it.'

I swallow hard, tasting the bitterness of guilt. 'Will their souls come back?' I ask.

'It's hard to say,' replies Caleb, rising to his feet with the help of his cane. 'But I'm hopeful their cleansed souls will reincarnate in future lives. And when they do, they'll be freer, happier and more grateful for life than they've ever been before.'

This eases my conscience a little. Then my gaze falls upon Tanas's body, her mane of black hair covering her face like a death mask. 'And what about Tanas? Is she ever coming back?'

Caleb turns to me with an assured and deeply proud look on his wrinkled face. 'Beyond doubt, Genna, *you* are the one foretold in the Soul Prophecy,' he declares, his blue eyes gleaming like diamonds. 'The one that lights the Darkness when no other can provide the spark! Just as the sun pushes back the night, so too has your Light sent the Darkness back from whence it came. Tanas's twisted soul is gone forever.'

The Soul Seer raises his hands in tribute to the night sky and the heavens appear to burst with stars, as if every lost and living soul now burns pure and bright. My fellow First

Ascendants and Protectors join in his celebratory ritual. Setting aside their weapons and holding their arms high, they softly chant like a heavenly choir.

As I gaze up in wonder, Nefe suddenly hisses and tenses in my arms. 'What's wrong?' I say, trying to calm her. But she leaps from my grasp.

'*Praise the Light!*' sings Caleb with unbridled joy as everyone turns their eyes to the heavens. 'For Genna is the one true sou–'

He chokes, his gleaming eyes widening in shock as he coughs up blood. The sharp point of a jade-green blade protrudes like a poisoned thorn through his chest. As Caleb slumps to the floor, Tanas rises up behind him, a scornful smile on her face.

'So much for the Soul Prophecy!' she snarls.

Acknowledgements

The Soul trilogy is proving to be the most challenging story arc that I've ever written. Each past-life Glimmer is a book in itself, requiring deep research and careful thought to ensure that the facts are accurate, the names are true to the time period, the locations are interesting and real, and any cultural references are respectful and appropriate. At the same time, I must endeavour to make each Glimmer exciting, relevant to the plot, logical within the timeline so there's no overlap, and a complete story in itself with a beginning, middle and end. This complex interweaving of history and present day means the Soul trilogy has become an immense plot puzzle set across time. I just hope I can solve it with the next book: *The Soul Survivor*!

Accompanying me on this epic journey are my editor Emma Jones, my excellent copy-editor Sarah Hall and my ever-constant managing editor Wendy Shakespeare. I thank you all for being supreme 'Word Hunters'!

Thank you also to my 'Protector', Charlie Viney. I truly value your advice, support and belief in me. I do hope you'll be my agent in the next life too!

I also wish to express my gratitude to all my friends for their support, love and wise counsel – life is best when shared with good friends. Among those I'm blessed to know are Hayley, one of my guardian angels; Karen and Rob (yes, you get *two* mentions in this book to make up for last time!); my dear friend and healer Mary; Mark, Kate, Thomas, Jasper and of course my goddaughter Lulu; my walking buddies Charlie, Matt and Geoff; Brian, my guru, running partner and fight-night organizer; and the fine gentlemen of the HGC – Dan, Dax, David, Dean, Larry, Siggy, Riz and Andy. Long live the HGC!

Para Marcela, tu amor es la Luz en mi corazón. Gracias por proteger y cuidar la llama que arde en ambos.

To my mum and dad, this has been another tough year thanks to the pandemic. While we couldn't be with one another much, you're always by my side in my heart and mind.

To my two boys, Zach and Leo: it is your strength, laughter and joy that gives me strength, laughter and joy. You mean the world to me, and I cherish every second I spend in your company. Each moment is a Glimmer to remember!

Finally, a heartfelt thanks to all my fans, librarians and avid readers. While I write the books, you breathe life into them every time you read my stories. Keep the Light burning . . .

See you all in another life!
Chris

Any fans can keep in touch with me and the progress of the Soul Prophecy series on Twitter @YoungSamurai or via the website at www.thesoulprophecy.co.uk

About the Author

As an author, Chris Bradford practises what he terms 'method writing'. For his award-winning Young Samurai series, he trained in samurai swordsmanship, karate and ninjutsu and earned his black belt in Zen Kyu Shin Taijutsu. For his Bodyguard series, he embarked on an intensive close-protection course to become a qualified professional bodyguard. More recently, for the Soul trilogy, Chris travelled extensively to experience first-hand the cultures featured in the story – from living with the Shona people in Zimbabwe, to trekking the Inca trail, to meditating in a Buddhist temple amid the mountains of Japan. His bestselling books are published in over twenty-five languages and have garnered more than thirty children's book awards and nominations. Chris lives in England with his two sons.

To discover more about Chris, go to
www.chrisbradford.co.uk

DON'T MISS
GENNA AND PHOENIX'S
NEXT THRILLING
ADVENTURE

2023